Someday
x

Debby Buxton

*With love
Deb.
x*

Someday x

Copyright © Debby Buxton 2024

The moral right of Debby Buxton to be identified as the author of this work has been asserted in accordance with the Copyright, Designs and Patents Act 1988.

All rights reserved. No part of this book may be reproduced or used in any manner whatsoever, including information storage and retrieval systems, or transmitted in any form or by any means, electronic, mechanical, photocopying, recording or otherwise, without the express written permission of the copyright owner, except in the case of brief quotations embodied in critical reviews and certain other non-commercial use permitted by copyright law. For permission requests, contact the author at the address below.

Second edition printed and independently published in the United Kingdom 2024.

A CIP catalogue record of this book is available from the British Library.

ISBN (Paperback): 978-1-0686511-0-6
Cover art: Andrew Buxton
Typesetting: Matthew J Bird

For further information about this book, please contact the author at:
www.debbybuxton.co.uk

*For Mum and Dad, Irene and Basil Young,
loved and missed every day.*

Someday
x

Debby Buxton

Foreword

My introduction to Debby took place during one of Michael Heppell's brilliant *Write That Book Masterclasses*, a group in which I had become a seasoned participant over the course of a couple of years. It wasn't long before Debby and I discovered a shared kinship, the pursuit of crafting narratives that blurred the lines between fact and fiction. She was immersed in the creation of a fictional memoir, a premise reminiscent of my own recently published book, *Certified* – a novel that weaves real-life events with a tapestry of creative license and imagination.

Enter *Someday x* – a beautifully crafted journey that traverses the spectrum of human experience with equal measures of laughter and heartbreak. Rooted in true events, the narrative unfolds the compelling tale of Lisa and Jason, guiding readers through the landscapes of their childhoods and the resilience that propels them beyond loss and heartache to discover each other. Debby's writing breathes life

Foreword

into the narrative, allowing the characters and their surroundings to leap off the page, immersing readers in a world where every emotion is palpable from the very first word.

A significant portion of this compelling narrative unfolds against the enchanting backdrop of Tuscany, a setting rendered so vividly by Debby's pen that readers will feel as if they have secured a ringside seat to witness Jason and Lisa's despair and secrets unfold, forever altering the trajectory of their lives.

Someday x is a lovely book that seamlessly interweaves humour, poignancy, and romance, serving as a reminder that triumph often emerges victorious in the face of adversity. As you embark on this journey through the pages of *Someday x*, be prepared to be transported not only through the captivating events of Lisa and Jason's lives but also to the sun-soaked landscapes of Tuscany, all meticulously painted by Debby's real experiences, and imagination.

Roger Wilson-Crane
Award Winning Author, *Certified.*

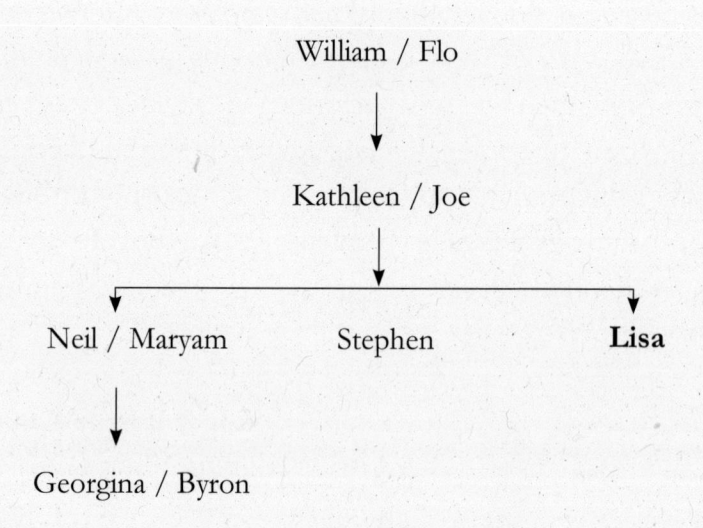

Lisa's Family Tree

William / Flo
↓
Kathleen / Joe
↓
Neil / Maryam   Stephen   **Lisa**
↓
Georgina / Byron

Jason's Family Tree

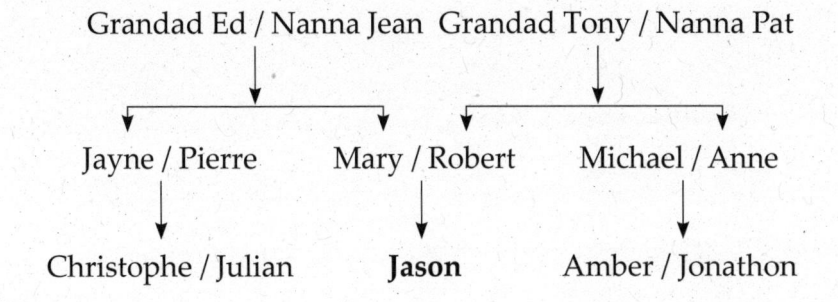

Grandad Ed / Nanna Jean   Grandad Tony / Nanna Pat

Jayne / Pierre   Mary / Robert   Michael / Anne

Christophe / Julian   **Jason**   Amber / Jonathon

Prologue

X

At precisely 12.25 pm on Friday, 14th June 2002, the Ryanair flight from Stansted landed on time, bouncing twice along Bologna Forli's main runway to a ripple of applause from the amiable but excited stag party seated in the four rows over the wings.

Lisa grinned. "See, I told you we wouldn't crash."

A few hours before, bleary-eyed from the early start that morning, she'd been leaning against the wall of the tightly packed gangway leading from the gate to the plane, hot and desperate for sleep.

She'd pitied the tall man in the white tee shirt and red baseball cap ahead of her in the queue, waiting to board with his wife and two very young and fractious children. He'd picked up and put down his screaming toddler several times already. As he gently lifted her and placed her over his shoulder again, he turned and momentarily looked straight at Lisa with intense, piercing blue eyes that she instantly recognised. She'd elbowed Jason in the ribs and whispered, "It's him! Off the tele!"

"Who off the tele? Where?"

"Shhhhhhh, keep your voice down! He knows I've clocked him. There, in the red baseball cap. Oh, what is his name? Chancer! That's it, he's Chancer!"

"Clive Owen? No, it can't be. Are you sure?" Reruns of the crime drama Chancer had recently aired on television. Surely the actor who played the all-action hero, Stephen Crane, couldn't be on their plane?

"There, look!" Lisa had pulled Jason across to her vantage point just as the man turned briefly to his daughter again.

"Blimey, you're right. It is him!"

"Well, at least we know we'll get there safely. The pilot wouldn't dare crash with Chancer on board!"

Lisa and Jason collected their panniers, the small bags used to carry their luggage on their bicycles, from the carousel and made their way, nervously, towards the excess baggage reclaim.

Jason had heard horror stories from his cycling friends of damage to bikes in transit. Some of them had even seen their precious steeds hurled around by unscrupulous baggage handlers, so he'd carefully packaged their new touring bikes in endless metres of foam pipe-lagging material and bubble wrap. The wide parcel tape had proven to be challenging and having removed almost all the hair on both forearms, Jason had started to wonder if he could be something big in depilatory treatment. It would be a minor miracle if the bikes arrived intact and they could enjoy their Tuscan adventure to the full.

As he watched the two large canvas bike bags loaned to them by generous friends emerging through the plastic curtains with no signs of damage, Jason was momentarily tempted to hug the burly member of the airport staff in charge. Rapidly discarding that idea, he retrieved one of the bags, heaved it onto a baggage trolley and then placed the second one alongside. They piled the four panniers on top and then carefully steered the trolley through the 'Nothing to Declare' exit and out onto the bustling concourse.

The price for the return flights from Stansted to Forli Bologna had seemed like a bargain, and it transpired there was a good reason for that. The airport was, in fact, nowhere near Bologna but at least an hour's drive away. Leaving Lisa with the luggage in the only quiet spot he could find, directly outside the gents' toilets, Jason headed off to purchase tickets for the shuttle bus. He returned several minutes later, triumphant, and they left the comfort of the air-conditioned terminal to step outside into the blazing heat of the day.

The Rough Guide to Tuscany recommended that cycling tours be undertaken in May, June or September when the weather is usually more amenable than in July and August. In June 2002, however, Italy was in the grip of a heatwave. The temperature was well into the 90s as Jason and Lisa made their way to the stand to board the waiting coach.

The same sense of unease he had felt that morning as they'd handed the bikes in at Stansted returned when Jason saw the coach driver approaching to load the bags into the hold. A trickle of sweat began to form a visible patch across the back of his tee shirt as he stepped forward to assist the man in carefully easing the bags in. The agitated driver, anxious to deal with the queue of waiting passengers and leave on time, muttered something in Italian that, fortunately, Jason couldn't understand and then the bags were inside.

Lisa and Jason boarded the coach, stashed their panniers on a spare seat in front of them and then settled back to relax and enjoy the journey to Bologna. Lisa was carrying a small bag that clipped onto the handlebars of her bike when she was cycling and contained all the main essentials for their trip; passports, money, credit cards and flight tickets. As she relaxed and closed her eyes, she wrapped her arms around the bag; for the next 16 days, she had no intention of letting it out of her sight.

The coach had barely left the airport when Jason pulled from his pannier the already well-thumbed Rough Guide to Tuscany they'd been studying for the last three months. The only accommodation they had booked was a Bologna hotel for the first night of their adventure and the final night before they flew home. The Hotel Manager had kindly agreed to store the bike bags and packaging until they returned.

With the aid of the Rough Guide, they intended to find other accommodation along the way. They had vaguely decided on the route they would take out of Bologna and, fuelled with excitement now that they were actually in Italy, Jason wanted to check a few details for the umpteenth time. But the low drone of the engine as the coach sped along the motorway and the oppressive heat that had utterly overpowered the ineffective air conditioning system combined to overcome him. Soon he, too, was sound asleep.

They awoke to the sound of crunching metal and the driver's harsh braking, which left the end of Jason's nose millimetres from the rear of the seat in front. Leaning into the aisle, he saw that the traffic ahead had concertinaed, and it seemed several collisions had ensued, judging by the altercations between the angry drivers. "Aagghh," the coach driver growled, raising his hands skyward whilst muttering in a low, menacing tone.

The minutes ticked by slowly, and gradually the drivers' anger abated. It soon became apparent, however, that a more severe accident had occurred ahead when a fire engine and two ambulances squeezed by, their wailing sirens still audible long after they had disappeared from view.

The opposite side of the motorway was devoid of traffic, and as the temperature in the coach became oven-like, Lisa and Jason decided to join some of their fellow passengers seated on the central crash barrier. The mid-afternoon sun was scorching, and Lisa frowned as she gazed absentmindedly into the distance.

"Penny for them?"

She smiled at his concern. "Oh, it's nothing. I found out last week that I've got to give a presentation when I get back, and I'm dreading it."

"You're thinking about going home already? But we haven't even arrived yet!"

"I know," she bit her lip nervously, "but you know what I'm like. I hate being the centre of attention; I'd rather resign than do a presentation."

Jason shook his head. "A woman as accomplished as you. You do realise you're nuts? It's no big deal, honestly. There's nothing I love more than being centre stage. The trick is to want to do it. You need to find a reason, something you will get from it, and it'll all be fine."

More than an hour passed before the traffic ahead began to move. Jason and Lisa were relieved when the dormant engine of the coach sputtered into life at last, and the frazzled driver could resume his route. They were subdued, hot, hungry and thirsty, but some of the earlier excitement returned when they reached the outskirts of Bologna. They gazed out of the window and were thrilled to catch their first brief glimpse of the Torre degli Asinelli through a gap between the buildings that lined the road.

According to the Rough Guide, the tower stood more than 90 metres high and, built in the 12th century, was one of the oldest medieval structures in the world. Climbing the 498 steps to the top for the fabulous views across the city was highly recommended.

They had hoped to watch the sunset from the top of the tower that evening before they ate, but the coach driver had resigned himself to the inevitable. He made his way slowly through the heavy traffic, carefully navigating the narrow streets and eventually arriving at the bus station a little after 4.30 pm, more than two hours late.

Lisa and Jason carefully extricated the bike bags from the hold. As there were no luggage trolleys, they staggered past several parked coaches, each carrying one of the heavy, cumbersome bike bags with the strap over one shoulder, their panniers in the other hand.

"I don't think we can walk very far like this." Jason moaned as they lurched through the main building, narrowly avoiding a collision with several passers-by.

"What about a taxi?" Lisa suggested as they emerged onto the white marble concourse. The heat from the sun was still overpowering, and although there was a canopy across the front of the building, it afforded no shade at that time of day. A fleet of taxis was parked by the kerb only a few metres away, but they were all relatively small vehicles; it was obvious that they would not be able to accommodate all their luggage.

Struggling to know what to do next, Jason watched as a lone cyclist weaved his way expertly through the stationary traffic. "Here's a thought, we could assemble the bikes, put the panniers on and wheel them to the hotel. Job's a good 'un!"

Lisa smiled. "Brilliant! Why didn't I think of that?"

They heaved their luggage to one end of the concourse, out of the way of the rushing commuters swarming around the main entrance. Another brainwave struck Jason as he gratefully jettisoned his heavy bike bag and surveyed the milling crowds strolling along the congested pavement.

"Lisa, I've had an idea! I know, two in one day's excessive, but how about I go and find the hotel first without the bikes, so we know exactly where we're going?"

She smiled again. "Inspired!" Whilst Jason propped the bike bags against the wall, Lisa began rummaging through the precious handlebar bag to find the booking confirmation for the hotel she had printed off the week before. At the bottom of the page was a small map indicating that the hotel was located about 15 minutes' walk from the bus station. Jason took a moment to get his bearings and then disappeared into the crowd.

Lisa piled the four panniers against the bike bags, sat down and leaned back against the improvised sun lounger. She clutched the handlebar bag, firmly secured across her shoulder by a wide canvas strap, as she closed her eyes and turned her face towards the sun. A slight smile played on her lips; Jason had told her to work on her tan, so why not?

"Found it!" he called, what seemed to Lisa like only minutes later. "Come on, sleepy head, let's get cracking." Lisa grinned as she took Jason's outstretched hand. His excitement and enthusiasm were infectious. It was going to be a great trip; she just knew it.

They laid the bike bags on the marble terrace, placed the four panniers between them, and then set to work, extracting the first bike and removing the packaging Jason had so carefully applied. When a momentary respite from the burning heat arrived in the form of a gentle breeze, Lisa scurried after the billowing bubble wrap, the handlebar bar bouncing uncomfortably against her hip.

Jason assembled his bike and, leaning it against the wall, inwardly groaned. The moment he'd been dreading was here, and it was now or never. As a safety precaution, he'd had to release all the air from the tyres for the flight; he'd rather poke himself in the eye with a bent stick than try to inflate them in this heat with a hand pump, but there was nothing else for it.

Grimacing, he began pumping. Within seconds he was sweating even more profusely than before and breathing hard. Sweat was running down his forehead into his eyes, making them sting. He could feel his kneecaps beginning to burn on the searing marble, even through his jeans, and his arms felt like lead weights. With the tyre only half inflated, gasping, he had to stop and take a break.

He turned to Lisa, struggling to unpack her bike, the handlebar bag swinging wildly, adding to her frustration alongside the unruly bubble wrap. She caught his glance and shot him a look of exasperation as she tugged the bag's strap over her head and placed it down on the terrace. After carefully positioning the four panniers around the bag so that it was completely hidden, she resumed her task with a satisfied smile.

Jason sighed and reluctantly applied himself once more to inflating the tyre, but then he heard Lisa's tinkling laughter. He turned to see a young man of Mediterranean appearance dancing around in front of her, holding one of her empty water bottles and pretending to drink from it. The young man grinned at Jason, tossed the water bottle back towards Lisa and then danced his way off into the crowd on the pavement.

They were still laughing at the friendly stranger's antics as they resumed their respective tasks. It was only when Jason was satisfied that he'd put sufficient air in the tyre and, utterly drained, walked over to assist Lisa that he noticed two of the panniers had fallen over. He bent to reposition them around the handlebar bag, and froze.

"Where is it?" he called out to her, trying to stay calm, his heart thumping in his chest. Before she had time to answer, she heard his voice again, this time more agitated. "Do you have it?"

"Do I have what?" Lisa could hear the note of irritation in her voice, but surely he could see that she was busy grappling with her bike, trying to hold the frame in one hand whilst inserting a wheel with the other.

"The bag. Have you got the bag?"

Clueless as to what he was talking about, she was about to chastise him for being so vague, when something about his tone stopped her. She turned to look at him and felt a rush of alarm as she watched the anguish written across his gentle face morph into a look of horror.

Lisa wasn't wearing the handlebar bag, and Jason couldn't see it near her. He stared down at the gap between the panniers where he had seen her place it. Stupefied, his brain scrambled to make sense of what he was seeing. *This couldn't be happening to them, surely.* "It's gone." was all he managed to mumble.

Still unable to comprehend what was going on, Lisa laid her bike down, walked over to Jason and placed a hand on his arm. "You're frightening me. What's gone?" she asked, looking down at the panniers Jason was staring at. She saw the space and thought she would be sick.

Where was the handlebar bag? It had to be here somewhere, maybe she'd kicked it out of position whilst she'd been struggling with her bike. She rearranged the panniers several times and, oblivious to the breeze, frantically tipped out the contents of both bike bags. The bubble wrap soared joyously in the air once more as her spirits went into free fall. The handlebar bag wasn't there, but the voice inside her head was screaming that it had to be. It contained everything they needed for their trip; it was simply impossible that it was missing.

Whilst Lisa searched the bike bags, Jason ran to check a nearby litter bin and another further on, but there was nothing. As his brain fought to keep up with events, he realised that the amusing 'dancing man' must have been a thief, and whilst he'd distracted them, an accomplice had stolen the bag.

They had been in Bologna for less than an hour, and now they had no money, credit cards, flight tickets or passports.

Part 1

Chapter One

Jason was born on 15th January 1975 at Stepping Hill Hospital, Stockport. His parents, Mary and Robert, were only 18, and they'd married hastily at Stockport Register Office only two months prior to Jason's arrival.

Theirs had been a whirlwind courtship after they met and fell in love at Stockport Technical College. Robert was an apprentice mechanic undertaking a day release course; Mary was studying full-time for a hairdressing qualification.

Their parents had thought they were enjoying a teenage romance that would soon pass, and they were surprised when Mary and Robert suggested a meal at the local pub one balmy evening in July 1974. They'd just taken their final exams; maybe they wanted to celebrate. But only minutes after sitting down, Tony, Robert's dad, was reeling. Was he going mad, or had his son just said that he was going to be a father? He glanced at Mary's parents, wondering what they were thinking; the four of them had never even met before.

"We thought you might need a drink after we told you. That's why we suggested meeting here," Robert grinned at the dumfounded faces surrounding him.

"I.., I.., I.." Not usually lost for words, Tony visibly grappled with his inability to continue.

"Your dad's trying to say he's very pleased for you both," Pat, his wife, finished for him, hellbent on saving the day. "As I think we all are. Aren't we?" She looked across the table, more in hope than expectation. Mary's parents obliged, nodding in unison, both equally stunned, unable to speak.

Mary and Robert excitedly told them of their plans to marry and somehow build a life together for themselves and their child. Accepting that they still had much to do to sort out the finer details, such as where they would live or how to pay for it, they flatly refused to heed their parents' recommendations for caution, both utterly convinced that everything would be fine. Their wedding four months later was a quiet affair but a joyous occasion, despite their parents' misgivings.

Jason arrived four weeks prematurely, small and underweight, with a tuft of fluffy blonde hair and blue eyes that sparkled when he laughed, which he did often. All four grandparents fell deeply in love with him at first sight and, united in their efforts to support the young family, quickly became firm friends.

Two years older than Mary, Jayne, her sister, was already working as a nanny for a French family in Chamonix. By all accounts, she was having the time of her life and wouldn't be returning home anytime soon, so her parents, Jean and Ed, could accommodate Mary, Robert and Jason for as long as necessary. Jean and Pat manoeuvred their working lives around so that they could help with childcare, enabling Mary to work part-time at a nearby hair salon. Neither of them could get enough of their baby grandson's company.

By the time Jason was two years old, Mary and Robert had managed to secure a mortgage on a two-up, two-down property close to both sets of grandparents, and they were thrilled when they were finally able to move into their own home.

Despite their limited income, they were intent on making their young son's life as happy as possible. He was the centre of their world, and they devoted every moment they weren't working to him. Jason's earliest memories were of a home filled with laughter and music. If the radio wasn't belting out the latest hits, his mum and dad would be playing their favourite records, and they all danced together. Robert played the guitar a little and practised lullabies every evening. He wasn't always note-perfect, but Jason never noticed.

Always on a tight budget, Mary and Robert taught their young son the joys of simple pleasures; jumping streams, climbing trees and flying kites in all weathers. They were frequent visitors to the park, and when Robert decided to invest in roller skates for all of them, they lurched around the footpaths, frequently falling and laughing together until they thought they would burst. "Who are your best friends?" Robert asked one day, struggling to his feet once more. "You are!" the little boy yelled in delight, and he meant it.

Ominous dark clouds scudded across the sky, and in the far distance, they could see the shadowy fingers of approaching rain as the family stepped onto the beach in Blackpool for their first holiday together. Five-year-old Jason ran ahead, heading straight for the choppy, grey waves, seemingly oblivious to the cool air. His uncle Michael, Robert's younger brother, aged 18, followed in hot pursuit whilst his parents and grandparents made camp with the obligatory windbreaks and umbrellas. A week of typical British summer weather couldn't dampen the family's spirits, and an era of annual holidays to Blackpool was born.

On the morning of his sixth birthday, trembling with excited anticipation, as instructed, Jason sat by his mum's side, clenched his eyes tight shut and held out his hands. He choked back a sob when he felt the warmth of a tiny, wriggling, furry body. Stunned and unable to speak, he gazed in wonder at his mum and dad's smiling faces and then down at Rolo, a chocolate brown Staffordshire bull terrier. The puppy clambered up his chest to lick his face; they were instantly in love and inseparable.

Rolo was like a second son to Mary and Robert; their two boys were rarely apart. If Jason joined his friends for a game of football, Rolo was there too, racing across the pitch like a demon, determined to get the ball. When Jason rode his bike, Rolo ran alongside, trying his best to get on. They landed in a mangled heap together more than once.

"If I didn't know better, I'd swear that dog is clock-watching," quipped a regular customer at the hairdressing salon where Mary worked. Rolo was in his usual spot, lying on his tummy with his head on his paws, looking bored and facing the clock.

"Oh, he does," Mary laughed. "Every day until we can collect Jason from school."

Mary and Robert's door was always open to all, and Michael was a regular visitor. Like Robert, he could strum a few chords on a guitar. They practised together for hours, hoping to form a duo and earn some money on the side playing in local pubs.

Soon other musician friends began stopping by, and Jason's parents slipped effortlessly into a Bohemian lifestyle. Casual visitors could be found most evenings, draped on the sofa or sprawled on one of the several large bean bags scattered around the lounge, a plate of something balanced on their knee.

Mary flitted around in her Indian-style clothing with her long, shaggy permed hair and wearing virtually no makeup, relighting scented joss sticks as the melodies of the rock ballads Robert and Michael preferred resonated through their home. Throughout his childhood, Jason fell asleep night after night, listening to the muffled sounds of the music drifting up from the lounge below, Rolo already gently snoring by his feet.

Growing up surrounded by performers, Jason was an outgoing child without an introverted bone in his body. He was popular, made friends readily and was notorious for his practical jokes. Only Jason could get away with hiding under the teacher's desk and startling her by flicking chalk from the blackboard rubber all over her as she sat down. But by age ten, he was already showing signs of academic ability and athleticism. He frequently got full marks on tests and held the school record for a 100-metre sprint for many years.

And, of course, he was musical. The headteacher liked to think of himself as a small-time drummer. He had a drum kit at school on which he performed at any given opportunity. When he broke his thumb just before the Christmas nativity, an urgent call went out in assembly for anyone who could play the drums.

Jason had only had a couple of goes on the bongos at home, but, in his usual uninhibited style, his hand shot up instantly and then he was out at the front, giving his all on the drum kit. A bit rough around the edges, it was apparent to everyone present that he had a good command of the rhythms required. Following some limited tuition, he went down a storm every night during the nativity the following week.

In the summer of 1986, Jason was leaving junior school, and his mum and dad were turning thirty. Jason's grandparents suggested a holiday abroad to celebrate. Michael and his girlfriend, Anne, had visited Crete the previous year, and their reports of wall-to-wall sunshine had sparked the interest of the rest of the family, none of whom had ever been abroad before. They booked a package holiday to the island of Corfu and, more by luck than judgment, managed to keep it a secret from Jason.

"Rolo! Rolo! Where are you?" The day before they were due to fly, Jason returned home from a visit to the cinema and was surprised that the dog hadn't virtually knocked him over in the doorway as usual.

"Rolo isn't coming this year. He's having a holiday at the kennels," Robert told him. Seeing Jason's look of dismay, he hastily added, "It's a lovely place; he'll have a great time."

"But why didn't you tell me? I don't want to go without Rolo!" Jason's face crumpled as he ran upstairs, threw himself on his bed and refused to eat.

The family had booked the same dog-friendly guest house every year since Rolo had come into their lives. He loved Blackpool as much as they did, racing across the beach and bounding into the sea. Jason couldn't imagine a holiday without him; what were his mum and dad thinking?

Nevertheless, he was intrigued when a minibus pulled up early the following morning. "Where are your cars?" Jason called out from the window, dressed in his pyjamas, his hair stuck up like forked lightning.

Michael glanced at his dad for reassurance, then jumped in with a reply. "Mine's broken down, and there wasn't room for us in Grandad's car. Everyone's been kind and shared the taxi. Get your skates on, the driver's waiting." He was more proud than ashamed of the small white lie that Jason accepted without further question.

"Can we get Rolo, Mum? Please?" Jason asked, his voice quivering as he took a seat by the window. The family glanced from one to another, concerned that Jason was upset, imbued with feelings of guilt. They hadn't given Rolo much thought; they'd assumed he'd be okay at the kennels. Ten days; it seemed like a long time, but it would soon pass, and he'd be home again.

"Wow! I've never seen an aeroplane that close before." Jason gazed out at the low-flying plane as it passed overhead. Then there was another, and in the distance, he could see yet another, climbing steeply. *Surely not!* He spun around in his seat. "Are we flying somewhere?"

Excitement flooded through Jason as the others grinned broadly at him. He craned his neck this way and that to try to spot more aeroplanes, and when the minibus parked up, he almost fell from the door in a rush to get out and help with the suitcases.

Only Michael and Anne had flown before; everyone else was nervous but not remotely prepared to confess to that. As they boarded the plane, however, Jason noticed that his grandmothers had become particularly subdued, and he insisted on sitting between them.

"Are you okay, Nannas?" he asked as the plane began to taxi along the runway. They murmured something he couldn't hear, and they both looked pale. Jason grinned at them. "Don't worry, it'll all be fine." That was what his dad always said. He took hold of their hands and then sat back in his seat, smiling, apparently completely at ease, waiting for take-off. Inside, his stomach was churning; he could feel his heart beating faster and faster, and he felt sick. He'd been watching the planes taking off.

How would it feel, moving that quickly along the runway and then climbing so steeply into the sky? What if his plane didn't get off the ground? It might crash into something, and then they would all die!

As the whining of the engines became a roar, followed by a burst of acceleration, Jason squeezed his grandmothers' hands in reassurance and smiled at them again, still revealing nothing of his inner panic. Then they were leaning back in their seats, and he heard Michael call out, "We're off!" His heart still felt like it was leaping around his chest as the aeroplane banked, and he gazed out at the expanse of landscape, hardly able to believe they were airborne.

They arrived at the small family-run hotel in Sidari in the early evening. Jason was delighted when everyone, including his Nannas, immediately changed into their swimwear and jumped into the swimming pool, the water still deliciously warm. As the sun set and the sky turned golden, the fairy lights around the bar twinkled, and the music got a little louder. With all his family splashing around him, Jason was in heaven.

The following morning, coated from head to foot in sun cream, the family strolled along the Canal D'Amour and found the sheltered beaches where they could swim safely in the sea. "Wow! It's not like Blackpool, is it?" Jason gushed as the turquoise water gently lapped the white sand beneath a cloudless azure sky. Basking in the warm shallows, Jason flinched when he noticed a shoal of tiny fish clustered around his arm. "Michael! Look!" he called out to his uncle, floating on his back close by. They were so close in age that Jason only ever called him by his first name.

"They won't hurt you. Here, try this." Michael walked over to his beach bag, pulled out a snorkel and showed Jason how to use it. "Stay still and see what happens." Soon the curious fish returned, nibbling at his legs, darting away as one if he moved. The men quickly purchased more snorkels, and Jason was thrilled when even his Nannas, who always flatly refused to swim in the sea at Blackpool, joined in exploring the coves and bays.

Jason was a favourite with the family who owned the hotel. The women fussed over him, besotted with his blonde hair, bleached almost white by the sun and every evening, the men got him up to participate in the Greek dancing and plate smashing. But the highlight of his holiday was the day spent on the pirate ship.

An hour after they set sail, there was a rumbling sound, like thunder. The captain, wearing an eyepatch and a shirt with a skull and crossbones on the back, growled that he was dropping anchor so that they could dive for treasure, and then he threw half a dozen bottles of champagne over the side. Robert and Michael watched open-mouthed as their father, a 50-something crinkly, yanked his tee shirt over his head, climbed onto the wooden handrail on the top deck of the boat and without a moment's hesitation, jumped over the side, clutching his knees to his chest as he did so.

"What are you waiting for? Geronimo!" Mary's father was the next to disappear over the side.

Jason watched as first his dad and then his uncle followed. He whooped with the crowd of onlookers as they hit the water; it looked a long way down. He turned to voice his concerns just in time to see his mum and Anne, clad only in their bikinis, approaching. "No, you're not going to..."

Before he could get the rest of the sentence out, they climbed onto the handrail using the rigging for support. They held hands, grinned at each other, grabbed hold of their bikini tops for security and then jumped together to the roaring cheer of the crowd on the boat.

That was it; Jason couldn't allow his mum to outdo him. His tee shirt was off in an instant; he ignored the protestations of his Nannas and climbed onto the handrail. *Don't look down, don't look down, jump!* He closed his eyes, swayed slightly for a moment, still clutching the thick rope with both hands and then he was free-falling before he felt the sudden rush of water in his nose and ears. He bobbed back up to the surface, laughing and spluttering simultaneously, trying with one hand to pull his trunks back down into a more comfortable position. "That was fantastic!" he yelled to his panic-stricken Nannas. "I want to do it again!" The family didn't manage to retrieve any of the champagne that day, but that wasn't important. They all returned to the hotel that evening exhausted and declaring it by far the best holiday they'd ever had.

"It's a shame we have to go home," Jason said, waving to the Greek family who had gathered to see them off. "I really like it here; I wish we could stay."

"But what about Rolo?" Mary asked.

Rolo! He'd forgotten all about Rolo! Suddenly Jason felt homesick. At that moment, what he wanted more than anything else in the world was to see Rolo bounding towards him.

Despite arriving home late in the evening, Mary, Robert and Jason arrived to collect Rolo as the kennels opened the following morning. Jason was beside himself with excitement as the kennel maid went to bring Rolo to them, but when the door swung open, they all gasped, horrified.

Chapter Two

The kennel maid had warned them that Rolo had been off his food, but they were unprepared for their first sight of him as he came through the door. He was a picture of misery with none of his usual vigour; he was thin, and his eyes had lost their sparkle. Before his parents had time to speak, Jason fell to his knees, wrapping his arms tightly around Rolo's neck and sobbing openly. In an instant, he knew that whilst he'd been away, having the time of his life and giving no thought to anyone or anything else, Rolo had spent all of his time pining for him.

On the way home, Jason sat in the rear seat of the car with Rolo, holding him close and promising he would never leave him again. Rolo leaned against him and gently licked his face, immediately forgiving him. Then he laid his head on Jason's knee as he'd always liked to do, relieved that, at last, his family had returned.

• • •

Jason remained steadfastly true to his word for the rest of Rolo's life. When the subject of the next family holiday came up, he would only agree to a destination where Rolo could go too, and so they returned to Blackpool the following summer. The family enjoyed their time together as much as ever, but they all agreed that, after the delights of Corfu, a week of mixed weather in Blackpool sadly no longer hit the spot.

By then, Robert and Mary were both doing well in their careers; Robert was a senior mechanic at a garage in Manchester, and Mary was a partner in a hairdressing business in Stockport. The family had moved into a semi-detached property on a corner plot with a drive, a garage and a large garden, ideally situated to accommodate their constant influx of visitors.

One bright spring afternoon in April 1988, Jason arrived home from school to find a VW camper van on the drive. Intrigued, he took a look around, stretching up to try and see in through the windows. A sudden shout startled him, and he nearly fell over backwards.

"What do you think of her then?" Robert called out from his hiding place behind a shrub.

"Dad! What are you doing here? You made me jump!"

"I finished work early to fetch the van."

"This is ours? You're kidding me! Really? No, it can't be. Is it? Really?"

"The door's unlocked, have a look."

Rolo wasn't entirely sure what all the fuss was about, but as Jason was very excited, he thought he had better be too. He did three laps of the van at top speed before leaping in to check out the interior.

Chapter Two

Jean, Mary's mother, was unusually subdued as the small convoy set out for Newquay in early August. She would have preferred a bed and breakfast, but Jason had insisted that they should all camp, something she had never done before and had no particular desire to try. Michael and Anne had complied and invested in a tent, but she couldn't go that far.

"It's a good job we all get on!" The glorious views over Fistral beach had chased away her apprehension when they'd reached the campsite. However, it returned, more potent than ever, as she surveyed the confines of the four-berth caravan she and Ed had hired together with Pat and Tony.

To her surprise, the compact accommodation proved to be surprisingly comfortable and catered for all their needs. The weather was warm and sunny, the surf was up, not that any of them could surf, but they all enjoyed trying, and it was such a good holiday they repeated it the following year.

On an icy cold evening in late January 1990, Mary and Robert's thoughts turned again to summer holidays. "What do you fancy, Newquay again?"

"I was wondering about somewhere different; how about Torquay?"

"Can I make a suggestion?" chipped in Michael, reclining on a bean bag, idly strumming a guitar. "How about France? I've heard Brittany is very nice. What about one of those Eurocamp places with the pre-erected tents?"

Robert laughed. "We'd never get your mum in a tent, would we love?"

But, much to their amazement, Jean thought it was a great idea, so in August, they had their first taste of life on a French campsite. They savoured the freshly baked baguettes and croissants delivered every morning by the cheery local baker, who announced his arrival with a blast of Chanson d'Amour played through a loudspeaker on his van.

They spent their days on the beach, swimming or fishing in the numerous rock pools, dangling tiny scraps of ham tied on a string into the salt water to entice the crabs from their hiding place, all of which were released to return home within minutes of being caught. The French practice of taking everything on holiday, including an assortment of pets, was a revelation for Rolo; cats on leads, rabbits, guinea pigs and hamsters in small hutches, parrots in cages suspended from tree branches, the campsite was an unparalleled utopia of scents and smells.

In the long summer evenings, when the twilight stretched almost until midnight, they played boules with their French fellow campers, keen to involve them in the fun. One evening, as the sun set and the shadows lengthened, their friendly neighbours invited them to join them for a walk to the nearby lake.

Unseen frogs croaked at a steadily increasing volume as they approached. The water was so perfectly still it was like a mirror, reflecting the fiery colours still splashed across the sky. Without speaking, their new friends pointed to a V-shaped echelon on the surface of the water, gradually widening as it came closer. They watched, mesmerised, as the sleek brown shape of an otter glided past them. From then on, they returned to the lakeside most evenings and right on time, the otter appeared and swam silently by on his usual route.

Chapter Two

They had been at the campsite for a week when Mary headed for a shower after a day on the beach and walked smack-bang into her sister. Jayne giggled helplessly at her younger sibling's startled expression before throwing her arms around her.

"But you told me you couldn't come!" Mary spluttered, not sure if she was dreaming.

"Mum rang me as soon as you'd booked. She wanted it to be a surprise for you."

Holding her daughters close, Jean surveyed the scene and decided that a fortnight in a tent had definitely been worth it. Only Pat and Tony had been in on the secret. Michael had quickly regained his composure after unexpectedly spotting Pierre, Jayne's husband, across the campsite and was busy introducing him to Anne. Jason was wrestling with his excited young cousins on the grass; Christophe, aged eight and Julien, aged six. When the families parted a week later, they had already agreed on a date to reconvene the following year; their love affair with Brittany had begun.

The annual trip to Blackpool that year was confined to a long weekend in September to see the famous illuminations. Whilst they were seated around the breakfast table at the dog-friendly guest house they had commandeered as usual, Michael tapped his teaspoon against the teapot and got to his feet.

"Anne and I have an announcement. We're pregnant!" he exclaimed before promptly sitting down again, flushed and with a smile from ear to ear.

Amidst the congratulations, Anne and Michael told them they intended to marry before the baby was born, and they would like Jason to be the best man. Still aged only 15, he was so outgoing and confident they knew he was perfect for the role. The wedding was set for Boxing Day.

Jason could play a little guitar and occasionally joined his dad and Michael on stage for a song at one of their gigs. He began work on his speech immediately and asked his dad to help him to compose a tune. When the wedding day arrived, everyone gave their speeches, and then it was Jason's turn. As he stood up and made his way to stand behind Anne and Michael, a waiter handed him a Spanish guitar, and to the surprise of everyone present, he sang his speech. Like all those years before when he had stood in for his headteacher on the drums for the nativity, he went down a storm.

On his 16th birthday a couple of weeks later, Mary and Robert gave Jason three packets of condoms, carefully gift-wrapped in the sheet music for the hit released by the British band Bad Company shortly before Jason was born, Feel Like Makin' Love. They were liberal-minded, and it was kind of a joke present, but not entirely.

Almost six feet tall, with blue eyes that twinkled mischievously and shoulder-length blonde hair that was always slightly dishevelled, they knew that Jason was already attracting the attention of several girls. More than anything, they didn't want him to follow them into early parenthood.

They realised how lucky they had been to find true love so early in their lives and to have the care and support of their parents. It could all have been so different.

Whilst still at junior school, Jason realised that his parents were remarkably young. From around the age of 13 or 14, virtually all of his friends had admitted that they were in love with his mum, captivated by her natural beauty, both inside and out. "Keep your hands off!" his dad told them, laughing when he caught them staring at Mary, but Jason knew that his parents only ever had eyes for each other.

"Mum! Dad! I don't even have a girlfriend!"

"That's what you tell us!" Mary smiled. "You have the power to break hearts; please don't do that if you can help it."

Jason did well in his GCSEs that summer, and two years later, although he passed his French A level with ease, being virtually bilingual thanks to his Auntie Jayne, maths had become his passion. He was ecstatic when he was accepted at Sheffield University, just across the Peak District from home, to do a maths degree.

During the summer holidays, Jason prepared for the move to Sheffield and worried about Rolo. They'd never been apart since the holiday to Corfu, and he wondered how the dog, now 12, would react. Riddled with arthritis, he could only manage short walks and spent much of his time asleep, with his head on Jason's lap whenever possible.

Earlier in the year, when the subject of the family holiday had come up, Jason offered to stay at home with Rolo rather than put him through a trip to Brittany. No one would hear of that, however, and agreed unanimously to postpone the holiday for the first time ever.

As August progressed, Rolo ate less and less and then the day came when Mary found him slumped in his basket, unable to move. Jason wrapped him in a blanket and gently cuddled him whilst Robert drove them to the vet. Mary stood quietly sobbing in the corridor, Robert's arm around her shoulders as Jason carried his beloved soulmate into the surgery and placed him in the arms of the vet.

"I'll stay," Jason told the vet. As he said the words, Rolo opened his eyes. The vet waited. Who could explain the unfathomable connection between animals and humans; he'd watched this scene played out many times before. Rolo's eyes held no fear, only a vast well of love for Jason, the boy-turned-man with whom he had spent his entire life. They held each other's gaze for what seemed like hours but were really only seconds, spellbound in their love for each other and then Rolo sighed and closed his eyes. As the vet had expected, Jason nodded to him, unable to speak, turned and left the surgery. They'd said their goodbyes. There was no need to stay longer, and his thoughts were only to comfort his parents.

Jason settled effortlessly into university life. He was a little homesick in the early days and returned home regularly at weekends, but he made new friends rapidly and enjoyed the social scene in Sheffield.

Initially living in the halls of residence, he obtained part-time work in a town centre bar, and within a few months, he and two friends began sharing a rental, a terraced property with a loft conversion. By invitation only, Mary and Robert joined their son for weekends in Sheffield, sometimes going to gigs at The Leadmill or the Polytechnic, other times just soaking up the relaxed student atmosphere that prevailed throughout the Crookes and Broomhill areas of the city.

They missed having their boys around, but two-year-old Amber, Michael and Anne's daughter, was a highly entertaining diversion. Their lives continued much as before, with a steady stream of visitors to the house, interspersed with the exciting weekends in Sheffield when they felt like youngsters again.

Chapter Two

In the summer of 1994, Jason invested in a secondhand Yamaha motorbike. Whilst the train journey between Sheffield and Stockport was very pleasant, on a warm, sunny day, there was nothing to match the exhilaration of riding the bike across the scenic expanse of the Peak District to visit his parents and grandparents.

"Wouldn't a car be better, what about Lesley?" his mum asked.

They had met Lesley for the first time at Christmas. Not entirely sure whether she was a friend or girlfriend, they liked her bubbly, easy-going manner, and that was all that mattered. Since then, Lesley had joined Jason for a couple of weekends in Stockport. The spare room was available, but Mary and Robert had no idea if she used it.

Jason laughed. "A car? You've got to be kidding. I can't afford a car! I'll get her a helmet."

A year had passed when Mary and Robert's attention turned to their son's rapidly approaching 21st birthday. "You're both 40 next year," Jason smirked, "and my birthday is so close to Christmas that nobody will be up for another bash then. How about a big summer party to celebrate all our birthdays?"

On the Friday evening before his birthday, Jason celebrated quietly at a restaurant in Stockport with his parents, grandparents, Michael, Anne, Amber and Lesley; Saturday evening was reserved for the usual musical soiree that still took place at his parents' home most weekends.

"Take these out for me, will you?"

Jason grabbed the bag of empty beer cans his dad was holding out to him. "Now? Are you having a laugh?" A blast of cold air hit him as he opened the back door. Shivering and muttering under his breath, he ran towards the drive, sparkling in the moonlight. In the lounge, the music fell silent, and the curtains twitched almost imperceptibly.

Someone stifled a giggle as Jason stopped abruptly, transfixed.

"Have you seen the bike outside?" Jason demanded to know, returning to the kitchen. "I can't believe someone's come on that. At this time of year? Mental."

"What bike?" someone called out from the lounge, and then everyone was on their feet, singing *Happy Birthday* and congratulating him.

Robert and Mary caught their son in a group hug. "We're a few days early, but we wanted you to have your gifts now, whilst everyone is here." Jason's grandparents had clubbed together with his parents to buy the bike; the helmet dangling casually from the handlebars was a gift from Michael, Anne and Amber.

"You're kidding me!!!! They're mine? No! They are? No, they can't be." Everyone laughed at Jason's perplexed expression; he was touchingly overwhelmed by his family's generosity.

It wasn't until a brief spell of warmer weather in early March that Jason got his first proper ride on his new bike when he rode it across the Peak District to Sheffield. On quiet stretches of road, he opened up the throttle and grinned as the power surged through the machine; he was in heaven. Two weeks later, he made the return journey for a weekend with his parents. The weather was crisp and wintry showers were forecast, but not until the following week.

"We can get the train. Please come; Mum and Dad would love to see you."

Chapter Two

Lesley had decided that the weather was much too cold to ride a pillion. She had watched Jason dismount after his first ride, so stiff with cold that he struggled to straighten his legs. It wasn't for her, but she knew he was desperate to ride the bike again as soon as possible.

"I'll come next time. Enjoy the ride, and make sure you're back before the snow comes."

It was just after lunchtime on Sunday when the rain started to fall. It turned to slushy sleet about an hour later and continued sporadically through the afternoon.

"Why can't the weather forecasters ever get it right? I'd better get the train back." It was about 4 pm, and Jason was standing by the window. It had stopped sleeting, but the road was wet, and there might be ice in the Peak District; not a night to be taking chances on the motorbike. "I'll leave the bike here and pick it up next time if that's okay?"

"Course," Robert replied. "But there's no need to get the train. We can drive you back, stay over tonight and come back early tomorrow. No one will mind if I show up a bit late for once, and you know your mum doesn't work Mondays."

Jason grimaced comically. When his parents stayed over, he slept on the sofa, which sank horribly in the middle and gave him backache. "Thanks, Dad. I'm meeting Simon at the pub later. You and Mum can join us; you'll love it."

Just before 6 pm, the three of them set off for Sheffield, taking their usual route over the Snake Pass, notorious for being the first road in the area to close in bad weather. Robert had been listening to the weather reports and was confident they would get through.

Ascending steeply along the road out of Glossop, they chatted happily about the forthcoming joint birthday celebrations. Robert drove at a steady 30mph. Soon they were at the top of the climb and then descending carefully along the pass, illuminated only by the beams from the headlights that sliced through the darkness all around. There was barely any other traffic, and they made good progress.

Moonlight pierced the heavy clouds as Ladybower reservoir came into view. Patchy mist drifted across the water, creating an ethereal, almost ghost-like scene. A short distance further on, they reached a junction with traffic lights. Robert saw the large delivery truck slowly approaching from the right. He intended to go straight across; the traffic lights were green, the truck was stopping, there was no need to brake.

Jason glanced up when he heard his dad shout, "What the...?" He saw the truck turning towards them on their side of the road as his mum began to scream. Almost instantaneously, there was a bang like an explosion, and then blackness.

It was some hours later when Jason came around in a hospital bed. He was unconscious when the emergency services arrived at the scene, and they'd sedated him for the journey to the hospital as a precaution. Fortunately, his injuries were confined to a cut across his right eyebrow that required stitches, a severe concussion and a broken wrist. His grandfathers were seated on either side of his bed; his Nannas were standing together at the end. They looked anxious and were holding hands. Surreal, thought Jason, in the sleepy haze of regaining consciousness.

Chapter Two

"How are you feeling, son?" Tony asked. *Son? What had made him say that? He'd never slipped and called Jason son before; naturally, it was a term reserved for Robert and Michael. But now? Was he somehow already adjusting, trying to close the gap?*

"All the better for seeing you guys." Jason attempted a weak smile. "Where am I?"

"You're in the hospital." Tony hesitated. He glanced across to Ed for reassurance and then forced himself on. "There's been an accident, your mum and dad were driving you home."

"Yes, I remember. Where are they?"

The older men each took hold of one of Jason's hands whilst his Nannas held each other and began to sob quietly. His voice barely a whisper, choked with emotion, his grandfather continued:

"They didn't make it, son."

Chapter Three

From his wheelchair, William reached forward to run gnarled fingers through his granddaughter's silky curls as she knelt in front of him, head bowed, working on her wooden jigsaw puzzle. He knew he was writing the final chapter of his life, but what a joy this young child was making it for him. He never failed to be amazed that she wanted to spend so much time in his company; they adored each other.

"There!" declared Lisa when all the pieces were in place. A triumphant smile replaced the look of intense concentration written across her face moments earlier.

"Well done you!" Her grandfather returned her smile.

Lisa's father, Joe, broke the puzzle and turned all the pieces face down. "If you think that's clever, Dad, watch this!" Lisa began to assemble them again, this time without the benefit of the picture, selecting each piece purely by the shape. When the jigsaw was complete, delighted with her efforts, the child climbed onto her grandfather's lap.

"Careful with Grandpa's legs Lisa." Joe knew that the shrapnel wounds suffered by his father during the First World War, when he was nothing more than a boy himself, gave him constant pain But the older man welcomed Lisa onto his knee with open arms. She flung her arms around his neck and settled her tiny cheek against his stubbly chin.

"You're scratchy, Grandpa, but I love you." Minutes later, they were both sound asleep in each other's arms.

Joe was born and raised in a small mining village in Durham. Both he and his mother had been lucky to survive his birth; there would be no more children. He didn't relish the prospect of working underground, hardly ever seeing daylight, nor did he want to follow his father into farming, which seemed to be relentless hard work.

Peacetime conscription was made mandatory in January 1948. Keen to experience something of the world beyond the quiet little backwater where he lived, in 1950, he joined the army to do his national service as soon as he was eligible to do so, aged 18.

Based in Aldershot, he stumbled on the Royal Army Dental Corps, and at the end of his two-year conscription, he successfully applied to join the unit. He enjoyed the work, but four years later, whilst on leave and travelling home by train, he passed through Sheffield station and noticed a recruitment billboard for a newly constructed dental teaching hospital.

For the remainder of the journey, Joe could not put the advertisement out of his mind. He enjoyed army life and was happy, but this sounded like something new and innovative; it might offer scope for promotion and development. He

Chapter Three

applied for a position, and in October 1956, aged 24, Joe began his new life in Sheffield.

Kathleen, a petite doll-like creature with huge green eyes and long, glossy blonde hair that fell to her waist, was a parttime dance teacher and dreamed of having a dance school one day. In the meantime, she had to take a part-time waitress job at the local cafe to make ends meet.

She noticed Joe the first time he visited the cafe. It was hard not to; he towered over her as she pointed to an empty table. He had the chiselled features of a film star and shiny, almost jet-black wavy hair that curled at the ends if he let it grow too long. He came in regularly after that, and if she caught his eye, he blushed and hastily looked away.

When her patience ran out, Kathleen took the plunge. "Would you like to go out with me?" Joe almost spat his coffee at her, startled by the unanticipated and forthright question. "I can meet you for a drink at the Red Lion at 7 pm tomorrow. I'll wait 15 minutes, and if you're not there, no hard feelings." With that, she moved swiftly to another table, leaving Joe wondering if he was hallucinating.

To be on the safe side, he arrived at the Red Lion 10 minutes early and waited outside anxiously, wondering if she had set him up. Kathleen appeared around the corner bang on time and they never looked back.

"When can I see you again, Kath?" Joe enquired as they parted.

"The name's Kathleen. I don't like being short, don't ever shorten my name."

Kathleen, the eldest of three girls, was two years younger than Joe. Her father had been killed in an accident in the steelworks when she was eleven, and her mother had suffered severe depression for several years afterwards.

Despite her grief, Kathleen had taken on the role of carer for her younger siblings and her mother. Her petite and seemingly fragile exterior hid an iron will and a determination to succeed, no matter what life threw at her. They were married within 18 months, and in February 1960, Kathleen gave birth to Neil and Stephen, virtually identical twins.

The 1960s were challenging for the couple, both striving for success in their chosen careers whilst simultaneously providing a loving home for their rapidly growing boys. In those early years, they hardly seemed to see each other, passing on the doorstep as Joe returned home from the hospital and Kathleen headed to the dance school. She'd been gradually taking over more and more classes as her employer aged, and when the still sprightly but elderly lady decided to retire, there was only one person to whom she would entrust her precious dance school. It was the fulfilment of Kathleen's dream, but now she had to work hard to succeed, not only for herself but for the lady who had put so much faith in her and was watching from the wings.

Slowly, the colossal workload paid off. By the end of the decade, Joe and Kathleen had secured a mortgage on a large, detached property in Dore, an exclusive district of Sheffield and began taking their summer holidays in the warmer climes of Spanish resorts.

Neil and Stephen had inherited their parents' work ethic, and both were doing well at school. Competitive by nature and determined, they constantly battled to out-achieve each other, academically and in sports. Whilst still at junior school, the glowing reports provided by their teachers suggested it was likely that both boys would go on to university.

And into this world of high achievement and success landed Lisa on 19th June 1972, when Joe was almost 40, Kathleen was 38, and the twins were aged 12.

Two years earlier, only weeks after moving into their new home, over breakfast, Kathleen had again broached the subject of extending their family. "My clock's ticking, you know?" Several times before, she'd mentioned to Joe how nice it would be to have a daughter, perhaps they could try for another baby, but the time had never seemed right.

"Is it, dear?" Joe replied absentmindedly. "I can't hear anything." He hadn't intended to sound sarcastic, but when the newspaper he was reading came hurtling towards him, knocking his half-empty coffee cup over, he realised his error.

"Joe! I keep telling you! I want another baby before it's too late!"

Joe carefully folded the coffee-sodden newspaper, trying to buy time to clear the myriad of thoughts darting around his befuddled brain. Images of crying babies, nappies, sticky fingers and the bags he'd seen under his own eyes for several years flashed in front of him.

"Let's not be hasty, sweetheart," he said gently. "We're only just finally getting on our feet; maybe we should enjoy that for a while?"

"Another reason to delay? We can't keep putting it off; we're running out of time!" Kathleen's beautiful green eyes clouded over and began to brim with tears.

In that instant, Joe knew there was nothing more to be said; he couldn't bring himself to deny the love of his life her chance to be a mother again. He felt guilty for secretly hoping it wouldn't happen, but Kathleen was pregnant just over a year later; and when he held his daughter for the first time, a beautiful, healthy baby, he thought his heart would burst.

Lisa had her mother's almost feline green eyes but otherwise resembled her father, both in looks and temperament. Tall for her age with a tousled mass of dark curls, it was soon apparent that she was timid and shy; the toddler avoided other children, preferring the company of her parents, her brothers and her grandparents.

Hoping to help her daughter overcome her shyness, Kathleen took her to the dance school when Lisa was almost three years old. Throughout the short class, Lisa refused to let go of her mother's hand. The following week she managed to stand by the side of the other children and shuffle her feet only briefly before tears of anguish streamed down her face. Distressed, Kathleen swept her daughter into her arms and hastily took her home.

"No, Mummy, no!" Lisa wailed the following week as Kathleen got her ready for the dance class, tears spilling down her small red cheeks again.

A smile crept across the little girl's face when her mother took her hand and showed her some basic dance steps. "Again, again!" She learned quickly, clapping her hands together with delight when she got the steps right.

Kathleen was thrilled by Lisa's enjoyment of dancing and the speed of her progress. She had a natural rhythm and quickly mastered the steps of a short dance, but she would not hear of re-joining the dance class.

A turning point came when Lisa agreed to perform her dance for her family. She had a couple of false starts but encouraged by the rapturous applause of her brothers and her daddy, her confidence grew, and she completed her dance several times. The following week her grandparents joined the audience; it was a huge step forward for the painfully shy toddler.

Spurred on by Lisa's pleasure in performing for the family, Kathleen talked to her about doing a 'test' of her dancing to win a prize. She showed photos of other little girls in their dance costumes, hoping the lure of the pretty dresses would incentivise her to try. If she could get her daughter over the first hurdle, surely she would take to dancing like a duck to water.

The ruse worked, Lisa was interested, and on the morning of exam day, Kathleen helped her into one of the costumes. The child's eyes widened when she saw her reflection; when could she do the test and win the prize?

Kathleen watched, horrified, as her daughter's pretty face crumpled when she told her the test would be at the dance school with the other little girls. Lisa turned and ran from the room, screaming. In hot pursuit, Kathleen followed her upstairs and found her in the bathroom, cowering in the tiny space between the underside of the sink and the toilet, distraught and gasping between sobs.

Almost in tears herself when Lisa refused to take her hand, Kathleen desperately tried to calm her. When she promised Lisa she would never have to dance again, the little girl crept forward and clung to her mother until her panic subsided. The dance lessons were over.

"I'm so worried about her, Joe," Kathleen said in a quavering voice later that evening. "It was horrible. Lisa isn't like the boys; I couldn't keep them off the stage when they were small."

As Joe wrapped an arm around her shoulder and held her close, he reminisced about the twins' younger years. It was true that they were both natural performers like their mother, lapping up the limelight at every opportunity, but they had always had each other for support.

He thought back to his childhood. As an only child, he had been painfully shy, just like Lisa. Nervous and unsure of himself, he didn't make friends easily, but his parents had told him to approach everyone with a smile, and soon friends would come to him. They had been right; in time, he must remember to pass the tip onto Lisa. "Don't worry, love, just let her be herself. She'll be fine."

Lisa had her fourth birthday in June 1976. A few weeks later, daily temperatures began to soar until they were comparable with those in Spain, and they stayed that way until the end of the summer. Neil and Stephen had taken their O levels and were confident they had done well.

They spent part of almost every day of their school holidays with their young sister, taking her to the packed lido or playing hide and seek in the cool shade of the nearby woods. They made rope swings for her and helped her to climb small trees. The three siblings were very close despite the age gap.

Often too hot to sleep, the family stayed outside late into the evenings, the French doors flung wide open, the twins squabbling over the record player in the lounge. Their taste in music was one of the few things they didn't share. When they played one of her favourites, Lisa joined in the dancing, naturally swaying and twirling to the beat; she seemed to have forgotten her panic attack the previous year. The summer passed in a glorious haze of Mediterranean-style weather and outdoor living. But then, it was time for Lisa to start school.

"Sweetheart, you are too clever for me to teach you," soothed William as he held her close.

Joe's parents had moved to Sheffield when the twins were young, and they both delighted in the company of all their grandchildren, but everyone knew there was a special bond between Lisa and her grandfather. To avoid distressing Lisa, the family agreed only he would discuss school with her that summer and try to prepare her.

Holding his sobbing granddaughter close to his chest one hot day at the end of August, William thought about this latest unexpected turn that his life had taken. Born at the turn of the century, he'd fought for his country when he was only sixteen, at the insistence of his brutish father, who had called him a coward if he refused to lie about his age and join up.

He had returned from the Great War, wounded both physically and mentally, grateful he'd survived when so many of his friends hadn't. He found work as a farm labourer, and within a few years, he married Flo, whom he'd known since infancy and who held him tight through the night terrors that continued.

Eventually, he worked his way up to be a Farm Manager and worked hard throughout his life to provide for his family. Now, with his body failing due to age and his old injuries, he'd expected to be on the scrap heap, not much use to anyone. It had come as a complete surprise when the family had unanimously agreed that it should fall to him to try to prepare Lisa for school, and he was immensely proud to take on the role of mentor.

He dedicated the summer entirely to Lisa, spending hours at the children's library selecting books that might catch her interest and helping her to read them, writing out sums for her to do and using both his fingers and toes to check her answers so that she was bent double with laughter. This latest challenge in his life, to help his granddaughter set out on life's journey, meant as much to William as anything that had gone before.

As Lisa began to sob once more, almost hysterical, he gently stroked her head to calm her, softly told her how clever she was and explained that she had learned everything that he could show her; now she needed a better teacher. He told her how proud of her he was and that he couldn't wait to hear everything about the school and her new friends. Joe, helping his mother to make tea in the kitchen, glanced through the open doorway and was momentarily transfixed by the scene. His father was a good, kind man, but he had never been tactile. The power of love, he mused. *So, old dogs can learn new tricks after all.*

Lisa's first day at school a week later was traumatic. Kathleen had taken her, and they sat together at a small table with three other little girls for an hour or so before the teacher came over and suggested to Lisa that maybe her mummy could go now and leave her to play with her new friends. As Kathleen stood to leave, Lisa let out a howl that sounded like she was about to be murdered. Unable to calm her, her mother had no alternative but to take her home. The next day wasn't much better, and by the third day, Lisa flatly refused to go. Bewildered, Kathleen and Joe almost carried her there, kicking and screaming. They stayed with her until lunchtime before they all returned home together, spent.

Each evening Lisa demanded to be taken to see her grandfather. Sobbing uncontrollably, sometimes gasping for breath, she pleaded with him to take over as her teacher, to make her mummy and daddy stop taking her to the awful school. "I need you, Grandpa!" she screamed at him on that third evening. "Please, please help me."

Holding her tight and soothing her gently as best he could, William struggled to find words to calm her fears. He told her he would be thinking of her all through the next day, looking forward to hearing all about what she had been doing.

He didn't know then that he could not keep his promise. That during the night, whilst he was asleep, his big, courageous heart would stop beating. When Flo broke the news to them the following day, Joe and Kathleen were devastated. William's passing was an enormous loss for everyone, but Lisa depended on him. How would their little girl cope now?

Chapter Four

X

There was no question of Lisa going to school; for days, she was inconsolable. Joe and Kathleen took time from work to comfort her, taking turns to sit with her during the night until she fell back to sleep following a nightmare. Kind neighbours entertained her whilst the family attended William's funeral. That evening, as Joe sat on the edge of Lisa's bed and prepared to read her a story, she suddenly looked towards the door and smiled. "What are you smiling at, sweetheart?" he asked.

"Grandpa!" she replied. Astonished, Joe turned and looked towards the door, but he could see nothing. "He came last night after you'd gone, and sat with me until I fell to sleep, didn't you, Grandpa?" Lisa continued, still smiling and gazing into what appeared to Joe to be thin air.

"Come on, Grandpa; you can sit here again." She patted the quilt on the unoccupied side of her bed.

"Would you like me to go now Grandpa's here?" asked Joe, uncertain what to do next.

"No, Grandpa likes this one," chirped Lisa, "he'd like to listen too." So, Joe read the story, peculiarly self-conscious at the thought that his father might be listening. He kissed his daughter, who was content to be left in the care of her grandpa again until she fell asleep.

Bemused, he headed downstairs to tell Kathleen. She immediately dismissed it as a child's fantasy, but she was happy their daughter had found some comfort. To her astonishment, however, two days later, Lisa announced at breakfast that she was ready to return to school the following day.

"Grandpa's coming with me," she told them. "He's going to sit with me, and we'll do the lessons together."

Sure enough, Lisa needed no encouragement to return to school the following day. She insisted the teacher place an empty chair beside her for her grandpa to sit on. Mrs Hall reluctantly complied but noted throughout the day that Lisa didn't speak to the other children. Instead, she'd frequently leaned towards the empty chair and, in hushed tones, had spoken to the grandfather she believed was sitting there.

The pattern continued for several weeks until half-term. Lisa was attentive in class and learned quickly, but Mrs Hall became concerned that some children were bullying her and invited her parents in for a chat.

"Of course, we are all pleased that Lisa finds comfort in her imaginary world with your father," Mrs Hall addressed Joe directly, grateful to have a moment to divert her attention from Kathleen's intense scrutiny. "But the other children find her behaviour difficult to understand. It's causing some, how can I put it, adverse reactions. Could you talk to her? Encourage her to move on, maybe relinquish the spare chair and engage more with her classmates?"

Joe and Kathleen took the opportunity to speak to Lisa about it over the half-term holiday. She was aghast, demanding to know what Grandpa would think if he had nowhere to sit, and so the use of the spare chair, together with the bullying, resumed after the holiday.

On a cold and icy morning in early December, Mrs Hall was on yard duty during break time. She noticed Lisa, characteristically standing on her own in a corner, her back turned to the other children, but suddenly she spun around.

As she did so, one of her classmates, Michelle, fell on the ice and cried out. By the time Mrs Hall reached them, Lisa was crouched beside Michelle. She was crying, and the teacher watched incredulously as Lisa instinctively placed her arm around the child's shoulders and began to stroke her hair.

"What a kind girl you are, Lisa. Would you like to come with Michelle to the office so we can take a look at that arm?" Lisa nodded and, to the teacher's further amazement, took hold of Michelle's hand as they walked gingerly across the yard. When they returned to the classroom, Mrs Hall seized the sudden opportunity. "Would you mind sitting next to Michelle for me, please, Lisa, and keeping an eye on her for the rest of the day?"

Michelle looked tentatively at Lisa. She, too, was quiet and shy; she couldn't imagine that this strange girl who spoke to no one would want to sit next to her. But Lisa carried her chair to the table where Michelle was seated and placed it next to her. From that day on, throughout their school years, Lisa and Michelle were best friends and were rarely seen apart.

"Do you know what was strange?" Mrs Hall recounted the incident to her colleagues in the staff room later that afternoon as they got ready to leave. "I'm sure Lisa turned before Michelle fell. I know it sounds ridiculous, but...., it was as though she knew the accident was going to happen before it did."

In junior school, it was already apparent that Lisa possessed the same academic ability as her brothers. "What happened to the other 5%?" Kathleen asked when Lisa rushed in, excited to tell her she had gained 95% on a test and a gold star again.

Kathleen intended to encourage and impress on her daughter how clever she was and that full marks were within her grasp; but what Lisa heard was that her best was not enough. It didn't matter how many correct answers she got; her parents were disappointed if she could not achieve that essential perfect score.

To outsiders, Lisa had it all; successful, wealthy parents, a beautiful home, foreign holidays from which she always arrived back tanned to the colour of honey and two older brothers who doted on her. But she remained racked by insecurities. Neil and Stephen excelled at sixth form, and both won scholarships to Oxford, from where they graduated in 1981. Lisa fully understood the enormity of their achievements. She worked harder and harder, locking herself away in her bedroom, relentlessly studying, telling no one why, and constantly grappling with her fear of failure in a family of high achievers.

By the age of 13, Lisa stood just short of six feet tall, almost a foot taller than her mother and her best friend, Michelle. And she hated it.

Still hopeful that one day she might relent and take up dancing, Kathleen encouraged her to help at the dance classes, watching the younger ones practise their steps whilst she instructed the others. To appease her, Lisa dutifully went along several times each week but flatly refused to dance herself. The reflection in the mirror said it all; she was a huge, ungainly, ugly lump at the side of her beautiful, vivacious mother, her tiny frame whirling and twirling to the music. How could she possibly ever dance?

To her surprise, however, Lisa was very popular with her small charges at the dance school. She had inherited her father's sense of humour, and as she slowly relaxed enough to let her personality shine through, she discovered, as Joe had told her she would, that both the children and their parents gravitated to her.

As anticipated by everyone who knew how diligently she had worked for them, Lisa left senior school in the summer of 1988 with eight grade A GCSEs. She had already discussed at length with Michelle her plans for the future. They had a mutual interest in psychology and sociology and had decided those were the subjects they would study in the next phase of their education.

"Are you sure about your subjects, love?" asked Joe. "They sound a bit woolly and might not get you as far as if you did a maths subject and a science or a language like Neil and Stephen." Neil was a barrister in London, and Stephen had gone into civil engineering. Neither career remotely appealed to Lisa, but Kathleen took up where Joe left off.

"It can be harder for a woman to succeed, Lisa. Think about technical subjects in preparation for your degree if you want to be considered a serious contender."

Torn between her interests, her desperate need to stay true to her closest friend, and her overwhelming desire not to disappoint her parents, Lisa agonised over her choices. When she told Michelle that she had ticked pure maths with statistics, physics, English and general studies on her enrolment form, they sat and cried together.

Lisa's first term in the sixth form was a disaster. She hated the maths and physics courses and saw virtually nothing of Michelle, who began to make friends in her classes. To make matters worse, she developed weeping eczema on her hands due to her constant stress, which drew horrified glances from her classmates. Struggling to contemplate the next term, she broke down at Christmas; Joe heard her sobbing in her bedroom.

"Sweetheart!" Joe opened his arms to her like she was a small child again. "What can be so awful to make you cry like that?" Between choking sobs, Lisa explained how much she hated the sixth form. "Well, let's talk, sort something out. There's no need to be so upset."

"I can't let everyone down," Lisa wailed, ignoring her father's placation. "I know Mum's disappointed already that I don't want to dance. I've got to make it to uni, but it's so hard. I want to make you and Mum proud."

Kathleen had heard the commotion and was standing outside the door, listening to the conversation, aghast. She rushed in and wrapped her arms around Lisa. "How could you ever think we are anything but proud of you? We love you, and we want you to be happy."

Chapter Four

They talked long into the night. Lisa didn't want to change courses at the sixth form, unable to bear the thought of being behind in the class. She decided to find a job and start over and with her parents' full support, left the sixth form at the beginning of the second term.

After several unsuccessful job interviews when, due to nerves, Lisa had been barely coherent, she started work in March 1989 as a trainee insurance claims handler. Jenni started on the same day as a trainee underwriter. Aged 18, she was a little older than Lisa, and she took her under her wing on that first day, suggesting a bite to eat together during the lunch break. From then on, they spent every lunchtime together and soon became good friends.

There were 21 members of staff in total in the open-plan office; aged only 16, Lisa was the youngest. Despite the volume of work and long hours, there was always plenty of friendly banter, and with her ready wit, Lisa gradually fitted in. She rapidly learned the basic techniques of claims handling, and in September, Alan, the Office Manager, encouraged her to sign up for a day release course. The remainder of the year passed swiftly, and then it was December and the Christmas party.

"Well, what are you going to wear then? Here, try this on." Jenni was swiftly gathering an array of glittering outfits to try on, all of which were too flamboyant for Lisa's taste. Frustrated, she held out a baggy sweatshirt to Lisa, who eventually settled on a black dress, plain by Jenni's standards, and a pair of flat black pumps.

Sitting alone at the table after the meal, watching Jenni gyrating on the dance floor surrounded by her admiring male colleagues, Lisa remembered the times spent watching her mother at the dance school; how she wished she could be petite and pretty.

"Lisa! There you are, I've been looking for you everywhere. Christmas kiss for Stu?" Her intoxicated fellow claims handler, sweating with his efforts on the dance floor, dropped heavily onto the chair beside her and almost suffocated her with a hot, slobbery kiss. Horrified by the encounter, Lisa caught Jenni's attention to tell her she was leaving the party early.

"You've never been kissed before? Lisa! Where've you been all your life? Get out there and bag some more." The two friends were in the ladies' toilets, and Lisa was almost in tears. Despite her friend's protestations, she headed to the pay phone and rang home.

"Would you like a lift?" She asked Jenni as she held out her ticket and reclaimed her coat.

Jenni laughed. "No thanks, I think I'm on a promise."

Throughout the next two years, Lisa worked hard at work and her studies. By August 1991, she had completed her day release course and progressed to handling motor claims. A few of her colleagues were already studying for the Associateship of the Chartered Insurance Institute exams, the equivalent of a degree. It would be a challenge, some were attempting the same subject for the second or third time, but she fancied having a go.

"If you don't apply, you'll have some explaining to do," Alan smiled when Lisa mentioned it at her annual appraisal. He wasn't entirely sure what had drawn him to the shy, timid, Amazonian-built teenager who had mumbled and stuttered her way appallingly through her interview. But after 40 years in the business, he considered himself a good judge of character, and she was certainly living up to his expectations.

Lisa signed up for courses in three subjects in the first year, which all her colleagues insisted was over-ambitious. Only Alan was unsurprised when she passed them all. In September 1992, she signed up for three more subjects. There were only a handful of other students for the evening class in Legal Liabilities, one of whom was Mark. He was doing the course for the third time and didn't appear overly concerned about that.

Mark worked for an insurance broker in Sheffield. He was 24 years old, slightly taller than Lisa, dark-haired and quirkily good-looking; his nose was too big and somewhat lopsided. Banter with the tutor was his speciality, and everyone agreed that he made what otherwise might have been a dry, tedious subject fun.

At the last class before Christmas, Mark suggested an early finish and a drink at the local pub, which even the tutor agreed was a great idea. Half an hour later, Lisa found herself standing next to him in the crowded pub, trying to shout something into his right ear about going home to make mince pies. He turned to face her with a meaningful look and moved towards her. "Don't even think about it!" she yelped, leaning backwards so fast that droplets of red wine splashed onto her white blouse. "I've been there, done that and never again!"

Laughing, Mark produced a biro from his pocket, wrote his phone number on a partially soaked beer mat and handed it to her. "Okay, ten-pin bowling it is. Call me over the holiday."

On a cold, rainy day between Christmas and New Year, Lisa checked that she could read the faded number on the crumpled card, still surprised that she had agreed to put the evil-smelling object in her handbag. *What had she got to lose? It might be fun.* After dialling only half the number before hastily replacing the receiver several times, she finally made the call. Mark picked it up on the second ring. "Hoped you'd ring, Mouse, free tomorrow night? I'll book it, and I'm warning you, I'm good!"

"I'm going out later," Lisa told her parents the following afternoon. "Ten-pin bowling with a friend."

"Oh, that's nice; I didn't know Jenni liked bowling," Kathleen replied, glued to the Sound of Music yet again.

"I'm not going with Jenni."

Kathleen spun around, staring intently at Lisa. "You're not going with Jenni, then who? You never go out with anyone else."

Lisa blushed. "Mark. From class. Please don't get excited, Mum, there's nothing in it. He's so full of himself; I'd never go out with him. He's just a friend, and I thought it might be fun."

Joe sighed as Kathleen leapt up, switched the television off and hauled Lisa upstairs, insisting that she choose something pretty to wear. As he expected, she looked perturbed when they reappeared half an hour later. Lisa had adopted her usual choice of black jeans, a baggy sweater and sparse makeup.

But the smile on Lisa's face when she returned home later that evening left nothing more to be said. She may have misjudged Mark; his humour hid insecurities. He'd confided in her that he had dyslexia. Although outward appearances might suggest he wasn't in the least bit concerned by exam failure, that wasn't true. They began meeting for a drink after class each week and, within months, were smitten with each other. Lisa invited Jenni and her current boyfriend to join them at the bowling alley one evening. To her delight, Mark and Jenni immediately hit it off, and Jenni began joining them regularly, with or without a boyfriend.

Lisa passed all three subjects again, and with her expert extra-curricular tutelage, Mark finally passed his liability exam.

In September 1993, Lisa enrolled for courses in the last three subjects; Mark needed only two to complete his qualification. Spurred on by Lisa's encouragement, he signed up for both and, to his utmost amazement, passed them. They celebrated their joint exam success with a gulet cruise in Turkey. It was the first time she had ever been away without her family. She returned radiant, and three months later, Mark invited her to move into the small, two-bedroom starter home he was buying.

"Everyone has to start somewhere. It'll make a perfect little love nest until we can afford something bigger," he told her. It took her a while to come around to the idea, but shortly after her 23rd birthday in June 1995, Mark carried Lisa over the threshold as proudly as if they were married. Life was good, they had both gained promotions on the back of their academic achievements, and over the summer, they worked hard to transform Mark's investment into a beautiful home.

By September, Lisa's thoughts were turning again to studying, this time for the Fellowship exams. Few people went on to study for the Fellowship; it would improve her chances of further promotion and make her family proud.

"You don't need to do it," Mark whined when Lisa told him her plans. "I'm certainly not studying anymore. Let's get out and have some fun. We work hard enough as it is without studying on top."

"Come on, don't be like that," she coaxed him. "By early April, the exams will be over. I only need to study hard for six months, and then we'll party as much as you like through the summer. Promise!"

Mark dejectedly agreed to Lisa's proposal, knowing he was beaten, but the first year was more demanding than either of them had anticipated. Lisa needed to pass five subjects for the Fellowship. Again, she signed up for three in the first year, but there were no college courses; it was all home study. She spent endless hours in the spare bedroom, which Mark had converted into a study for her. He helped out with cooking and cleaning, but it was a struggle for them both. They were relieved when Lisa passed the exams, two with distinction.

In September 1996, Lisa enrolled for the last two subjects. "One more year, that's all it is, and then I'm through with studying for good." She desperately wanted Mark to enjoy the winter months more than he had the previous year, and so, at her insistence, they worked out a strategy.

She would study at Sheffield Central Library two evenings per week, straight from work. Mark would stay in town with colleagues, and she would drive him home at the end of the evening. By mid-December, she was pleased that the arrangements seemed to be working well, and Mark was much happier.

Chapter Four

Lisa was now a team leader, dealing with sometimes complex injury claims in addition to supervising her colleagues. Occasionally she was required to visit the offices of solicitors to discuss tactics. One such occasion arose just before the Christmas holiday. It was an afternoon appointment; afterwards, she planned to go straight to the library.

"Merry Christmas!" The solicitor smiled as he held the door open for her when she left. A gust of cold air hit them as several wet snowflakes landed on the tiled floor and immediately transformed into tiny puddles.

"And to you." She quickly found her umbrella and launched herself into the dark, wintry early evening. The meeting had gone on longer than anticipated as the friendly solicitor plied her with mince pies and chocolates to celebrate the festive season. She would usually have been at the library half an hour ago, but it wouldn't matter for once.

Running along the wet pavement, head down and trying to hold her umbrella steady, she suddenly heard laughter, a laugh she vaguely recognised. She looked up briefly into the sleet that whirled against the backdrop of the sparkling Christmas lights. Ahead, she could see two people walking close together, one much taller than the other.

Light spilt onto the pavement as a door opened, and then she heard that familiar sound of exuberant laughter again. Lisa hurried on; when she reached the entrance to the small and slightly shabby-looking back-street hotel, she hesitated and then pulled the door open. She saw the receptionist smile at Mark and Jenni as she held out their room key, and then her world shattered like glass.

Chapter Five

χ

Jason surveyed the surreal scene below him. It was as though he was hovering about six feet above the bed; he could see his body lying prone, his skin so pale it was almost grey against the white sheets. Grandad T was sitting on one side of the bed, Grandad E on the other, their heads bowed. His grandmothers clung to each other, openly sobbing. *Was he dead?*

He watched as his grandfathers raised their heads and looked at each other and then at him. Grandad T was saying something, Jason could see his lips forming the words, but he couldn't hear anything. His grandfather seemed agitated; leaning forward, he placed his free hand on his grandson's right shoulder and shook it. "Jason! Can you hear me?" Suddenly Jason was back in bed, feeling the pressure of his grandfather's touch. He blinked. "Thank God. For a moment there, I thought....."

"I'm okay, Grandad." Jason looked at each of his grandparents in turn, a quizzical frown deepening across his brow. "Can I just check? Did I hear right..., did you say Mum and Dad....."

Before anyone could answer, the door swung open, and a nurse bustled in. "Ah, Jason, you've surfaced, good. How are you feeling? Can I get anyone some tea?" The chink of mugs and teaspoons was strangely banal in the heavily charged atmosphere. The nurse helped Jason to sit up against his pillows. He managed a few sips of tea, but that was all.

"With any luck, you won't be here too long." Grandad T broke the silence, desperate to find something to say that sounded remotely positive.

"Come and stay with us for a while." Nanna Jean stepped forward to take Jason's mug from him, stroking his hair as she spoke.

Nanna Pat followed and slipped an arm around his shoulders. "And then with us, let us look after you, Jason." He looked at them blankly, unable to contemplate anything other than that moment.

"One step at a time," Grandad T interjected gently. "When Jason can come home, we'll sort things out. Let's not worry about it now."

The nurse breezed in again and, with the ease of someone with extensive experience in such situations, took charge. "Everyone drunk up? Lovely. Now, shall we let this young man get some rest?"

In turn, each of his grandparents kissed Jason before they left. Surreal, he thought again as he lifted his hand to wave. He couldn't remember the last time either of his grandfathers had kissed him. "This will help you to sleep," the nurse handed Jason a small glass of water containing a light sedative and then helped him to lie back down. She opened the door and turned to look at him, her eyes glistening in the dim light. "I'm so sorry, love."

The sound of voices, the clatter of crockery and a vacuum cleaner somewhere in the distance awoke Jason. *Where was he?* With some effort, he opened his eyes and gazed around the small, sterile room, two plastic chairs stacked in one corner. A memory played out in his mind like a film clip; he could see himself lying in a bed, his grandfathers sitting on chairs on either side, his grandmothers standing together, their arms around each other. He knew this place; he was in the hospital. And his parents were dead.

Surely that couldn't be true? He looked towards the door, hoping they'd walk through it, laughing, telling him it had all been a silly mistake. When the door suddenly swung open, he gasped. *Please, God.*

"I didn't think you'd be awake yet, Jason. How are you feeling?" The day sister had read the notes at the start of her shift. "I'm sorry for your loss. Breakfast is on the way. Try to eat something if you can, the doctor will be round to see you later." Still staring at the door as he listened to her footsteps tapping away along the corridor, Jason realised he felt strangely calm. *So that was it then. His parents wouldn't be coming through the door; they really were dead. Surely, he should be sobbing hysterically? The two people he loved most were gone, and he hadn't even shed a tear.*

Jason was munching on a slice of toast when his grandmothers arrived, looking exhausted, their eyes red from crying. He felt guilty for being able to eat, but he'd been ravenous when breakfast came.

"Where are the grandads?" he asked, puzzled.

The women looked at each other, not sure how to answer. Nanna Pat cleared her throat. "They'll be here soon. They've just got a few.......... formalities to deal with."

His grandfathers arrived looking pale and ashen. Horrified, Jason instantly realised where they'd been. He'd seen enough crime dramas and knew the procedure when someone died; they'd come from the morgue. Watching his grandmothers stand to comfort their husbands, tears streaming down their faces, the enormity of their suffering struck him. *Mum and Dad were their children; they've lost their children!* He couldn't begin to imagine how dreadful that must be.

"I'm very sorry," the doctor said as he entered the room a short while later. "No, no, you don't need to leave." He motioned to Jason's grandparents to remain seated as he approached the patient. "You've had breakfast? Any headaches? Double vision? Vomiting?" enquired the doctor, hesitating only briefly for Jason to answer. "Well, if you're still feeling okay after lunch, I think we can let you go into the care of these good people then."

He smiled benignly at Jason's grandparents, seemingly ignoring the anguish on their faces, a deliberate ploy. Their lives would never be the same again. They needed something to do, a role to play, a focus. He hoped that was what he had just given them.

"Some of your clothes have blood stains, love. From the cut above your eye," Nanna Jean hastily added. "Can we collect some fresh ones for you? In case we can take you home today." She pulled the plastic bag of clothing from the locker by the bed and crouched out of range of Jason's vision to search for the door key in the pocket of his jeans.

Chapter Five

Jason's grandparents had never visited him in Sheffield, and images of the generally appalling state of the bedsits of his fellow tenants flashed through his mind. He managed to give them the address and some basic directions.

"I live on the top floor, in the loft at the top of the second staircase. If any of the other doors are open, whatever you do, don't look inside. My clothes are in the divan."

Nanna Pat went to fetch more tea, leaving Jason alone with Grandad T. "We haven't told your Uncle Michael yet; he doesn't even know there's been an accident." Suddenly, Jason's grandfather could hold his composure no longer. He'd fought to be strong and comfort his wife when the police arrived to tell them of the accident and insisted on breaking the dreadful news to Jean and Ed in person before driving them to Sheffield. Telling his youngest son that his brother was dead was too much to contemplate.

Jason watched, stunned, as his grandfather's face crumpled and tears tumbled down his cheeks. He leaned forward in his chair to hide his face, but his body shook with the raking sobs that tore through him. Unsure what to say or do, Jason placed his hand on his grandfather's shoulder and waited for his sobs to subside. "Sorry about that," Tony dabbed at his eyes and blew his nose loudly into his handkerchief.

"Don't worry. I'll tell Michael."

"No, no, I can't let you do that. It's my job."

"Please, Grandad," Jason continued. "I want to help you; I need to help you. Please."

The doctor returned to check on Jason just after 1 pm and confirmed that he was fit to leave. Feeling slightly unsteady, he managed to dress, and his grandmothers linked arms with him as they entered the corridor, leaving the quiet stillness of his room behind. Jason was mesmerised by the activity all around; there was the hum of people chatting interspersed with laughter, music playing somewhere, a telephone ringing, someone calling for the next patient. His world had collapsed, yet everything else was still normal and unchanged. How could that be?

Sandwiched between his grandmothers in the rear seat, Jason gazed out through the rain-streaked windows as his grandfather drove them home across the Derbyshire hills in silence, everyone lost in their thoughts. Was it really less than 24 hours since he'd been in the back of another car, happily discussing plans with his mum and dad to celebrate their birthdays? It seemed like a lifetime ago. There were more hugs and tears when they dropped Jean and Ed, ashen-faced, at home. They planned to ring Jayne immediately and stay on the phone with her for as long as she needed them, the rest of the day if necessary.

As soon as they'd got Jason settled in a large armchair with a cup of tea, Grandad T rang the large shopping centre where Michael was the Assistant Manager. "Any chance you can call by sometime later?" he asked, trying hard to sound nonchalant.

"Course, Dad, everything all right?"

His father hesitated. "Great, see you later. Bye."

Shortly after 5 pm, they saw Michael's car pull up outside. He'd left work early. His dad never called him at work; something wasn't right. The door slammed shut behind him as he bounced into the kitchen with his usual vigour. "Where're you hiding?" They heard him call out as the door to the lounge swung open. "Oh, hi Jason. Shouldn't you be in class? Hey, what's happened to your arm, you've not come off your bike?"

"Sit down, son." His father gestured to a space on the sofa next to his mother. With a puzzled frown, Michael did as he was told, bemused. Jason began to recount the events of the weekend and the journey home the previous evening, of his memory of the hazy moonlight over the reservoir, and then he faltered.

"That's the last thing I remember. The next thing I knew, I was in the hospital." Jason shook his head sorrowfully. "I don't know what happened."

Perched on the edge of the sofa, Michael was even more alarmed when his mother put her arm through his. His father took over the remaining details; the arrival of the police and the terrible news of an accident with a truck. He paused, struggling to maintain self-control for the sake of his son.

"Mum and Dad," Jason said softly. "They've gone."

Michael was motionless as he stared at Jason, a look of disbelief creeping across his gentle face, but then his mother gasped, feeling the pressure on her arm as he slumped towards the floor. Flinging herself backwards, she dragged him with her until they were both in a heap on the sofa.

Jason watched from across the room, unable to help as his grandparents tended to their son, bringing him around within seconds and then they were all holding each other tight as Michael wept uncontrollably. Quietly, he slipped out of the room to the kitchen, shocked and ashamed by a sudden stab of envy. For one dreadful moment, he'd almost resented his uncle for still having his parents. Never again would his mum and dad hold him like that. He was alone now, an outsider.

The thought left as quickly as it came. His broader family had all suffered the terrible loss of someone special; a son, a daughter, a brother, a sister, an uncle or an auntie. He was being selfish, thinking only of himself and his loss.

Waiting for the kettle to boil, Jason made a decision; instead of wallowing in self-pity, he would make it his mission to help his family cope. As he reached the door to the lounge with the laden tray, however, he overheard Michael talking to his parents, his voice low, weighed down with sadness.

"What about Jason? The poor boy, what will he do now? We must put him first and look after him."

Later that evening, when Michael had left, Jason began to think about Lesley and his housemates. They would be wondering where he was. "Where've you been?" she almost shouted, relieved to hear his voice. "I've called you at yours and left a message on your parents' phone. I've been worried sick and panicking that you've had an accident on the bike. Please tell me you're okay?" Jason slowly began to tell Lesley about the events of the weekend. When he told her about driving past the reservoir, she interrupted.

"Wait. There was something on the evening news about a dreadful accident at Ladybower last night. Two people were killed." Jason remained silent, unable to confirm her worst fears. He listened impassively when she broke down, sobbing loudly into the phone. *Why wasn't he crying? What was wrong with him? Was it because, deep down inside, he was still hoping this was a vicious nightmare from which he would soon awake?*

Chapter Five

Lesley sighed. "Where are you? Can I come over?"

"I'm staying with Grandad T and Nanna Pat for now. Can I call you in a couple of days? We're all struggling a bit here just now."

"Of course." Lesley began to sob again. "Does Simon know?" Simon was one of Jason's housemates and probably his closest friend.

"No, I was going to call him later."

"I can do that for you if it would help?" Lesley offered, glad to have found something she could do for him.

"Please, if you're sure, I'm worn out, to be honest."

"Try to get some rest if you can, and I'll see you soon." She wanted to add "I love you," but she had never said it before, and decided it wasn't the right time. Unbeknown to her then, it would be two more weeks before she saw him, and nothing would ever be the same again.

The next few days passed in a haze. A kind and friendly police officer arrived to take Jason's statement about the accident. Over tea and biscuits, he asked gently probing questions to establish precisely what Jason could recollect. "I remember seeing the reservoir. It looked eerie, like the River Styx. I half expected to see the Grim Reaper paddling across; we all commented on it. I can't remember anything after that, sorry."

The officer glanced up from his notes, startled by the sudden macabre reference. He realised from the distant look in Jason's eyes that he was recounting a memory, oblivious to the sinister fact his parents were killed only moments after they'd seen what looked like the gateway to the underworld.

He shook his head sadly. "You're probably in deep shock. If your memory starts to come back, get in touch, will you?"

Following the meeting with the funeral directors, Jason felt like his head was in a vice. His grandparents hadn't wanted him to attend, but he insisted on supporting them. The questions had seemed endless. How did they know if his parents wanted to be buried or cremated, what hymns they would like or what they would like to be dressed in? It was implausible that his parents had ever given any thought to such things themselves. Eventually, his grandparents concluded that burial might be the most appropriate. Jason hadn't expressed an opinion; either option was too horrific to contemplate.

But in the middle of the night, Jason awoke from a terrible nightmare, gasping for air. The sheets on his bed were wet with sweat as he sat bolt upright, trembling, but the horrendous images in his mind persisted. He'd watched in horror as two coffins were lowered slowly into an open grave, first his dad's and then his mum's. Nanna Jean leaned forward to throw a rose down onto her daughter's coffin and was pulled back just as she was about to topple into the grave. Then suddenly, he was in total darkness, in a cold, confined space. He could hear the thud as shovel after shovel of earth landed on the wooden slab inches above his face.

Too distraught to sleep, Jason crept downstairs and selected a book from his grandparents' bookcase. He was still reading the same page at daybreak, and when Grandad E and Nanna Jean arrived mid-morning, he voiced his concerns. "I've been thinking about the funeral arrangements."

No one spoke, but the sadness in their eyes as they looked at him spoke volumes. How could it be that their beloved grandson, so young, was saying these words?

Chapter Five

"I don't think Mum and Dad would want to be, you know....., be put into the ground. It's too dark and cold for them. I wondered ...."

He'd been about to suggest scattering their ashes in the open air where the sun would shine down on them but found himself unable to continue.

"I've spent most of the night thinking about it too," Nanna Jean said softly, tears coursing down her cheeks again. Someone automatically pushed the ever-present box of Kleenex across the table to her. "I wondered if cremation might be better, then maybe we can choose a special place in the remembrance gardens, where the sun shines? Occasionally," she added, managing a wry smile. Jason glanced at her, surprised that she had virtually spoken his thoughts.

Within minutes everyone agreed it was a much better idea and Grandad T headed towards the phone in the hallway. "I'll call the Co-op."

"There's just one more thing, Grandad."

His grandfather returned to the table and sat down again. "You've been thinking about this a lot, haven't you? Are you okay?"

Jason nodded, not entirely convincingly. "About the..., buffet afterwards." He couldn't bring himself to use the word 'wake'. There'd been a lot of talk about the wake the day before. Virtually everyone in Stockport knew Robert and Mary somehow, through the schools they'd attended, their jobs, Jason's schools, and the gigs in the pubs.

A vast turnout was expected for their joint funerals, and a large venue would be necessary to accommodate everyone afterwards. "I've been thinking," Jason continued. "The last time I was with Mum and Dad, we talked about plans for the birthday party. They were excited about it." He could barely continue but forced himself onwards. "The funerals should be a celebration of them and what they meant to everyone, but I don't think any of us will be up for celebrating, do you? Shall we postpone the buffet and continue with the plans for the party in the summer? Make it a tribute to them and invite everyone then?"

A hushed silence fell around the table as they struggled to comprehend how joy and excitement could have turned so swiftly to tragedy. Grandad T cleared his throat. "I think that's a brilliant idea, Jason, and what's more, your mum and dad would love it. Shall I go and tell the Co-op now?" Jason's grandparents nodded their agreement as the Kleenex was pushed from one to the other around the table.

Jayne and Pierre arrived in Stockport three days before the joint funeral. During one of many tearful phone calls with her parents, Jayne had made a special request. "Do you remember the necklace I bought Mary for her 21st? Could I wear it for the funeral, please? To feel close to her?"

No one had stepped inside Robert and Mary's home since the accident. They couldn't face it, but everyone agreed that Jayne must wear her sister's necklace. "I'll get it," Jason offered. He knew where his mum kept her jewellery box; she'd often sent him running upstairs at the last minute for a piece of the chunky, brightly coloured costume jewellery she favoured. She hadn't wanted anything expensive, utterly satisfied with the treasured gold necklace from Jayne and a gold bracelet from her parents, both given to her on her 21st birthday and which she wore only on special occasions.

Chapter Five

The evening before the funerals, the family insisted on accompanying Jason to retrieve the necklace. Tony's hand visibly trembled as he turned the key until he heard the familiar click and, with a deep sigh, eased the door open.

Chapter Six

Jason swallowed hard when he saw everything precisely as he had left it a fortnight ago. The crockery he had washed that evening whilst his parents prepared for the journey was on the drainer, a large saucepan still soaking in the sink; how much his world had changed since then.

"Ugh, what a terrible smell!" Nanna Pat lifted the lid from the casserole dish on the hob where Mary had left it and hastily replaced it as the stench of the putrid leftovers filled the air. The aromas emanating from the fridge and the pedal bin weren't much better. Without uttering a word, Nanna Jean joined her in an onslaught on the kitchen. The men headed off on a tour of the house, persuading themselves that they needed to check on security.

Jayne, 20 years older than her nephew, was intent on supporting him, but as she entered the main bedroom, the sense of her beloved sister overwhelmed her. Burying her face in the softness of the jumper left strewn across the bed, she wept as the lingering scent of Opium, Mary's favourite perfume, jolted her back to happier days. Jason cradled her in his arms until the tears slowly subsided. "I shouldn't have asked for the necklace. Look what I've put you through," Jayne stammered between sniffles.

"You haven't put me through anything. Coming here for the first time had to happen sooner or later, and I'm just glad you're here."

Wiping her eyes and hugging Jason tightly, Jayne wondered when the golden-haired boy had grown into the young man towering above her, yet so gentle and kind. Her sister would be proud of how he was coping.

The jewellery box, given to Mary by her parents as a child, was tucked away in the back of a drawer. As Jason lifted the lid, the tiny ballerina twirled to the strains of Swan Lake, and Jayne sobbed again. He found the necklace quickly, but the sudden silence when he closed the lid was oppressive and crushing. "It's yours now." Jason's voice was barely a whisper as he placed the precious necklace in the palm of his aunt's hand and gently curled her fingers around it as he led her from the room.

Lesley had called Jason most days since the accident; she desperately wanted to be with him, but he'd resisted. "I spend every day just trying to help everyone else," he'd gently explained. "I'm always busy, we wouldn't have any time together. Besides, it's your last year, you need to concentrate on uni."

She'd tried to understand but was beginning to feel excluded, shunned almost. Stung when Jason told her only close family members would be attending the committal service at the crematorium, she'd tentatively suggested some private time afterwards so that she could comfort him. Her

Chapter Six

feelings of rejection intensified when he instantly rejected the idea, insisting he would need to be with his family. Reluctantly, Lesley had agreed to Jason's suggestion that she and Simon arrive early at his grandparents' house for coffee before the funerals.

As he waited for them to arrive, Jason thought about Lesley. He knew he was distancing himself from her and felt terrible about that, but he had to do it. The nightmares persisted relentlessly; night after night, he dreamt of the imaginary death and funeral of everyone he loved.

Frightened by the future, all he could see ahead was loss and grief. Through no fault of theirs, his beloved parents had gone and left him behind. Life is precarious; he couldn't and wouldn't allow himself to love anyone that much ever again.

So, when they arrived, Jason hugged them both and discussed mundane things over coffee around the kitchen table; strenuously avoiding the imminent enormity of the day. He avoided looking into Lesley's pleading eyes as much as possible, and when it was time for them to go, he held her only briefly and barely brushed his lips against hers. Lesley hugged Jason's grandparents, but as she left for the church with Simon, she wasn't sure whether her tears were for the family or herself.

As expected, hordes of people turned out for the funerals. Many people stood outside the crowded church, unable to hear the service but just wanting to be there to honour Mary and Robert.

Waiting to enter the church behind the coffins, as he had done on the aeroplane ten years before, Jason positioned himself between his grandmothers and took hold of their hands, consumed by fear but determined not to show it. He smiled in turn at each of them. "Don't worry, it'll all be fine." They smiled back briefly, recognising Robert's much-used phrase. Despite all his nightmares of collapsing in the aisle, the weight of grief making it impossible for him to breathe, Jason walked between the throngs of people gathered in the church, head held high for his parents, holding tightly onto his grandmothers all the way. It was another consummate performance.

On what had started as a dank, dismal day, seated in a pew of the small chapel at the crematorium later that afternoon, Jason noticed that sunlight was streaming through the stained-glass windows, creating tiny rainbows that danced around the two coffins placed side by side. He barely heard the muffled voice of the vicar saying the final prayers whilst he watched in fascination as the sunlight steadily gained strength.

The scent of spring flowers greeted them as they left the chapel, tributes of every hue cascading far beyond the confines of the display area. "Shall we go back to the house?" suggested Jayne. She was returning home to France with Pierre in two days; this might be her last chance to spend time in her sister's home.

"That's a lovely idea." Her mum linked arms with her. "Let's go."

"Good turnout for them, wasn't it?" Grandad E did his best to sound casual despite the tense atmosphere in the lounge, where they sat quietly drinking tea and coffee; no one was hungry.

"I'm so glad the sun came out; the chapel looked beautiful." Jason glanced at Nanna Jean in surprise. *That was the second time she'd spoken his thoughts; was she reading his mind?*

Chapter Six

Michael broke the pensive silence, clearing his throat as he tapped his teaspoon against his mug. "I have some news. I don't know if it's the right time or place to tell you, but I'll do it anyway, as I don't want the last time we're all together in this house to be an entirely sad occasion. We've all had too many good times here for that, so here goes."

He stopped to take a breath and smiled at Anne. "We're having a baby, due in November."

Stunned silence followed the unexpected happy announcement in a home shrouded in tragedy before a babble of congratulations broke forth, everyone speaking at once. As Michael looked around at the faces of his family, smiling at least for now, he knew that he'd done the right thing. In future, they would all have to grab snippets of happiness wherever and whenever they could.

They returned to the crematorium two days later and slowly made their way through the tranquil gardens of remembrance, searching for a suitable resting place. Eventually, they selected a sturdy young cherry tree in full bud and almost ready to flower.

As his grandfathers scattered their children's ashes, their faces grim, a study of indescribable misery, Jason held his grandmothers tightly whilst they sobbed for several minutes. Pierre did his best to comfort Jayne, and Anne clung to Michael. But Jason could not equate the flimsy particles of dust with either of his parents, so full of fun and vivacity. Waiting as his family fought to regain self-control, he was horrified by his complete lack of emotion; he felt nothing and wondered again what was wrong with him.

Weeks passed before anyone could begin to face clearing Mary and Robert's house in preparation for sale. During a discussion at the group bereavement counselling sessions that started after the funerals, Jason had been adamant that he did not wish to keep the house. "There's no point. They've gone," was all he said.

The earnest young councillor encouraged everyone to participate freely in the sessions and volunteer how they felt. Still, week after week, Jason could contribute nothing. "I don't feel anything." Even to himself, it sounded like he was being obtuse, refusing to cooperate, so he tried hard to add something more. "I'm not happy, but I'm not desperately sad either, and I feel bad about that. It's as though I'm watching all this happening in some miserable soap opera, and none of it is real."

Amber provided a version of straightforward, no-nonsense counselling that only young children are capable of, which proved far more effective than the bereavement sessions. When Ed asked Michael how he was doing, he replied that he was okay. "No, you're not, Daddy. I heard you crying in the bathroom last night," Amber interjected. And when Jean gently asked Pat if she was sleeping, Amber, who had stayed over a couple of times, leapt in and answered for her.

"No, she isn't. She reads downstairs in the middle of the night, I've seen her."

"That girl should have ears the size of an elephant's and eyes that glow in the dark," mused Tony one evening when they were all together after Amber had gone to bed. "She misses nothing!"

Everyone nodded and smiled in agreement. The little girl's direct, honest approach led to many conversations that wouldn't have happened otherwise; she forced them all to admit to feelings they hadn't intended to share. Everyone, that is, except Jason. She was never able to catch him out.

They began clearing the house around the end of April. There were many tears the first day, no one knew where to start, but slowly, room by room, they worked together to decide what should go where. They packed all of Mary and Robert's most personal possessions into two large boxes to be stored until Jason was ready to go through them. In addition, Jason packed a large floppy hat and an Afghan coat his mum had treasured in the 1970s, together with a half-empty bottle of her favourite perfume and his dad's guitar.

As the end of May approached, Jason began toying with the idea of a visit to Sheffield to wish his friends well in their final exams. He'd spent every day since the accident with his grandparents, and they were keen for him to take a break. "Of course, you should go. We'll be fine here, we've nearly done," Grandad T reassured him.

It came as no surprise to Jason that Lesley was not at the station with Simon to greet him when he arrived on a warm, sunlit evening. Since the day of the funerals, they'd spoken on the phone only when she called him. He had deliberately frozen her out of his life, and he would never be able to make her understand why. "Fancy a beer, mate?" Simon adeptly circumvented the customary preliminary greetings and cut straight to the main feature of the evening, the consumption of alcohol. Within minutes they were ensconced in a real ale pub with friends taking a break from revision on Friday night.

"If anyone else comes up to me and shays I'm sshorry, I'm going to knock them to the floor and jump on their throats!" Jason slurred to Simon a few hours and several pints later.

Simon gulped. "Have I ever told you how very sshorry I am?" he enquired before throwing himself to the floor, gripping his own throat with both hands, his eyes rolling. Laughter exploded from Jason for the first time in months; it was only then he realised just how much he had missed his housemate.

They spent Saturday recovering from the mother of all hangovers. Lesley dropped by in the afternoon but didn't stay long due to the incoherent nature of the two friends and the overpowering smell of stale beer. "I think I've lost her," Jason remarked when she'd gone. Simon said nothing.

On Sunday, they haphazardly packed Jason's things into bin liners. Simon's parents were collecting him at the end of term and had kindly offered to make a detour to drop them off.

As he locked the door to his bedsit and handed Simon the key, Jason sensed he was walking away for good. They were both subdued as they walked to the railway station. "Thanks for this weekend, just what I needed." Impulsively, Jason hugged his friend, knowing it was the end of an era. Afterwards, embarrassed, he laughed and quickly boarded the train. Simon feigned a ridiculous expression of horror at the sudden unanticipated embrace but gave him a thumbs-up as the train glided into motion.

The inquest was scheduled for the end of June 1996; the party to celebrate his parents' lives was to take place one week later. Jason didn't know which was scaring him the most. He was required to attend the inquest as a witness. Still unable to recall anything of the accident, he could only confirm the events up to that point. The thought of coming face to face with the man who had killed his mum and dad, a Spanish lorry driver, filled him with dread. How would he feel? What would he want to do to this man? Worst of all, would he lose self-control in the courtroom and scream at him or even break down?

And then there was the party, all those people wanting to be there to celebrate his mum and dad; how would he cope? The nights passed in a morass of nightmares; he was exhausted. As the day of the inquest drew nearer, Jason distracted himself with the arrangements for the party.

The family had decided to hold it at a pub where Robert and Michael had often played; the premises were large, with a beer garden at the back. Jason spent time preparing collages from the hundreds of photos he had found around the house and had some enlargements done. It was an opportunity for everyone to remember all that was special about his mum and dad; he wanted to do them proud.

On the day of the inquest, Jason arrived at the Court with his grandparents. Michael had wanted to attend, but a hiccup in Anne's pregnancy kept him elsewhere. There were four witnesses, the Spanish lorry driver, the driver who had come upon the scene a short time after the accident, the reporting police officer and Jason. The coroner had Jason's statement and asked him to take the stand only to confirm the details he had provided and that he still had no recollection of the accident. The car driver gave his evidence, and then the reporting officer. Jason held his grandmothers close as it was confirmed that his parents had been killed instantly.

It was then the turn of the lorry driver, who spoke no English and had an interpreter. Jason watched as the man, in his mid-thirties, about 5' 8" tall, lithe and with shiny black hair, got to his feet and walked forward to give evidence. He answered all of the coroner's translated questions without hesitation. The accident had occurred on only his second trip to the UK. He'd been driving most of that day and was lost and tired.

The road was quiet, there was no traffic around, and on the approach to the junction, he'd been trying to check which way to turn. Engrossed in checking the map, he hadn't noticed the traffic lights, and as he turned left in a wide sweeping arc, he momentarily forgot to move back over to the left side of the road. The glare of oncoming headlights suddenly lit up his cab, blinding him, and then there was an almighty bang like an explosion.

The coroner thanked the man for his evidence and bade him sit down, but he turned to look directly at Jason and his grandparents, a torrent of Spanish pouring from his lips. Tears raced each other down his cheeks, and it was apparent to everyone present that he was distraught.

"What is he saying?" the coroner asked the interpreter.

"He is apologising to the family, sir," the woman replied, "telling them of his heartbreak, that his life will never be the same again. He cannot ask it of them now, but he begs them to forgive him for his terrible mistake someday."

The coroner indicated that the colleague who had accompanied him could assist the distressed driver from the witness stand. He summarised his findings, and everyone left the Court.

Relieved that the proceedings were over, Jason and his grandparents made their way outside into the light rain just as a taxi pulled up by the kerb. The Spanish driver's colleague opened the rear door and got in. The driver was about to follow when Ed, quiet and reticent by nature, seized the opportunity. It was now or never; he would not meet this man again. The driver turned around when he felt the tap on his arm, a startled look on his face when he saw who it was, but Ed held out his right hand. Hesitating for the briefest of moments, the man gripped Ed's outstretched hand between both of his. Tony followed, and the scenario was repeated.

Then the Spaniard looked over to where Jason was standing, watching bemused as the scene unfolded. He moved swiftly, half-running and in an instant, he was standing in front of him, his eyes pleading and awash with tears as he gazed at Jason before reaching up and resting his hands on his shoulders.

Looking down into the eyes of the man he had so dreaded seeing, Jason was astonished by what he saw there. This man was not a killer; sadly, he'd been in the wrong place at the wrong time. He had made an error, as people do every day, but in this terrible instance, that error had resulted in the death of his parents. Jason could see in his eyes that, like him, this man would suffer for that for the rest of his life. Taken aback by his unexpected surge of compassion, Jason rested his hands on the driver's outstretched arms for just a moment to acknowledge his apology, a cathartic moment for them both.

Ed walked across and patted him on the shoulder. "Well done, Jason," he said, his voice filled with emotion. "Your mum and dad would be proud."

"I did it for the two of you, Grandad. I'll never know how you did that."

Ed sighed, tears welling in his eyes. "We'll never forget, but we can forgive. It was an accident."

Eight days later, the party took place on a warm sunny day. Jayne, Pierre and the boys had come over for the weekend, and the entire family danced and sang through the afternoon and late into the evening to the music performed by Robert and Mary's musician friends.

Michael couldn't be persuaded to join in; he hadn't played a single note since the accident but enjoyed spending the day with his family and musician friends far more than he expected. It was the music that touched him the most. The joyous sound of the notes as they fluttered along on the light breeze, the harmonies of the voices and the drum beat that pulsated through the songs like lifeblood soothed him as nothing else had since the accident.

Anne was putting a very tired and sleepy Amber to bed that evening when she thought she heard a sound downstairs. *She must have imagined it; no, there it was again, the notes so soft and gentle they were barely audible.* Amber stirred, listened intently and then smiled at her mother. "Daddy's playing the guitar." Another page had turned.

After all the guests had finally left, Jason took down all the photos and carefully prepared collages, packing them in a large storage box in the bar. Shock reverberated through his body as he turned one of the enlargements over and found himself gazing straight into his mum's eyes, full of laughter as she grinned at him. In the dim light of the bar, his fingers reached out to touch her face, but instead of warm, silky-smooth skin, he felt only cold glass beneath his

Chapter Six

fingertips. As two large tears slid down his cheeks, the first he had cried since the accident, he heard a woman's voice softly calling his name.

Chapter Seven

Lisa watched as Mark and Jenni turned to look at the door, their smiles fading almost in slow motion and replaced by a look of horror.

Instinctively, she turned and ran along the slippery pavement as fast as she dared. Mark was shouting her name; he would surely come after her. Out of sight as she turned a corner, she ran a short distance further and spotted a passageway between some shops. Without the slightest hesitation, she ran along in the darkness, turning her ankle on a grate at the base of a fall pipe halfway along.

The passageway provided access to what would once have been the rear gardens of a row of large stone-built terraced houses, but modern extensions and storage areas had consumed the gardens on either side.

Afraid someone might see her and think she was a trespasser, Lisa crouched out of sight around the corner of the wall at the end of the passageway and waited. She felt dizzy and hot, suffocated even as she swallowed great gulping gasps of air. Feeling faint, she opened her coat and the sudden blast of cold air brought her around a little. Images of Mark and Jenni's smiling faces spiralled in her mind, but she made no sound as tears flowed down her cheeks.

Lisa didn't know for how long she had remained in that crouched position when she noticed she was violently shivering. Barely able to move, she slowly struggled into a standing position and then felt the pain of her twisted ankle as she hobbled back along the passageway. When she reached the street, the sleet had turned to snow, and it was beginning to settle.

Desperate to go home to her parents, she began to limp towards the bus station, her head down against the bitterly cold wind and the falling snow. Caught up in a turbulent whirlpool of painful thoughts, at first, she didn't hear the voice of the taxicab driver as he pulled up alongside her and asked if he could help. He'd sensed something was wrong the moment he saw her limping, her coat flapping and clearly unfastened, a broken umbrella dangling from her right hand. When she didn't respond, the taxi driver drove a little further on, stopped and jumped out.

"You alright, love?" he asked, stepping in front of her. I was right, he thought, appraising Lisa's tear-flooded eyes and reddened face, pinched with cold as she glanced up at him, startled. "Please, let me help you. Where can I take you?" He gestured to the black cab parked by the roadside.

"I can't pay," mumbled Lisa. "I'm getting the bus, but thank you."

Chapter Seven

"Some buses have already stopped running in this, love. Come on, get in and tell me where to take you. We'll worry about payment later."

He rested his hand lightly on Lisa's shoulder, guiding her towards the cab. Twenty minutes later, she was home; the kind taxi driver helped her to the door and rang the bell. She made a pitiful, bedraggled sight when her mother opened the door; icy water pooled on the floor from her sodden coat as she stepped into the luxurious warmth of the kitchen, tendrils of wet, windswept hair stuck to her cheeks.

"Lisa! My God, what's happened? Has someone attacked you, are you hurt?" Kathleen, usually such a strong, formidable character, was so shocked and distressed to see her daughter in such a state that tears ran down her own cheeks as she threw her arms around her. Unable to speak coherently, Lisa could only shake her head to reassure her mother she was uninjured.

Hearing the commotion, Joe hurried to the door. The taxi driver explained where he had found their daughter before refusing to accept the generous tip Joe proffered. "No need for that, mate, it's Christmas. I'm just glad I spotted her and got her home."

As she ran a hot bath, Kathleen plied Lisa with questions, still anxious and alarmed by her obvious distress and the lack of a response. "Sweetheart, let's leave the questions for now, eh?" urged Joe. "Let's get Lisa comfortable and sort things out tomorrow." Whilst Lisa bathed, Kathleen busied herself making a warming soup and took it up to her, leaving Joe to answer the shrill ring of the telephone.

"Is Lisa there? Is she there? Please tell me she's there."

"Steady on, Mark," Joe replied as calmly as he could. "What on earth's going on?" The line went quiet. "Are you still there, Mark? What's happened?"

"Lisa......... saw me. With another........., with someone. At a........., a hotel," Mark stammered. "I've been searching for her. I don't know what to do. Is she there?"

"Yes, she's here." There was a long, droning buzz as Mark hung up before Joe could say anything more.

When Kathleen came down, she was still visibly shaken. "She's sleeping, thank goodness. What could possibly have happened?"

"Sit down, love." Joe handed her a large glass of brandy and told her about the phone call with Mark. Kathleen was distraught, angry and incredulous in quick succession, and for once, Joe put his foot down and forbade her to ring Mark. Knowing that hell hath no fury like a petite woman who believes her precious daughter has been wronged, he could not allow her to unleash herself on Mark at that moment, no matter how badly he had behaved.

The next day was the last working day before Christmas, but her mother had already called in sick for her by the time Lisa awoke. Over brunch, Joe told Lisa about the phone call with Mark and put his head in his hands as she fled back upstairs. *It had been the wrong thing to say, but how could he have known that?* Kathleen moved to stand by his side and wrapped her arms around him; this was unknown territory for them both.

Lisa spent the rest of that day and most of the following day in bed, sleeping fitfully and saying very little. When she finally surfaced that evening, still dressed in the old pyjamas she had found at the bottom of her wardrobe, she curled,

Chapter Seven

childlike, on the sofa between her parents and fell asleep watching a Christmas film. They looked at each other and sighed; what had this latest trauma done to their beautiful but fragile daughter?

Knowing that Lisa and Mark planned to spend Christmas with his parents, Joe and Kathleen had accepted an invitation to spend Christmas with Neil, his wife Maryam and their twins, Georgina and Byron, at their large house in Walton-on-Thames. Neil and Maryam had met at university, where they both studied law. Neil had become a defence barrister, and Maryam was a partner in a law firm dealing principally with conveyancing.

Maryam had grown up in Tehran, where her parents owned a small retail chain. Her siblings had all gone on to work in the family business, but even in her early years at school, it was apparent that Maryam was highly academic. With the full support of her family, she studied hard and was rewarded with the offer of a scholarship to Oxford.

The opportunity to study overseas was too good to miss, and in September 1978, nervous and uncertain, she arrived in England to begin her degree. She had intended to return home when she completed her studies, but her life took a different path when she met Neil, and they settled in London.

Remaining close to her family was a vital part of her life, but she also immersed herself in the culture of the family into which she had married. Enthusiastically enjoying Christmas with them each year was a particular pleasure. She dearly loved her young sister-in-law and was saddened when Kathleen rang to tell her what had happened. "Of course, you can't leave Lisa alone," agreed Maryam. "Please don't worry if you can't come, but we have enough food to feed a small army, and we would love to have Lisa too. It would make the children's Christmas."

The following morning, Kathleen broached the subject with Lisa. "Christmas Day tomorrow," she said as brightly as possible.

"Is it?" Lisa murmured without turning her head. She was sitting by the patio doors, staring listlessly out into the garden.

"Yes, I think Georgina and Byron will be very excited by now." To Kathleen's delight, the seemingly throwaway remark had the desired effect. Lisa spun around, her interest sparked, but then her face crumpled again.

"Oh no, their presents! They're at his!" She couldn't bring herself to speak Mark's name. Images of the gifts piled beneath the Christmas tree swam before her eyes, each carefully chosen and wrapped in bright, glossy paper, adorned with ribbons and bows.

"I haven't got anything to give anyone!" she wailed. Lisa's eyes began to brim with tears again as Kathleen rushed to comfort her. Joe emerged from the kitchen where he was preparing his legendary sherry trifle, overdoing it as usual with the sherry.

"Let me finish up here, and then I'll drive over and collect the presents."

"Oh no! No, you're not going anywhere near that, that, that......," Kathleen blustered, her face turning scarlet with the effort of finding the words to express herself.

Still clutching the sherry bottle in one hand, Joe stroked his wife's shoulder soothingly with the other. "Can you come up with a better idea? I'll ring and see if he's there. If not, I can always leave a message, let myself in with Lisa's key and get them. Job done!" He allowed himself a self-satisfied smile when Kathleen and Lisa both reluctantly nodded their heads in agreement. He could still look after his girls.

Joe heard the ringing tone several times before a click and Lisa's happy voice announcing they were out. He was halfway through the door when Lisa called, "Dad! I'm really sorry, but,....." She hesitated. "Could you bring me some clothes, please? My things are in the wardrobe, and my.....underwear is in the top drawer of the dressing table." Lisa cringed at the thought of her poor father grabbing handfuls of her bras and knickers from the drawer, but he just smiled at the mortified look on her face and went in search of a holdall.

Anticipating no one home, Joe still knocked several times loudly before letting himself in with Lisa's key. Carefully stepping between the empty beer cans strewn across the lounge floor, he found Mark sitting at the kitchen table with his head in his hands. He had three days' beard growth, and it looked like he hadn't changed his clothes for a while.

Mark raised his head as Joe entered; the grey bags beneath his hollow eyes proved he hadn't slept. "I've come to collect the Christmas presents for the family," Joe told him, not knowing what else to say. He turned and began removing the gifts from beneath the tree, loaded them into the car and then returned with the holdall. "Lisa needs some clothes, Mark, will you help me to get them? I don't much like the idea of poking through your things on my own."

Mark slowly shook his head, so reluctantly, Joe headed upstairs alone. As quickly as possible, he emptied Lisa's underwear drawer into the holdall, threw her items in the wardrobe, complete with hangers, over his arm, and hurried out to the car. He started the engine and was just about to drive away when he hesitated, switched the engine off again and got out. Joe walked back in just as Mark let out several gut-wrenching sobs.

"I love her! I love her so much! I don't know why I did it. I was just fed up with being on my own. She was always working and studying, and I wanted some attention. I'm so sorry."

Listening to Mark, Joe's mind flashed back to a memory from more than thirty years before. The twins were born half an hour apart, and it was almost two years before the babies' sleeping and eating patterns synchronised. Both he and Kathleen were exhausted, working hard to provide for their young family and working equally hard at home to look after them. There was no time for each other.

Whilst attending a two-day conference, a young, blonde hygienist had shown interest in him, and he'd been sorely tempted. They had a few drinks in the bar that evening and left together to walk back to their rooms. At her door, she leaned forwards to kiss him, and the next thing he knew, he was in her room, removing his shirt. Reality suddenly snapped in, and to her disgust, he apologised and left. He adored his wife and had been shocked for many years by how close he had come, in an unguarded moment, to being unfaithful to her.

Looking at the troubled young man standing before him, Joe knew how lucky he had been to avoid facing this same dreadful situation all those years ago. He was horrified by the distress his daughter was suffering, and he could never condone what this man had done to her, but he understood

Chapter Seven

how it had happened. He placed his hand on Mark's shoulder, squeezed it briefly, then turned and left.

Kathleen and Lisa ran out to greet him as he pulled onto the drive, visibly brightening when he opened the car boot so they could see the carefully wrapped parcels nestling there.

As Lisa began unloading them, her mother grabbed the opportunity to discuss their invitation to London. "How about giving Georgina and Byron their presents in person? It will be a lovely surprise for them if you feel up to it."

Kathleen knew that Lisa would have refused if she had asked her to go with them to enjoy Christmas herself. Suggesting that her presence might make it memorable for the children would, she hoped, entice her daughter to join in the festivities. The ruse worked.

It was early evening when they arrived in Walton-on-Thames. On the way, Kathleen confessed to Lisa that she had given Maryam some brief details to avoid any awkward questions, and as she stepped forward into her sister-in-law's welcoming arms, both women's eyes were brimming with tears.

They held each other tightly for several moments until Maryam neatly skipped out of the way as the twins hurtled along the hallway, shrieking with delight at Lisa's unexpected arrival. Suffused with the children's excitement, Lisa put all thoughts of Mark firmly aside, and the evening passed happily in a riot of laughter.

Although the twins, aged just five, were allowed to stay up much later than usual, they still woke at an ungodly hour the following morning, their squeals reverberating around the house when they found the small sacks of gifts that Santa had left for them on the end of their beds.

"Back to bed, for goodness' sake!" cried Maryam. "It's the middle of the night!" To her amazement, the noise subsided, and peace resumed. Intrigued, she went to check on them and found their beds empty. The door to Lisa's room was slightly ajar; there they were, their heads resting on her shoulders as she wrapped her arms around them, all three sound asleep, the small gifts littering the bed.

After breakfast, Joe brought the parcels in from the car and present opening for everyone began in earnest. Neil stepped in as Georgina and Byron tore the paper from their gifts. "Shall we look at who the presents are from before we open them?" They dutifully nodded in unison, fidgeting only slightly. He handed each of them a gift from their pile. "Try to read the label."

"This one says, to Georgina, lots and lots of love from... erm..., Lisa! Auntie Lisa and Uncle Mark!" She guessed correctly, anxious to get the reading task over and discover what was inside. "With lots of kisses." The little girl spun around to face Lisa. "Where is Uncle Mark?"

Maryam saw the sudden cloud that passed across Lisa's face and quickly replied for her. "He's gone to see his mummy and daddy, to have a special Christmas time with them."

"Oh. That's nice." Georgina was satisfied with the answer and returned her attention to her gift, all thoughts of Mark departing as swiftly as they had arrived.

"Are you okay, Lisa?" Maryam whispered later that morning, tapping lightly on the door before she entered. Lisa was sitting on the floor in a corner, almost hidden by a

Chapter Seven

large chest of drawers. She looked up from hugging her knees as Maryam crouched in front of her, silently stroked her hair and kissed her forehead.

"She was my best friend," Lisa mumbled after a few moments.

"I'm sure he was," Maryam said softly.

"No, **she** was my best friend, the woman he was with." Through a sea of tears, Lisa saw the startled look in Maryam's eyes.

"Jenni?" The name was spoken so softly it was almost a sigh. "Your friend from work?" Lisa nodded and rested her head on her knees again. "My poor sweet girl." Maryam wrapped her arms around Lisa and wept with her.

"Mummy, Mummy, where are you?" The twins were thundering up the stairs.

"Go!" Lisa urged Maryam. "Please don't say anything to anyone. I'm sorry I've upset you. I'll be down in a minute. Let's have a happy time, and thank you so much for letting me come."

Between sniffles and dabbing at her own eyes, Maryam gently chided Lisa. "Don't ever thank me again like that; you're my sister, and we'll get through this together."

For Georgina and Byron, that Christmas was one of the best. Three days packed with nonstop fun and laughter; family walks, games, watching television whilst snuggling up to their beloved auntie and jumping into bed with her first thing each morning to rough and tumble together.

They knew nothing of the effort Lisa was making to join in with the celebrations or that when she said she needed to rest for half an hour, in fact, she could suppress the tears no longer and needed somewhere to sob in private.

Lisa had arrived at her brother's home feeling irreparably broken. Her partner and her best friend, two people she loved and trusted, had let her down badly. *How could that be? Why would they do that to her? Did she deserve it? What had she done wrong?* The questions bounced around inside her head incessantly, but at least she had enjoyed some respite over Christmas, cocooned in the love of her family, smothered in the adoration of the twins. One day, when they were old enough to understand, she would tell Georgina and Byron of her memories of that Christmas and the part they had unknowingly played in helping her through some bleak days.

As they said their goodbyes, holding each other close, Maryam whispered into Kathleen's ear. "Jenni."

Kathleen stepped back, confused. "Jenni?" Maryam nodded and then glanced meaningfully across at Lisa, her arms wrapped tightly around the twins, laughing as she tried to lift them both off the ground.

"She asked me not to say anything while you were here."

A look of shock slid onto Kathleen's still lovely features. *Jenni???*

"Anything you want to tell us, sweetheart?" she eventually ventured over a glass of wine when they arrived home. Lisa looked into her mother's eyes.

"You know, don't you?" she said softly. "Maryam told you."

"Only as we were leaving," Kathleen replied, aghast as she saw tears welling in her daughter's eyes, wishing she could turn the clock back when Lisa said goodnight and headed for her room.

"What did I miss?" Joe was perplexed by the short exchange. He couldn't believe what he was hearing as his wife quickly brought him up to date. *Of all people, Jenni? The lovely girl who'd brought so much happiness into his daughter's life, who had encouraged her to do things and helped to build her confidence? The same girl they had welcomed into their home for years, and who was almost one of the family? How much harder could this be?*

Chapter Eight

The light on the answering machine was flashing, and Joe listened to the messages from Mark, ranging from just a few sobbing sounds before he hung up to increasingly long, pleading monologues, begging Lisa to call so that they could talk. He poured a large glass of brandy, his solution to any crisis, and tapped lightly on the door to Lisa's room before entering.

"How about a sip of this?" He sat on the edge of the bed and proffered the glass towards the mound hidden beneath the quilt. There was no reply, only the muffled sound of weeping. "Please come out of there and try this because if you don't, I'll have to drink it myself, then I'll be tempted to have another, and then...."

He groaned dramatically, and Lisa's tear-stained face emerged with just the slightest flicker of a smile playing around the corners of her mouth. Despite everything, her father's humour never failed to amuse her. As the warm, soothing liquid slid down her throat, Joe told her about Mark's messages.

"Delete them," she snapped. "I don't want to hear his voice or set eyes on him ever again."

"Are you sure, sweetheart? He's quite desperate to speak to you." The look on Lisa's face told him she was sure; there would be no reconciliation. Joe deleted all the messages, but whilst Lisa was safely out of earshot in her room, and Kathleen was still ensconced in the kitchen, he took the opportunity to ring Mark. He answered on the second ring. "Lisa?"

"Afraid not," replied Joe. "We've been away for Christmas, just got back. Lisa won't listen to your messages and doesn't want any contact, please don't ring again. I'll be in touch to collect her things." He hesitated, knowing what he wanted to say next, making sure he was sincere. "I'm sorry." Without waiting for Mark to reply, he put the phone down.

The next few days passed in a haze of misery. To her mother's distress, Lisa withdrew again and insisted on spending much of her time alone in her room, refusing to be comforted. Not knowing what else to do, Joe attempted to inject a little humour wherever possible, allowing himself a small pat on the back when rewarded with a smile. "You'll be taking a few more days off work?" Kathleen enquired as Lisa helped to prepare a celebratory lunch on New Year's Day. She was due back at work the following morning.

"I've resigned."

Kathleen spun around, incredulous, dropping the potato she had only half-peeled. "You've done what?"

"Well, I can't go back, can I? I... I can't face Jenni. She was my best friend, Mum. Alan will get my letter tomorrow; it's finished."

"We need to talk."

"I don't want to talk, there's nothing to talk about." Lisa turned and made for the door.

"Don't you dare walk away from me again. Sit down."

In the next room, Joe's heart sank; he hadn't heard Kathleen raise her voice to Lisa for a long time. *As if things weren't bad enough already, what would happen now?* Lisa recognised a tone in her mother's voice she hadn't heard for many years that commanded respect and compliance. Like a small child, she complied and abruptly turned to sit back down.

"I've never told you much about my early life," Kathleen began. "When my dad died, your nan suffered terrible depression, and I looked after her for years. It was horrible, there were many awful times, but we never gave up. We are not a family that gives up, Lisa. It's not our way to run away from things; we stand and fight."

Listening from the safety of the lounge, Joe wished he had been the one to make this rousing speech. "I know quite a lot about depression, and I think you may be suffering from it," Kathleen continued.

"I'm not suff..." Lisa began but was cut off mid-sentence as her mother continued her impassioned lecture.

"Now is not the time to be making big decisions. Do you like your job?" Lisa hesitated. "Well? Is it yes or no?" Lisa nodded. "And what about your colleagues? Other than Jenni, of course. And your Manager?"

Lisa slowly nodded again. "Have you studied extremely hard to be able to do your job?" The almost imperceptible nod came again. "May I call Alan tomorrow and ask him to tear up your resignation then?" Kathleen continued briskly. "We are in this together, Lisa. Let us help you get through this dreadful time so you can make good decisions. Can I start with the phone call tomorrow? Please?"

Joe watched through the open doorway, frightened to breathe in case they realised he was there. He saw Lisa nod her agreement, and it was as though the whole house sighed with relief.

"Good, well in that case, you're dismissed," Kathleen said, her mouth beginning to twitch as she fought hard not to smile.

Lisa got to her feet and moved around the table to stand beside her mother, so petite in stature but with the heart of a lion, and hugged her. Joe watched mother and daughter in a deep embrace for a few moments before returning to his book. Now was not the time to tell his wife how proud he was that she was still every inch the brave, fiery girl he had fallen in love with all those years ago; he would wait for the right moment.

Kathleen rang the following morning and provided sparse details to a perturbed Alan. "Thank you for letting me know. I can assure you I'm tearing up her letter as we speak, please tell Lisa she must not come back until she's ready."

Mark was out when Joe arrived to collect Lisa's few remaining belongings; she wanted none of the things they had bought together for their home. Emptying the bags her father had collected, she found a letter from him and stashed it, unopened, in the back of her wardrobe, together with a pile of photos he had sent. Many more years would pass before they saw the light of day again.

Despite their best efforts to support their daughter, a week later, it was clear that Lisa was not well enough to return to work. Kathleen arranged an appointment with the GP and almost manhandled her daughter into the car to get her there.

"Could I please speak to the patient?" the doctor asked politely when Kathleen finally paused for breath after rapidly appraising him of the facts as she saw them and demanding a sick note. "How are you feeling, Lisa?"

"Sh..." Lisa began and then corrected herself. "Rubbish, I cry at anything, which isn't me, is it, Mum?" She glanced at her mother for confirmation, the ever-present unshed tears glistening in her eyes. "The worst thing is, I don't want to return to work. And I do love my job."

"Right, I'll sign you off for a month, and you can try these. Come back if you don't feel any better." The doctor handed Lisa a prescription for Prozac.

"I don't want to take these, Mum. Please don't say I have to." Outside the surgery, Lisa's pleading eyes told Kathleen her daughter was so distressed she would do anything she was told, even at 24.

"We'll get through this without them." Kathleen scrunched the prescription into a ball and put it in her pocket. She didn't tear it up, just in case. A few days later, she walked over to where Lisa was sitting in her favourite spot, gazing out of the patio window at nothing in particular. "How about having a look at your course books, Lisa?"

"I'm not interested," came the curt reply.

"Come on, sweetheart. You've put so much effort into your studies for so long. Let's have a look together, just for 10 minutes?"

Reluctantly, Lisa brought her work bag down from her room and slowly extracted the course book, dreading the sight of the cover and the memories that went with it, but much to her surprise, it was like looking at the face of an old friend. She opened the book and read a few lines, but the words made no sense, and the tears flowed again.

"Well done, well done." Kathleen quickly removed the book from the table and placed it on a shelf nearby. "That's enough for today; we can try again tomorrow."

With her mother's encouragement, Lisa spent a little longer each day looking at her course book, and soon Kathleen and Joe were thrilled to see that she seemed to be absorbing herself more and more in her studies, giving herself some much-needed respite from her thoughts.

Halfway through January, Maryam rang and asked to speak to Lisa. "I've got a few days holiday I need to take, and Neil has to work. Fancy coming down and doing some girly stuff?"

Maryam was waiting for her at St Pancras, waving enthusiastically from the other side of the ticket barrier. "Lunch and a glass of something fizzy to start us off?" she suggested.

"It's only 11.30 am, Maryam."

"And your point is?"

Within minutes they were on the tube heading for Covent Garden. Over a bowl of steaming minestrone, Lisa told Maryam about her mother's encouragement to resume her studies. She was beginning to enjoy that but still had huge misgivings about returning to work. "I can't face it; what must everyone think?"

"Do you think your colleagues might be taking a dim view of things?" asked Maryam. "They might be very concerned about you." That hadn't occurred to Lisa, but she still didn't feel she could bring herself to walk through the office door. "What you need is a costume, a disguise," Maryam declared, grinning broadly as their drinks arrived. "Soup and champagne, my favourite!" She raised her glass. "Here's to the new you!"

Lisa frowned as she toasted her sister-in-law. "I'm sorry, I'm not with you."

"Do you remember our wedding?" Lisa nodded; how could she ever forget it?

When she had first met Maryam, only slightly taller than her mother, with her luscious jet-black hair, eyes like melted chocolate and full lips that framed a dazzling smile, her heart sank. Another stunningly beautiful woman in the family to highlight her hideousness was the last thing she needed.

Lisa was only 13 then, and the age gap of twelve years was significant. She didn't spend much time with Maryam, but she liked her, and Maryam always spoiled her with the most thoughtful gifts at Christmas and birthdays.

In the autumn of 1988, Lisa was horrified when Maryam and Neil asked her to be an attendant for them at their wedding the following year. Initially, she had refused, desperate to fade into the background as much as possible at the celebration. She was head and shoulders taller than her mother and Maryam and two inches taller than her brothers. Only her father was slightly taller, so it would be hard enough not to stand out without having a starring role in the proceedings.

Maryam had insisted on Kathleen and Lisa's opinion of the wedding outfit she had chosen before she committed to the purchase. Whilst in London, she carefully steered them past a glamorous bridal boutique. In the window was displayed a dress of shimmering jade satin, the simple lines enhancing the luxurious fabric. "Oh, Lisa! Why don't you try that on?" Maryam asked innocently.

Despite her reservations, Lisa couldn't resist trying on the beautiful dress, and when she emerged from the changing room, both Maryam and her mother gasped. The delicate shade emphasised the colour of her eyes, green like her mother's with flecks of gold, and the shimmering fabric against her fading summer tan was exquisite. Against her better judgement, Lisa had agreed to let them purchase the dress. Panic-stricken about the forthcoming wedding for months, she had to admit that she'd felt like a princess on the day.

"I remember it very well," Lisa smiled at the memory. "But I could only do it because everyone looked at the beautiful dress, not at me."

That wasn't Maryam's recollection of the day at all, she had overheard her guests telling Lisa how beautiful she looked, and she was pretty sure they hadn't been referring only to the dress.

"Exactly," she said. "The dress empowered you, you felt able to do anything when you were wearing it, and that's what you need now. Actors do it all the time, you know? Lots of them are very shy, but when they put on a costume, they become someone else and perform without a problem until they take it off again."

"Really? I didn't know that."

"You need a costume now so that you can walk into the office feeling confident. Your colleagues will be looking at your costume, not you. Get it?"

Lisa nodded and smiled, her first genuinely happy smile in weeks. Over the next couple of days, the two women hit the shops. Eventually, Lisa settled on two fitted suits and a selection of plain shirts, silk blouses and tops that went with both. "Now, shoes!" declared Maryam. "Something with a stiletto heel."

"Have you gone completely bonkers?" Lisa was incredulous. "I can't wear stilettos; I'll look like a giraffe!"

She chose two pairs of low-heeled pumps, one black, the other red, with matching handbags. "Red?" she'd yelped, but Maryam wouldn't take no for an answer a second time, and she put all the purchases on her credit card.

"You can pay me back when you get paid," she smiled, inwardly pleased with her plan to give Lisa another motive to return to work.

"She looks stunning." Kathleen rang to tell Maryam a few days later when Lisa returned home and bashfully modelled her new outfits for her parents. "You've worked miracles; I can't thank you enough."

"My pleasure," replied Maryam, and she meant it. Life hadn't always been easy for her. Since coming to England, her olive skin tone and Middle Eastern features had sadly attracted more adverse racial comments than her family and friends could imagine. Years before, she had learned how to put on an impervious persona, akin to a deflector shield, with a set of clothes. Now she hoped the technique would work for Lisa.

But as the date the sick note ran out loomed, Lisa became more withdrawn. "Don't worry," Kathleen urged her. "If you don't feel ready to go back, we can always visit the doctor again."

That was the last thing Lisa wanted, but she was so fearful of seeing Jenni. She'd dreamt about her numerous times, remembering the many happy times they'd shared, but the dreams always ended the same way, with her friend's betrayal.

One night, shortly before she was due to return to work, in her dream, she was at the office. She pushed open the door and walked in, her heart pounding. Ordinarily, she would have reached Jenni's desk before her own and dreaded seeing her, but in the dream, she came to her desk first. Positioned on either side of her office chair were two grey, plastic children's chairs, the type used in primary schools years before. She stopped and stared at the chairs, puzzled. *What were they doing there? And where had they come from?* She had never seen them before, yet they looked oddly familiar.

The flash of memory jolted Lisa awake. Lying in the darkness, the dream still so vivid, she felt like a small child again. She hadn't thought about the spare chair at her primary school for years, but that was what she had just seen in her dream. Only now, there were two of them.

Although she had never thought about it since the day she'd helped Michelle in the playground, Lisa remembered her dread of going to school, not unlike her fear of returning to work. She recalled her grandfather's promise that he would always be with her and the comfort she had taken from that. *But in her dream, there had been two chairs. Was that a sign that her grandparents would both be with her when she returned to work?*

Joe had lost his mother four years before; he'd gripped her wedding ring tightly in his hand as Kathleen drove him back from the hospital. At home, they broke the news to Lisa, and as she held her father and sobbed with him, he offered her the ring.

A few days later, on a short, solitary walk to try to clear her head, Lisa sat in the late afternoon sunshine, twisting the wedding band around the fourth finger of her right hand. Lost in thought, she noticed a tiny white feather as it floated down on invisible air currents and landed close to her feet. Moments later, a second feather followed and settled almost entirely over the top of the first. Lisa gazed around for several minutes but could see no birds, and she'd returned home elated, convinced that the feathers were a sign that her grandparents were together again.

Stop grasping at straws; of course, they can't be with you, don't be ridiculous, she reprimanded herself harshly. But the dream had left her feeling calmer, somehow reassured that everything would be all right, and she fell into a deep, restful sleep for the first time in days. She told no one about the dream, but Kathleen and Joe were pleased she seemed brighter and ready to return to work.

On a dull, rainy morning at the beginning of February, she selected the dog tooth suit; a fitted jacket and pencil skirt with a short split. She teamed it with the red silk blouse, the red handbag and the red shoes; if she was going to do this, she might as well do it right.

Her mother arranged her shoulder-length curls in a high ponytail and helped with a light dusting of makeup before stepping back to admire her work. "You look fantastic, I'm so proud of you. Go and show them what you're made of."

Joe drove Lisa to the office. "Shall I come in with you?"

"No thanks, Dad, that would make it even worse!" She smiled at her father, knowing he would understand what she was trying to say. She had to do this on her own.

She summoned the lift, stepped out on the third floor and walked towards the double swing doors. Taking a deep breath and imagining her grandparents on either side of her, she entered. From the far end of the office, her Manager, Alan, looked up and smiled encouragingly at her.

And seated at the nearest desk on the right, with her back to Lisa, her head bowed as she concentrated on a file, was Jenni.

Chapter Nine

"Jason, are you there?" Nanna Pat called softly again.

"In here, Nanna," Jason quickly wiped his eyes, placed the last picture in the storage box, and dragged it to the door.

"Are you ready to go, love? It's been a wonderful celebration for your mum and dad. Thank you so much for preparing all those lovely pictures." In the dim light, Jason could see her eyes were glistening with tears. He wrapped his arms around her and held her for a few moments. That night, he fell into bed exhausted but satisfied that the party had been a fitting tribute to his parents.

The remainder of July and August passed in a blur as the family began the awful process of dealing with Robert and Mary's estate. *What's the point of living? There must be some reason for all the striving and aggravation, only to die at the end of it.* What is it? Jason wondered yet again, sat in the back of the car one afternoon as his grandfather drove them home from yet another meeting with the solicitor.

His parents, so vibrant and full of life, were now reduced to 'the deceased,' just names on death certificates that spelled out the injuries that had taken their lives from them. Everything they had worked for, all their treasured possessions, now had to be listed, valued, and disposed of somehow. It wasn't that Jason didn't want to live; he couldn't help wondering what all the effort was for when life could be snuffed out in an instant.

Shortly before his family home was placed on the market, Jason arrived to empty the garage. Dreading the sight of the camper van in which he and his parents had spent so many memorable holidays and the gleaming red motorbike he had only ever ridden twice, he braced himself and swung open the garage door. There they were, the camper van taking up most of the space, the motorbike squeezed at the side, where he had wheeled it just a few hours before the accident.

Nanna Pat watched from the bedroom window as her tall, broad grandson stood motionless on the driveway, seemingly frozen by what he saw inside the garage. Tears rolled down her cheeks again as she wondered what was going through his mind.

Wanting so much to run out and hold him, she understood how hard he was fighting to come to terms with what had happened, and this was something he needed to do by himself. Jason disappeared into the garage and reappeared a few minutes later, pushing the motorbike. He stopped a short distance along the drive, placed it on its stand, and then stood back for a few heart-wrenching moments, staring at it, his shoulders hunched. His grandmother couldn't watch any longer; she hurried downstairs to make strong coffee for them both.

Chapter Nine

Jason turned his attention to the camper van; his heart lurched when he started the engine and heard the familiar tick over. Instantly, it called to mind his excitement when that sound had signified the start of another holiday. He drove the camper van out onto the driveway and quickly checked to ensure that no personal items had been left inside. In the glove box, he found a few maps, a first-aid kit, and a small guidebook entitled *Camping in Tuscany and Umbria*. Surprised, Jason flicked through the pages of the book. Written on the inside front cover, in his dad's scribbly handwriting, was a message clearly intended for his mum.
Someday x

"Did Mum and Dad ever mention anything about going to Italy?" he asked Nanna Pat as she handed him his coffee when he returned to the kitchen. "I've just found this." He was surprised again when his grandmother read the title of the guidebook and laughed out loud.

"Oh, yes. Do you remember that silly advert on the tele that your mum used to love? It's a few years ago now, I think it was for some kind of pasta sauce. Anyway, the advert showed a Tuscan farmhouse and views of the hills, and she kept asking your dad if he thought they could get the van that far. It was all a bit of a joke, but it looks like he had ambitions."

Jason slid the guidebook into his pocket, a memento to remind him just how much his dad had loved his mum and how determined he had been to give her everything he could.

Handing the keys to the van over at the local dealership proved more heartbreaking than Jason had anticipated.

Another ending in his life; never again would there be any more happy holidays in the camper van. The friendly man who had offered him a lift back attempted conversation, but Jason was lost in thought. He felt exhausted by the omnipresent weight of grief and decided he would put off dealing with the motorbike for a few days. But when he saw his grandmother, up to her eyes in soapsuds, vigorously cleaning the already sparkling cooker to justify being there, he felt obliged to plough on.

The Ferrari red paintwork shone brightly in the sunlight as Jason walked past the motorbike, but he took no pleasure from that. He'd decided to sell it and needed to take it for a short spin around the block to check that everything was working. Steeling himself again, he opened his bedroom door; his helmet, jacket, gloves and boots were still on the floor, exactly where he had left them that fateful day. He quickly retrieved them and left. There were lots to sort out in there, but it would have to wait for another day; he could only stand so much.

The machine fired up the first time, thanks to his grandfathers' regular visits to put the battery on charge. He marvelled again at the capacity of the two men to continue to function when they had suffered such a monumental loss. Not once had he thought about his motorbike, yet alone the battery and he was too young to realise that focusing their minds on mundane things was a coping strategy for all his grandparents, a brief but welcome break from their relentless distress.

It felt surprisingly good as he turned out of the driveway, waving to his grandmother, who was mouthing something at him. He couldn't hear what she was saying but knew she

Chapter Nine

was telling him to be careful. The grin he gave her as she walked across to him when he returned told her all she needed to know. The bike was going nowhere.

"We'll clear our garage out and make room for it until you want it," she told him.

Jason kissed her. "Thanks, Nanna, you're wonderful. I'll get another helmet and take you for a ride."

She looked at him thoughtfully. "I think I'd like that."

When the house was finally empty, Jason took one last look around with his grandparents. They were all very emotional, but as he closed the front door for the last time and locked it, Jason felt no emotion at all. It was just a silent, empty house. The people who had made it such a happy, loving home had gone, and it was nothing without them.

At the end of August, Simon answered his parents' phone. The exam results had just been announced, and he had a good idea who the caller would be. "Hello," he said, doing his best to sound disgruntled and miserable.

"Well?" came Jason's reply, as Simon had anticipated.

He hesitated in what he hoped was a dramatic pause. "I've only gone and passed the bloody lot!" he yelled, unashamedly ecstatic with his success.

Jason grinned. The two friends had met in the maths classes, and it was evident from the start that Simon was highly intelligent, but as with many people with an exceptionally high IQ, he seemed to have no common sense whatsoever. Jason had never doubted that his friend would do well in his exams, but he really could do with someone to look after him. "Let's celebrate when we can. What's on the cards for you now, then?"

"Well, I have more to tell, dear friend. I have, wait for it, drumroll please, ... got myself a job!"

"Unbelievable!" Jason was genuinely impressed as Simon supplied details of the role he had secured with a large firm of accountants in Sheffield.

"I'm starting in a couple of weeks, so I'm renting the house again if you're interested. I presume you're going back to uni?"

Jason hadn't given any thought to uni; he had no idea where his life was going. All he'd been able to concentrate on was being there for his family. "We'll see."

"There's something else," Simon continued. He'd heard the slightly subdued tone in Jason's voice when he'd mentioned university, but he needed to press on and get this out. "It's about Lesley."

"Are you seeing her?" Jason's tone had rapidly moved from subdued to incredulous.

"No, no, idiot! I've got my eye on a dame at the pub, not that it's any of your business."

"God help her, what then?"

"She might be seeing somebody. I saw her in the pub with a guy just before I came home, and they looked kind of........ well, friendly. I just thought you should know."

The sense of relief that swept through Jason surprised him. He'd spoken to Lesley a few times since the funerals, but the calls were stilted and had become shorter and further apart. He felt awful about what had happened, but he was sure it was for the best. It was impossible for him to love anyone but his closest family ever again, and he was glad that Lesley was moving on.

"Thanks for letting me know, mate. See you soon, yeah?"

Chapter Nine

"September," Simon replied and hung up.

Jason thought about the conversation long after it had ended. University, his courses. Simon assumed that he would go back and complete them, but could he? He hadn't been able to put his mind to anything since the accident. Still struggling to read anything and make sense of it, his powers of concentration seemed to have deserted him entirely. And he would know no one; all his friends had graduated, so it would be like starting all over again.

But would that be such a bad thing, he pondered. It might be good to spend time with people who knew nothing about what had happened, talked to him about mundane things, and treated him like he was just some ordinary, everyday bloke who wasn't reeling from personal tragedy.

On Friday evenings, the family had taken to meeting for a bar meal at the local pub, and between courses, Jason took the opportunity to mention the conversation with Simon. "I hadn't thought about it before, and I don't want to leave you to manage on your own." He spoke to everyone, but especially Nanna Pat and Grandad T, with whom he'd been living since the accident.

"Don't worry about us, son," Grandad T replied. "You have your own life to live, and it's important that you finish your degree. Of course, you must go." Everyone wholeheartedly agreed.

"And don't forget, in a few weeks, we're hoping you'll all be busy helping us out," said Michael, smiling and patting Anne's tummy, shaped like a space hopper minus the ears.

Amber leapt to her feet and addressed her mother's stomach. "Yes, I hope you'll be here soon, brother or sister. I'm tired of waiting for you." Everyone laughed, and Jason realised for the first time that life was moving on. His beloved family were all slowly moving forward into new circumstances. They were all still suffering the pain of their grief and would do so for a long time, but they were coping. He was free to go.

As Simon had hoped, Jason arrived with his grandparents in a car laden with food, clean bedding and freshly laundered clothes early in September. "You've got the ground floor," he announced as Jason headed towards the stairs.

"But you always have the ground floor?"

"Yeah, well, I figured you'd be bringing the bike over, and you'd want to be near it, so I'm on the first. The new bloke gets the loft." he grinned.

The property had a rear yard with a small garden, accessed by a passageway that was just wide enough for Jason to wheel the motorbike around the back. He had kept it there for the few weeks before the accident, but he'd been worried about security. Being a light sleeper, on the ground floor he'd be able to hear if anyone tampered with the lock on the gate.

"That's great, mate. Thanks." Jason was mildly surprised by his friend's thoughtfulness.

"That's okay, the folks suggested it." Simon's parents knew their son was only continuing to rent as a favour to his friend. What they had actually said was that it might be difficult for Jason to return to the same place where he had lived before.

"The problem is, I know the landlord well now, and he'll give me a better deal than I can get anywhere else." he'd explained to them. The best he could do was to allocate Jason the room furthest from where he had lived before on the pretext of being closer to his bike.

Jason threw himself into his courses. Initially, he found it hard to concentrate and was frustrated by his seeming inability to keep up with the class. With perseverance, however, the complex equations gradually began to make sense again. With his friendly, outgoing personality, he had no difficulty settling back into university life, dividing his free time in roughly equal measure between studying conscientiously and drinking heavily with his new friends.

"Do you think you need to ease up a bit, mate?" Simon tentatively suggested one midweek evening in late November. He'd heard Jason fall over in the hallway as he came in and went down to help him up and into his bedsit. "I'm starting to worry about you. Nobody enjoys a bender more than me, but not five nights a week. You're overdoing it, pal."

The following morning, Jason's alarm sounded like a pneumatic drill, and it felt like it was being applied to his skull. After throwing up twice, he made some strong coffee and a slice of burnt toast. *Simon's right, this has to stop.*

The problem was, with no one else to think about or worry for, he was slowly beginning to realise the permanence of this dreadful situation. The absence of his mum and dad wasn't for this year or even the next ten years; it was forever. He couldn't ring to tell them about something amusing or to chat; he couldn't practise something to play in the pub with his dad. There would be no more invitations for a fun weekend in Sheffield, no more holidays or parties. EVER.

The nights were the worst time for Jason when the house was dark and quiet, and he was alone with his thoughts. His mind relentlessly went over and over again about the life he had enjoyed with his parents, his hopes for the future and the accident that destroyed everything. When he finally fell asleep, usually not until the early hours of the morning, his dreams were often nightmares but sometimes, even worse, he dreamt that his parents were alive. He would be doing something with them, having a great time and loving every minute, but then he would wake suddenly, only to realise that it had all been just a dream and they were dead.

He'd been the one to suggest a midweek drink with his new-found friends towards the end of September. Everyone had enjoyed it, he'd arrived home only slightly the worse for wear, but he had slept reasonably well for the first time in weeks. Over the next few months, the number of times he went out each week and the amount he consumed steadily increased. If his circumstances had been the same as the previous year, he wouldn't have been able to afford his social life, but money from his parents' estate was beginning to filter through, so he had no financial constraints.

That evening, feeling contrite and oddly nervous, Jason knocked tentatively on Simon's door. "Sorry about last night. Thanks for the pep talk."

"So, at least your ears were functioning then?" Simon scowled.

"I'm struggling, mate. I don't sleep."

"I can imagine, but being constantly bladdered isn't going to help, is it? Have you thought about the gym? If you knacker yourself enough every day, you might sleep." Jason glanced at Simon's podgy, untoned frame. *What the hell does*

Chapter Nine

he know about the gym? "I can't afford the membership, but you can," Simon quickly added, correctly interpreting his friend's look of disdain.

Jason stared at the floor dramatically, mulling the suggestion over, but only for a matter of seconds. "Sounds like a plan, when are we joining then?" he asked, grinning and ignoring the lie his friend had just told.

Simon groaned, instantly aware it was a done deal. *Why me? Why do I feel obligated to try and drag him out of the mire?* "Saturday. Now, leave me alone to stuff myself senseless before they tell me I've got to cut my carbs." He slammed the door shut in Jason's face, but he could hear him laughing outside, and he was pleased. It was a sound he hadn't heard for a while.

"It's alright for you," moaned Simon a week later, slowly ascending the stairs to his bedsit, virtually on his knees. "I should never have given you the ground floor." Through December, the two friends trained several times a week at the local gym. They were competitive, constantly trying to outdo each other, and returned home absolutely spent.

"Have a good one!" Simon called out as Jason boarded the train. It was four days before Christmas, and he'd helped Jason to carry the mountain of presents he'd bought for his family to the station.

Christmas shopping was another new experience. In previous years, Jason had bought only for his parents; his mum had sorted out all his other gifts, including wrapping them, and he'd gotten away with just giving her the money.

Easy! But not anymore.

Jason wasn't sure everyone would appreciate his selections, and the presentation was bordering on awful.

Neither he nor Simon, who had been a willing assistant, were adept with paper or Sellotape, but at least the gifts couldn't be seen. That was probably the best that could be said about the standard of the wrapping.

The busy evening train ground to a halt in Stockport and disgorged the multitude of passengers, leaving Jason alone in the carriage to gather all his parcels together. He struggled to get them and himself through the narrow doorway, then braced himself to greet his waiting grandparents. Christmas, the first without his parents. He was dreading it.

Chapter Ten

All four grandparents jostled with each other to greet Jason when he eventually disentangled himself from the ticket barrier, surrounding him in a group hug. They had discussed at length how best to approach this challenging milestone, and as usual, they'd settled on facing it together.

Seated between his grandmothers in the rear of the car, insistent on hearing every tedious detail of his life at uni, Jason struggled to appear upbeat for their sakes. It wouldn't be the same without his parents; how could it be? He recalled his mum's child-like pleasure in all things bright and sparkly, how she'd decorated her home each year until it resembled Santa's Grotto. Momentarily lost in his memories, he was suddenly dazzled by the hordes of multi-coloured lights adorning Christmas trees inside and out as his grandfather turned into the driveway. "Surprise, surprise! We're trying to pick up where your mum and dad left off, love," Nanna Pat told him, her voice quavering ever so slightly.

To his utter amazement, Jason enjoyed Christmas that year, overawed by his grandparents' determination to make it a happy time in honour of their children and to continue the traditions they had started, including several rowdy games of musical chairs on Boxing Day.

Amber was permitted to win virtually all of them and was graceful in defeat when her brother, Jonathon, gurgling happily in his father's arms, was declared the winner of a round. The little girl was ecstatic to be in the company of her favourite cousin for several days and refused to let him out of her sight. She'd been encouraged to talk about her auntie and uncle, and she did so readily, with no trace of sadness.

"Wouldn't Auntie Mary have liked this?" she asked Jason, gazing up at the new fibre-optic tree. "Oooohh, Uncle Robert would have loved this!"

Her eyes widened like saucers as she bit into a piece of the yule log, rich chocolate buttercream squishing across her top lip to form a gooey moustache. Everyone spoke of Mary and Robert often, and Jason basked in his family's warmth and the shared memories of his mum and dad.

The oasis of happiness at Christmas was brief. Bleak thoughts quickly returned when he was back to living alone in Sheffield, and they seemed harsher than ever. Jason's life of studying, more moderate drinking and ever-increasing efforts at the gym resumed through the winter months, but the cold, gloomy days and long dark evenings reflected his grim thoughts. He felt guilty for concocting a reason why he couldn't get to Stockport for his birthday, not wanting to burden anyone with the truth that he wasn't interested in celebrating this year or possibly ever again.

Over the following weeks, Simon noticed the steadily increasing frequency with which Jason attended the gym; he was now going every day and spending longer and longer working out. He was developing muscles where previously there had been nothing, and Simon could no longer compete with him. "Can't you take your foot off the gas, mate?" he panted when Jason encouraged him to try to match his efforts.

He knew the first anniversary of the accident was looming, St Patrick's Day. He'd been looking forward to celebrating with Jason in their usual fashion when he returned from his parents' the previous year. It was a great night out at the local Irish Club. The Hippies, Simon's nickname for Jason's parents only because they had lived through the 60s, would have loved it. Now he suspected that Jason might never want to celebrate the occasion again. "Fancy a jar and some fodder at the pub Monday?" Simon enquired as Jason got ready to head to the station on Friday afternoon.

"Yeah, great." They hadn't discussed it, but Jason was confident Simon would be aware of the significance of the date. He knew that his friend was trying to be kind, sacrificing his night out. The pub was alright, it didn't serve the best food in the world, but it would be quiet compared to the Irish Club.

"You can meet the lovely Amy. My girlfriend."

"Girlfriend? You're kidding me! You've got a girlfriend? No!" Jason was stunned. Simon never seemed to show any interest in girls, and he thought he'd been joking about the dame he fancied at the pub. But, come to think of it, there had been a few changes lately. Simon had to look reasonably smart for the office but otherwise tended to dress on the scruffy side of casual; recently, he seemed to have smartened up his act.

Secretly, Simon had always envied his friend's good looks, casual charm, and ability to mix with anybody and everybody effortlessly. He was also an only child; he'd been shy at school, didn't make friends easily, and spent a lot of time in his room alone, demolishing packets of cheese and onion crisps and custard creams, sometimes both at the same time.

For years he'd regarded himself as an ugly, spotty, overweight lump that would interest no one. He hid his insecurities behind a bawdy sense of humour, which he knew offended more people than it impressed. He'd been surprised when he and Jason had hit it off so well in their first few weeks at university and valued his friendship greatly, although he had no intention of ever telling Jason that.

When the terrible accident left Jason an orphan, he couldn't begin to imagine the depth of his friend's suffering or how he would have coped if it had happened to him. From then on, Simon had made it his business to look out for his friend whenever he could. What he had not anticipated was that, in doing so, he would start to lose weight and get fitter than he had ever been in his life before.

Various girls had caught Simon's eye in the past, but he'd never had the confidence to approach any of them. Amy was different. She was studying at Sheffield Hallam University, a year younger than him, and worked part-time in the local

Chapter Ten

pub. On quiet evenings, when he was in having a pint on his own, they had a laugh together.

Her sense of humour was as outlandish as his own, and he soon started to look forward to seeing her. His muscles weren't exactly rippling, but he was pleased with his new shape and decided to take a risk, discarding his usual baggy attire and investing in a tighter pair of black jeans with a couple of decent tee shirts. He hadn't thought for one minute that she would agree to go out with him but feeling more confident than usual one evening after downing a couple of chasers with his pint, he took the plunge. "Do you get a night off, and if so, would you like to spend it with me?" He knew precisely which evenings she worked, and he hoped to pass the question off as a joke when she laughed and turned him down. But, to his astonishment, she hadn't turned him down, and that was where it had all begun a few weeks before.

17th March 1997, the first anniversary of the accident, was as cold, dank and grey as the days around it. The day before, in the rain, Jason, his grandparents and Michael had made a pilgrimage to the crematorium. They placed their bouquets by the side of the small plaque beneath the cherry tree that read 'Mary and Robert, Together Forever', then huddled together only briefly in the cold wind, each lost in their thoughts. "Will you be okay tomorrow?" Jason had asked his grandparents later over coffee. "I can always stay another night and bunk off for the day."

"They'll all be fine," Michael answered for them. "Anne and I have got them on child-minding duties with Jonathon for the day, and then we're all having a fish supper. Your mum and dad would like that. More to the point, will you be alright?"

"I think Simon's got something planned," Jason scowled. "He's going to introduce me to his girlfriend."

"Nice." Michael smiled at Jason's comic expression. "Good mate you've got there."

"You have my sincere commiserations," Jason told Amy the following evening, focusing hard on trying to be good company and ignoring the hands of the clock as they slowly moved around to the time when, a year before, his life had changed forever. "Couldn't you have taken on some other charity project like Help the Aged? It would have been much easier."

Amy was rushing downstairs from Simon's bedsit one morning a few weeks later, her Doc Marten's clattering on every stair, when Jason handed her an envelope with her name on it. Inside was a badge from Blackpool, proudly proclaiming, "I Rode The Big One And Survived!" She loved it.

As the days began to warm and lengthen around mid-April, Jason started to ease up on his gym sessions; the exams were nearing, and he was now throwing himself into his revision. He had never taken his studying seriously before, always doing as little as possible and relying heavily on his natural academic ability. But there was no room for error this time; already a year behind everyone else, he couldn't afford to fail these exams.

"Got any plans for when you've passed? The graduate scheme I'm doing's not bad, shall I put a word in if they're running it again this year?" Simon asked casually. The truth was he'd already enquired about the graduate scheme; his employers would be recruiting three more people that year and were interested in personal recommendations.

"I wish I had your confidence that I'll pass," Jason groaned. "But yeah, I would be interested, thanks, mate. If you're sure you don't mind me tagging on."

Simon turned away to hide his smile and headed back upstairs to his bedsit. *Mind? Jason was the best friend he'd ever had; it would be brilliant!*

Despite his heavy workload of study and revision, Jason insisted on returning to his grandparents every other weekend to check up on them. Deep down, he knew that Michael and Anne would be excelling at supporting them all, but his continued sense of responsibility kept his thoughts away from himself.

One warm weekend in late April, he decided to ride the motorbike back to Sheffield. He carefully planned and memorised a route that took him well away from the Snake Pass and Ladybower Reservoir. Determined to enjoy the experience to the full, he forced all thoughts of his previous rides across the Peak District from his mind. Instead, he focused entirely on the scenery and the curving sweep of the bends. The sight of the occasional cyclist struggling wearily up the hills reminded him of the bike rides he'd done with his parents as a child.

Relaxed, he opened the throttle to climb a steep hill, enjoying the sudden surge of power and at the top, he turned right; onto the Snake Pass. *No! How had that happened?* Jason realised too late that, lost in the pleasure of the ride, instead of concentrating on the planned route, he'd made turns familiar to him. Now he was heading straight for

Ladybower. *He could turn back, but he was starting to feel cold. The sensible thing to do would be to keep going.*

The reservoir came into view on his right, and his mind instantly returned to that last evening, the mist, the moonlight. He shivered. As he rounded the gentle bend, the junction came into view. The traffic lights were green; there was no other traffic around, no need to slow down. Virtually at the junction, he was suddenly dazzled by a flash of bright, white light. He pulled up a short distance further on, confused. *What the hell was that? Was he ill? The junction was shaded; it couldn't have been sunlight.*

Cautiously, he returned to Sheffield, still puzzled by the flash. A couple of nights later, he awoke to the sound of a woman's piercing scream. He leapt out of bed and looked outside, but there was no one. Several times he dreamt of the sudden flash and heard the woman's scream before he realised what had happened. Being back at the junction had awoken his memory. The flash was the headlights of the truck; the scream was his mum's.

Using all his strength of will and determination, Jason somehow continued to bury himself in his books throughout May and then suddenly, it was the end of the first week in June; the madness was over. He wasn't confident, but he'd given the exams his all. Now what?

Too much time on his hands wasn't a good thing. Even when he was busy, there wasn't a single waking minute when his parents weren't in the forefront of his mind, but his new nightmares left him exhausted and frightened to sleep. He dreaded seeing the flash of the headlights again, hearing the terror in his mum's scream.

Chapter Ten

Jason was satisfied that no one knew of his inner turmoil spiralling out of control. He had perfected the art of appearing okay when he was anything but; his family marvelled at his strength and how he had coped. They were pleased for him that his life was blossoming, a job already waiting if he passed his exams. It would shock them to know the truth, that he wasn't coping at all but slowly falling further and further into a black morass of despair.

He could never burden them with his misery; it would remain his secret. He'd thought about talking to Simon but was frightened that if he ever revealed how he was really feeling, the genie would be out of the bottle and he wouldn't be able to stop. There was every chance he would make a complete fool of himself and probably wreck their friendship.

Counselling wasn't an option either. He didn't want to face questions he might not want to answer or even like to think about, and what benefit would it be anyway? It wasn't like anyone could suddenly make everything right and bring his parents back from the dead.

Locked into a world of make-believe, he fought to persuade everyone around him that he was fine in the vain hope that, one day, he would be. But it was better if he had plenty to do; distraction helped. If he passed his exams, he would start work in September; how could he fill his time until then? He secured a part-time job at a restaurant, resumed his strenuous gym sessions and rode his motorbike regularly, but still he had time on his hands. On his forays into the Peak District, Jason noticed more cyclists challenging themselves with the gradients. *He had the time to have a go, why not?*

"Tour de France next, is it? Count me out, mate," Simon yelled from his first-floor window, watching Jason weaving up the street on his newly acquired secondhand bike, saddle-sore and exhausted.

Despite all attempts to quell his mounting anguish, Jason knew it wasn't working. The effort required to maintain the self-imposed pretence of normality was becoming too much. He was at breaking point, and he knew it. He needed his own space, somewhere where he could give in to the rising tide of depression he was fighting to hold back. *But how could he break it to Simon?*

He tapped lightly on his friend's door and then entered. Simon was wearing marigold gloves, trying to catch up with a week's worth of pot washing and didn't seem interested in a chat, but Jason needed to tell him now. "The house has sold," he blurted at Simon's back as his friend stooped over the sink, vigorously applying a pan scrubber.

"Good, that's a weight off. Give me five."

Jason slumped down on the battered couch to wait and retrieved a dog-eared paperback that had virtually disappeared down one corner. "*The Unexplained*. What's this, your autobiography?" Flicking through the pages, he saw an image that he instantly recognised, an artist's impression of a person lying on a bed with their spirit floating above them, the two attached by a silver cord about five or six feet long. The picture described precisely what had happened to him in the hospital. It was captioned 'Out of the body experience.'

"So, what else?"

Now that he had Simon's full attention, Jason stuffed the book back where he'd found it. "I thought I might buy something myself. There's enough for a decent deposit, maybe a bit more." He held his breath, fearing he was letting his friend down, dreading his reaction, but Simon grinned broadly.

"Thank the Lord! Now I can start looking."

"What? But I always thought you liked it here; I've been worried sick about telling you."

"Like it here?" Simon guffawed. "I hate it here, mate. Nice area and all that, but this house is the pits, particularly the first floor." He grimaced.

"Then why.......?" Jason tailed off as realisation began to dawn. They'd found this house when they were first-year students with no money. Simon's circumstances had changed considerably since then, so why was he still here?

"Somebody had to watch out for you, didn't they; and while we've been paying low rent on this dive, I've put more aside for a deposit myself, so all's good, buddy."

A good mate, that's how Michael had described Simon, but Jason had never before realised just how good. He stepped forwards, feeling compelled to hug his friend. "Back off!" growled Simon, making the sign of a cross with his yellow-gloved forefingers. "You caught me out like that once before; I'm not falling for it again!"

Jason read the advertisement in the estate agent's window.

A well-proportioned three-bedroomed semi-detached property with garage and front and rear gardens, located on a quiet estate with easy access to the motorway and bus routes into the city.

The photo looked appealing; he went in and arranged a viewing.

The house was well decorated; he could move straight in. The gardens comprised a rectangular lawn at the front, and a patio at the back edged with shrubs, easy to maintain. Whilst inspecting the garage, Jason noticed a fancy road bike propped against the wall. "You're a cyclist? Nice bike."

"I do a bit, not as much as I'd like to with the second nipper coming along." The young man sighed, smiling. "But there's plenty of good cycling around here and some decent clubs if you're interested."

A week later, when the financial checks were complete, Jason rang his grandparents. "I've bought a house!"

"Really?" Grandad T was unable to disguise his startled surprise. "You said you were thinking about it, but......., how many have you looked at?"

"Just the one, I liked it."

His grandmothers threw themselves into ideas for furnishings and colour schemes, studying room sizes, the location of doors and windows and which areas of the house got the sun as keenly as any professional interior designers. When the day came to move in, Jason drove the hired transit van containing his belongings and the items donated by friends and family whilst his grandparents followed in the car. "Are you sure you'll be okay?" Nanna Pat asked at the end of a hectic day, teary-eyed, not wanting to leave him alone, not knowing that was what he wanted most of all.

"I'll be fine, Nanna, don't worry." Jason felt guilty as he waved them off. He loved his family dearly and was incredibly fortunate to have Simon as a friend, but he was relieved to be alone at last.

Chapter Ten

He went to the garage, where he'd deposited the storage box containing the pictures he'd prepared for the party over a year before, took several of the largest ones out, carried them upstairs to his bedroom and leaned them against the walls. As twilight fell, he sat on the floor, surveying the pictures in the dim light.

His eyes began to swim; he could see his parents' faces moving and hear them faintly laughing and chatting. Tears began to roll down his cheeks slowly, then more and more. His body shook with the effort to keep self-control, but then he gave in. Huge sobs left him gasping for air. He lay on the floor, the carpet muffling the sound of the wounded animal he could hear somewhere in the distance. He didn't know that the sound was coming from himself.

Chapter Eleven

Jenni heard the door swing closed with a click. So, this was it; the moment had arrived. It was precisely 8.30 am, the time that Lisa always arrived at the office. Jenni didn't usually start until 9 am, but she wanted to get this encounter over with as soon as possible. She'd been dreading it and had thought of nothing else since that snowy evening in December; she would never forget the look on her friend's face, so brief but which spoke volumes.

Sleep had eluded her for weeks; she was tired, unable to concentrate, and barely able to work. She lived alone in a small, draughty rented flat and, in those last few days before Christmas, had hardly left her bed. Since Mark ran out of the hotel in pursuit of Lisa, he hadn't returned any of her calls, and she couldn't talk to anyone else about what had happened. She desperately wanted to contact Lisa, but how? And even if she did, what could she say?

Her parents had split up when she was only a toddler; due to her dad's infidelity, her mum always said, but they had both gone on to have several relationships and children. Jenni had been shunted around between her parents and their various partners for several years until her dad's mother called a halt to it when she was aged eight. "This poor child needs a stable home life. Let me have her for a while." Both parents, battling with the needs of younger children and transient partners, readily agreed.

Life with her grandmother was happy, but looking back, Jenni realised she had always been searching for something more. She craved the attention that had so often been absent during her early years, mistakenly searching for it with the young boys at school who made her feel special but, in fact, had just gladly taken advantage of the girl who was prepared to go further than the others.

The troupe of Moroccan acrobats she met at a travelling show when she was fifteen were more than willing to give her all the attention she could possibly want. Pursuing them on weekends as they moved around the county had proved to be exhausting in more ways than one, and when her grandmother found out, she was sent back to her mum. As soon as she could leave school and start work, she'd managed to rent a tiny, damp and dingy bedsit and started out on her own.

Jenni was 18 when she met Lisa. By then, she'd been working and living alone for more than two years, and the contrast between the two girls could not have been greater. Lisa was timid, shy and still dependent on her parents; Jenni was streetwise and self-sufficient.

It was an unlikely pairing that might never have happened at all, but for the fact that they'd started work on the same day. After spending the morning together on the induction course, Jenni had suggested lunch, and in no time at all, they'd become firm friends. During their lunchtime discussions, it soon dawned on Jenni that her friend had limited experience with men. She frequently entertained Lisa with tales of her encounters with the opposite sex. "I bumped into my hairdresser last night in Isabella's. I've fancied him for a while. We had a few drinks, then a bit of a boogie and I invited him back. Snores like the devil."

Lisa never offered any anecdotes in return, and Jenni knew she didn't have a boyfriend, but she'd been astonished when Lisa confided at the Christmas party that she'd never been kissed before. "You've never even snogged? Where the hell have you been all your life?" she'd demanded to know. "You're missing out on so much fun!" But Lisa hadn't thought that the sickly, slobbery encounter with Stuart had been anything approaching fun.

The first time Jenni met Mark was at an Insurance Institute bowling evening when Lisa had introduced them. She'd mentioned a guy from college a few times, and Jenni had been surprised that someone seemed to have finally gotten under her skin.

She was impressed that he was reasonably attractive and fun; knowing Lisa, a studious-looking geek in glasses who spoke to no one would have been more her type. Thinking back, Jenni recalled with horror that she had mildly flirted with him on that first meeting. It meant nothing; it was just what she did. She couldn't help herself.

Much to Jenni's amusement, Mark had called Lisa 'Mouse' throughout the evening. She had used the nickname at work the following day, and in no time, everyone in the office knew her as 'Mouse'. Lisa had taken it all in her stride and never complained; only now did Jenni realise how demeaning it must have been for her, an insult to her experience and ability.

Why did I do that to her? Jenni wondered, over and over again. She wanted to believe that it had been just a little joke, but was there something more to it? Was she jealous of her friend, younger than her and so determined to achieve success, cutting a swathe through the exams that she was failing, already one pay grade ahead of her and likely to gain further promotion at any minute?

As Lisa's relationship with Mark progressed, she had sought help and advice from Jenni, her more worldly friend. "Mark keeps inviting me to his. For a meal," she added hastily.

"Hallelujah! You're gonna get laid."

"That's what I'm worried about, I don't know what to do."

Jenni rolled her eyes, unable to believe that she was having this conversation with someone rapidly approaching 22 years of age. "Please tell me you know what goes where."

"Don't be ridiculous." Lisa blushed crimson. "I think.... that's what he's hoping for and.... I don't want to be a disappointment. I don't know what to expect and ..... I'm scared." Jenni smiled, both delighted and intrigued at the same time by her dear friend's innocence and naivety, so very different from her own life experience.

"Mark will lead the way, but for God's sake, be a willing participant."

Lisa looked like a rabbit caught in the headlights. "Don't say anything to him," she pleaded.

"I promise I won't." But the next time they'd all met for a drink and Lisa had disappeared to the toilet, Jenni had leaned across to Mark conspiratorially and tutted. "Our darling Lisa's a virgin, look after her." *Had she gone against Lisa's wishes out of concern for her or to undermine her again?* Sadly, Jenni didn't know the answer.

As her relationship with Mark flourished, Lisa was determined not to forget her friend and regularly invited Jenni to join them for meals or a drink, making up a foursome if she had someone in tow at the time.

So, when Mark struggled with Lisa's commitment to her studying, it was to Jenni he turned for a shoulder to cry on. He suggested a drink after work to talk to her about things, genuinely believing that if he told Jenni what was going on, she could subtly influence Lisa into easing up and enjoying life more.

That first evening they'd sat in the quiet little bar, both drinking pints, and as she played the scene repeatedly in her head, Jenni realised too late that she had been too understanding of his predicament. Ever the fun-loving party animal, she'd instantly empathised with him and wholeheartedly agreed that life was all about enjoyment. "I don't know why she does it either. She's doing well at work; she's already a grade higher than I am. She's got her qualification; she doesn't need to do any more studying. She should be paying more attention to you." *There it was again, that word, attention. The very thing she had been searching for all her life.*

During that first meeting, she'd felt guilty about going behind Lisa's back, but she'd recognised her own need in someone else; they had a mutual understanding. When Mark rang the following week to ask her to meet him again, she'd readily agreed. They enjoyed the light-hearted couple of hours together, both pretending, she could see with hindsight, that it was just a drink and a laugh. But then Mark had leaned over and kissed her. Between relationships again herself, she had ardently returned his kiss. Alarmed, they had quickly left, determined they must never meet alone again.

But the following week, she had been unable to resist Mark's request to meet for a drink, supposedly to discuss what had happened and clear the air. *She'd known what was going on; why hadn't she put a stop to it there and then, for Lisa's sake?*

Within half an hour, they were heading for the little back street hotel, Jenni convincing herself that it would never have happened if Lisa had just been more attentive to Mark. It was just sex, nothing more. She had no feelings for him, and she was pretty sure he had none for her. They were both just satisfying each other's need for attention whilst Lisa was committed to studying. It would only last a few months, then everything would be back to normal, and Lisa would be none the wiser. Sadly, that wasn't how it had worked out. On the third or was it their fourth visit to the hotel, Jenni couldn't remember, suddenly there she was, standing in the doorway, as still as if she'd been turned to stone.

Jenni couldn't get Lisa's expression out of her mind. The look of blank confusion, followed by such horror and agony that she looked as though she feared for her life. *How could she ever have thought that it wouldn't matter, that they could get away with it, that life would ever be the same again?*

She had wounded the best friend she'd ever had as deeply as if she had taken a knife and plunged it into her chest. For the first time in her life, Jenni felt ashamed; self-loathing, a feeling she had never experienced before, settled on her and seemed to suck the very life out of her.

There was no one she could turn to. "My best friend has found out I've slept with her partner; what should I do?" wasn't a question she could ask anyone. So, she had spent most of her time in her flat alone, endlessly going over the same scene, considering how she might contact Lisa and deciding against every option. When she returned to work after Christmas, Jenni discovered that everyone in the office somehow knew what had happened, and now she was a pariah. No one spoke to her unless they had to; worst of all, she could understand why.

And now the dreaded moment had at long last arrived. She could sense that Lisa was only feet away and had no idea what to expect. *What will she look like, what will she say, will she say anything at all, will she hit me? Whatever happens, I deserve it!*

"Morning, Jenni." Lisa's voice shattered the silence within the half-full open-plan office. Several staff members had arrived early, not wanting to miss the spectacle of the two women meeting for the first time since the 'incident'. Jenni looked up into the smiling face of the stunning creature who once upon a time everyone knew as 'Mouse'; the beautiful green eyes made to look even more cat-like with just a hint of eyeliner at the corners, the long lashes, the slick of red lipstick, the figure-hugging suit that clung to every curve.

"Morning," she mumbled as Lisa proceeded to greet all her colleagues in turn before sitting at her desk, facing her team. Attempting to introduce an air of normality, Keith, a claims handler, jumped to his feet and grabbed the tea tray from the top of the filing cabinet. "Coffee, anyone?" Taking a slight detour on his way to the kitchen, he walked past Lisa's desk, grinning. "You look bloody great!"

"I could have got the bus, Dad." Lisa had left the office at 5 pm as usual and almost ran past Joe, waiting for her in the car.

"No, not on your first day back, maybe later in the week," he grinned, with no intention of letting her travel on the bus until spring arrived. He relished this unexpected opportunity to spend a little time alone with her each day and didn't want to squander it.

"How was it?" Kathleen threw her arms around Lisa as she entered the kitchen.

"Not bad, to be honest." Lisa smiled. "Two of the girls invited me out for coffee at lunchtime, and the guys have all been very complimentary about my new look."

"There you go, you see. And Jenni?"

Her mother had left Lisa in no doubt about what she would like to say to Jenni. She had told her that she must not be taken in by any half-hearted apologies. Right up to the previous evening, Lisa hadn't known how she would react when she saw Jenni. Her emotions chopped and changed from feeling distraught that her closest friend could let her down so badly to being utterly outraged. She wasn't sure if she would burst into tears or punch her.

But as she lay in bed, anxiously anticipating the day ahead, a calmness had come over her, and her head had cleared for the first time since she had seen Mark and Jenni together. *Did she really want this to be a defining event in her life, or did she want to put it behind her and move on? Would she allow herself to be eaten alive by anger and bitterness or be the bigger person?*

Her decision to greet Jenni as she had always done before, without any sign of malice, had been a tough one. She'd felt exhausted with the effort when she sat down at her desk, but then she suddenly felt the sensation of arms around her shoulders, holding her tight, supporting her. *Could her grandparents really be there with her? Had the friendly greeting been their idea?* Throughout the day, she'd only spoken to Jenni when necessary, but when she did, it had been with a smile. She had made it through her first day and could do it again; their friendship was over, but they could be colleagues.

"I can rub along with Jenni, " she replied. Kathleen glanced at Joe, bemused, but he only smiled. Stuck in traffic on the way home, he'd enjoyed an enlightening chat with his daughter, and he'd been thrilled to discover she was made of sterner stuff than perhaps any of them had realised.

"Well? I can't wait any longer, how's it going?" Maryam sounded more like an excited schoolgirl than a respected senior partner of a London law firm on the other end of the telephone at the end of Lisa's first week back.

"Great!" Lisa replied, giggling at her sister-in-law's enthusiasm. "The costume works so well. I feel like Boadicea when I go into work, ready to take on all-comers and then when I'm back in my jeans, I'm just boring old me again."

"There's nothing boring about you, girl. Get out there and buy some more costumes. It works for anything, you know, not just the office." Maryam replaced the receiver and punched the air, delighted.

"I need a transfer, if possible, please," Jenni told Alan at the end of Lisa's second week back. It might have been easier if Lisa had come in screaming at her or at least ignored her completely, but she could not bear it that she still smiled at her after all that had happened.

Four weeks later, insisting that no one should know until afterwards, Jenni worked late and then cleared her personal belongings from her desk. A sob caught in her throat as she looked around the office one last time. It had been a harsh life lesson, but she was determined never again to hurt anyone so badly to satisfy her own needs. She started at the Nottingham office on Monday morning, a straight swap with another young underwriter who lived in Sheffield and couldn't believe his luck.

Lisa arrived that morning and found a folded sheet of paper in the centre of her desk. She recognised Jenni's scrawl as she read the words, I'm so sorry. That evening she filed the piece of paper in the back of the wardrobe with the photographs and Mark's unopened letter.

Due to sit her final exams in the second week of April, through February and March, Lisa spent virtually every waking hour she wasn't at work studying and revising. "Do you think you're doing too much, sweetheart?" It was the third time that week that Kathleen had heard Lisa creeping down the stairs to the study at 5.30 am.

"I don't want to fail, Mum, and I've lost so much time."

A few weeks later, stepping out into the bright sunlight after three intense hours in the gloomy college hall, Lisa gazed around as she walked back to the bus stop. The birds were singing, the trees already had a full canopy of fresh new leaves, and the grass was lush, almost emerald-green. Hopefully, she had completed her last exam; it felt like a new beginning.

Chapter Eleven

"Will you come to this with me, Mum?" Lisa pushed the recruitment flyer she'd picked up at the gym, detailing the date, time and location of the Samaritans open evening into Kathleen's hand. She'd forced herself to join the local gym a month before, only days after her last exam, self-consciously rushing in and finding a space at the back just as her chosen class was beginning.

Kathleen read the flyer to Joe whilst Lisa showered. "I don't think it's a good idea. She should be out having fun, not spending her time talking to people who're thinking of killing themselves."

"Why not go along with her and see what it's all about love?" Joe felt absurdly offended that Lisa hadn't asked him to go with her; she would surely know that he would be supportive of anything she wanted to do.

But that was precisely the reason why Lisa hadn't asked him. She and her dad were like peas in a pod, both in looks and temperament; their relationship was so easy, they understood each other without even trying. Lisa and her mum were very different people; she had always admired her mother's incredible strength of will and determination. Even now, aged almost 25, she still needed Kathleen's approval.

"Are you sure you want to do this?" Kathleen asked Lisa as they drove back from the open evening a few days later. "It sounds like hard work to me, all that training and then a minimum commitment per month. You've studied so hard for so long; don't you want to take a break, sweetheart?"

Lisa bit her lip. *Was it the right thing to say or not?* She'd been longing to ask ever since her mum had made her sit at the table and listen to her. *Oh, why not go for it?* "Mum, will you tell me about my nan, please?"

Kathleen glanced at her, startled at the request. She'd forgotten about the lecture and telling Lisa of her mother's long years of severe depression when she was only a child. Taking a deep breath, she began, hesitantly at first, and then the words spilled forth in a torrent as she shared with her daughter things she had never told anyone else.

Why aren't they coming inside? Joe wondered as he looked through the curtains again at the car parked on the driveway. They'd been sat there for almost half an hour. He hoped that Kathleen wasn't trying to talk Lisa out of becoming a Samaritan; it would be good for her to have something else to do in her spare time besides the relentless pounding at the gym. "Come on, girls, I've got the coffee on." Joe pulled open the passenger door and was horrified to see Kathleen and Lisa clinging together, their faces glistening with tears. *What on earth had happened now?*

"No one's really ever asked me about Mum before," Kathleen told Joe as he held her close in bed that night. "She tried to drown herself in the canal more than once. It broke my heart, made me tough."

"But as young as you were, you must have helped her through it, love. That's where Lisa gets it from, wanting to help others. She takes after you." Kathleen said nothing, thoughts of this unexpected connection with her beloved daughter whirling through her mind. "Are you okay?"

Kathleen could hear the concern in his voice. "Yes, yes, I think I am. I've always thought Lisa takes after you...., in everything."

"Most things, yes, especially her good looks. But she gets her very best bits from her mother." Even in the darkness, Kathleen could sense her husband was smiling.

Chapter Twelve

X

"Happy Birthday to You!" In unison, Lisa's parents planted a kiss on her cheeks. She opened her card and gifts; a bottle of her favourite Amaretto liqueur and a NEXT gift voucher, then hugged them in turn. "Thank you so much; it's way too much, but thank you."

"Champagne?" Joe asked at the fancy Italian restaurant that evening.

"I'm 25, Dad, not 21." Lisa frowned. *A quarter of a century old already; how had that happened?*

"Well, actually, it is a special occasion," Joe smiled as Kathleen passed Lisa a slim white envelope. Inside was a certificate detailing the amount of the trust fund her parents had set up when she was born, which became hers on her 25th birthday; it was for a sizeable sum.

Overwhelmed by their generosity, Lisa caught her breath and turned to look at her parents. "Cheers!" they chorused, smiling. "No tears, not on your birthday!" Joe reprimanded her, before explaining they'd done the same for Neil and Stephen, and swore them to secrecy.

"We wanted to give you all a helping hand," Kathleen continued, "but not too early on in life. We wanted you to find your feet first and make your own way. You've worked so hard, Lisa, done so well; you more than deserve this."

No one in the family was surprised when, in early August, Lisa received confirmation from the Insurance Institute that she had passed her final exams with distinction and was now a Fellow. When Stephen was in London on business, the family celebrated at Georgina and Byron's favourite restaurant, Pizza Hut.

Squashed into the corner of a booth between her delighted nephew and niece, Lisa finally felt she belonged in this family of high achievers, grinning as her parents, brothers, and Maryam toasted her success. It had come at a high price; there was no doubt the failure of her relationship with Mark was somehow her fault, but right now, she was the happiest she had been in a very long time. She had made her family proud, and that meant everything to her.

"Congratulations!" Alan, her Manager, beamed broadly at Lisa as he clinked his wine glass against hers over the celebratory lunch he'd insisted on, despite her protests. Looking at her now, he could scarcely remember the gawky young teenager who had given such a poor account of herself at her interview that he'd almost decided to discount her. It was only when he'd asked her about her ambitions that a fierce look of determination had settled on her lovely features.

She'd told him of her desire to learn, do well and make her family proud; the pleading look in her eyes had persuaded him to give her a chance. How that chance had paid off; he'd expected her to do well, but not this well. There were relatively few women who held the Fellowship in what was still a male-dominated industry, and she was undoubtedly a great asset to the company; the problem now was that she would inevitably be head-hunted by other companies.

He was nearing retirement, and if he could hand his carefully nurtured protege over to the higher echelons of the company, she would surely make a remarkable legacy. "I have a confession to make," Alan continued. "I haven't invited you here purely to celebrate. I have something I want to discuss with you. What are your thoughts about being put forward for the Major Loss Team?"

The Major Loss Team comprised a small group of claims-handling experts distributed among the main offices around the country who dealt with the highest-value personal injury claims received by the company. The other experts had gradually worked their way into the team through years of experience and were much older than Lisa.

Alan suspected Lisa's intellect and commitment might make her senior management potential in years to come, but, for now, joining the Major Loss Team would be the highest accolade the company could give her, and it might be enough to keep her.

"Wow, are you having me on?" Lisa couldn't quite believe what she was hearing. To be considered for the team at this stage in her career would be an honour.

"Think about it, Lisa. It would probably mean a transfer to the Leeds office so that you can train with the other team members. It's by no means certain that you will get in, but I didn't want to put you forward until I'd discussed it with you." He watched a shadow pass across Lisa's face and instinctively read her thoughts. "Don't worry. If you're successful, we'll keep in touch."

Lisa lay awake long into the night, touched but deeply troubled at the same time by Alan's unexpected question. He'd always encouraged her and given her every opportunity to progress, and even though there was no prospect of further promotion in the small office, she'd given no thought to moving on.

The idea of leaving behind the support of the only Manager she'd ever known was daunting, to say the least, but what he proposed was a huge compliment, a virtually unheard-of opportunity for someone her age.

But being a member of the Major Loss Team was a very prestigious position; if she got in and didn't enjoy it, she wouldn't be able to ask to go back to what she had been doing before. The team would invest a lot of time and effort in her training, and she would need to commit to delivering her best in return. *Why are you wasting your time thinking about it? You haven't got a chance! For God's sake, go to sleep and forget about it!* The ever-present voice of her insecurity butted in as she tossed and turned in bed that night, pondering for hours over what to tell Alan the following day.

"I'd like you to put a word in for me, please," she told him, feeling distinctly nervous.

"The team would like to meet you," Alan told Lisa a week later. "You're invited to the conference in London at the end of September." He put his glasses on to read from the email he'd printed out for her. "They'd like you to do a presentation, only something short, for about 30 minutes." Lisa thought she might pass out as she took the email from him.

Chapter Twelve

A presentation? In front of the company's most qualified and experienced team of claims handlers?

"I can't!" She sobbed to her parents, relieved to be home at last and able to pour out the distress that had consumed her throughout the day. Kathleen stroked her daughter's hair, soothing her, recalling so many previous instances when Lisa had been distraught due to her total lack of self-confidence. *Would this ever end?*

Mortified, Lisa trembled in her mother's arms. She'd thrown every ounce of effort she possessed at her career and been offered an incredible opportunity as a result, but it was all to come to nothing because she couldn't stand up and present to her colleagues. Her disappointment in herself was overwhelming, but she could do nothing. The mere thought of the presentation was already giving her panic attacks.

"It will all be fine, Lisa. Or should I say, Boadicea?" Maryam tried to reassure her over the phone later that evening. "Don't panic; remember how different you feel when you wear your costume. Treat yourself to a special outfit that transforms you into that confident person who knows how much she deserves this success."

"I can't do it; I'm sorry. Please withdraw the application," Lisa told Alan wearily the following morning, the dark circles beneath her eyes evidence of her lack of sleep.

He sat her down and brought her a coffee. "Now listen to me, young lady. You know as much, if not more, about liability than anyone else who will be there because you've recently studied it at a very high level. You can do this; I'll help you with some slides and then blind them with your knowledge. They're not trying to catch you out; they want to meet you and discover what you can do. Choose something you can reel off in your sleep," he suggested, "then we can work on a few slides together."

She tried, but soon Alan noticed that the skin on her fingers looked increasingly red and sore, and small white particles, like dandruff, fell to her shoulders. "Are you okay, Lisa?" He asked, concerned; the conference was scheduled for the following week.

"Not really, to be honest. I've got eczema and psoriasis. I used to suffer both as a child, something to do with nerves."

Kathleen and Joe had also noticed that Lisa was struggling. "Why don't you let it go, sweetheart?" Joe had asked her. "It's not worth making yourself ill; there'll be other opportunities."

Lisa sighed, desperately wanting the pressure of the impending conference to stop. "If I give in now, it will all have been for nothing. I have to try."

But she wasn't sleeping, and her skin complaints worsened by the day. Without telling Lisa, Alan contacted the director who had invited her to the conference. "Mr Young would like to speak to you, Lisa. Are you happy to call him? I've told him you're making yourself ill; I thought it was for the best in the circumstances."

He glanced meaningfully at her fingers. "Sit here and use my phone, away from prying ears. I'll make us a coffee." Then he was gone, grinning back at her briefly over his shoulder as he strode away in the direction of the kitchen, giving her no chance to refuse. She could feel her heart pounding in her chest as she carefully tapped out the number scrawled on Alan's blotter. *What a prize idiot you are, applying for a senior position and then your first-ever conversation with a director is because you're making yourself ill. What's he going to think of you? You've made yourself a laughing stock. Well done!*

"Lisa!" Mr Young's voice boomed from the receiver. "I've heard a lot about you; good to speak. Now listen, there's no need to worry about the conference. Could you manage your presentation sitting down, operating the projector, with your back to us if necessary? Thinking about it, that would be a much better option for you than facing our ugly mugs. If there are questions at the end, we'll all be sitting around the table, just like in a group discussion. Do-able? Great, I look forward to meeting you next week."

"They want you in the team, Lisa," Alan enthused when she told him about the call. "If they're willing to do what they can to help you get through this, they already want you. Remember that when you get down there."

The conference went much better than she'd expected. All the team members and the several directors present made her welcome. Still consumed by nerves as the time for her presentation approached, she delivered it well to the appreciative applause of her audience. Relaxed, she answered the questions that followed competently, unknowingly displaying her extensive knowledge to the full. Within days, she was offered a position in the team, based on the unanimous decision of the directors and all the team members present. Alan was so happy for her; he breached every code of conduct and kissed her.

In mid-October, Lisa completed the three-month training programme and became a fully-fledged Samaritan. The course had been a revelation; she'd always assumed that a Samaritan's sole remit is to dissuade suicidal people from killing themselves and was amazed to discover that's not the case at all. The skill of the role is to encourage deeply distressed people to open up, talk, and gradually try to find a way forward for themselves.

She'd enjoyed studying the aspects of psychology the tutors considered most beneficial for the difficult task of identifying different types of people from a disembodied voice at the other end of the phone line. Fleetingly, she wondered what life might have held in store for her if she had pursued her preferred A levels with Michelle.

The familiar self-doubt kicked in on her first shift at the sound of the shrill ring from the phone on the desk in front of her. She hardly dared pick it up, afraid of being unable to provide the comfort the caller needed. But, with the support of her mentor, Denise, she handled the call and several others.

The national outpouring of grief following the death of Diana, Princess of Wales, still flowed unabated, and her three-hour shifts, sometimes at weekends but often in the evenings straight from work, were intense and tiring. As her confidence steadily grew, Lisa thrived on the unexpected sense of well-being she derived from trying to help others and the companionship of the other Samaritans, an eclectic mix of ages and backgrounds.

At a Christmas fundraiser, Lisa introduced Denise to her parents. "We're very fortunate to have her," she told Joe and Kathleen as Lisa headed to the buffet. "Especially now. She has amazing empathy for one so young. Has she been hurt herself?"

"Her best friends ripped her heart out," Kathleen sneered, still wishing she'd been allowed to vent her anger with them.

Chapter Twelve

Taken aback by the intensity of the reply, Denise was relieved to see Lisa returning with her food.

Nervous but determined not to show it, Lisa joined the Major Loss Team at the beginning of January 1998. "It's almost as though she has become two people," Kathleen remarked to Joe as they watched Lisa rushing along the pavement early one morning in the direction of the railway station only a short distance away.

She looked every inch an executive in a pillar box red, almost ankle-length coat and boots to protect against the cold weather, briefcase in hand, her tumbling curls tied back in the high ponytail she preferred, her makeup subtle and immaculate.

Her job involved meetings with solicitors, barristers and sometimes her opposite number from another insurance company; it was essential to look the part. When she returned home in the evening, she immediately changed out of her work clothes into jeans and a sloppy jumper or her pyjamas if it was late, removed her makeup and then she became almost child-like again, curling up between her parents on the sofa, telling them of her day. Inevitably the conversation would turn to the things that were worrying her, usually the high-level meetings and discussions to which she would have to contribute. They talked through her concerns each evening, and then the following day, she set off again, dressed to kill, ready to do battle with her insecurities above all else.

The train journey between Dore and Leeds each day was tedious and fraught with problems. It was necessary to change at Sheffield; sometimes, Lisa missed her connection.

She came to dread the echoing tannoy announcement that her train was running late and was grateful when winter gave way to spring, the days lengthened, and it wasn't quite so cold standing on the draughty platforms.

By the time summer arrived, she was thoroughly enjoying her new role, and as Alan had anticipated, he was hearing glowing reports of how she was progressing.

"I'm not looking forward to another winter on the train, though," Lisa told him as they sat in the early evening sunshine, enjoying one of their monthly catchups. Although he knew Lisa thought highly of him, Alan was constantly surprised that this lovely young woman wanted his company and insisted at each meeting that they schedule a date for the next one.

"Well, is there anything else you could do? Drive, perhaps?"

"I don't think so," Lisa replied. "I don't have a car for a start."

"Buy one then."

"The traffic's crazy first thing, it would take me forever to get across Sheffield to the motorway."

"So? Move closer to the motorway."

Lisa laughed. "You make it all sound so easy."

"That's because it is."

Alan smiled, but Lisa gasped, suddenly startled. He turned to see what she was looking at; there was nothing behind him. "What is it, Lisa?"

She quickly recovered herself and smiled. "Sorry, I was just mulling over your extraordinary idea!" They both knew that wasn't true, but Alan didn't pursue it further. Everyone has their secrets.

Chapter Twelve

Kathleen and Joe didn't relish the prospect of Lisa leaving home again, but, as had now become the norm, they were poring over the property pages with her. She'd viewed several houses and apartments, but nothing had appealed. "Oh, there's a new one here. A three-bed detached, quiet cul-de-sac, five minutes' drive from the motorway. I'll give them a ring." Lisa bounded out into the hallway and returned a few minutes later. "I can have a look at it on Saturday at 3 pm. Can you make that?"

"I'm meeting Sue for coffee on Saturday; your dad can go with you," Kathleen replied for them both.

"Hey! I have a social calendar as well, you know?" Joe spluttered. "I'm golfing Saturday afternoon. Can you make it in the morning, Lisa?"

"It's okay, Dad. They're busy Saturday morning; I'll be all right on my own, and I'll probably not like it anyway."

"You can take my car," Kathleen offered. "I'm sure Sue won't mind picking me up."

Lisa laughed. "Thanks, Mum. I'd not thought about how to get there. Duh!"

The owner of the property had told her to follow the main road through the estate to the end and then take a left and a right. *Or was it a right and a left?* Lisa checked the route again in the A to Z before setting off and wrote down the directions. Drive to the end, then right and left.

She set off in plenty of time and found her way to the estate easily. Turning left and right at the end, she spotted the 'For Sale' sign in the corner of the cul-de-sac.

"Can I help you?" The lady who came to the door appeared to be in her early to mid-70s. She was clearly not the younger woman Lisa had spoken to on the phone and seemed surprised to see her.

"I'm Lisa. I've come to look at the house. I'm sorry I'm a little early; my appointment is at 3 pm."

"Your appointment?" The lady looked confused. "The board only went up yesterday, I haven't been contacted by anyone yet." Before Lisa had a chance to answer, the lady smiled. "Oh, I know; I bet you've arranged to see the house on the next road. That one went up for sale last week, but you can look at mine if you like, as you're here."

Lisa glanced at her watch. It was 2.50 pm; she didn't have much time, but this lady seemed nice, and she didn't want to refuse her offer. "That would be lovely, thank you, but I'll have to hurry I'm afraid."

"No problem at all, dear. I like to be punctual myself." Precisely ten minutes later, Lisa waved goodbye to Irene. "You have a beautiful home. Thank you so much for your number, I'll be in touch." Irene returned the wave with an odd sensation that she had somehow already made a sale.

Idiot! Lisa chastised herself as she drove to the end of the cul-de-sac. She'd written the directions down for goodness' sake, how could she have got the last bit wrong? Nearing the junction, she noticed the tall young man with fair hair wheeling his red motorbike out onto the drive. She glanced down to check her directions again, still unable to believe her incompetence, and so she didn't see him nod his head in acknowledgement and smile at her as she drove past.

Chapter Thirteen

Jason awoke stiff and cold, still curled in a ball on the floor, where he had eventually fallen into a fitful sleep. At first, he wasn't sure where he was, but as his eyes became accustomed to the darkness and focused on the pictures around him, he remembered. Feeling a surge of reassurance as he surveyed his parents' smiling faces in the gloom, he climbed into bed, still fully clothed and fell into a deep sleep.

The hazy morning sunlight that flooded the bedroom despite the curtains eventually woke him again. He made coffee, took the radio upstairs and selected Radio Hallam, the station his parents always favoured when they were in town. As he sat back against his pillows, listening to the strains of local band Pulp pulsing out from the crackling transistor, he knew that this was what he needed; a place to be with his mum and dad. He wouldn't, in fact, couldn't let them go, and this room was where he could be with them.

He extracted the remaining pictures and photographs from the box in the garage, carried them upstairs and laid them on his bed. Tears began to fall again as he wrapped his strong arms around a large, framed photograph of the three of them together, taken by his grandparents at Anne and Michael's wedding and held it tightly against his chest.

Grief poured from him like a swollen river bursting its banks. At first, Jason felt overwhelmed, drowning in his despair, but slowly his sobbing eased, and he felt calmer, relaxed almost, spent. He became aware of a new sensation ebbing through him, relief. At last, there was no more need for pretence. Here, he could collapse, given in to the grief that was eating him alive, and no one need ever know.

His bedroom had a large, fitted wardrobe along one wall and a picture window opposite. Within days, he had filled the available wall space with pictures of his parents. The two packing cases containing their most personal possessions stood side by side in the garage, his dad's guitar case laid across the top of them.

Jason took the guitar up to his bedroom and propped it in a corner by the side of the window. He'd intended to drape his mum's coat over a kitchen chair placed by the side of the guitar, but it smelled like an Afghan hound after a long walk in the rain and so, smiling to himself, he threw it over the rotary drier on the patio for the day. *That should cause some consternation amongst his new neighbours if anyone saw it. Perhaps he could convince them he was a Mark Bolan impersonator?*

Later that evening, he applied a squirt of his mum's favourite Opium perfume to the coat to overpower any lingering odour and then carefully positioned it over the back of the chair, stretching out along the carpet, the floppy hat perched on top. He took the guitar from the case and

Chapter Thirteen

placed it on the stand. "Cheers!" Jason raised his glass as he turned and gazed at the images around him. For the first time since the accident, it felt like they were a threesome again.

There were ten houses on the cul-de-sac, referred to as 'The Close' by the locals and most of his new neighbours stopped by to introduce themselves. In the adjoining semi lived a young couple with two young children, and then came Pietro, an Italian in his early thirties who lived on his own and drove an Alfa Romeo Spider.

Next door to Pietro lived Tracy, Ian and their large Alsatian, Gnasher. Within days of moving in, Jason began to look forward to seeing Ian pass his house around teatime in the pose of a water skier, holding on to the lead for dear life as Gnasher dragged him along at speed in the direction of a nearby field.

Irene and George, both in their seventies, lived in one of two detached properties at the end. George wasn't in the best of health, but Irene had invited Jason around for coffee and cake within days of him moving in. In the opposite corner lived a middle-aged couple with a daughter who looked to be about Jason's age, and next to them lived a divorced lady, Jan, who brought her two young daughters over to meet him. "You look like Dad," commented one of them, referring to Jason's shock of fair hair, so like their own.

"Only 20 years younger," remarked Jan, fluttering her eyelashes.

Another middle-aged couple lived by the side of Jan. Shelagh quickly informed Jason that she had OCD and not to worry if he saw her on a ladder, cleaning her windows at all hours. Next to Shelagh and her husband Jim lived a gay couple, John and Phil. Jason had never met any gay men before but could not help but take to them instantly. They'd knocked on his door one evening after tea.

"Hi, we thought we'd come and introduce ourselves. I'm John, and this is the lovely Phil." The man's broad smile suddenly faded, replaced by a concerned frown. "We live together. I hope that doesn't put you off?"

"I'm very pleased to meet you both." Jason hoped his face didn't reveal his shock at John's introduction.

"Oh good," John enthused, "We have the best parties ever; you really must come!"

Phil smiled benignly and steered John towards home. "Come on, let's leave the poor man to think about it."

Lastly, opposite lived 'The Colonel' and his wife, Diana. They were heavily into wall art and adorned the exterior of their home with large multi-coloured butterflies and other insects. "Why do you call him The Colonel?" Jason asked Pietro at the local pub a couple of weeks after he'd moved in.

"Dunno. Something to do with the way he marches about everywhere, I think. We've already got a nickname for you."

"You have?" Jason was surprised.

"Adonis!" Pietro pulled a face. "I've no idea why!"

Shortly after moving into his new home, Jason began full-time employment on the graduate scheme recommended to him by Simon. The dramatic change in his circumstances in only a few short weeks had left his head spinning, but he was grateful for the distraction from his ever-present demons. His days were filled with meeting his new colleagues and learning the skills of managing client investment accounts.

Chapter Thirteen

At his first team meeting, as requested, Jason stood to introduce himself formally to his colleagues and the Manager. With no preparation, he delivered a short but hilarious account of his life to date, portraying himself as the fun-loving, gregarious, untroubled young man he had once been. His warmth, humour and charm captivated everyone present, male and female alike, and as Simon had anticipated, he rapidly fitted in and became part of the social scene.

As the vibrant hues of autumn began to fade, Jason was feeling distinctly better. Looking back now, he could see how perilously close he had come to a breakdown, but things were looking up. He enjoyed his job and the company of his colleagues. Simon worked on the floor above, and they met at lunchtime at least twice per week.

The Colonel and Diana had invited him over for a meal; he'd been out to the local pub a couple of times with Pietro, and Jan flashed her eyes at him whenever she got the opportunity. But the best times were when he went to his bedroom at the end of each day to be with his mum and dad. He'd started to go through the packing cases in the garage, extracting any remaining photographs he'd missed when preparing for the party, and now they cluttered his bedside tables and drawers. His grandparents had generously bought him a television as a housewarming gift, but it was too large for the bedroom. The small portable he'd purchased was perfect for the haven he'd created with his mum and dad.

"Aren't you lonely, Jason? You must miss Simon?" Nanna Jean asked.

"Like a hole in the head." Jason smiled at his grandparents sitting around the restaurant table. He kept in regular contact by phone, but this was only his second weekend with them in the two months since he'd moved in, and he could see in their faces that they were concerned for him. Actually, to his surprise, he did miss the comforting sound of his friend thundering around above as he stumbled headlong, yet again, over some discarded item, but Simon had his own place now, and Amy had virtually moved in. Things had worked out well for them all. "No, I'm not lonely at all, Nanna. I'm lucky, I have good neighbours." He would never be able to tell them the real reason why he wasn't lonely, that he had the company of his mum and dad. Convinced that no one else would ever understand, he'd decided to keep that a secret.

When not invited out somewhere, Jason began spending the long, dark winter evenings in his bedroom, taking his meal up there and then reading, watching tv or listening to music on his Sony Walkman. "You spend a hell of a lot of time in your bedroom, what do you do up there?" Pietro demanded to know one Saturday morning. "What you need is a woman. Get yourself out with me and the lads tonight."

Jason had already seen Pietro in action in the local pub; no reasonably attractive, unaccompanied woman under 50 was safe. Grappling with his situation, he hadn't had any contact with the opposite sex since the split with Lesley and hadn't even noticed the absence of female company. As he began to feel a little better, he had to admit that the thought had crossed his mind that it would be nice to be with a woman again. But he recalled the conversation with his mum on his 16th birthday, her voice soft and gentle when she'd asked him not to be a heartbreaker. He had no intention of ever getting into a relationship again, so what was to be done?

"Thanks, but I'll pass if you don't mind. I don't want to get hooked up just now," he told Pietro, who could hardly get his breath for laughing.

"Who the hell does?" he gasped, bent double. "Love 'em and leave 'em, my friend. They can't get enough of it. Why do you think I bought this pulling machine?" He lovingly stroked the bonnet of the Spider. "Suit yourself, Adonis, but think about it!"

On a cold mid-November evening, Jason heard a knock at the door; it was John. "Invitation!" He beamed, holding out a small square envelope. "We're having a Christmas Eve party. You really must come; everybody's coming."

"Thanks, but I'm sorry, I can't make it." John did his best to hide the stab of rejection but failed miserably. "I always spend Christmas with my grandparents in Stockport," Jason felt obliged to explain and instantly regretted it. He didn't usually volunteer any information about his family to anyone, and now John would surely ask about his parents.

"You still have your grandparents? How wonderful! We'll do something earlier in December as well then, so that you can come."

"No, please don't go to any trouble," Jason called out hurriedly as John turned to run back to the warmth of his home.

"No bother! I love a party; you can never have too many, can you?" he called back without turning around.

"Are you going to John and Phil's party next week?" Jason asked over a bowl of lasagne a couple of weeks later.

Pietro was an excellent cook. Jason could get by with cooking, but couldn't rustle up anything to compete with the Italian's delicacies, so he supplied the beer.

Pietro choked: "You wouldn't get me in there if you paid me. It's not my scene, fella."

"Why not? John says everyone's going. They're doing the party for me cos I can't do Christmas Eve, so I'd better go."

With a level of trepidation he hadn't experienced for some time, Jason carried his beer and wine over to John and Phil's. He could hear the party was already in full swing, hesitated briefly at the door, then knocked.

"Oh, you came, I'm so pleased. J's here, everyone!" John called out as he took Jason's carrier bag and led the way through the open-plan lounge and dining room, throbbing with disco music and flashing strobe lights. "What can I get you to drink?" In the light of the kitchen, Jason could see that John was wearing something that was a cross between a dress and a toga, black and sequinned, which he'd teamed with fishnet tights. He was wearing black eyeliner and just a trace of lipstick.

"Beer, please." He felt the need to make conversation as John opened a new case of cans but struggled for words.

"You look ..... great."

"Oh, thanks, J!" John gushed with pride. "I just saw this old thing in the wardrobe, and I thought to myself, why not, it's Christmas!"

"Nice to see you, thanks for coming." Jason turned as Phil entered the kitchen, expertly balancing empty wine glasses and paper plates strewn with remnants of finger food. He wore jeans with a grey tee shirt and nodded at the food laid out on the worktop. "Help yourself when you're ready."

Chapter Thirteen

Jason stood by the door with his plate of food, watching the dancers. Most of the people present were neighbours, and there were a few people he didn't know who might or might not be gay friends of John and Phil. There was no way of knowing, and what did it matter anyway?

"I know what you must be thinking," Phil said, returning to the kitchen as Jason watched John dancing with Jan and the girls, spinning around, totally uninhibited and not at all drunk.

"How are we together? It's what everyone wants to know. The truth is, he is the most wonderful person. He has the biggest heart of anyone I've ever met; he loves everyone. Yes, he's over the top, and he knows it, but what you see is what you get. He gets so upset when people judge him or avoid him; you've made his night by coming over. Thanks."

When Jason drifted off with the last of the guests around 2 am, slightly the worse for wear, he meant it when he told John and Phil it was one of the best parties he'd ever been to. "You should come next time," Jason told Pietro when he called round to check that his new friend had survived the evening. "There was no one there for you to pull, though. Jan's girls aren't old enough yet, thank God."

In the office the following week, Dawn glided past Jason's desk carrying a pile of files and wearing a split pencil skirt that fitted like a second skin. "She fancies you," Daniel, his colleague, sighed.

"I don't think so."

"What do you want her to do, carry a placard? Don't be an idiot, ask her out. Christmas do next week, perfect timing." Like every other man in the building, Jason had noticed Dawn. She was attractive and had a figure to die for, but under no circumstances would he allow himself to get involved with anyone, so he kept his head down and ignored her as much as possible. He spent Christmas and New Year in Stockport and returned two weeks later to celebrate his birthday.

"You sure spend a lot of time with your parents," Pietro grumbled.

Jason decided against informing his friend that he was referring to his grandparents when he spoke of the family, not his parents. "It was my birthday last Thursday."

"Well, why didn't you say? You're definitely coming out with us Saturday, no excuses." Faced with his friend's stubborn refusal to take no for an answer, Jason reluctantly agreed to a pub crawl around Sheffield with him and his mates, followed by a visit to a nightclub.

As expected, Pietro pulled, and Jason felt obliged to dance with the girl's friend to keep her company. When they left, Pietro suggested that the four of them share a taxi, but Jason hesitated; he had no intention of going anywhere with this girl. Eager to get home, Pietro had sighed, exasperated. "Well, here, make the most of these." He pressed a packet of three condoms into Jason's palm before flagging down an approaching taxi and leaving Jason standing on the pavement with the friend.

"Come back to mine?" The friend giggled and then reached up and kissed him deeply. The warm, soft touch of her lips was intoxicating. He felt the pressure of her fingers on his back as her embrace tightened. The following morning, he awoke in a strange bed, in a strange room, initially oblivious to where he was, a dull headache pounding somewhere deep in his skull. A note on the bedside table

Chapter Thirteen

read: **Great to meet you, hope to see you again. Lou. Xx,** and there was a phone number.

"So, how was it?" Pietro had been watching out for Jason and dashed around immediately he saw the lights go on. "I've been waiting for you all day. I thought you'd moved in with her!"

"I haven't seen her; she'd gone out by the time I woke up." Jason remembered the hot, urgent kisses on the back seat of the taxi, the girl's hand between his thighs. They'd reached her bedsit and crept upstairs as quietly as they could, closed the door behind them softly and then he had taken her against the door; an explosion of mutual desire they repeated, more leisurely this time, in the warmth and comfort of her bed before falling into an exhausted sleep.

"And?" Pietro persisted. "How many have you got left?"

"One," Jason replied honestly.

Pietro pulled a face. "Can't have been that good then, but it's a start. See if you can do better next week."

"She left me this." Jason passed the note to Pietro. He quickly read it, scrunched it up and stuffed it in his pocket.

"She's just being polite; she won't be expecting to hear from you again. Onwards and upwards!"

The following weekend, Jason visited his grandparents, and the weekend after, he invited Simon and Amy. "To what do we owe the pleasure?" Simon demanded to know over a lunchtime pint. "You've only lived there for about six months, and you've never invited us before. I thought I'd been passed over for Spiderman!"

Jason recounted in as sparse detail as possible the events of his 'night on the town' with Pietro. When he'd finished, Simon exploded with laughter. "So let me get this right.

You've had a one-night stand, and now you're frightened to death of going out in case it happens again, so you're inviting us instead?"

"Something like that," Jason mumbled. "I'm just not sure that's how she saw it, I think she might have hoped for something more, and I feel bad. Anyway, sorry I've not invited you before; you know I don't cook that well."

"You don't need to remind me of that! Remember the time when the neighbour's cat nearly turned itself inside out after trying your spag bol?"

Jason hadn't invited anyone to stay, too fearful of someone stumbling on his secret. He'd managed to get away with the excuse that it was better if he went to Stockport and saw everyone at once rather than any of the family come to stay with him. His grandmothers wanted to fuss over him and do some cleaning, but he'd managed to gently resist. He was taking a gamble inviting Simon and Amy, but they were his friends and needs must if he was going to avoid another onslaught from Pietro.

Simon pondered theatrically for a moment. "Okay, count us in, but we'll get a takeaway. And I'm telling Amy the full story."

"I thought you might."

When they arrived, Jason took Amy's overnight bag from her and carried it upstairs to the spare room. She went straight over to the broad picture window. "Lovely garden, you're so lucky."

"I know. I've got great views across to Rother Valley from my window," he added without thinking.

"Really? Amy turned to face him. Can I see?"

Chapter Fourteen

"Gotcha!" Amy laughed, delighted by the look of horror that suddenly swept across Jason's face. "If your pit is anything like Simon's used to be, there's no way I'm going in there. I've not had enough jabs."

The three friends quickly settled into the banter they'd always enjoyed, and the weekend passed swiftly. "Been good, mate. We should do it again." Simon clapped his friend on the shoulder as he loaded the bags into the car. Watching them drive away, Jason wondered why he hadn't asked them over before. They were so relaxed and easy-going; he should have known it would be okay. In fact, it had been far more than that; it had been fun, something to be repeated and soon.

As the end of February loomed, Dawn began to feel concerned. The graduate scheme necessitated spending time in each team for six months to gain experience in all aspects of the business before specialising. There were six teams, two on each floor of a multi-storey office block leased by the company. She'd overheard that Jason would be moving into one of the teams on the floor above in a few weeks. "I need to do something," she told her friend, Julie. "When he gets up there, they'll all get their claws into him, and that'll be that!"

"Why don't you just ask him out?" Julie suggested. "Ask him to go for lunch or just a coffee. What have you got to lose?"

Time was running out, and urgent action was necessary, so the following day, when she saw Jason heading towards the photocopier, Dawn grabbed a handful of papers from her desk and followed him. As the tired contraption clicked and clanked ominously into life, Dawn smiled at Jason.

"Fancy a coffee at lunchtime?" she asked, just as the machine began copying.

"Pardon?"

Speaking louder this time, Dawn repeated the question just as the machine completed the task. She blushed to the roots of her hair as she heard her voice resound across the office as clearly as if she'd been using a loud hailer. Several colleagues looked across and grinned, nudging each other, but ever gallant, Jason smiled at her.

"Yes, I'd like that, please." He turned and gave his watching colleagues the thumbs up as he returned to his desk.

"I'm so sorry about that," Dawn apologised as they headed to a nearby coffee shop a few hours later.

"No problem, it's nice to be asked. I'm buying." Jason enjoyed the hour with Dawn. She insisted on buying her lunch, a surprisingly large sandwich; he'd assumed she ate virtually nothing. "So, how do you stay so slim?" he asked

Chapter Fourteen

as she finished the last mouthful. "You must have a fast metabolism." Too late, he hoped he wasn't being rude.

"I'm quite a keen cyclist. I time trial, you know, race against the clock."

"Really?" Jason was amazed. Beautifully made up every day and with every hair in place, he hadn't for one moment imagined that she was in any way sporty. "I'm trying to do a bit of cycling myself. It's been hard over the winter, and my bike's only an old secondhand thing, but I can do about 30 miles now. On a good day, that is."

"Well, that's not bad. Perhaps we can go for a ride sometime if you like?"

"Yes, I'd like that." The sentence was out before he could stop it. He was on dangerous ground, and he knew it, but surely a bike ride couldn't do any harm, could it?

Jason arrived home from work that evening just in time to see George, wrapped in a blanket on a stretcher, being wheeled towards a waiting ambulance. Irene followed, ashen-faced, aided by a paramedic. A couple of hours later, lying on his bed watching tv, Jason heard a car. He watched as Irene got out of the taxi and went in, then he walked over and tapped gently on the bay window.

"It's only me, Jason," he called through the letterbox as he heard Irene unlock the door. She allowed him to make her a cup of tea. George had been watching the television that afternoon. She had gone to make a drink, and when she returned, she'd found him slumped, unconscious in his chair. They'd made him comfortable at the hospital, but it had been a shock for her. Three days later, Jason answered a knock at the door and caught Irene as she stumbled towards him. "I've lost him, Jason."

He sat her down on the sofa and made some strong tea. Between her sobs, he let her talk uninterrupted for more than an hour, spilling out her shock and sorrow. Only when she had eventually calmed a little did he speak. "I know how it feels to lose someone you love deeply, Irene."

"You do?" She looked at him in surprise. "But you are so very young."

Now he'd done it. Should he tell her more or not? "Can I let you into a secret, Irene?" She nodded, intrigued. "I don't tell anyone about it; it's not something I like to discuss." He hesitated. "I lost both my parents in a car crash two years ago." *There, he'd managed it. For the first time ever, he had spoken the words.*

"Oh, my dear boy." Irene's eyes filled with tears again as she leaned across to hug him. "They'll be looking out for you, you know. Just because you can't see someone doesn't mean they're not there."

"Please don't tell anyone else."

"I promise, it will be our secret." Jason wondered whether he could tell her more. Tell her that they had been his best friends as well as his parents, tell her that he couldn't live without them, maybe even show her the myriad of pictures that now filled every conceivable space in his bedroom. *No. Maybe one day, but not now.*

Irene's sister arrived the following day and stayed until after the funeral. When she returned home, Jason began calling on Irene regularly and soon she was cooking for him once or sometimes twice a week, delighting in the company of her young neighbour.

"You can't possibly be jealous of Irene?" Jason accused Pietro a few weeks later.

Chapter Fourteen

"Well!" Pietro was indignant. "You spend more time with her than me!"

"Because she's 70-something and very lonely, in case you hadn't noticed. You've never been lonely in your life. And you're not likely to be, are you?" he smirked.

"John's always around there as well. You could take a night off now and then."

"Or you could join me occasionally and get to know Irene? She's lovely." The following week Irene found herself at Pietro's, seated with not one but two handsome young men, sampling a rich dish of pasta with gorgonzola and walnuts washed down with a glass of red wine. She only wished George could have been there to enjoy it with her.

In early April, Jason moved into a team on the third floor, where Simon worked. The company had a private car park, and as the weather warmed, Jason began travelling to work on his motorbike. "It's not big, and it's not clever, you know? You're making yourself very unpopular," Simon told him at the coffee machine. "The girlies hear you arrive on the bike, rush to the window to watch you park up and drag your helmet off like sodding Brad Pitt, and then stampede to the toilets to titivate themselves up. Some of these guys have been trying to get off with them for months, they're not impressed."

Jason laughed, clapped his friend on the shoulder so that he spilled his coffee and left him crouched by the machine, paper towel in hand, drying the floor. Simon watched him walk away. All the women turned to look at him as he passed their desks, and he realised that Jason had no idea of his impact. He could have virtually any woman he wanted in the entire building, and he was utterly oblivious to that.

"Well?" Julie demanded to know over lunch with Dawn. "Have you heard from him?"

"Nothing." Dawn had returned to the office ecstatic after her lunch with Jason. They'd hit it off well. He'd seemed quite keen when she'd suggested a bike ride, but that was over a month ago, and he hadn't been in touch. She hardly saw him now he'd moved teams; she had no reason to go up onto the next floor, and he didn't come down. Like everyone else, she heard him arrive on his motorbike each day, and she'd tried to engineer a meeting on the stairs, but so far without success.

"Be proactive," Julie encouraged her. "Ring him and remind him about the bike ride."

"I can't. I don't want to seem pushy."

"Nothing ventured, nothing gained. You don't want him to be snapped up by one of them upstairs, do you?"

He answered the phone on the third ring just as she was about to put it down. "Hi Dawn, this is a surprise!" She cringed, biting her lip; *she'd been right, he hadn't been hoping every time he received an internal call that it might be her.*

"I just wondered, now it's getting warmer, if you still fancy that bike ride?" she asked, trying hard not to sound too keen and fearing that she did.

The recent events in Irene's life had overtaken everything else, and Jason had forgotten entirely about the bike ride. Caught off guard, he said the first thing that came into his head. "Yeah, that would be great. Saturday any good?" Dawn flushed with excitement as she replaced the receiver, and Julie smiled. On the floor above, Jason panicked. *Was it the right thing to do? Too late now!*

"Shall we meet in the Peak?" Dawn suggested when they met in reception later to plan the ride. "How about Edale? There's a decent car park."

"I don't have a car."

"You don't have a car? I thought everyone had a car." She smiled, but Jason said nothing. *Oh no, this was going all wrong already.* "Well, how about I bring my bike to yours? We can ride from there?"

The last thing Jason wanted was for Dawn to know where he lived. He already had Jan popping across far more than she needed to; she'd made it quite plain that, despite the age gap between them, she would like an affair with him. He didn't want to have to fend off anyone else, however gently. "There's a place a couple of miles away, Ulley Reservoir. There's parking there, and I can just about drag my sorry carcass up the hill."

Dawn knew the area; there were some time trialling courses nearby. The terrain wasn't too hilly, but she had no idea of Jason's fitness, so on Saturday morning, she selected an old touring bike and pulled a pair of battered three-quarter-length cotton trousers over her padded Lycra shorts. Jason's bike was heavy, but he set a remarkably good pace, and she was genuinely impressed.

"I've really enjoyed that; we should do it again sometime." She worried about the comment all the way home, had she sounded casual or desperate?

Over the next few weeks, Dawn was thrilled Jason regularly requested her company to discuss bikes and visit sports shops at lunchtime. With her expert guidance, he'd invested in a new, lighter road bike with more gears in no time.

"Who the hell do you think you are then?" Pietro called out to him as he set off to meet Dawn one bright Saturday morning on his new bike, dressed in his new Lycra shorts and top, helmet, glasses and cycle mitts. "You could have just come to the pub with me to pull instead of going to all that trouble."

Determined to improve his stamina Jason began doing mid-week rides, acknowledging the same Lycra-clad cyclist he saw most evenings, travelling at speed in the opposite direction. "I'm on my way to a time trial, ten-miler. Give it a go, next one's Thursday," the young man shouted over one evening, breathing hard. On Thursday evening, Jason was waiting as the cyclist came into view, grinning when he saw him there. He pedalled hard to catch up as the man shot past him, warming up on his way to the start of the course.

"Not bad, but you'd do better with clipless pedals to hold your feet in place when you're putting big efforts in," Craig told him as they cycled back together at a steadier pace. Dawn had mentioned them to him a few times before, but so far, he'd resisted. The pedals were expensive, and the specialist shoes with the cleats that went with them cost a fortune, but he was already hooked on time trialling. Competitive by nature, he couldn't wait to improve his time the following week. If the pedals would help, he'd get some.

"No! Not again!" Jason yelled on a Saturday ride with Dawn, realising too late that he'd forgotten again to turn his foot to release the cleat from the pedal as he stopped. Over he went, landing on the tarmac with a clatter for the second time that morning.

"Don't worry, you'll soon get the hang of it." Dawn acknowledged the patient motorist carefully navigating the sudden obstacle and then bent to help Jason untangle himself from his bike.

"If I don't kill myself first! I've done a couple of time trials and they told me to get these damned pedals!" he complained. "I wasn't going to tell you until I'd managed to get a decent time."

As usual, Monday lunchtime, Julie wanted a full resume of the progress of Dawn's romance. "He's not interested, Julie! We only ever cycle together, he hasn't invited me to his, even though I think he lives close to where we meet, and he hasn't kissed me. I'm giving up!"

"No, take it to the next level," Julie laughed. "Sprawl on his bed naked. If that doesn't do the trick, nothing will!"

To Jason's surprise, Dawn turned up at the Thursday evening time trial the following week. "Dawn! We don't often see you around these parts. What brings you here?" Craig called out as they arrived at the start, just as she was extricating an expensive-looking bike from the rear of her car.

"You two know each other?" Jason was amazed, but Craig grinned as he planted a kiss on Dawn's cheek.

"Dawn and her family are some of the best time trialists in the area," he replied. "Everyone here knows her." She was the last of the women to set off, slender and sleek in a one-piece Lycra skin suit, bent low over her tri-bars, as aerodynamic as possible. When she had completed the course her skin glistened with sweat, and she'd beaten Jason's time by almost three minutes.

"OK, you've proven your point. I have work to do." Jason feigned a grimace.

"Do you live near here?" Dawn asked as she loaded her precious bike back into the car. "Any chance of a shower, please, before I drive back?"

Alarmed but unable to come up with an excuse fast enough, Jason provided the directions for the few miles back to his home and set off on his bike. He turned into the cul-de-sac just as Dawn stepped out of her car, and Pietro drove by with Irene in the Spider. There was a sight he'd never expected to see, he thought, as Pietro pulled up and began removing Irene's shopping from the car boot. So, the man has a heart after all!

Jason took Dawn inside, showed her the bathroom and went downstairs to make a drink. Sitting on the sofa at the bottom of the open-plan staircase, he heard her leave the bathroom twenty minutes later. But instead of footsteps on the stairs, there was a familiar click as she pressed the handle of the door to the front bedroom and then the squeak of the hinge as the door began to open. "What are you doing?" he shouted, hurtling up the stairs instantly.

Dawn looked flushed, wrapped only in a bath towel, her hand still on the door handle. "I ...., I....., thought.... maybe...."

"I'm afraid not. Will you please leave. Now." He saw the shock flash across her face but was powerless to say or do anything more. She walked past him to the bathroom, and within minutes she had gone.

Pietro arrived moments later. "Who the hell was that?"

"A colleague."

"Wow! Any jobs going? Why'd she leave so soon?"

"Lover's tiff." Jason closed the door leaving Pietro standing on the doorstep, for once utterly speechless.

Chapter Fourteen

"The word on the street is that you threw Dawn out of your house last night," Simon told Jason over their Friday lunchtime pint.

"That's not true."

Simon looked relieved. He'd been alarmed since Julie had come up to use the photocopier earlier whilst the one on her floor was being repaired yet again and hissed at him, "Your friend's not a nice guy!" before informing him of the events of the previous evening.

"I politely asked her to leave. She was trying to get into my bedroom, uninvited."

Simon's lower jaw dropped and hung there, limply, for several moments whilst he looked at Jason in perplexed bewilderment. *Good job he hadn't mentioned she was wearing only a towel at the time. Simon would probably have passed out.*

"You've lost the plot, dear friend. Do you know what the guys in the office would give for that to happen to them?"

Jason was inclined to agree. After Dawn had left, he had gone up to his bedroom and looked at himself in the mirrored door of the wardrobe. He was 23, not too bad looking, relatively fit, and quite a decent guy, he hoped. How had he become trapped in this life of driving everyone away? Studying the numerous photographs surrounding him, he knew the answer. He was damaged; he couldn't live without his parents, he couldn't share his secret with anyone else, and he didn't ever want to be close to anyone but his family ever again. So this was how life had to be.

"You'll be pleased to know it's done nothing to dampen the girls' interest, anyway," Simon continued. "On the way out I overhead them clucking about their plans to succeed where Dawn failed!"

As he took their overnight bag up to the spare room the following weekend, Simon thought about Dawn walking along this very landing, and he glanced at the door to Jason's bedroom. On the top right corner of the door was a small bolt secured with a tiny padlock, painted white, so they were almost invisible. He was sure they hadn't been there before.

Strange, Simon mused, heading back downstairs to where he could hear Jason and Amy laughing in the kitchen. He thought he knew his best friend well, but obviously not. His mind raced; was Jason a closet transvestite? Maybe he had a collection of inflatable dolls? He tried to imagine his friend attired from head to toe in the skin-tight leather garb reputedly favoured by the average sadistic masochist but, to his immense relief, failed. So, what could it be? What was he hiding? Reaching the kitchen, Simon decided to say nothing.

"You're not leaving us, Irene?" Pietro sounded genuinely dismayed, bent over the oven, removing a tray of olive ciabatta he'd baked for a starter despite the soaring temperature of a gloriously hot day in August.

"My sister has been asking me to move closer since I lost George; it would be better for both of us. The board will be going up tomorrow, but I'll probably be here for a while yet."

But less than a week later, the property was sold. "A lovely girl, Lisa, is buying it," Irene told Jason and Pietro. "It was very strange; she came only the day after the board went up and was at the wrong address. She was looking for the house over the way and took a wrong turn, but as it turned out, she liked the layout of mine better. Her parents came over to have a look, and you know the rest."

Kathleen and Joe helped Lisa move in at the beginning of October. By the end of the first week, she wasn't sure if it had been a good move or not. Used to having her retired parents constantly around, she wasn't enthralled with her own company and didn't particularly enjoy her first taste of living alone.

Saturday morning; a whole empty day stretched ahead of her. At least she would be eating out with her parents later. It was as she was heading to the shower that she heard an almighty crash in the living room. Panic-stricken, she crept very slowly down the stairs, shaking. In front of the marble hearth lay the carriage clock her parents had bought for her some years ago and which she had carefully positioned on the mantlepiece. A framed picture of her with her parents was lying face down by the clock, fragments of glass scattered across the carpet where it had struck the edge of the hearth.

Lisa gasped in fear, and her knees buckled. *What could possibly have happened, she was alone in the house.*

Chapter Fifteen

Lisa sat on the stairs, trembling, for what seemed like an age but was really only a few seconds before suddenly something black shot across the living room and into the kitchen. She couldn't see what it was, but there was a large white splodge in the middle of the carpet. Still shaken, she stood and cautiously descended the last three stairs.

Through the open kitchen door, she could see the blackbird pacing agitatedly along the worktop, seemingly every bit as panic-stricken as she was and evacuating its bowels for all it was worth. She stepped forward, and the bird winged her as it hurtled back out of the kitchen and flew straight into the lounge window. Whilst the dazed creature recovered on the windowsill, Lisa grabbed the key for the patio door and then closed the kitchen door behind her. She flung the patio doors wide open, and as she approached the bird again, it flew straight over her head and out without so much as a backward glance.

The doorbell rang whilst she was still trying to clean up. Through the window, Lisa could see the tall, fair-haired young man from the end house, holding something behind his back. *Oh no, that was all she needed!*

"Hi!" He smiled as she opened the door. *Blimey!* He'd seen her a few times on the drive, but he hadn't realised she was so tall. She must be almost six feet, and she looked even taller with her hair dragged up on top of her head in the unbecoming shape of a pineapple.

"Jason." He was surprised and, for some inexplicable reason, pleased she knew his name; she must have taken the trouble to ask someone. "Sorry I can't invite you in, I've just had a blackbird down my flue. The place is a mess." Not entirely sure how best to respond, Jason raised a quizzical eyebrow as she reached for the A4 piece of paper Irene had kindly left for her, on which she had drawn boxes to represent the houses and annotated them with the names of the people who lived there. "But I'll tick you off, thanks for calling round," she continued dismissively.

He noted with satisfaction that there was no tick in Pietro's box. *So, he'd beaten him to her door, remarkable.* "Cupcake?" With a flourish worthy of a magician, Jason offered her the pack of four calorie-laden treats.

Lisa relented, she knew she was giving him the brush off, and he'd only come to welcome her into the neighbourhood. "My name's Lisa, actually. Pleased to meet you, Jason."

Her sudden smile transformed her features, and he grinned back. *She's got a sense of humour; we'll get on well.*

She thought about him as she placed the cakes in the fridge. Close up, he looked younger than she'd expected, and even though he'd smiled a lot, she sensed something sad

CHAPTER FIFTEEN

about him, something lurking in the depths of his eyes. *Nonsense, you've only just met him. How can you possibly know anything about him?* And even if she was right, what did it matter to her? She had no interest whatsoever in learning what it was that troubled him.

Mid-afternoon, Lisa unexpectedly received a phone call from her brother, Neil. She spoke to Maryam far more often than Neil, he was always tied up with some complicated case and working very hard, even at weekends, but he'd wanted to discuss a suggestion. Stephen, his twin, would be attending a conference in London at the end of October and, as usual, would be flying in the weekend before to spend time with the family. If possible, they'd like to come up and spend the weekend with her, just the three of them together for the first time in 20 years. "I'd love that, Neil. What a great idea, I can't wait!" Over the meal that evening, however, she was anxious to ensure her mother wouldn't feel left out, knowing how much she missed Stephen.

"Maryam's called, sweetheart. You know what she's like, all excited about your plans. She's invited us to spend the weekend with her and the twins. We can catch up with Stephen for a few evenings when the boys get back to London."

Neil met Stephen from the direct flight from San Francisco to Heathrow. "Good to see you, bro. How was it?" He smiled, knowing his brother's employers flew him everywhere business class.

"Oh, you've got the car," Stephen exclaimed, pursuing Neil toward the pay station. "I thought we'd be on the train." He knew how much his twin hated driving in the heavy traffic that prevailed throughout London.

"I've got my car," Neil replied.

"Your car? I thought you'd decided years ago you don't need one?"

"I've changed my mind." Neil smiled. He led the way to the car park and stopped by the side of a highly polished Ferrari F355. "Well, what do you think of her?"

Stephen burst out laughing. "This can't possibly be yours?"

"Get in!" As Neil eased into the early evening traffic on the M25, to his amusement, Stephen was still quite clearly absolutely flabbergasted.

"I just don't get it," he repeated again and again. "All these years you've said that you don't need a car of your own and you've put up with that, that......." For a moment, words failed him. "........heap of a people carrier, and the next minute you're driving a Ferrari!"

"It's all your fault! You keep telling me I've become a middle-aged family man, dull as ditch water, and I seem to recall the last time we met you insinuated I have a paunch!" Neil frowned.

Stephen had never married; he worked hard and played hard in equal measure. Tanned and fit, he was a very youthful 38. Chuckling, he reached over and poked his fingers into his brother's ever-so-slightly flabby flesh. "Too many business lunches, I suspect."

"Well, I decided you have a point. I've worked hard forever, it's time I had some fun!"

"What about the kids' education?"

"What about it? They'll have to make it on their own like we did."

Chapter Fifteen

Stephen couldn't believe what he was hearing. His brother was a family man through and through; he always put them first. His questions kept coming all the way up the M1 to Sheffield. "Why didn't you tell me about the car? When did you get it?"

"Last night. We're pleased it was ready in time for your visit, we thought it would be a good surprise."

"What does Maryam think of it?" Neil rolled his eyes dramatically in reply.

Stephen could imagine his sister-in-law's reaction. A diminutive font of perpetual excitement, she must be beside herself. "Has she driven it?"

"Not yet, I think she's a bit frightened of it."

"Likely!" Stephen scoffed. "What engine is it?"

"3.5 litres."

"How fast can it make 60?"

"Under five seconds."

"How many to the gallon?"

"A handful."

"What's it like for insurance?"

"Diabolical."

They arrived at Lisa's just after 8 pm. She heard the low rumble of the powerful engine as the car turned into the drive and looked through the curtains. *Was that really a Ferrari?* As she opened the door to greet them, her brothers wrapped her in a warm embrace, as delighted as she was to be together again, just the three of them.

"So, do you own that monster out there?" Lisa asked Neil, amusement dancing across her face as she took their overnight bags from them. It was unlikely but not impossible.

"No, of course I don't!"

"What?" Stephen spun around to face his grinning brother, incredulous. "You told me you do!"

"I never did! I merely invited you to get in."

"But I've been asking questions all the way here!"

"Indeed, and I answered all of them truthfully. Economically I admit, but I'm a barrister, after all. It is mine for the duration of the hire, only four days, sadly. You didn't ask the right question, and this clever girl did." Lisa blushed at Neil's compliment. "It's cost me an arm and a leg, but it was worth every penny to see the look on your face in the car park."

Neil sidestepped as Stephen swung a playful punch at him. Both men still thoroughly enjoyed the amiable competitive rivalry they had always shared, and this was undoubtedly a high-octane prank. They toasted each other with the champagne Lisa had bought. "To us!" She raised her glass. "The three musketeers!" Neil and Stephen glanced at each other in surprise. Lisa could only have been six years old when they had last been able to spend the summer with her, taking her out to the woods to climb and swing. They had called themselves the three musketeers, and what a summer they'd had. They hadn't known that she remembered it.

The next day, Pietro was desperate to take a closer look at the Ferrari. Stunned, he'd thought he must still be feeling the effects of the previous evening's alcohol when he'd ambled around the corner from the bus stop and saw it parked there. After taking a long look from his bedroom window to make sure he wasn't hallucinating, he raced around to Jason's and barged in without even knocking. "Jason, where are you? Quick, give me the gen."

Chapter Fifteen

Jason grinned; he'd anticipated Pietro's visit. "You're so nosey! I was in my bedroom last night," he began, slowly.

"No surprises there, then!"

"I heard the car turn in. The sound of the engine was incredible, and I looked out to see what it was."

"Yes, yes. And?"

"Well, it stopped. Where it is now, on Lisa's drive." Jason paused for effect, gaining maximum pleasure from his friend's frustration as he waited agitatedly for further details. "Two men got out with overnight bags. One seemed to be wearing a suit, but the other was more casual in jeans and a leather jacket."

"Jeez, what's the story there, then, with our not-so-little Lisa?" Jason laughed out loud when Pietro, still gazing at the Ferrari, stumbled and almost fell when he veered from the pavement onto his neighbour's front lawn as he returned home.

The three siblings didn't leave the house for the entire weekend, utterly engrossed in each other's company, making the most of the opportunity to reconnect. Lisa basked in her brothers' attention and their interest in everything she was doing. She had always been in awe of them, both successful in their chosen professions. Now they wanted to know in detail about her new role at work, her ambitions and prospects for promotion, her training for the Samaritans and her punishing regime at the gym. For the first time, she was talking to them on a level; the age gap between them had disappeared.

"Are you sure you don't want a quick ride in the car before we go?" Neil asked, reluctantly gathering his things together.

"Go on. I'm a big boy; I can survive here on my own for a while," Stephen urged her.

"Okay then, but just around the block." As the engine roared into life, Pietro ran to the window to watch the car depart. Embarrassed, he acknowledged Lisa's wave but paid particular attention to the older man beside her. *Who the hell was he? And where the hell was the other guy?*

He rushed around to bring Jason up to speed with developments the minute he returned from his bike ride. "They were back ten minutes later," he finished, frowning and perplexed.

"Great!" Jason replied wearily, not remotely interested and starting to shiver, barely listening to Pietro's animated account. "I'm going in to get a shower, I'm shattered."

"Just a minute, they're going." Pietro grabbed Jason's arm, and in the falling twilight, they surreptitiously watched as the two men placed their bags in the boot of the car. Lisa hugged and kissed each of them before they got in, and the low growl sounded again as the engine started. "Quick, in! I don't want to be caught watching again." Pietro shoved Jason in the direction of his front door and rapidly followed, slamming it shut behind him.

"We seem to have got your neighbours talking anyway!" Stephen called to Lisa through the open window, laughing as she waved them off.

"Must you go so soon, the night is still young?" John wailed a few weeks later as Lisa stood to leave. She smiled, still unable to believe how much her life had changed in the few short months since she'd met John and Phil. "Irene said you're moving in alone? Unbelievable, you're so gorgeous!" John had gushed only a couple of days after she'd arrived.

"Please come over for tea, can you do next week?" She'd never met anyone quite like him, so open and guileless. Despite her shyness and reserve, she'd felt unable to refuse the invitation, and they'd eaten together every week from then on, alternating between their respective homes. They'd both been so kind to her, such good fun, and she felt at ease with them; after all, they would never be interested in her.

"Night, gorgeous, see you next week. Love you!" Knowing that John would watch till she reached her home, she turned to wave as Jason and Pietro came into view on the way back from the pub. For the sake of politeness, she enquired about their evening before turning back to John.

"Shall I invite them to join us next week?"

"That would be lovely. The more, the merrier!" Confused as she hurried home in the cold night air, Lisa wondered what had just happened. Inviting Pietro and Jason to join them was a spur-of-the-moment thing, very out of character for her and probably the most spontaneous thing she'd ever done in her life.

Pietro turned to watch Lisa as she trotted home in the instantly recognisable gait of a woman attempting to run in heels and a pencil skirt. "Are you thinking what I'm thinking?"

"Unlikely!" Jason frowned. "It'll be a first if I am."

"The detached property, the sexy black Golf GTi, the guys in the Ferrari staying for the weekend, now the expensive suit; Lisa's loaded. Do you think she might be one of those high-class hookers?"

"Pietro, for God's sake! Do you ever think about anything other than sex? No, I thought not. Maybe she's a businesswoman?"

Much to his amazement, Pietro enjoyed the meal at Lisa's the following week, despite a moment of pure panic when John and Phil arrived. "Oh, Pietro, we never get a chance to talk. Can I sit next to you?" John had asked, his hands clasped together in a beseeching pose. Alarm written across his suave features, Pietro had nodded - what else could he do? - but John had turned out to be surprisingly good company; funny, self-effacing and knowledgeable about anything and everything that cropped up. When Pietro tried to steer the conversation towards Lisa's unknown visitors and the Ferrari, to Jason's amusement, John leapt in with a detailed account of the spec of the vehicle compared with other high-performance cars.

"I didn't find out anything about her at all," Pietro moaned to Jason as they headed home.

"Well, it wasn't an entirely wasted evening. Everyone's looking forward to your cooking next week, and you accepted the invitation to John and Phil's Christmas bash for the first time, so you've made some progress. And I did discover something."

"You did?" Pietro was suddenly animated, anticipating some juicy snippet of information.

"Lisa works in insurance."

"Is that it? Insurance? What does she do?"

"I don't know, she didn't tell me." Usually able to engage in easy conversation with anyone, Jason had struggled with Lisa. Good conversationalists always take an interest in others, he'd once read somewhere, but she seemed very reluctant to disclose anything about herself. Her obvious discomfort made him feel he was prying, so instead, he'd regaled her with anecdotes about his life at university.

They'd all enjoyed his tales of sharing a house with Simon. "You must meet him," Jason told them. "Life will never be the same again."

A month later, Lisa sat back and gazed around her lounge in wonder. It was almost two years to the day since she'd dragged open the door to the little back street hotel and saw Mark and Jenni, her partner and her best friend, standing there.

They had been her only real friends; her world had collapsed, but now, here she was in a room full of friends. Jason was perched on a chair in the corner by the Christmas tree, strumming a guitar as Pietro, John and Phil, sitting on the floor, beer in hand, sang along at the tops of their voices. Simon and Amy held hands on the sofa. It was the first time she'd met them, but they'd all heard a lot about them from Jason, and it was as though she'd known them for years; they'd hit it off immediately.

Jason grinned when they all applauded as he placed the guitar down. It had remained on the stand in his bedroom, untouched, for almost a year until one day, a song his dad and Uncle Michael had sung together came on the radio.

He'd picked up the guitar; it felt familiar in his hands even after so long, and he'd strummed a few chords. Tears fell as he remembered the pleasure the precious instrument had given his dad, but then he tuned it and tried out a few more chords. As he did so, he felt strangely comforted; it was a link, a bond with both parents.

He'd started playing regularly, practising the old songs. When he'd mastered the music, he began singing along, and from the depths of his memory came the sound of his dad's voice singing the harmonies. But this was the first time he'd played for an audience since the accident; he had never expected to do that again.

Only Simon knew the significance of the guitar. Listening to the songs, he'd been lost in memories of other evenings spent like this when Jason had invited him home for the weekend. He thought of Jason's parents; young, vibrant, so full of life. As time passed, it seemed that those happy evenings filled with music and laughter had gone forever, but not so; they would go on with Jason. His friend had some dark secrets, but after all he'd been through, it was hardly surprising, and he was pleased to see him getting his life back together. He said nothing, just winked at Jason knowingly as he went to get another beer.

Chapter Sixteen

"That's it, the last wedge!" John was ecstatic. "I've only got to get to the middle now, I might win for once!" The friends were playing what had become, during the winter months, a regular mid-week game of Trivial Pursuit. It had become so competitive that even Pietro had taken to glancing through an encyclopaedia over the weekend. They'd all half-expected that, as the days began to lengthen in March, their weekly get-togethers would cease, but by then, they all got on so well that there was no possibility of that.

"I can't make it next week," Lisa announced after joining everyone in a toast to John's first, but decisive, win. Dipping out was unheard of; they gazed at her, stunned.

"Why the hell not?" Pietro demanded to know, never one to mince his words. "May I remind you it's your turn to host?"

That's torn it! Jason glanced nervously at Lisa, still visibly uncomfortable when asked anything about herself. She never gave much away; maybe this was a question too far.

"My niece and nephew, Georgina and Byron, are coming to stay. They're only seven, a bit young to join in." She smiled, relishing the prospect of their company. For the first time ever, they would be holidaying without their parents, four days with Lisa and then four days with their grandparents.

"Twins! How wonderful! Can we meet them? Please?" Not surprisingly, John adored children.

"Steady on," Phil urged, "we don't want to frighten them."

Lisa laughed. "I'm sure they'd love that. A takeaway at mine and a game of Frustration? It's their favourite, I just didn't think you'd want to spend the evening with two seven-year-olds."

"I'll cook pizzas and an ice cream bomb," Pietro offered, feeling guilty. "Twins, that's nice," he continued, still trying to make amends for his outburst.

"Yes, they seem to run in our family. My brothers are twins." Jason and Pietro glanced at each other, realisation slowly dawning. "The Ferrari," Pietro hesitated, not wanting to put his foot in it again. "Those men were your brothers?" Lisa laughed again as the memory of Stephen's look of utter incredulity suddenly came into sharp focus.

"Yes, that was them. Neil, the twins' dad, hired it for a prank." A look of relief swept across Pietro's face. "Why? Who did you think they were?"

"You don't want to know," Jason quickly replied for him, fearful that Pietro might blurt out his initial conclusions.

Chapter Sixteen

It was almost lunchtime on Saturday when Jason saw the trio walking past. "Halt! Who goes there, and where are you taking my friend?" Georgina and Byron turned to stare, open-mouthed, at the tall, fair-haired young man running along the drive towards them. Standing one on either side of Lisa, their arms linked through hers, they edged just a little closer to her as he approached, grinning.

"This is our auntie," Byron ventured in a small voice.

"I'm Georgina, and he's Byron. We're going for a walk with Auntie Lisa," Georgina added.

"Nice! I'm Jason. So, what else will you be doing with her while you're here? Swimming?" They looked up at Lisa.

"Can we, please?"

"Bowling?" Jason continued, now on an enthusiastic roll.

"Please, Auntie Lisa." The twins were hopping from foot to foot.

"Cycling?"

"No, Auntie Lisa can't ride a bike." Byron looked disappointed.

"Oh!" Lisa's sudden frown told him he had overstepped the mark. Keen to make amends, his mouth racing ahead of his brain, he heard himself say: "Well, I can take you if you like."

"Wow! Will you?" Georgina grabbed her brother, her eyes shining. "Can we go? Please, Auntie Lisa, please!"

"What were you thinking of?" Lisa growled at him later that afternoon as John crouched on the opposite pavement, deep in conversation with Georgina and Byron, even though he'd met them only minutes before. "All they've talked about is the bike ride, how are you going to pull that one off?" That very conundrum was all that Jason had thought about since the conversation earlier.

"Sorted it. I can meet you at Clumber Park tomorrow afternoon. They can hire bikes and helmets for an hour, and we can do circuits around the lake, so we keep passing you. Any good?"

Surprised, Lisa hesitated for a moment. Maybe she had underestimated him? Then she nodded and smiled.

"Ingenious!"

"I'm turning back early today," Jason told Craig on the Sunday club ride. When the time-trialling season ended, Craig had suggested joining a club to keep their fitness level up through the winter. They rode together every Sunday, weather permitting.

"Date?" Craig grinned.

"Yeah, with seven-year-old twins at Clumber."

They were waiting in the car park when he got there. Both children stepped back, not recognising him as he rode up to them in his black Lycra leggings, a dazzling fluorescent yellow and blue top, blue helmet and dark glasses.

"You look like a racer!" Byron was immediately impressed.

Soon kitted out with bikes and helmets, Lisa watched as Georgina and then Byron set off behind Jason, a look of pure joy to be riding with a 'racer' mixed with grim determination to keep up etched across their young faces.

They lapped her three times as she walked along the lakeside, their faces flushed with both exhilaration and exertion, depositing another layer of clothing with her each time they passed. At the end of the ride, the twins spontaneously hugged Jason between them.

Chapter Sixteen

They insisted on playing as a team with Jason when everyone went ten-pin bowling, and Pietro was suitably gratified when, on their last evening at Lisa's, the twins declared his pizzas were the best they'd ever had. Even better than their favourites at Pizza Hut!

"I have a bit of a strange request," Lisa told her friends the next time they all got together.

"You want to play Strip Twister?" Pietro guessed. Incorrectly, he assumed, judging by Lisa's look of total disdain.

"My parents have asked if they can meet you. Georgina and Byron did nothing but talk about you all whilst they were staying with them; they'd like to meet you sometime."

"Oh, how wonderful that the children talked about us." John's pleasure was almost palpable. "We can't wait to meet them, can we, Phil?"

"Make sure you wear something sensible." Pietro barked at him with a twinkle in his eye. "And ditch the makeup and nail varnish." As John forced out his bottom lip, not in the least bit offended, everyone laughed with him, and Jason was reminded again of how far the friendship between them all had come since Lisa's arrival.

"You interrogate the father, and I'll do her mum," Pietro instructed Jason on the way to Lisa's to meet her parents. "This is our best chance of finding out more about her."

"Why do I get the father?" *Surely Pietro couldn't have designs on the older woman, could he? He wouldn't put it past him!*

"Don't you remember them helping her to move in? He's massive! I'll get a crick in my neck if I spend the evening with him, her mum's more my size."

As it turned out, no interrogation was necessary. Kathleen and Joe were far more forthcoming than Lisa, and when someone commented on Joe's Geordie accent, he volunteered the story of his early career and how he'd met Kathleen, making her blush.

"How wonderful that Lisa should meet such lovely people through the necessity to move for her work," Kathleen remarked. And when it became apparent they knew little of Lisa's employment, she was only too happy to proudly fill them in with details of her daughter's academic and career achievements as Lisa cringed with embarrassment.

"It's been a lovely evening, we have a lot to thank all of you for," Joe said as they were leaving." Georgina and Byron can't wait to come again and want to stay longer next time."

But as he kissed his daughter goodnight at the door, he whispered: "Watch the blonde. With those looks, I bet anything he's a butcher's dog, not to be trusted." Surprised her father even knew the term, Lisa nodded in agreement.

"I've had an idea," Jason told Lisa when she returned to the lounge. "Why don't you learn to ride a bike as a surprise for the twins when they come up next time? I've got a spare one, I could teach you."

John was beside himself as they walked back to their own homes. "I'm so pleased for you and Lisa, J. You'll be great together!"

"No, no, you've got it all wrong!" Jason was aghast. *Might she think he was trying to get off with her?* He turned to go back.

"Where're you going?" Pietro caught his arm. "Don't spoil it now, imbecile! She might actually go for it." He'd been

Chapter Sixteen

pleasantly surprised when Jason had asked her about the cycling; he'd started to think he hadn't got it in him.

Jason hurried back and tapped lightly on Lisa's door. "Forgotten something?" she smiled, handing him his door key.

"Oh, thanks. No, I hadn't realised. I just came back to make sure that you didn't think I was, well, you know, trying to get off with you. They all seemed to think that I was." *What was it Pietro had called him? An imbecile. He certainly sounded like one, even to himself.*

"No, I didn't think that. And to clarify, you have absolutely no chance of ever getting off with me." Her eyes twinkled with amusement at the mere thought of it, and relief flooded through Jason.

"Thank God for that. Sleep tight." As he walked away, he heard her call after him.

"But I'm up for a go on the bike."

Standing outside the bike hire at Clumber Park on a dull Saturday morning, she wondered if it had been a good decision. The mechanic had taken one glance at the length of her legs, promptly produced an Allen key, and was now busily raising the saddle on a bike.

"You've never ridden a bike before? Not even once?" Jason asked, amazed. Lisa explained that living on a busy main road, her parents had always thought it was too dangerous. They wheeled their bikes to a quiet, level track where she hoped and prayed they were out of sight.

"Get your hands off!" She almost screamed at him when he took hold of the handlebars with one hand and the back of the seat with the other.

"I need to hold you up!"

"But you're touching my bum!" She was momentarily incensed.

"Not deliberately, I can assure you!" He pulled a face and then placed his arm around her waist, his shoulder against her arm to support her.

"No, no, you're too close. Hold the seat, but don't touch my bum again or else!" It was a tall order in the circumstances, but he somehow coped, and after half an hour of going first one way and then back again with Jason holding her up, Lisa was beginning to manage a few pedal strokes unaided.

When they returned the bike at the end of the two-hour hire period, she was thrilled that she could stay upright for a short distance on her own, but she was exhausted from the effort. Every muscle was tense, and her hands ached; she'd been gripping the handlebars as tightly as if she were on a white-knuckle ride. "Can we come again next week?" she asked Jason on the way home.

"Only if you promise not to hit me again."

The following week, after a bit of practice, Jason ran alongside Lisa as she teetered along, weaving slightly, ready to catch her if necessary, but as her confidence grew, he couldn't keep up.

"You're riding solo, well done!" he called out, causing her to panic and stop. As she placed her foot down, she overbalanced and fell, still astride her bike. "Oh no, are you okay?" He took her hand and helped her up.

She was laughing despite a small cut on her elbow and another on her shin. "I think I'll live."

Dressed to kill as usual on Monday morning, her colleagues noticed the sticking plaster when she removed her

Chapter Sixteen

jacket and smiled indulgently when she described the accident.

"Been out on your bike again, Lisa?" someone called out the following Monday morning, observing more sticking plaster. She groaned at the sudden recollections of Saturday morning. She'd been doing well on her first attempt at a lap of the lake with Jason. Unbelievably she'd overtaken someone, a small child on a bike with stabilisers. Moments later, she had ridden over a small branch, inexplicably causing her head to bounce around like it was supported by jelly and down she went again.

The toddler had caught up and stopped, his small face full of concern as he jumped off his bike and crouched to examine her leg more closely. "Oh dear, bleeding." The irony of the situation wasn't lost on her. She spent hours and hours each week poring over detailed medical reports on the most complex and sometimes horrific injuries, and here was a child of about three, studiously assessing hers.

"You've got staying power, I'll say that for you!" her Manager commented several weeks later when she arrived on a warm sunny day dressed in trousers with a long-sleeved blouse to hide her latest wounds. She'd progressed to riding Jason's old bike short distances on the road but discovered tarmac is far less forgiving than the soft earth of the tracks at Clumber when she inadvertently clipped the edge of the kerb. Jason heard the clatter behind him and instantly recalled his first ride with the clipless pedals, the sickening sensation of falling and being powerless to do anything about it.

"Lisa! Are you okay?"

"I'm fine." Blood trickled down through the road dust sticking to her legs as she climbed back on her bike.

"I'm not sure this was such a good idea. Let's head back and get you patched up." Jason began to turn in the road, but Lisa refused, her acute fear of failure instantly kicking in.

"No, no, let's carry on. I want to be able to do this." A week before the twins were due to arrive, Lisa followed Jason the short distance along the road from her home to Rother Valley Park, did several laps of the lake and rode back, a distance of about twelve miles and, most importantly, without falling off. She was ready!

As before, Kathleen and Joe dropped the twins off early on Saturday morning. They were desperate to go cycling with Jason, and he'd happily obliged that afternoon. Their faces had been a picture when Lisa hired a bike as well, even more so when, after she'd pretended to struggle, she caught them up and passed them, laughing as they pursued her.

Jason took a few days off work, and they'd all gone cycling several times during the twins' week-long stay with Lisa. When it was time to leave, they hugged Jason between them. "I can't believe it," Byron shook his head, still amazed. "We've had the best time ever. Thank you for showing Auntie Lisa how to ride, you're the best!"

Jason enjoyed teaching Lisa; she was good fun and surprisingly resilient. He would miss her on Saturday mornings now their mission had been accomplished. But to his surprise, Lisa appeared on his doorstep the first Saturday morning after the twins left, dressed for cycling.

"Oh, I'm sorry, my mistake. I hadn't realised...." She'd so enjoyed the cycling lessons with Jason that it hadn't occurred

Chapter Sixteen

to her that once she could ride, they would end. Now she'd made a fool of herself; he was clearly surprised to see her.

"You want to go out? Really? I thought you were putting yourself through it for the kids. Give me five and I'll be with you." Three hours later, they were back and sitting on his front doorstep, enjoying a cool drink.

"Will you help me to buy a decent bike?" Lisa asked, wishing she could bite her tongue in half when she realised what she'd implied. "Not that there's anything wrong with yours!" she added hastily.

Laughing at Jason's attempt to look offended, she impulsively linked her arm through his. "I'm sorry." It was his turn to burst out laughing when she realised what she'd done and retracted her arm with such speed that she nearly fell backwards through the open door.

Simon and Amy arrived early in the evening for one of their regular weekend visits, and everyone piled into Jason's. "You get on well with Amy," Lisa commented as she was leaving around midnight.

She'd seen Jason in the kitchen with his arm around Amy. They were laughing about something, and then he'd leaned towards her and kissed her on the cheek. At the time, Simon was in deep conversation with Pietro, and Lisa had suddenly felt sick. *Was she watching a rerun of her own life? Would Jason one day let his best friend down?*

"I adore the girl," Jason replied. "I'll never know how she puts up with Si. But I love him too, I suppose," he grudgingly conceded. "They seem very happy together, I'm pleased for them."

His blue eyes were so crystal clear as he spoke, without the merest trace of guilt; Lisa had no choice but to believe him.

By the end of September, Jason and Lisa spent much of almost each Saturday cycling together. Feeling that he now knew her well enough, he tentatively probed further about her private life on one of their lengthy rides. "Any more holidays planned? I thought you'd be heading abroad."

"I take my holidays with family. I'm the twins' only auntie in this country, so I spend my time with them, and we're stuck with school holidays. We usually get away at half-term for a blast of sunshine, but Neil's got a big case this year, so it's not looking good." Jason thought about his family holidays as a child. He'd like to tell her about them, but he couldn't; one question would lead to another. *Best left well alone.*

"So, how come there's no other half then?" The words were still spilling from his mouth when he realised that he'd gone too far. Again. As he turned to Lisa, she looked down at the road and didn't reply. "Bad relationship?" he felt obliged to fill the uncomfortable silence.

She barely nodded, and he quickly changed the subject, but Lisa remained quiet for the rest of the ride. Over a meal with her parents later that evening, she mentioned the conversation with Jason.

"I think I was quite rude to him, and I feel bad about it, he's been so kind. So, I've phoned Maryam and asked if I can invite him down with us at half term, just for the weekend."

"You want to invite Blondie for the weekend? Lisa?" Joe couldn't believe what he'd just heard.

Chapter Sixteen

"He's just a friend, Dad," she protested. "I just thought it might be a nice idea, and you know Maryam's itching to meet the racer Georgina and Byron can't stop talking about." On their bike ride the following weekend, she issued the invite.

"You jammy devil!" Pietro declared when Jason broke the news. "Jeez! How the hell did you wangle that?" The smaller man turned and peered up into his friend's face. "Are you screwing her?"

"For God's sake, Pietro! No, I'm not. How could you even think that?"

"Sorry, maybe I was hoping. Is this the last trip out for you, then? Before you join the monastery? You might as well."

Jason hadn't wanted to refuse the invitation; he felt honoured in light of Lisa's insurmountable reserve. But he was concerned. She'd filled him in with some brief details about her brother and sister-in-law, a top-notch barrister and a partner in a London law firm no less; *how could he possibly fit in?*

He needn't have worried; he couldn't have been made more welcome. The twins were thrilled to have him in their home and Maryam and Kathleen fussed around him like he was one of the family. Neil and Joe asked about his work and were friendly enough, but he had the distinct impression they were weighing him up.

When they were briefly alone, Neil warned him, "Look after my sister. She's been hurt badly before."

Jason swallowed hard, fighting back the instant surge of alarm. "I'm not her boyfriend, we're just neighbours." Neil didn't look convinced.

At the next get-together, John wanted full details of the weekend. "Were the children pleased to see you, J?" Enthralled by the tales of the happy family gathering, he demanded to know every minute detail from Lisa and Jason.

"Where did you sleep?" Pietro interjected, staring pointedly at Jason.

"He slept on a camp bed in Byron's room," Lisa answered for him. "Why? What are you trying to insinuate?"

"I just thought there might be something going on?"

Lisa almost exploded with laughter. "In your dreams."

"Anyway," Pietro turned again to Jason. "Changing the subject, when do we all get to meet your parents?"

Chapter Seventeen

X

Jason hesitated as they all looked at him expectantly, waiting for his answer to Pietro's question. *Should he lie, evade the question, or simply tell the truth? These were his friends, after all.* He decided to go for the latter option. "I don't have any." Pietro grinned, ready to make a suitably unsubtle remark, but Lisa's sudden elbow in the ribs silenced him.

Looking like he might burst into tears, John stood and placed a hand on Jason's shoulder. "Really? How dreadful."

"It's okay." Jason lied. "I don't talk about it much. Or at all, really." The conversation moved on, but it was stilted, and the evening had ended earlier than usual.

"It was a conversation stopper, up there with the best of them. "Jason told Simon over their Friday lunchtime pint.

"Well, someone was bound to say something sooner or later. It sounds like you dealt with it pretty well to me. Anyway, if you're in the mood for disclosing personal details, can I ask you something?"

Simon had waited more than a year to raise his question. He still wasn't sure the time was right, but it seemed as good as any other. "What's with the padlock on your bedroom door?"

Jason smiled, touched by Simon's concerned expression. "You know why it's there, to keep out unwanted visitors." He'd anticipated the question a long time before and had worked out his answer, which was perfectly true.

But Simon knew there was more to it, and when Jason saw the flash of disappointment in his eyes, he felt a stab of guilt and sadness that he couldn't tell him more. The situation wasn't improving; if anything, it was getting worse. Time is a great healer, that's what everyone had told him after the accident, but as time passed, he didn't feel any better, only increasingly desperate to hold on to the parents he cherished.

Besides visiting his grandparents, he hardly ever spent a night away from home. His bedroom, crammed with photos, mementoes and memories, was the last remnant of a life he couldn't let go.

A few weeks later, Lisa was lying in bed, wide awake in the middle of the night, slightly breathless, and the tiny beads of perspiration on her skin made it feel prickly. The dream that had awoken her was familiar; she'd had it about three or four times now. It had all started after she had returned from the week at Neil's.

The dream always began the same way; she was lying in bed, curled around the body of a man facing away from her, sleeping. As the musky smell of his skin overwhelmed her, she gently dotted kisses on his back and ran her fingertips slowly along the length of his arm and then his thigh. The man stirred and turned towards her.

She rolled onto her back and took hold of his shoulders, pulling him towards her. As he entered her, she gasped and gazed up into intense blue eyes, full of desire like hers but still with that ever-present hint of sadness - Jason's eyes.

What is happening to me? she wondered yet again, with the now familiar sense of unease. She certainly didn't fancy Jason, or anyone else for that matter. As her father had succinctly pointed out, even if she was ever to decide to chance another relationship, Jason was far too good-looking for his own good and to be avoided at all costs. He was just a very good friend, so why had she started having this ridiculous dream? She tried to sleep, but the images of the dream persisted.

The situation worsened later that evening at John and Phil's when Jason brushed her arm as he reached for his beer, and her body suddenly tingled from head to foot, like she'd been plugged in at the mains.

At the weekly get-togethers, she tried to sit as far from him as possible, but it wasn't easy. Safe in the knowledge that she had no interest in him whatsoever, Jason had started playfully flirting with her, thoroughly enjoying her vicious retorts to his advances which had them all in fits of laughter. But he always had to have the last word. "Well, when you change your mind, you know where I am."

"So tonight, I'm gonna party like it's 1999!" John sang tunelessly, completely drowning out the voice of his hero. "It is 1999! I can feel a spectacular New Year's Eve party coming on!" It was early December; he had almost a month to prepare, and his friends looked nervously from one to another. Phil hung his head in his hands and pretended to weep.

As virtually everyone in the neighbourhood had something planned for New Year's Eve, the party was held on the first Saturday in January.

"Let's start the millennium with a bang!" insisted John, and they did precisely that, with fireworks throughout the evening and late into the night. A minor stampede ensued when one went off almost horizontally, forcing a path through the hedge towards the house, fizzing and flashing before finally emitting an ear-splitting bang as it dropped, spent, onto the patio.

As the worse-for-wear partygoers made for the shelter of the kitchen, Jason caught hold of Lisa's arm to steady her. There it was again, that instant surge of attraction, like an electric shock, not diminished in the slightest by the unusually copious amounts of wine she'd consumed.

By 3 am, the last of the revellers had left. The kitchen looked like a small bomb had exploded, but no one was capable of clearing it up; Lisa and Jason assured John and Phil they would return later to help. They offered to drag Pietro, comatose on the sofa and snoring loudly, back to his own home, but John covered him with a quilt, carefully tucking it around him.

"I'll walk you home," Jason laughed as Lisa wobbled along the pavement.

"I'm okay." She watched him walk away, turning to wave just before he reached his home. *What was she doing? It was three years since the split with Mark; she was now 27. There wouldn't always be a good-looking man inviting her around. A new millennium, maybe it was time to move on?*

Chapter Seventeen

It's the drink talking, a voice in her head cautioned her. Don't be an idiot, be content with his friendship. But she knew it wasn't just the drink. After what she'd gone through with Mark, she had never expected to feel desire again. And she hadn't, until these last few months, but now she couldn't get him out of her head.

She hoped no one was watching as she stumbled along in the darkness. The light was still on in Jason's bedroom. She tapped lightly on the door, but there was no response. Bending to pick up a small stone, she fell forward onto her hands and knees and struggled to get back up again.

Hideous! The voice in her head was screaming at her now, go home with your pride intact while you still can! Staggering slightly along the drive, she turned and aimed, not expecting to hit the target, but she heard a tap, and then Jason appeared at the window.

Seconds later, he opened the door and ushered her in. "God, are you okay? What happened?" There was mud on the knees of her jeans and a muddy streak across her face where she'd pushed her hair back.

"Fine. I'm absolutely fine," replied Lisa, oblivious to her appearance. "I, ... I've....... decided to come."

"Oh, good." Jason was still confused. He'd only left her minutes before, what had happened?

"You keep saying I know where you are," she continued. "So, I've come." Through the fuzzy alcoholic haze that surrounded him, understanding was beginning to dawn.

"I do? You have?" The look on his face sobered Lisa instantly, as if someone had just thrown a bucket of cold water over her. He didn't want her here, it had all been a joke and she had made a fool of herself.

"Sorry, I've misunderstood." She turned and headed towards the door.

"No, no, don't go." Jason caught her arm. He'd never anticipated this happening; she had so vehemently made it clear that they were friends and nothing more. As she turned to look at him, tears of shame glistening in her eyes, he couldn't stop himself and leaned forward to kiss her. She turned her face swiftly to the side so that his lips connected with a wad of curly hair.

Puzzled, he stepped back. "Sorry, I thought ...."

"I can't do the whole kissing thing, I thought maybe we could just ..... do it?" Seeing Jason's look of stunned surprise, tears trickled down her cheeks. This had been a bad mistake, possibly the biggest of her life to date.

Clank, clank, whirr; Jason could feel his brain struggling into motion. Was she really suggesting what he thought she was? *Dear God, if he got this wrong their friendship was doomed.* "Yes. Of course." *Had he just said that? What was he thinking? Was he thinking? This was the problem with drinking to excess!*

Lisa took a step towards him, caught her foot against the armchair and lurched forwards. Already off balance as he grabbed her, the back of Jason's knee struck the arm of the sofa, and then he was sprawled on his back with her on top of him.

Before he could move, she had rolled onto the floor and knelt beside him, pulling up his shirt and dotting kisses over his chest and stomach, following the line traced by her fingertips to his belt. She recognised the musky scent of his skin, she'd dreamt of it so often, and she wanted him right there. There was no going back now. "Do you have a condom?" she breathed, fumbling with the buckle.

Aaaaaaggggghhhhh! No, he didn't! At Pietro's insistence, he'd been out several times with him and his mates and had a few more one-night stands, which had only served to confirm it wasn't for him. He wasn't attracted to the girls who Pietro insisted wouldn't give the encounter a second thought, and his conscience wouldn't allow him to take advantage of someone who might want more. The upshot was he currently had no need for condoms.

"Just a sec." Lisa heard several drawers opening and banging closed in the kitchen before he called out, "Ta-dah!" and reappeared, wearing nothing other than a length of cling film from which he had tried, unsuccessfully, to fashion a makeshift condom.

Lisa gaped at him. She'd expected him to have industrial-sized stocks of condoms, but presumably he had none at all; otherwise, surely he would never have made such a complete spectacle of himself. *So much for being a butcher's dog!* As he moved towards her, the edge of the cling film lifted and slowly began to uncoil; he tried to distract himself as she made a clumsy attempt to tighten and secure the wrapping.

"His name's Rolo."

"Whose is?" she asked, not looking up from the task in hand.

"His." She glanced up as Jason looked meaningfully downwards. He'd hoped to amuse her with the anecdote, but it was met with a look of bemusement. "An initiation ceremony at uni," he continued lamely. "We all had to name our……. Ouch! That's a bit tight."

"This isn't going to work, is it?" She frowned. "I'd better go."

When he awoke at lunchtime with a headache from hell, Jason wasn't entirely sure whether the surreal events of the early hours had actually occurred or not. Only the patches of dried mud on the sofa and the carpet confirmed it.

Occupied with attending to his hangover, he forgot about helping John and Phil with the clearing up, and it was several days before he saw Lisa again. He'd wondered what to do next. The situation had taken him completely by surprise, and he deeply regretted going along with her suggestion. Obviously, she'd been drunk at the time; he should have done the right thing, helped her back home and left. There was every chance their friendship was over, and that would be a real shame.

It was just after 10.30 pm when he heard the gentle tap at the door on Wednesday evening. "Sorry it's late, I've just finished at the Samaritans. Have I got you up? I saw the light on in the bedroom." Jason was thrilled that Lisa was still talking to him. "I need to go, early start tomorrow," she told him when he invited her in. "I've just brought these." She pressed a small packet into his hand. "For Rolo."

There was a condom machine on the wall in the ladies at the All Bar One, where she'd had lunch with a colleague. Never having made such a purchase before, she'd been frightened to death of anyone seeing her. It had felt like a miracle when she stowed the packet in her handbag and walked away, her mission undetected. Jason glanced at the packet and caught Lisa's arm as she turned to go.

"I need to talk to you, five minutes." Standing in the same spot where they had fallen together onto the sofa a few nights before, Jason explained, as gently as he could, why he thought it was a bad idea. "We're such good friends," he told her, "I don't want to lose that."

"I see. It's been a long day." She turned away to hide her shame. *How stupid can you be? It was bad enough when you had alcohol as an excuse, now you're messing things up big time!*

"No, I don't think you do. I like you, Lisa, a lot. But I don't want a relationship, not with anyone. I'm sorry."

She turned to him again. "And neither do I. Ever. So, it would be a perfect arrangement for us both."

Soaking in the warm, scented bathwater ten minutes later, Lisa wondered again if she had done the right thing. She was still dressed in her business suit when she'd called at Jason's, having gone straight from work to do her shift at the Samaritans. Was that what had given her the confidence to be so forward? What would Maryam say if she knew to what use she had just put her technique? *But then, did she really need a costume to feel at ease with Jason? He'd seen her makeup-free countless times, even grovelling in the dirt and bleeding.*

It came to her then; why she'd had the dream about Jason. With him, she could relax and be herself; there was no need to hide behind a disguise. She hadn't realised it until then, but she spent more time with him than anyone else; he'd become her closest friend.

The following Saturday was cold and crisp but dry, and on a short bike ride together, Jason broached the subject of the proposed 'arrangement'. "I need to be straight with you, Lisa. I can't ever be more than a friend."

"Likewise."

"Well, if you're absolutely sure you won't get hurt and it's what you want, ..., maybe we could give it a try?" Despite his fears that it could all go horribly wrong, Jason was beginning to question the sense in turning down this lovely young woman who was offering him the best possible solution to his predicament.

"I won't get hurt," Lisa assured him. She'd thought this through endlessly and knew she could handle it. Her heart had already been smashed to smithereens; there was nothing left to break. "I do have a few rules, though."

Jason's heart began to thump. "I thought you might."

"There are only two; no kissing on the mouth and no one else must ever know." She and Jason were single people, free to do whatever they wanted, but she was ashamed of the needs of her treacherous body. This wouldn't be a love affair; she didn't want people making assumptions and asking awkward questions. "It's just sex, is that okay?"

"I think I can live with it." He grinned. "I thought you'd want to know if there was anyone else and stuff like that?"

She shook her head. "I'm not interested."

Later that evening, she knocked lightly, and Jason handed her a glass of wine as she walked in. They were both confident that Pietro would be out with his mates and unlikely to return home, but she wouldn't stay long in case anyone else had seen her arrive.

She sat in the armchair, and when Jason went to pick up the empty wine glass, the look in her eyes made it clear she had no doubts. He knelt in front of her, and as she loosened the buckle on his belt, he eased her long skirt up over the silky smoothness of her legs that seemed to go on forever.

They'd both been nervous and restrained that first time, but as the weeks passed, they relaxed and threw themselves wholeheartedly into this new dimension of their friendship.

Jason was delighted by her response to him. As her breathing got faster and she arched and shuddered beneath his touch, she made him feel like the most accomplished lover in the world, a powerful aphrodisiac.

Now, watching Lisa writhing on his dining room table, seemingly oblivious to anything but her own pleasure, he recalled his mum talking about people who are free spirits, unencumbered by the usual mental restrictions that human beings place on themselves. He wondered if, by some stroke of good fortune, he had been lucky enough to meet one.

Chapter Eighteen

They never spoke of their liaisons; it was an unspoken rule, but Jason was becoming preoccupied with questions about Lisa's past. So shy and timid at the start, he'd concluded she must have had limited sexual experience.

Now that she was rapidly becoming possibly the most confident, inspired and uninhibited lover he'd ever had, he wanted to know more. But Lisa had lost none of her reticence in revealing personal details, so how could he ask her?

Cycling alongside her one bright spring morning in April, he took the plunge. "I need to tell you something, Lisa." He hesitated, knowing he was taking an enormous risk. "You're very good."

"Oh, thanks." She smiled and accelerated away from him with a sudden burst of speed. The endless hours spent at the gym on the exercise bikes were starting to pay off. He caught up with her and cleared his throat nervously.

"That's not what I was talking about."

She glanced at him, and even though she was wearing a helmet and sunglasses, he knew she was frowning. "I'm 'very good'? What's that supposed to mean? Sex isn't a competitive sport. What do you do, score me out of 10 for content, performance and star quality?"

She was angry, as expected. What had possessed him to open his big mouth? "No, no, not at all, I just wondered......" He faltered, not daring to continue.

"Well? Go on, you wondered what? Out with it."

Jason swallowed hard. "I just wondered if you've had many..... if there've been.... many others. In your past?" He gulped. *That was it, right there, game over. He should have kept his thoughts to himself.* The silence that hung between them for several miles was deafening.

When they reached Oldcotes, Jason suggested a cafe stop to refuel; unusually, they ordered their food separately before sitting down. Stony-faced, Lisa looked across at Jason, mortified and fiddling unnecessarily with his change. *He was so open and revealed so much of himself freely; she owed it to him to answer his question.*

"I've only had one partner."

"Oh!"

"You're surprised?"

"Well, I just thought, maybe...... no, no, I'm not...... oh God, yes, yes I am."

Lisa couldn't help but smile as he struggled to be honest and inoffensive at the same time. "The way you're so.....free, so uninhibited, I just thought......, maybe........" he tailed off, not wanting to say what he'd thought.

Chapter Eighteen

She hadn't thought about Mark and their life together for a long time. Jenni had advised her to be 'a willing participant', and she'd done her utmost to comply with everything he asked of her.

Painfully shy and with no confidence whatsoever in her own body, it had been excruciatingly difficult for her to become the uninhibited and experimental lover Mark had wanted her to be. She'd persevered throughout their relationship, doing all she could to satisfy his needs and desires, hoping he would have no reason to look elsewhere. But she'd failed.

Not once had she given any thought as to whether she pleased Jason. Why would she; their friendship meant everything to her, and if she lost that, she'd be devastated, but the sex was just a pleasurable add-on until he met someone. She'd never thought about it before, but with him, she felt liberated, free to let herself go and enjoy every sensation that tore through her body, unrestricted by the pressure to please someone else.

Over their toasted sandwiches, she filled him in with brief details of her only relationship, including the traumatic ending. "So, now you know. My first foray into the world of love ended so disastrously that I have no intention of ever setting foot there again."

"God, that's awful. I can't believe they would do that to you. But I'm surprised to hear that you were ever painfully shy, you're so confident and outgoing."

Lisa pondered for a moment. *Should she tell him anything more? She'd already shared far more with him than she'd ever intended, but didn't he deserve that?*

Over a second coffee, she told him of the insecurities that still lingered, the technique that Maryam had given her to deal with them and about the 'costumes' that she still invested heavily in, disguises to hide behind. "So, you see, it's all just an image, a show I put on to be able to cope. I'm not confident about anything." Alarm bells pealed loudly in her head. *She'd said too much, left herself exposed.*

Jason nodded; he could relate to the concept of creating an image far more than she would ever know. His mind was racing as they made their way back home. He'd known Lisa for over 18 months, and she had always been such a closed book, giving nothing of herself away.

What she had told him over lunch had left him reeling. This confident, statuesque, beautiful businesswoman was, in fact, shy, insecure and terribly hurt? Could that be true, or was she playing games with him? He didn't think so; she'd seemed so sincere. So much for her being a free spirit! Maybe he could tell her something about his situation? Might she understand? He waited until he could ride alongside her.

"There's something else I've been meaning to talk to you about, ..." His lips continued to form words, but there was no sound; he simply could not speak them. He coughed and spluttered loudly to hide his embarrassment. "Are you okay?"

"Yep," he squeaked.

"So? What do you want to tell me?"

He cleared his throat again. "I have an aunt who lives in France, and there's talk of a family celebration in the summer to celebrate my cousin's 18th. I wondered if you might like to join us and meet some of my family?"

What? Remember the golden rule, engage brain before mouth! It was one thing to falter and stall when he'd attempted to open up to her, another thing entirely to blurt out something that hadn't even been in his head! *He'd had no intention of inviting her to France. It had never even occurred to him; where had that come from? More to the point, how could he backtrack?*

He nearly fell off his bike when she smiled. "Thanks. I'll think about it."

They were nearly home when Jason realised Lisa had asked him nothing about the proposed trip; she hadn't wanted to know about his family or where they lived. Come to think of it, he couldn't recall her ever having asked him anything about himself. He was intrigued but tried his best to sound casual. "You know, you never ask me anything."

"I don't need to ask you anything." Her reply stung; he wasn't sure why.

"Don't tell me, you're really not interested." He contorted his handsome features into a comical caricature of misery, but Lisa sensed that, behind his antics, he was hurt.

"Oh, for goodness' sake, don't look so put out. Are you familiar with the phrase 'Ask no questions, get no lies'? I'm sure you'll tell me whatever you want me to know whenever you're ready to tell me. I don't need to ask you anything."

Jason thought about her words long after they'd completed their ride and parted. He would have said that they were good friends, but he'd been shocked when she'd revealed that much of the time, she hid behind a charade. Perhaps he didn't really know her at all.

But then, wasn't that precisely what he did himself? And what had she meant about not asking him anything? Didn't she trust him to answer her truthfully, and if that was the case, why did it make him feel sad?

The impending trip to France, still almost three months away, weighed heavily on Jason's mind. It would be his first holiday with the family since the accident four years before. To his chagrin, he'd told several white lies in the past to explain why he couldn't join in with long weekends and holidays. He wasn't convinced his family had believed his excuses, but, fortunately, they hadn't pressed him.

He still made regular trips to Stockport, and he'd spent time with Jayne, Pierre and the boys when they came over, but family get-togethers only served to emphasise his parents' absence. He would never get used to that. It was hard enough to steel his way through a couple of days together; a holiday was unimaginable. There would be too many memories of happier times.

And then there was the other issue. It was over two-and-a-half years since he'd moved into his own home and created the haven in his bedroom where he could be with his parents. Since then, he'd only spent a couple of nights away at a time, and when he did, he couldn't wait to get back. It was ridiculous for a man of his age to be so entrenched in the past and so utterly stuck fast, but that's how it was. And he could tell no one.

But there was no possibility of avoiding Christophe's 18th birthday celebrations, no-one would forgive him that. After inexplicably inviting Lisa, he thought more about it and realised it might be a good idea after all. She would add a different dynamic to the group, which would be no bad thing, and it would be an excellent way to repay her for inviting him to London.

Chapter Eighteen

He provided her with more details on their bike ride the following week. "Auntie Jayne is Mum's sister. Apparently, she went to work in France as a nanny, fell in love and never returned. She's married to Pierre; they have two sons, Christophe, who's turning 18 and Julien, two years younger. Pierre has his own business. They live on the outskirts of Limoges in a renovated farmhouse with outbuildings and a swimming pool. It's nice, you'll be able to have your own room," he assured her. "I've told them about you, they know we're just friends. Mum and Dad's parents will be going, and Michael with his wife, Anne and children, Amber and Jonathon," he continued. "Michael's Dad's brother, I never call him Uncle, he's only 13 years older than me. The rest of the crowd will be French."

Lisa noticed that Jason spoke of his family's relationships with his parents in the present tense. She also noted the age gap between him and his uncle was only slightly more than that between her and her brothers. That could only mean one of two things; either Michael had been much younger than his brother, or Jason's parents had been very young when he was born.

"Sounds great, count me in. But only on condition that no one else knows we're going away together. You know what Pietro's like, we'd never hear the last of it!"

In the shower later, Lisa wondered for the hundredth time why she'd accepted the invitation. Other than her own family, she'd only ever been away with Mark, and that was years ago. *What if his family didn't like her? She couldn't back out now; he'd been so pleased when she'd accepted. Oh no, what had she done?*

"Fancy going to see the Tour de France?" Jason asked Lisa, tongue-in-cheek, a couple of weeks later. "It's going through the Pyrenees a few days after Christophe's party, about five hours drive from Limoges. The highest mountain on the French side is the Tourmalet, it'd be something to see the race come over there. What do you think?" He grinned as she gave him the anticipated withering look.

"Drive? I thought we'd be on the train. I've never seen you in a car, have you asked me along so I can do the driving?"

"No! No, of course not. I've held a licence since I was 17. It's been a few years since I had a go, but it can't be that hard. Can it?" He flashed her his most disarming grin, and Lisa sighed.

"I think you're a crackpot. Is there anything you're not over- confident about?" *Think about it. You'd only have to spend a few days with his family, with a legitimate reason to leave. Perfect!* "But why not?"

Jason's mind whirled, and his face shone with the giddily excited expression of a young child. "You're kidding? Are you up for it? Really? No! You are?" They had less than two months to get organised before they left for France. "We'll need to hire a car large enough for both bikes and the tent."

"Bikes? And a tent?" Lisa was horrified.

"It would be nice to do some riding in France, and unfortunately, there aren't any five-star hotels on a mountain top."

Another week passed before Lisa plucked up the courage to tell her parents about their plans.

"You're going camping? With Blondie? Lisa!" Joe was so stunned he could barely speak, convinced that the charming, good-looking young man would one day break his daughter's heart, and he couldn't bear the thought of that happening to her again.

"We're just cycling mates, Dad, he's only invited me because he came down to London last year. It's nothing, honest."

They decided to break the journey to Limoges to try out the small two-person tent they'd purchased for the trip. It wasn't a promising start to camping for Lisa, unnerved at the thought that the flimsy material was all that protected her from the outside world. She felt restricted and claustrophobic in her new sleeping bag, shaped like an Egyptian sarcophagus, and didn't sleep well.

But the following day, Jayne and Pierre greeted her like a long-lost friend, kissing her on both cheeks, continental style. Lisa commented on Jayne's necklace, a delicate chain with a pendant formed into the back-to-back profiles of the Gemini twins. "How beautiful, I'm a Gemini too."

"Thank you," Jayne said nothing more but glanced at Jason as she momentarily held the pendant between her fingers. He knew she had worn it every day since her sister's funeral.

She showed Lisa to a beautiful single room overlooking a field of sunflowers; their faces turned towards the sun as they gently swayed in the light breeze, and then took her to meet the rest of the family. Jason's grandparents seemed only slightly older than her parents, confirming what Lisa had already suspected; his parents had been very young when he was born. And when they died.

Before Michael and Anne could say hello, Amber bounced up to her side. "Wow, you're so tall and pretty. I'm tall for my age, I'm nine. I hope I look like you when I'm grown up."

"And this is my cousin Amber." Jason laughed as she tried to wriggle free of the headlock he'd just applied.

Lisa smiled at the child. *So, that explained how he got on so well with the twins; his cousin was only a little older.*

"Lovely to meet you, Amber, my nephew and niece, Georgina and Byron, will be nine in November."

"Oh, we're nearly the same." Amber twirled until her full skirt billowed around her like the petals of a flower, delighted with the connection.

"No, no, Lisa doesn't want to get dirty playing with you, Jonathon." Anne remonstrated with the toddler a little while later when he held his tractor out to her. But Lisa knelt beside him in the dry dirt and soon had him giggling uncontrollably as she remembered the happy hours she'd spent entertaining her mother's youngest pupils at the dance school years before.

In the early evening, Christophe and Julien returned from making the preparations for the party the following day. Jason introduced them to Lisa and gawped, open-mouthed, as she conversed with them in fluent French. "You never told me you speak the lingo!"

She laughed at his stunned expression. "You never asked! When Neil and Stephen were doing French at school, they practised with each other at home. I was only four or five and just started picking it up, it continued from there."

The party weekend was a success from start to finish. Pierre's family joined them for a celebratory brunch and in the late afternoon, everyone headed to the local hall, festooned with the balloons and banners the brothers had been working on the previous day. Around 60 local friends were waiting for them there, and after a leisurely meal, the party had really got into full swing with a live band on the outdoor stage, dancing and fireworks.

Halfway through the evening, the band took a break, and two of them passed their guitars to Michael and Jason, waiting by the side of the stage. Michael's hands trembled as he took hold of the instrument. He'd dreaded this moment ever since the telephone call with Jason just after the party was announced.

"Do you think we could do a couple of the old songs as a surprise? So that Mum and Dad aren't forgotten," his nephew had asked, and although he'd felt immediately sick with nerves, he hadn't felt able to refuse. Now the moment was here, but as Jason began to walk forwards onto the stage, Michael caught his elbow, panic-stricken.

"I'm sorry, Jason, I can't," he whispered, mortified. But Jason turned and smiled, gently strumming the first notes of Eric Clapton's *You Look Wonderful Tonight*, and everyone watched in silence as he encouraged his uncle, clearly filled with emotion, onto the stage. The two of them held each other's gaze, oblivious to everyone else, as Jason began to sing. To Michael's surprise, he found himself joining in, hesitantly at first but gradually with more confidence, his voice blending as one with his nephew's, his fingers effortlessly finding the familiar chords.

Looking on as the family huddled together, dabbing at their eyes, Lisa knew she was witnessing something special. Amber caught her arm. "Uncle Robert used to sing this song with my dad." She insisted on leading Lisa over, and the family parted to make room for her to join them.

The audience sang along in English as uncle and nephew performed another of Robert and Mary's favourite rock ballads and then an encore before they took a bow and Michael announced: "From Jason's parents; my brother, Robert and his beautiful wife Mary, who would have loved to be here with you tonight, Christophe." The rapturous applause and the stamping of feet were deafening.

The following day everyone enjoyed the treasure hunt, followed by a barbecue and in the evening, Jayne helped Jason re-pack the car. "The time has gone too quickly; having you both here has been wonderful. But I was wondering, are you sure Lisa's just a friend, nothing more?"

"Absolutely certain," Jason smiled.

"Well, we've all fallen in love with her even if you haven't."

The following morning, Lisa felt oddly reluctant to leave as the family hugged her one by one and told her how much they hoped to see her again. As she bent to hold Amber close, to everyone's surprise, the child shed a few tears, sad to be losing the company of her new best friend so soon. "I promise I'll ring you when we're all home," she whispered.

Watching them drive away, Jayne thought again about the coincidence that Lisa was the same birth sign as Mary. *Similar qualities, maybe? Was that why she and Jason seemed to get along so well, and all the family had taken to her so quickly?*

She recalled the day many years ago, not long after she had met Pierre in Chamonix when they'd decided to take a ride on the highest vertical ascent cable car in the world over the top of Mont Blanc to Courmayeuer, situated on the Italian side of the mountain.

Chapter Eighteen

The morning was grey and overcast, and as they reached the Aiguille du Midi, just below the summit, they were a little disappointed that cloud cover hid the reputedly incredible views of the valley. Still, they'd been excited at the prospect of spending the day in Italy.

But only a few hours later, Jayne spotted the necklace in a shop window, perfect for Mary's 21st birthday gift. Pierre had kindly pooled his money with hers to enable her to purchase it. They'd had nothing left to buy a meal, so they cut the day short and returned earlier than planned. But the cloud had lifted, and the return trip had been spectacular. The cobalt blue of the cloudless sky was the perfect backdrop to the dazzlingly white snow-capped mountain that sparkled like diamonds.

They'd stayed at the Aiguille du Midi until sunset when the sky turned to blush pink and then fiery red, the drama in the heavens reflected on the snow so that the whole mountain seemed alight. She held the precious pendant again in her palm; it held so many beautiful memories, especially of her beloved sister.

As Jason drove south, the landscape changed, becoming steadily hillier and then mountainous and gradually, the enormity of the challenge Lisa had accepted, to watch the Tour de France on the top of the highest and most iconic mountain in the French Pyrenees, began to come into sharp focus. Later, in the cool air on the top of the Col d'Aspin, helping Jason to erect the tent in the breezy conditions before sunset, she nervously wondered what the following day would bring.

Chapter Nineteen

"You're going to see the Tour de France? On the Tourmalet? Incredible! You've got to bag the climb then, it's the 'must have' for your cycling CV," Craig had enviously informed Jason on a club ride in early May. Inspired, Jason had mentioned it to Lisa.

"Ride up a mountain? Are you insane? This time last year, I couldn't even stay upright! I thought we were going to camp on the top?"

"We can camp on a mountain top, the next one along, the Col d'Aspin. It's another famous one, so we'd get two for the price of one." Lisa shuddered at the thought, but Jason's eyes were full of excitement as he continued: "There's always a big party the night before the race arrives. We can join in with that and then, on race day, ride down the Aspin and up the Tourmalet before they close the road."

"Close the road?"

"Yeah, the police close the road hours before the race arrives for safety. It would mean an early start, but what an adventure. Maybe...?" he tailed off.

Lisa shook her head. "No chance." But, like a persistent wasp that refuses to be swatted, the idea buzzed around her brain incessantly. That week she began selecting harder gears on the bikes in the gym, pushing on the pedals till her thighs burned, and on their next ride, she suggested a route with as many hills as possible.

"What's going on, Lisa?" Jason groaned as they approached yet another short but steep ascent. "Are we in training for something?" Lisa only grinned, breathing hard as she climbed, but he understood the reply. The challenge was on.

Now, huddled in her sleeping bag, Lisa was questioning the wisdom of her decision. She seemed to have been asleep for only minutes when Jason nudged her and told her it was time to get up if she wanted to do the ride.

The previous evening, they had eaten in the small town of Arreau before driving up the Col d'Aspin to camp, about 25 kilometres from the summit of the Col du Tourmalet, where they intended to watch the race go by. They'd been lucky to find a space on a grassy bank, barely large enough to accommodate their small tent, amidst the multitude of campervans and tents strewn across the mountaintop.

During brief periods of exhausted sleep despite the crescendo of airhorns, music and singing that continued well into the early hours, they involuntarily rolled into a suffocating heap against the side of the tent, threatening to break through. It had been a very long night.

Chapter Nineteen

Pulling herself together, Lisa fought to don her cycling gear in the confines of the tent before emerging, bleary-eyed. Jason had been looking forward to this for months, was she going to back out now? Of course not.

After a quick breakfast of croissants and fruit, taken standing by the side of the tent, they set off. Carefully wending her way down the switchback that formed the mountain road, Lisa couldn't help but wonder if she had bitten off more than she could chew this time. It was a long way down, and the Tourmalet was much higher than the Aspin! "Okay?" Jason had waited for her at the bottom and was grinning broadly, exuding excitement.

"Fine," she somehow smiled back.

They rode along the valley floor together to the signpost that signalled the left turn to the Col du Tourmalet, still almost 15 kilometres from the top. The road climbed gradually but soon became steeper. "I might not make it, you go on ahead," Lisa called out to Jason. It was several hours until the race was due to come through, but they were unsure how soon the police would close the road. The last thing she wanted was to deprive him of achieving his mountaintop view of the spectacle if she couldn't get there in time or even at all.

"No, no, we'll stay together." He wouldn't hear of leaving her behind, but Lisa was adamant.

"Please, I'll be gutted if you miss it."

She watched as, unwillingly, he slowly pulled away from her, calling out, "I'll be watching for you at the top," before he disappeared around the next bend.

Lisa rode on slowly. She suspected her erratic breathing had more to do with her mounting sense of panic than the gradient of the road. *Just ride as far as you can. You don't need to get to the top, aim for the next kilometre marker.* A cluster of motorhomes parked on either side of the road came into view, and people readying tables, chairs and awnings in preparation to party before the race arrived. Around the next bend were a few more, and within a few kilometres, the vans were already lining both sides of the road with only a few gaps between them.

Some people were already sitting out in the warm sunshine, and they waved to her as she passed or called out "Bravo!" as did other cyclists, mainly young men built like whippets, who shot past her as though she wasn't moving at all.

As the road got steeper still, Lisa stopped to take a drink, and when she set off again, a smiling French man ran to her side. "Allez, Allez, Allez." He planted a firm hand in the middle of her back and began running, projecting her forwards with as much impetus as possible when he could no longer keep up, much to the amusement of the groups of people now gathering on either side of the road. Other gallant male observers stepped out into the road, ready to take their turn in assisting Lisa.

Clapping and cheering broke out, interspersed with the occasional blast from an air horn. Onlookers up ahead leaned out to see what all the fuss was about, and seeing the lone woman struggling up the mountain road, they too began clapping and cheering her effort, encouraging her onwards.

This is it, I'm just going to die right here. She was living her worst possible nightmare. The shy, timid girl who couldn't bear to be the centre of attention, who only a year before could barely ride a bike, had somehow become the focus of attention of all these spectators who had come to watch the most elite cyclists in the world do battle to be the first to reach the mountain top. She willed the ground to open up and swallow her.

As the road wound up the mountain, the tree cover disappeared, and it was hot. Constantly thirsty, Lisa began to feel hungry, and the muscles in her legs were burning. *For God's sake, you idiot, stop and get off!*, the voice in her head screamed at her, but slowly, now only half a kilometre at a time between stops, she ground her way upwards.

Reaching the ski village of La Mongie, she could see and hear the hustle and bustle of celebrations in full swing; music playing, people dancing, enjoying the day and full of anticipation. What on earth was she doing, she wondered yet again. Why was she straining every sinew, sweating profusely and enduring the worst day of her life so far when she could stop and watch the party? But still, she ploughed on. *Just around the next bend. Good, now the next one.*

And then, suddenly, she could see the top; it was only just ahead, maybe another kilometre at the most. But the road reared up to the steepest section of all. The roadside was crowded, and the now familiar clapping and cheering thundered around her as though she were a famous rider.

When the road eventually levelled off, Lisa couldn't quite believe she was still alive. She would never forget the last excruciating two-and-a-half hours for as long as she lived.

But another problem loomed immediately. The crowd at the top of the mountain was already five or six deep; there was no chance of finding Jason. She walked along, pushing her bike, looking for any small space where she might join the throng. Suddenly, through the excited clamour, she thought she heard her name, and then again. "Lisa, Lisa, over here!" She turned as the crowd parted slightly to let Jason reach the roadside. "I can't believe you made it! So, so well done!" Aware that Lisa hated any sign of affection, he couldn't help but hug her, and the crowd cheered again.

The air began to cool as they waited for the race to arrive. Clouds scudded across the sun, and then a grey, seething mass of mist slowly crept up the mountainside, obliterating the view of the valley below, eventually forming a dense shroud on the top. The approaching cavalcade of vehicles, imaginatively adorned to advertise the wares of the numerous French sponsors of the race, could be heard long before it could be seen, and the crowd jostled to catch the titbits hurled at them from the passing vehicles.

Another half hour ticked by slowly. The temperature had dropped several degrees, and Lisa shivered, her thin rain jacket providing scant warmth in the cool mist that parted now and then to give tantalising glimpses of the valley far below. Then a disembodied voice called out through the gloom, "Ecoute, écoute!!" The excited chatter of the crowd dramatically fell silent, everyone straining to hear the faint pulsating beat, the sound of rotor blades. A roar went up; the approaching helicopters signalled that the race was nearby. The sound grew steadily louder until it was almost deafening as the helicopters hovered low over the mountaintop, the film crews inside doing all they could to capture the moment the first man made it to the summit.

Knowing the stage leader's arrival was imminent, the crowd peered into the gloom, and suddenly, there he was. People surged forwards as he sped through the ear-splitting cacophony of air horns, cow bells and cheering, desperate to glimpse the hero.

Only seconds later, a small group of riders in hot pursuit flashed past, followed half a minute later by the main peloton, the riders filling the road and causing the crowd to step back hurriedly or risk being run over. Just a few stragglers off the back, warriors suffering their own private hell, came through and then it was over. The race had passed by in only a few short minutes.

Sipping coffee with her parents in the comfort of their kitchen a few days later, Lisa attempted to describe her experience. "He left you to ride up the mountain on your own? Despicable!" Joe was appalled by her account of her trip.

"It wasn't like that, Dad. I made him go."

"And was it worth it?"

She thought back to what had become a damp, dismal day on the top of the Col du Tourmalet. What had impressed her the most? The sight of the stage leader, almost waif-like, yet his legs pumping with a ferocity that completely belied the severity of the incline he'd just climbed; or the young men at the back with their weary faces, their teeth gritted, desperately fighting their way to the top, refusing to give in, determination personified. What words could ever describe what she had seen?

"Absolutely."

"I think he's good for her," Kathleen told Joe that evening whilst Lisa rang Stephen during his lunch hour in San Francisco to tell him of her exploits. "Could you have ever imagined her doing anything like that before?"

Stephen was interested in all sports; he knew of the world's most challenging bike race and the formidable iconic mountain. "My kid sister's ridden up the Tourmalet? I'm impressed!" Lisa allowed herself a slightly self-satisfied smile; this was high praise indeed from the James Bond of the family. "I'll have to give it a go," he continued, unable to prevent his innate competitive streak from coming to the fore again.

"But it won't count unless you do it on race day with thousands of spectators," she laughed, still unable to believe she had done that. Later that night, at home and luxuriating in her own bed after the rigours of four consecutive nights in the tent, she thought about the ride again, remembering the tumult of emotions that swept through her as she climbed and climbed for what seemed like forever.

Why had she done that? Jason had given her a way out, telling her she could wait in the valley for him. She didn't need to ride up the mountain at all and certainly not to the very top, so why had she put herself through that? In fact, why had she fought to learn to ride a bike in the first place and then trained so hard even to be capable of riding up a mountain?

Come to think of it, her parents had always told her that all they wanted was for her to be happy. They'd put no pressure on her to study or further her career, so why had she pushed herself relentlessly to attain the highest qualification in insurance and then moved into the Major Loss Team?

Alone in the darkness, realisation struck Lisa like a light bulb flashing on in her head. She remembered an old story her mother used to tell her, something about her doing jigsaws upside down when she was very young, pushing herself even then to recognise the shapes without the benefit of the picture. "We couldn't believe it when you did it the first time, the boys had never done that."

All this time, she'd been wrong about herself. Her thirst for success wasn't so that she could belong within her high-achieving family as she'd always believed; the need to challenge herself came from within. She was the same as them; she had belonged right from the start.

The first weekend after they got back from holiday, Pietro invited everyone around to a barbecue. He'd asked nothing about Lisa and Jason's respective trips; by some extraordinary feat, they seemed to have got away with their elaborate plan to throw him off the scent, despite the uncomfortable few moments when they'd told everyone a couple of weeks before their departure that they were both taking holidays and would coincidentally be away at the same time.

"J! A holiday! At last, fantastic, where are you going?" John had asked as Pietro scrutinised Jason's face, incredulous at this sudden development.

"France. I'm staying with family near Limoges and then going to see the Tour de France."

"Oh, how lovely!" John was delighted. "And you're leaving us too, Lisa! What are you up to?"

"I'm spending time with family, too." She'd learned the art of being economical with the truth from her brother, Neil. She hadn't told a lie; she just hadn't mentioned whose family she would be spending time with. Reluctantly, Pietro had left it there, knowing better than to press her for more information than she wanted to divulge.

Lisa had stayed with her parents for a couple of nights before they set off, and Joe had muttered something menacingly about his drive looking like a car park, as Jason loaded the bikes into the hire car the night before they were due to leave. Not taken in at all by Lisa's pitiful excuse that her drive was not large enough to accommodate her car and the hire car, Joe had correctly interpreted the situation. "You're hiding here! Skulking about late in the evening to bring Jason's bike over, what's going on, Lisa? What are you covering up?"

"We don't want our friends putting two and two together and coming up with five," she replied honestly.

"Like I'm doing, you mean?" Joe groaned. Matters hadn't improved the following morning when Jason arrived on his motorbike, loaded up to make it look like he was going touring, with panniers he'd borrowed from a colleague, the tent and his sleeping bag strapped on top. He'd made sure that Pietro had seen the heavily laden bike the night before and had even told him the route he would be taking. Thankfully, the ruse seemed to have worked.

The weather couldn't have been better for Pietro's barbecue, a rare scorching Saturday afternoon. Simon and Amy were over for the weekend, and everyone was relaxed, enjoying a beer and each other's company, when Pietro innocently asked, "So, how was the holiday then, you two?"

Jason glared at Simon, sprawled on the grass, his plate balanced on his stomach while his food cooled. "You told him?"

"I never did! Now look what you've made me do." Simon began carefully removing grass from his assortment of chargrilled sausages and burgers, sent flying as he struggled into a sitting position to remonstrate with his friend.

"Aha! So, you did go away together. I knew it!" Pietro brandished his tongs like some wild orchestral conductor.

"You told Simon?" Lisa was astonished. She punched Jason hard on the shoulder, and beer splattered all over his tee shirt as he almost fell out of his deckchair.

"You knew Lisa and Jason had gone away together and never told me?" It was Amy's turn to be outraged. She swiped at Simon's arm, knocking the carefully cleaned food back into the grass again.

John chuckled. "Have you all been rehearsing this? It's the best slapstick I've seen in ages."

Still intent on defending himself, Simon pointed a sausage accusingly at Pietro. "He asked me weeks ago if I thought you were going away together. Too much of a coincidence that you were both going away at the same time, he said."

"Yeah, and you lied to me, tried to make out that you didn't know anything," Pietro jabbed the tongs, sabre-style, at Simon.

"I didn't lie at all!" yelped Simon. "Jason hadn't told me by then."

"Told you what, exactly?" Lisa interjected, standing behind Jason, holding her beer directly above his head at a perilous angle.

"Just a minute, first things first," Jason croaked, frantically trying to deflect the conversation somehow to give himself time to think, firstly, how to extricate himself from this nightmare and then how to kill Simon as slowly and painfully as possible. "Why didn't you tell me Pietro had guessed we were going together?" he fired at Simon, who was wolfing down his food at a rate of knots before it could be launched from his plate a third time.

Beads of sweat were beginning to form on Simon's forehead. *Why were they all suddenly shouting at him? It wasn't his fault that he'd been caught in the middle, he'd done nothing wrong, and he'd said nothing to anyone, not even Amy.* "I couldn't tell you; he swore me to secrecy." He managed to reply, looking like a lopsided chipmunk, one cheek bulging out around half a sausage.

"So many secrets, I can't keep up," John wailed, bewildered.

"So, back to my question, what exactly did you tell Simon?" Lisa was still dangling her beer precariously above Jason's head. He shot Simon a warning glance as he cleared his throat, suddenly distinctly dry despite the swig of beer he'd just gulped.

"I told him that I was going away, and he was surprised and wanted to know who with. He's my best mate...." Jason hesitated, briefly halted mid-sentence by Simon's grimace. "I confided in him, explained that the invite to the party was a chance to repay you for inviting me to London." *Surely that would win him back some brownie points?* "Then I told him about our planned bike adventure."

Excited to hear all about the party and the bike adventure, John plied them with questions and was beside himself when Lisa described her ride up the mountain. "Oh, you're just so... so... wonderful!" He hugged her, tears welling in his eyes.

"So, you slept together in this awful tent thingamy, then?" Pietro persisted. "That's cosy."

"Separate sleeping bags," Jason replied honestly. "Zipped up to the neck," he added, "it's cold on a mountaintop."

Late in the evening, Simon stumbled as he turned to wave when Pietro closed the door behind them, and Lisa caught him. Inebriated and in high spirits, he giggled. "Shohh Lisa," he slurred conspiratorially, "you must know why Jason has a padlock on his bedroom door? Come on, tell yer mate Shi."

"Sorry about that!" Amy forced her way past a stunned Jason, grabbed Simon by his tee shirt and began hauling him away, but Lisa burst out laughing.

"Can't help you there, Simon. I've never been anywhere near his bedroom. Uggghhhh!"

Simon was confused. A few weeks before, over their Friday lunchtime pint, he had been incredulous when Jason had told him about the planned bike trip with Lisa. "You've lost the plot, mate. Lisa's from a wealthy family, and you're planning to stay in a two-man tent on the top of a mountain? Has she ever camped before?" Jason shook his head, and Simon looked horrified.

"She's up for it, she wants an adventure."

"Yeah, well, she's going to get one. How long have you been together? It's not going to last beyond your hols, is it?"

"We're not together, we're just friends. You know that."

Simon carefully placed his pint down on the table and turned to give Jason his full attention. "I'm a graduate, I'm reasonably intelligent. Unless I'm losing my marbles, you've just told me you will be sharing a tiny tent with a stunning woman on holiday, but you're not together?"

"That's right," Jason nodded.

"Bloody hell!" was all Simon said when Jason recounted Lisa's tale of her failed relationship and the betrayal of her best friend as well as her partner.

"So, she doesn't want a relationship, we just have an... arrangement." *What the hell are you doing, why did you say that? If Lisa ever finds out you've told Simon, she'll kill you!*

"What kind of an arrangement?"

Jason sighed; he'd done it now. He and Simon had become so close over the years that they were almost like brothers, and he felt bad that he still couldn't bring himself to share with him what lay behind his padlocked bedroom door.

Could he somehow make amends by taking his friend into his confidence about Lisa? Was that why his mouth had humiliatingly run away with him yet again?

Simon's eyes widened, and his lower jaw almost struck the floor when Jason explained. "You're not together, but you make the beast with two backs with her?"

"No, it's not like that! For God's sake, don't ever say anything, or I'm dead!"

"You lucky sod!" Simon declared. "What made her pick you?" *Need he ask?* The golden-haired, super-fit and sickeningly good-looking man sat opposite him, endowed with far more than his fair share of charm and charisma, could have virtually any woman he wanted. He nearly choked when Jason replied.

"My convenient location, apparently."

Now, Simon turned to look at Jason, bent double with laughter. Even in his semi-drunken stupor, he realised he'd been had and wagged his forefinger meaningfully at his friend.

Chapter Nineteen

Idiot!, he berated himself. Jason's tale of their arrangement had sounded too good to be true; how could he have fallen for it so easily?

Chapter Twenty

Jason's smile evaporated as he watched Simon stagger away, supported by Amy, hissing like a viper. *Now he was for it!* As well as demanding to know what he'd told Simon, Lisa would surely be interested in the padlocked door. But as he turned, she was already walking away, her head down and shoulders hunched, dejected.

"I'm sorry," he called after her. He saw a flash of her fingertips above her right shoulder as she flicked her hand dismissively. So that was it then; finished, and tragically, he knew he deserved it. But to his amazement, she stopped, hesitated momentarily and then turned and walked back to him.

"You're on extremely thin ice."

Jason winced. "I thought I'd gone through, to be fair."

"You had; I threw you a line."

"Yes, I was surprised by that. Thank you."

Lisa frowned. "Me too, it won't happen again."

Jason could see the pain in her eyes. "I know. Listen, I...." Before he could say anything more, Lisa nodded towards his home.

"They're waiting for you, I'll see you later."

Lying back in the warm, perfumed water, Lisa thought again about the afternoon's events. She'd been disappointed, to say the least, wounded even, that Jason had confided something to Simon, although she didn't know what exactly.

Why was it so important to her that no one else knew just how close friends they were? Perhaps it was part of her strategy for keeping tight control of her emotions, for ensuring that she would never want anything more from him than friendship. She'd told him right from the start that their situation must always remain secret; she'd put her trust in him, but just like her previous close friends, he'd let her down.

Her gut reaction had been to tell him at the first opportunity what she thought of him, how despicably badly he had behaved, that he'd ruined their friendship. But then, at the very last minute, there was Simon's weird question which in turn had sparked a rare, heated reaction from Amy, usually so laid back she was practically horizontal.

They all knew that Simon was Jason's closest friend; he often regaled them with tales of shared escapades with Jason during their days at uni. The two men always seemed as thick as thieves, so she'd been taken aback when Simon had suddenly asked her about a padlocked door.

If there was such a thing, did it have anything to do with the shadow that persisted in Jason's eyes? There had to be some secret so significant to him that he couldn't tell even

Simon, and that was intriguing. Was that why she'd suddenly relented, she wondered, still astonished that she'd given him a second chance. She hadn't intended to, but the words were out of her mouth before she could stop them.

Although not remotely interested in his secret, she sensed that behind the ever-confident, extrovert exterior, he hid something, some vulnerability. Probably against her better judgement, she decided to remain his friend, at least for now.

The following day, after Simon and Amy had left, Jason wondered yet again what was happening to him and how, if ever, he could escape. Life was actually very good; he enjoyed his job and the friendship of his colleagues, Craig and the other cyclists in the club. He knew how lucky he was to have the constant support of a caring, loving family and on top of all that, he was blessed with special friends.

So why was he messing up with his closest friends, Simon and Lisa? He was pushing it to the limit with both, he realised that, and it was distressing.

Simon hadn't dropped him in it at the barbecue, he realised now; he'd fallen into Pietro's trap himself. He knew he could trust Simon with anything; his friend had always gone out of his way to help him, putting his own life on hold almost. *So why can't you tell him about this?*, he asked himself yet again as he looked around his bedroom. The pathetic attempt to appease him had failed spectacularly, and for the first time, he understood it was the fact that there was any secret between them that was such an issue for Simon.

And what about Lisa? Not only his friend but also his lover, the person with whom he'd just shared such an incredible adventure. If anyone deserved to know what was going on, it was her. After all she'd been through, now he'd let her down, betrayed her trust, and he felt awful for that.

At the very least, he should explain to her why he'd felt the need to confide something to Simon.

But deep inside, he already knew that he would never tell them. Four long years had passed since the accident, during which everyone thought he'd been incredibly strong and had coped with his loss remarkably well.

If they knew the truth and saw his room, they'd think he was insane! Maybe he was? What other 25-year-old man spent part of most evenings trying to recreate a happy atmosphere with his dead parents? DEAD! DEAD! DEAD! It was time to face up to that and deal with it.

He took hold of one of the enlargements, whispered, "I'm sorry," removed it from the wall and laid it face down on the floor. Tears rolled down his face as he piled more on top and pushed them under the bed. It was a start. He didn't know then that they would all be back on the walls by the end of the week.

"Fancy a swift half at lunch?" Simon called over as he walked past Jason's desk on Monday morning.

"It's only Monday, Simon."

"I'm not thick, I want to talk."

Over the lunchtime drink, Simon profusely apologised for his behaviour at the weekend, and Jason felt even more guilty. "There's nothing to apologise for, Si."

"Yes, there is. Amy's been spelling that out to me since Saturday!"

"I should be apologising to you. The padlock's not important, honestly." They studied each other for a long moment; they'd become so close they were almost telepathic, and neither of them believed a word of what Jason was saying.

"It's a well-known fact, you know, that if someone has to say the word 'honestly' at the end of a sentence, they're lying. But it's okay, buddy, let's not let it spoil things." Simon grinned and downed the rest of his drink in one, furious with himself that, despite what he'd just said, he was still sad that there was something Jason couldn't share with him.

The following Saturday, Jason was thrilled when Lisa arrived on his doorstep bright and early with her bike. As they headed off into the quiet, hedge-lined lanes, she told him of her long telephone call with Amber, who had filled her in with the details of the family's remaining days in France and made her promise to ring again soon. He felt his ego collapse when she added, "For the child's sake, I decided to keep cycling with you, so I've got something to talk to her about."

She didn't reappear later that evening, and Jason wasn't surprised. He'd assumed the 'arrangement' was at an end; he was just grateful their friendship was intact, thanks to Amber, and the debacle of the previous weekend seemed to be behind them. Until, that is, a couple of nights later, when everyone was invited around to Lisa's and Pietro handed her a pile of brochures advertising luxurious holidays. "I think this is more you when Jason drags you away from us again," he leered.

To Pietro's surprise, Jason suggested a visit to the pub a few days later. He selected a table in a quiet corner, and Pietro eyed him suspiciously. "What's up then? You never ask me out for a pint."

"Just needed a quiet chat. Can you ease up with the laughs when we're all together? It's getting to Lisa."

"You're telling me to back off? That's a sure sign something's going on. But as you've asked nicely, I'll behave. Promise."

Just then, the door was flung open, and in crowded at least a dozen giggling young women enjoying a hen party. "Yee-hah!" Pietro beamed at Jason. "There is a God, after all. What are you drinking?" Within seconds, he was ensconced at the bar, surrounded by a bevy of beauties.

Watching from the corner, Jason knew Pietro had forgotten him instantly and was amused when he eventually returned, looking shaken. "What's up with you? You look like you've seen a ghost."

Pietro slumped down next to him on the bench seat. "I've just met my wife."

"What?" Jason wasn't sure that he'd heard right. "You never told me that you're married!"

"I'm not." Pietro looked every bit as stunned as Jason felt. "But I'm going to be." Swiftly downing almost half of his pint in one go, Pietro explained that he'd been talking to some of the girls when another had turned around to join in the conversation, and the moment he'd looked into her eyes, he knew that he would marry her.

"Rubbish," Jason laughed. "You, of all people? I've told you before about watching too many films."

But to his astonishment, Pietro wasn't laughing. "There, the short one with the dark hair."

"But she's nothing more than a child!" Jason protested.

"Oh God, they're getting ready to move on. I need to get her number. Pen, pen!" Pietro snatched the biro Jason found in his pocket, grabbed a beer mat and headed back into the crowd of girls again, leaving Jason wondering if he was dreaming. He heard laughter, then cheering and then the girls had gone.

"Well? How did that go?" Jason presumed the cheering meant that he had somehow obtained her number. Pietro held the beer mat aloft like a hard-won trophy; one corner stripped back where he had written the number.

"I asked her! To marry me!"

"You did? No! Really? What did she say?" Unable to believe his ears, Jason studied his friend for signs he'd been drinking before they set out for the pub.

"She's going to think about it. Her friends are already looking forward to another do."

Melissa was introduced to 'the gang' a few weeks later. Aged 21, she was almost 15 years younger than Pietro. She lived locally with her widowed mother and younger brother, and it was clear to them from the start that Pietro was besotted with her.

He was bewitched; transformed overnight from a fun-loving bachelor who thoroughly enjoyed sowing wild oats in every direction possible and had no intention of ever settling down, into an attentive, adoring and completely infatuated boyfriend. "Incredible!" John was over the moon as they all left earlier than usual with the odd sensation they were intruding. "Pietro, in love! Who would ever have thought it!"

"I'm with you," Jason agreed, bemused by the sudden and dramatic change in his friend. He'd asked more than once what had made him so instantly certain that Melissa was 'the one'. "I mean, when you asked her to marry you, you didn't even know her name did you?"

Pietro laughed, obviously sublimely happy. "I can't explain it, not even to myself, but I just knew. It was like I recognised her. Thank God you suggested the pub that night!"

Within weeks a new bedroom suite arrived, and then new carpets, curtains and a sofa. In a short time, Pietro converted his bachelor pad into a cosy home for two, and Melissa had moved in by Christmas. As she toasted them with champagne, Lisa remembered the day Mark had swung her into his arms as though she weighed nothing and carried her, laughing, into his home. She'd been so happy then, but it had turned into a disaster she knew she would never truly get over; she could only hope for a better outcome for her friends.

The wedding was set for early June. John dabbed at his eyes with the hem of Phil's tee shirt as he read the invitation to the main reception Pietro had just handed him.

"You know the drill, for God's sake, wear something sensible," Pietro snapped at him, grinning, but John was already wearing the concentrated expression of someone deep in thought.

"We must have a party before the nuptials, Phil, a last blast for Pietro, the single man. I'm thinking Rocky Horror."

On a dry but cool Saturday evening in mid-May, as Amy was still strenuously attempting to tighten a bulging corset around a squealing Simon's hairy chest, Jason stepped into the outsized stilettos supplied by the fancy-dress shop and, teetering alarmingly, made his way to Lisa's. A convincing Frank N Furter with his black curly wig, heavy makeup, basque, short skirt and stockings, he made the most of the opportunity for a bit of exhibitionism, to the delight of his neighbours already heading to the party in various guises.

Lisa watched him approach, alarmed by the sudden stab of attraction. *What on earth did that say about her?* He attempted a twirl, nearly breaking an ankle, before staggering in through her open front door. She gazed at him wordlessly, then reached out and twanged his suspender. He laughed as it snapped back resoundingly against his thigh. "Aren't I supposed to do that to you?"

"Some chance, I've never worn stockings in my life."

He followed her into the kitchen, where she turned, pinning him against the worktop as she slid both hands under his skirt and up over the lacy fabric of the black French knickers he'd borrowed from her and which she was amazed to discover he was wearing. She hooked her thumbs under the elastic and slowly slid them down over his narrow hips. They joined the party ten minutes later, their 'arrangement' well and truly resumed.

After a week of unseasonal wet and windy weather, the wedding took place on a beautiful, bright, sunny afternoon. The bride looked radiant in a froth of white tulle and lace, accentuated by the vibrant colours of the outfits worn by Pietro's female relatives over from Italy, carefully selected so that together they formed a near-perfect rainbow. Greeting his guests at the reception, Pietro stepped back to appraise John's attire; a pin-striped suit, shirt and tie, rounded off with black shoes, polished until they shone. "Jeez, you look smart!"

"Aww, thanks Pietro, big congrats." John cupped Pietro's startled face in his hands and kissed him on both cheeks before Phil could stop him.

In late September, the friends were shocked when Pietro replaced his cherished sports car with a family saloon. All became clear a few days later when he and Melissa revealed they were expecting a baby, due at the end of March.

Lisa was thrilled for them but beginning to take stock of her life. How could she be turning thirty in June; where had the time gone? And her life was so unlike what she'd envisaged; she'd expected to be married by now, maybe with children. Finding Mark and Jenni together had thrown her life off course forever.

The decision to remain single was hard; she wasn't lonely now but knew she would be, one day, a bleak prospect. Her mood didn't improve when, in January 2002, her mother began raising suggestions for a party to celebrate her impending birthday. "I'm thirty this year," she told Jason on a short but freezing ride, her voice unusually forlorn as they pounded through the icy mist that clung to them.

"Thirty? You're older than me then, I had wondered," Jason teased her. Pietro had tried repeatedly over the years to discover Lisa's age, but, as with anything else that she didn't choose to disclose, Jason had known better than to ask.

"Mum wants me to have a party."

"Well, that's nice of her. Isn't it?" He had a distinct impression that his responses were somehow totally unsuitable.

"No!" She replied vehemently. "I hate being the centre of attention. I don't want to celebrate it at all, to be honest.

Chapter Twenty

What's to celebrate, getting older?" Flummoxed by her unusually downbeat mood, Jason cast around his brain rapidly for something positive to say.

"Well, you should do something special. How about another cycling adventure? Prove to yourself age is just a number." *What? Where had that come from? Of course, she wouldn't want a cycling adventure!*

The few photos she'd passed around, at John's request, of her fortnight in a large villa in Florida with her family the previous summer had indeed confirmed Pietro's theory that she was more suited to luxury than adventure. But to his surprise, she smiled.

"That might be nice." Lisa had often thought about their trip to France; it had somehow changed her. Now, whenever she felt daunted, she remembered the day she'd ridden up a mountain surrounded by spectators. Nothing could ever be that hard; she could do anything if she believed it. Not thinking for one minute that Jason would ever want to share another adventure with her, she would never have suggested another trip, but she felt a sudden buzz of excitement at the prospect.

"What shall we do, then?" Jason glanced around at the dismal weather. "A tour, somewhere warm and sunny. Nothing too strenuous, no mountains, just nice rolling hills and beautiful countryside. Somewhere as different to this as you can imagine!" he grimaced.

"That sounds lovely," she mused, still smiling. "I can see it now, vineyards, cypress trees, old rustic farmhouses. Tuscany, here we come!"

Tuscany? How odd! Of all the places! As soon as he got home, Jason ran upstairs and began rummaging through his bedside table. In the bottom corner, he found what he was looking for, the little guidebook he'd found in the glove box of his mum and dad's camper van. He hadn't looked at it for years; how strange that Lisa had mentioned Tuscany.

The idea that had started as a flight of fancy on an icily cold day gradually gained strength, and by the end of February, Lisa was ready to tell her parents that she intended to be away for her birthday.

Feeling obliged to accompany her, Jason was having palpitations as Lisa drove. Without a doubt, they would blame him entirely for the developments, and he wouldn't put it past Joe to punch him. "You're going away? But Lisa? All the plans!" Kathleen was distraught as Joe sighed and went to put an arm around her shoulders.

"I'm so sorry, Mum, but I just can't cope with a party." Lisa hated disappointing her mother, and tears began to well in her eyes. Jason looked down at the floor, waiting for the onslaught that was surely coming.

"I have an idea," Joe spoke slowly, thinking aloud. "How about a joint party for our birthdays, Lisa? I could be the star attraction if you like. I'll be turning 70, and I've never had a party in my life, what do you think? We can do it when you get back."

Lisa threw her arms around his neck; two peas in a pod, they understood each other so well. He'd offered her a way out while still having the party her mother wanted so badly. "Perfect, Dad! I'd love that."

Watching the three of them embrace, Jason briefly remembered the plans for another joint party that didn't happen. *Please let this be different*. He smiled at Joe, grateful for his unexpected help in paving the way for the trip, but the look Joe flashed him in return told him the man had no more faith in him now than he'd had two years before.

They spent the next few months preparing for the trip, poring over the Rough Guide and a touring map of Tuscany, purchasing the necessary touring bikes and the panniers to carry their luggage. They decided only to book accommodation for the first and last night, so they could leave the bike bags at the hotel and go anywhere they pleased. There were so many beautiful places to visit Lisa tentatively suggested extending the trip to a fortnight.

"And exactly how are we going to explain both of us being away for two weeks at the same time to the others?" Jason asked her, frowning deeply as he recalled how the debacle following their previous trip had nearly ruined their friendship.

"I don't think they're interested, do you?" she replied, smiling. Chloe, Melissa and Pietro's daughter, had arrived two weeks early, and Lisa had invited everyone around in early April to celebrate. Cooing over the sleeping baby, John had almost collapsed when Pietro asked if he would be her godfather. "Me?" he spluttered, fanning himself furiously with his right hand.

"Yeah, you." Pietro grinned. "None of my other beer-swilling reprobate mates is up to the job, but you? Now I think you'd probably give your life for my little girl if you had to, am I right?"

Tears almost spurting from his eyes, John had hurtled out, completely overcome. "Shouldn't you go after him?" Jason asked Phil.

"Nah, he'll be back when he's calmed down. You've not just made his day, Pietro, you've made his life."

Since then, John had devoted himself to his new responsibility as much as the new parents. Amy and Simon would be in Paris where, unbeknown to her, he was going to propose. *They were all busy with their lives; why would they be interested in what she and Jason were doing?*

Jason was nervous about being away from home for two weeks, it was years since he'd been away that long, but he couldn't bring himself to disappoint her; it was her birthday celebration, after all, and he'd somehow suggested it. "Okay, let's do it!"

And so, they had set off for their adventure early that morning, 14th June 2002, full of anticipation and excitement. But it had all gone so terribly wrong. Now they were standing on the marble forecourt of the bus station in Bologna, incredibly hot, thirsty and tired, without a credit card or a solitary penny between them.

Part 2

Chapter Twenty-One

Afrim and Erjon had been hovering around the entrance to the bus station since lunchtime, watching for unsuspecting victims. Erjon's head still throbbed with the after-effects of his latest fix, but he knew that soon, his body would once more succumb to the familiar overwhelming cravings.

Respite on shady street corners was all too brief before they were moved on by the Carabinieri undertaking their regular patrols. He had no alternative but to maintain his vigil through the burning heat of the day, desperate to purloin sufficient means to purchase another fix before nightfall. Pickings had been slim, a small purse with a few coins here, a rolled-up 10 euro note there, a cheap camera that had looked like a bulging wallet in someone's trouser pocket and would make virtually nothing.

In desperation, he was about to suggest trying elsewhere when he spotted the couple struggling with their enormous bags on their shoulders and what looked like luggage in their hands. Now, this did look interesting.

Afrim was leaning against the wall, dozing, when Erjon tapped him on the shoulder, and the two young men watched and waited. The couple seemed unsure of what to do next. A large wet patch on the back of the man's tee shirt revealed he was sweating profusely, like everyone else. After a minute or two, the woman searched for something in her small shoulder bag and passed it to him.

He helped her to move the two bags and the luggage to the end of the concourse, well away from the main doors and then left. The woman sat down and leaned back against her luggage, facing the blazing sun, both hands secured across the shoulder bag. Afrim and Erjon glanced at each other, wordlessly agreeing on their target.

As a patrol car approached in the heavy traffic, the two men slipped further into the shadows of the small alleyway opposite the bus station. The last thing they needed now was the Carabinieri to move them on.

They resumed their vantage point when the car had passed, the officers oblivious to their presence. The man returned, looking excited and to their amazement, the couple began opening their bags and assembling their bikes. They continued to watch as the couple struggled in the heat, and the slightest breath of breeze dispersed their packaging. Erjon gasped as the woman removed the shoulder bag and placed it at the centre of the pile of luggage; experience told him they wouldn't get a better opportunity that day.

Glancing at Afrim, who immediately understood, the two men ran towards the couple, dodging the slow-moving traffic. Erjon hung back as Afrim jogged behind them and

Chapter Twenty-One

grabbed a plastic drinking bottle from one of the open bike bags.

Passing by the man, who was concentrating on inflating a tyre with a hand pump and looked like he might be about to pass out, Afrim reached the woman, bending over her bike and attempting to do something with the front wheel.

He called out to get her attention and began to dance in what he hoped was a comical fashion, pretending to drink from the bottle and flailing his arms around as though he was drunk. The stunt achieved the desired effect; she laughed at him, and the man looked across to see what amused her. At that precise moment, Afrim saw Erjon strike with the lightning speed of a cobra attacking its prey.

In the blink of an eye, he sprang forward, grabbed the shoulder bag and disappeared into the crowd. Afrim grinned, tossed the bottle back to the still-laughing woman and danced away along the crowded pavement. It had taken the experienced thieves less than 20 seconds to steal all of Lisa and Jason's most essential items for their trip.

The two friends met at the rear of the bus station and headed towards a park a couple of blocks away. Finding a quiet spot in a corner by a high hedge, Erjon quickly tipped the contents of the bag onto the grass. He was relieved to find a wad of notes in the wallet, a mixture of euros and sterling. There wasn't time to count it, but there appeared to be enough from his share to purchase the fix his body was already starting to demand.

He took the credit cards from the wallet and passed them to Afrim. The camera looked expensive and new; he could get something for it. He wasn't interested in the flight tickets, passports or the car key, which he scooped up quickly and thrust back into the bag before throwing it beneath the hedge. He stuffed the wallet and the camera in his pocket and then headed across the park nonchalantly as Afrim turned back towards the city's busy streets and the banks.

Jason's head was swimming. He stared at Lisa, transfixed by her open-mouthed, perplexed study of utter disbelief, a reflection of his own inner turmoil. *How could this be happening to them? Was it happening, or was he somehow caught up in a nightmare from which he would be forever grateful to awake?*

He ran towards a patrol car in the line of vehicles steadily moving past them. Lisa watched as he spoke to the officers through the open window, agitatedly gesticulating with both hands in an effort to explain what had happened before running back to her, the strain etched across his features. "They want me to go with them to try and spot the thieves. Will you be okay?"

"Of course." Lisa was surprised by the sound of her voice, calm and steady, trotting out the well-used phrase. She hadn't understood the question; her brain hadn't yet caught up with the sudden turn of events, but her mouth had somehow emitted a response. As if in slow motion, she watched Jason run to the car, jump in the back, and then he was gone.

Jason looked frantically to his left and right as the car moved slowly forward in the traffic jam, even though he was sure the thieves, there had to be at least two of them, would be long gone.

He desperately wanted the officers to put on the siren, cut a swathe through the traffic and find the culprits. But as the car plodded along, they seemed relaxed, chatting in Italian so that Jason couldn't tell if they were even talking about the

Chapter Twenty-One

theft. For some reason, he suspected they weren't; they would have seen it all before, probably several times that day already. They were going through the motions, following procedure.

Having never suffered travel sickness in his life, Jason suddenly felt the need to get out of the car as quickly as possible before he threw up. Ten minutes later, having merely accomplished a circuit of the bus station, the patrol car pulled up again. Lisa was standing exactly where Jason had left her. "They want one of us to go to the station to make out a report, can you do it?" He felt ashamed to ask; it was his duty to take charge and look after her, but he couldn't bear one more second in the stifling heat of the car.

"Yes, I'll do it," Lisa replied. "Are you okay?" Jason didn't answer as she hurried to the car, where the officers were beginning to fidget. As the car pulled away, in broken English, one of them asked her to look out for the thieves. Her eyes scanned the young men with jet-black hair dressed in what was almost a uniform of black leather jackets and jeans, but none of them bore a resemblance to the good-looking, smiling man she had laughed with such a short time ago.

She would recognise him instantly if she saw him again and, with a shudder, realised how perilously close she was to hating someone for the first time in her life. The officers did another circuit of the bus station before heading to the police station located by the railway. By the time they arrived, more than 30 minutes had passed since Lisa had left Jason, and she was anxious to get back to him.

Waiting alone in the small reception area where the police officers had deposited her, Lisa's eyes slowly became accustomed to the gloom of the windowless compartment, lit by a single lightbulb dangling from the end of a dusty cord.

Several minutes passed before a different officer appeared and led her to a seat at a large wooden desk in an office with small windows, only marginally lighter than the reception. Lisa's blank stare told him she could not understand Italian, so he tried again. "Thief?" She nodded, and he disappeared. Fighting back the tears, Lisa glanced at her watch and then around at her surroundings, trying to distract herself from her appalling predicament. It was almost an hour since she'd left Jason; he would be wondering what was happening.

She'd taken to counting the resounding clicks emitted by the keys of an ancient typewriter as an officer painfully tapped out his report using only his forefingers, promising herself she would get to one hundred before beginning to scream when the officer dealing with her finally reappeared with a piece of paper and a chewed biro.

The black print of the questions on the form swam before her eyes as she saw only incomprehensible words written in Italian, and her racing heartbeat climbed a little higher. Suddenly, the acrid smell of stale cigarette smoke combined with the body odour of the officer standing close by and the musty smell of paper files long since closed and archived threatened to choke her.

She sat back, trying to regulate her breathing. *A panic attack*; the police officer had seen it all countless times before. He stepped forwards and traced his finger beneath the heavy type of the first question to show her the English translation in italics below. As she bowed her head to

Chapter Twenty-One

concentrate and began writing her name in the first box, he left to get her some water. It seemed to Lisa that it took hours to complete the double-sided form as she struggled to answer even the simplest of questions in the surreal world in which she had suddenly found herself.

Exhausted by the end, she waited, chewing at her nails fretfully as the police officer checked her answers, fully expecting to be asked to do it again. Relief swept through her as he nodded and walked away again, this time to the photocopier in the corner, an incongruous misfit in the otherwise antique office. He handed her a copy of the report and indicated she could leave.

Lisa had been sitting at the wooden desk with the shiny black telephone for over an hour. The impulse to lift the receiver from the cradle, dial her parents' telephone number and hear the calm reassurance of their voices was overwhelming. "Can I call home, please?" she asked in a small, almost childlike voice, pointing at the telephone. The officer shook his head emphatically. Stunned, Lisa tried again. "Well, can I call the insurance company?"

"Visa only, free call." As Lisa began to lose control of her breathing again, the officer passed her a card detailing the free phone number for Visa in America that she could use to cancel the credit cards.

She hesitated momentarily. "No?" the officer enquired as he reached out to retract the card. Hastily grabbing it, Lisa lifted the receiver, her hand shaking as she pressed it to her ear and began to dial. After a long pause, she could hear the phone ringing. If only miracles could happen, and she could hear her mother's voice, but instead, a man answered in a sing-song tone.

"Good morning. How can I help you?" Lisa stammered her way through a brief explanation of what had happened.

"What an awful start to your trip." The man sounded genuinely sorry for her. "The department is in a meeting just now; can you call back in half an hour?"

Replacing the receiver, Lisa remembered the hotel confirmation folded in her skirt pocket. She took it out and copied the free phone number onto the back before the officer led her back to the reception area. Looking around the tiny, dimly lit space once more, it took all of her determination not to slump into a corner and burst into tears, but it was almost two hours since she'd left Jason, and she had to get back to him.

The evening sunlight momentarily blinded her as she opened the door. Quickly donning the sunglasses she'd been clutching like a comfort blanket, she looked left and right, unsure which way to walk. To her left, she could see the entrance to what must be the railway station, with throngs of people scurrying in every direction.

"Bus?" she asked a young woman, who pointed along the road. Lisa half ran to the next junction before checking with another passerby. She hurried along for a few more minutes, and then there was the entrance to the bus station; Jason was sitting on the concourse in the sunlight, holding his head in his hands. She called out his name as she reached him, and he slowly looked up.

"Where have you been?" he whimpered, barely able to speak. Lisa gasped when she saw his reddened face and cracked, white-tinged lips. After two hours in the intense heat reflected from the marble all around him and with no water, Jason was severely dehydrated. When he complained

Chapter Twenty-One

of nausea and exhaustion, she suspected he might also have heatstroke.

"Let's try to get to the hotel." She urged him to try to stand, holding him as he swayed precariously and sat down heavily again several times before he could finally stay on his feet.

Thankfully, Jason had busied himself completing the bike assembly before succumbing to the heat; the panniers were on, the bags folded and laid over the cross bars ready to go. They made slow progress to the hotel. Jason could recall the directions, but he barely had the strength to walk; wheeling his bike was almost impossible. He could manage only a few slow steps before resting for a moment, leaning against Lisa for support. Eventually, they reached the hotel and turned down the small alleyway into the car park.

Rosa was sitting at the reception desk, carefully inspecting her radiant reflection. Thank goodness her shift was almost over; as usual on Friday evenings, her boyfriend was collecting her from the hotel, and they were going straight out to eat, then onto a club.

She glanced up as the two people lurching across the car park with their bikes caught her eye through the glass doors. Oh no, this was all she needed. The guy was struggling to walk, presumably drunk, and the woman weaving along beside him, trying to hold him up, didn't look much better.

Watching as the woman leaned her bike against the wall before taking the man's bike and leaning it against hers, catching him just before he fell, Rosa sighed. She steeled herself for the inevitable as the woman guided the man to the steps leading to the ornate hotel entrance, sat him down, and the doors opened with a swish as she approached. Reluctantly, Rosa stood to greet her. "Buonasera."

"Do you speak English?" Lisa felt rude for failing to respond to the girl's greeting, but she needed to get help for Jason as quickly as possible.

"A little," Rosa replied.

"We have a reservation in the name of Kilbride." Tapping rapidly on the computer keyboard, Rosa frowned. She passed a small piece of paper to Lisa with a pen.

"Write the name, please." Lisa swiftly printed Jason's surname in large, unmistakable capitals on the small square and thrust it back, agitatedly hopping from foot to foot.

Rosa gazed at the screen again for several moments. "I'm sorry, no booking."

Chapter Twenty-Two

A burst of adrenalin struck Lisa like an electric shock. *No booking? Now what were they going to do?* Her head spinning, she suddenly remembered the slip of paper in her pocket. *Thank goodness she'd put it there and not back in the bag!*

"But I have this?" She passed the paper to Rosa, who unfolded it and, still frowning, studied it and then returned to the computer screen. Lisa glanced at Jason, slumped on the steps, his head again in his hands. "Could I have some water, please?" She pointed to the bottles neatly lined up like soldiers on the shelf behind the reception desk.

"One euro," Rosa held out her hand.

"I don't have any money," Lisa replied. As Rosa looked at her in bewilderment, she snatched the watch from her wrist and offered it to her. "Here, have this until I can get some money, I need the water, quickly, please." She pointed to Jason.

Alarmed, Rosa refused the watch but handed the water over. Lisa ran outside to Jason and urged him to drink as much as possible. Returning to Rosa, she was overwhelmed with relief when the girl smiled and confirmed she'd found the booking. "Passports, please." Rosa held out her hand expectantly again.

"I don't have the passports, they've been stolen." The words tumbled out in a torrent as Lisa hurriedly recounted the earlier events, and when Rosa couldn't understand, she passed her the copy of the police report. Reading the form swiftly, the girl gasped.

"Thief?" Lisa nodded. "Oh dear, oh dear. Not Italian?"

"I don't think so," Lisa reassured her, and it was Rosa's turn to look relieved as she quickly checked them in using the police report as identification.

"Keep it safe, it's your passport now until you get a new one." She urged, returning the document to Lisa, together with a room key. "Take him up, I'll watch everything here," she gestured to the bikes and panniers outside.

Wrapping her arm around him to support him, Lisa got Jason into the lift and then the short distance along the corridor to their second-floor room. Not even noticing the view from the window, she quickly closed the curtains and set the air conditioning as high as possible.

Jason fell onto the bed and closed his eyes. He heard the door close softly when Lisa slipped out and groaned out loud, grabbing the chance to release the pent-up tension inside. Devastated by the turn of events, after Lisa had left in the police car, he'd relentlessly scanned the endless sea of passing strangers, desperately searching for the heartless thieves who had ruined their trip within minutes.

Chapter Twenty-Two

But in the incinerating heat on the marble concourse, he'd soon started to feel ill, so he'd turned his attention back to assembling the bikes to distract himself. His head began to throb; he felt dizzy and had to sit down. Already incredibly thirsty, he'd been sick twice in the bushes by the corner of the concourse. Afterwards, he knew he was dehydrating rapidly; his tongue felt swollen and was sticking to the roof of his mouth, and his skin felt like sandpaper.

Still Lisa hadn't returned; he was beginning to wonder if she ever would when, to his immense relief, he heard her voice by his side. Now all he wanted was to get home as soon as possible, back to where he belonged; the safety of his bedroom and his parents.

Lisa returned to reception, but Rosa wasn't there. She found her outside with the bikes, trying to remove the panniers but unable to work out how to release the clips, her glossy black hair, so carefully arranged, falling across her face and her manicured nails in imminent danger of chipping.

"Please, let me do that." Lisa removed the panniers, but Rosa insisted on helping her wheel the bikes into the garage before carrying the luggage inside.

Waiting for the lift, Lisa suddenly remembered she needed to call Visa again. "It's a free call," she explained to Rosa, showing her the number. "No cost."

"Please, please." Rosa placed the phone on the counter so Lisa could make the call.

"How terrible for you, honey. Let me take the details. I'm Margot." The American woman at the end of the phone announced. Fighting to make her brain work, Lisa supplied all the necessary information to cancel the credit cards.

During the lengthy pauses between questions, she could hear gentle tapping, like morse code, as Margot input her answers. "Good. Now what about emergency cash, how much do you need?"

"Emergency cash?" Lisa repeated, dreamlike.

"Yes, to be able to continue your vacation. You have no money at all, am I right?"

"Yes," Lisa confirmed. "How much might we be able to get?"

"Well, you're both with the same bank and if you're good customers, they might give you enough to continue. Work some figures out and call me back asap honey, the name's Margot. I already told you that, sorry. Call me."

As Lisa replaced the receiver, Rosa passed her two litre-bottles of water. "What will you eat?" she enquired, concerned.

"I don't think we can, we have no money." Lisa reminded her. Rosa led her into the cool air-conditioned dining room to a laden table covered with a large tablecloth.

"Breakfast for tomorrow." She lifted the tablecloth to reveal baskets of bread rolls and small pots of honey and jam, covered plates of ham and cheese and jugs of fruit juice. "It's all we have, but please, eat."

Lisa was touched by the girl's kindness. "Thank you so much." Jason was showering when she returned to the room but, in an effort to raise his spirits, she quickly told him about the food they'd been offered and suggested she could bring some up.

"I'll go down with you," Jason replied weakly. "Could you pass my toilet bag? I'm desperate to clean my teeth."

Chapter Twenty-Two

They'd each brought a nylon drawstring bag containing only minuscule amounts of toiletries to keep the weight of their luggage to the absolute minimum. Lisa opened the main compartment of one of Jason's panniers, extracted the contents and piled them neatly on the end of the bed until she found what she was looking for and passed it to him.

While waiting for her turn to shower, she opened the little guidebook she'd discovered during the search and read the inscription - *Someday x*. Intrigued, she wondered who had written it and who the message was intended for, but quickly returned Jason's belongings to his panniers, not wanting him to know that she'd seen it. *The book had some special significance; otherwise, he would have told her about it. And so did this trip.*

On the way to the dining room, they felt a blast of warm air as a tall, handsome young man, elegant and unflustered by the heat, strolled in and kissed Rosa on both cheeks. She gushed something in Italian and headed over to Lisa and Jason. "Cappuccino, Latte, Expresso?"

"No, no, please go. You've been so kind already." Lisa gently refused her offer, but her boyfriend joined them, extending his hand to shake Jason's.

"I'm sorry to hear what has happened, sorry on behalf of Italy. I will help Rosa."

The young couple insisted on delaying the start of their evening to make coffee before they left, and over the small meal they were able to eat, Lisa told Jason of the phone call with Visa.

"I just want to get on the next plane out of here and go home," he told her. "Continuing with the holiday is the last thing I want to do."

"But without plane tickets or passports, we can't do that." She saw a look of despair settle on his face and immediately regretted her words. In addition to their awful situation, he was ill; she wouldn't burden him anymore with it tonight.

Still feeling weak and nauseous, Jason undressed and got into bed. The sound of laughter drifting up from the street below as groups of friends walked by, looking forward to a Friday evening out in the city, jarred his ears, and he remembered another time when happy sounds had grated on his nerves. It was as he was leaving the hospital with his grandparents, astonished that the world around him was exactly as before despite the cataclysmic event in his own life. He'd never dreamt that he would experience that feeling again.

To Lisa's surprise, minutes later, Jason was snoring. She doubted that she would get any sleep that night, she had a banging headache, and every muscle was as taut as a spring. *What had the woman said about emergency cash? Come back with a figure that might be enough to complete the holiday.*

But Jason wanted to go home. The problem was, how could she begin to calculate how much they might need to make that possible when she had no idea of the price of anything other than the cost of bed and breakfast at the hotel where they were staying?

Overwhelmed, she could feel the sting of tears welling again but pulled herself together sharply. *Make a start!*, she told herself, grabbing the pad and pen from the bedside table and locking herself in the bathroom where she could put the light on without disturbing Jason.

The hotel where they were staying had been a treat, more expensive than other places they intended to stay, so she multiplied the cost of the hotel by 14, then added on 30 euros per day each for food, which was hopefully excessive, and another 500 euros for miscellaneous expenses, including rebooking flights and purchasing passports. Doing a rough conversion into sterling, she calculated a total of £2,500. *Surely the bank would never agree to that?*

Lisa realised she'd worked out how much money they might need to be able to continue the holiday, but Jason didn't want that. They could probably manage to get home with a fraction of that amount, but she was sure the little guidebook held a secret, and if he didn't make the trip, Jason might one day regret it.

Deciding to request the full amount first in case, by some miracle, the bank approved it; her backup plan was to halve the amount and hope it was enough to get them home. *And if it wasn't?* She quickly pushed the thought from her mind, a potential problem for another day.

The Night Manager was aware of the situation and placed the phone on the counter for her. He watched her, his expressive face full of concern, as she dialled the lengthy long-distance number and then waited for what seemed like forever until she got through to Margot again, who didn't seem to be in the least bit fazed when she asked for the equivalent of £2,500 in euros. "I'll contact the bank. Can you call me about 4.30 pm my time, honey?" she crooned. "That's 1.30 am in Italy. Have a nice..... What am I saying? Try to get some sleep."

Lisa set her alarm and lay down, fully clothed. It was the first time she and Jason had ever shared a bed, there'd been no twin rooms left when they booked, but she had never felt more alone as she lay by his side in the darkness.

How could this have happened? How could they be in a foreign country without a penny between them and no means of contacting anyone to get help other than Visa? She knew nothing of the procedure for getting back home, and even when they did, there were still more problems to be faced; driving back from Stansted without the car key wouldn't be easy.

As the thoughts swarmed around her head like bees around a honey pot, her breathing became shallow, her body tensed until she was rigid with panic, and she thought she might cry out. She'd turned off the rattling air conditioning to avoid disturbing Jason, and in the stifling heat, she could feel rivulets of sweat trickling across her skin. Fighting to regain self-control, she desperately tried to think rationally. *Problem-solving, she could do that. What was the main problem here? What did she need to sort out first?* As her thoughts began to overwhelm her again, the voice in her head shrieked, WORK IT OUT!

The answer came to her when she stood beneath the cool soothing water of the shower. *Money, that was it. With some cash, they could begin sorting everything out, one step at a time. Forget everything else; concentrate on getting money.* Forcing all other thoughts from her mind, Lisa watched the luminous lime green hands on the clock face slowly inch around to 1.20 am, then she crept out of the room and down to reception, pleased that Jason had never stirred.

But he heard the door softly close behind her for the second time. Feelings of guilt coursed through him for leaving her to shoulder the burden of trying to dig them out of this appalling mess alone. He'd steered a course through life's difficulties by thinking of others and putting them first, but he couldn't do that this time. The callous thieves had

Chapter Twenty-Two

broken him; he desperately wanted to look after her, to make everything right, but he couldn't even lift his head from the pillow.

His thoughts turned to the thieves. He'd always tried to follow the example his grandfathers had so admirably set at the inquest when they'd shaken the hand of the Spanish driver. But that was different; that man had made a mistake. These men hadn't; they'd deliberately targeted them, and for the first time in his life, Jason tasted the bitterness of hate. He couldn't wait to get home.

The Night Manager smiled as he placed the phone on the counter, and Lisa dialled the number she almost knew by heart.

"The bank has approved the request, honey, no prob," Margot trilled, to Lisa's utter amazement. "Be at Great Western Union Bank, opposite the Town Hall, at 10.30 am. They'll give you the money in three batches, jot down these numbers."

Carefully writing down the eight-digit codes, one for each of the batches, Lisa checked several times that she had noted them down correctly. "Now, identification," continued Margot, warming to her task. "Tell me precisely what you'll be wearing. Sounds swell, honey and a list of identifying marks, moles, that kind of thing? Oohh, maybe wear shorts if you're going to show that one! Shall we change the clothing details? Good, we're all done here, have a great vacation, honey."

Overwhelmed at the prospect of having money within hours, Lisa ran up the stairs back to the room and crept in. As she laid back down, Jason mumbled sleepily, "Okay?"

"Yes, go to sleep." He suddenly wanted to hold her but thought better of it; she would never forgive him.

Lisa felt as exhilarated as if she'd just climbed to the top of the Tourmalet again. In the intervening two years, she'd often used the analogy of cycling up a mountain to help her deal with difficult situations; *don't think about it, ride to the next bend, then the next and eventually, you'll be at the top.* That was all she needed to do now, take one step at a time; soon, they would have money, and then she could concentrate on the next issue and then the next. Exhausted, she fell into a deep sleep.

The following morning Jason was determined to accompany Lisa to the bank. After a light breakfast, they found their way to the Town Hall, located in a large square. They paced up and down several times, looking for the bank, before Jason spotted a small yellow sign displaying the words Great Western Union by the entrance to a large building.

They entered a dimly lit lobby and, in one corner, found another only slightly larger yellow sign. Behind a cracked Perspex partition sat two bespectacled middle-aged ladies, each with a queue of at least ten people and both already looking hot and flustered.

Still not well enough to stand in the queue, Jason found a wall to lean against as Lisa joined the end of one of the lines. Slowly making her way forwards, she eventually reached the partition 30 minutes late, but there was nothing she could do about that.

She pushed the paper on which she'd written the three codes beneath the partition and tried to explain matters to the cashier, who leaned forwards to place her ear next to the

Chapter Twenty-Two

tiny holes in the Perspex and asked Lisa to speak slower. Tapping away on her keyboard for several moments, the cashier then pushed the paper back, shaking her head and motioned to Lisa to move away. "What's wrong?" Lisa asked.

"The codes, I don't have these." The cashier replied and motioned her away again.

"Just a minute." Lisa stood her ground. "Please check with Visa, I've been careful to ensure the codes are correct." She returned the paper to the cashier.

The woman sighed, mopped her brow with an already damp hankie and then picked up the telephone. Lisa couldn't hear what she said, and the queue of people behind her was becoming agitated, muttering and pressing forward. After a few minutes, the woman put the phone down. "No good." She pushed the paper back again. Jason had moved to where Lisa could see him. With misery etched across his handsome features, he signalled to her to move away from the window. Lisa looked at him, bit her lip and then turned to face the lengthy queues behind her.

"Excuse me!" The agitated jostling continued. "Excuse me!" she called out again, a little louder this time. "I'm sorry that I'm holding you all up, but we've had our money stolen, we have nothing. I'll be as quick as possible but I must sort this out. Please be patient."

Turning back to the cashier, she pointed to the phone. "Please, ring Visa again and pass me the phone so I can speak to them." With a deep sigh, the woman did as she was asked, forcing the handset beneath the Perspex whilst someone in the queue who had understood relayed the message in hushed tones to everyone else. The lines edged back, and one elderly lady squeezed Lisa's arm before tapping her own chest, offering her sympathy.

Several minutes later, Lisa's persistence was rewarded with success. The cashier checked her identifying marks, counted out the three batches of euros and then asked her colleague to check them whilst both queues waited patiently. Everyone smiled when she turned to thank them for their patience, clutching the thick wad of notes in her hand.

The sensations tumbling through Lisa as she held the bank notes were like nothing she had ever experienced. Relief flowed in like a rip tide, but there was so much more; she felt triumphant. Her surroundings suddenly seemed brighter, people seemed friendlier, and the day held so many more prospects; she was ecstatic.

"Blimey, how much did you get?" Jason was astounded. "We'd better put it away quickly." Lisa passed him half of the money, a look of pure exhilaration on her face.

"There, how does that feel? We have money, I can hardly believe it!" They quickly divided the notes into small batches, secreting them in various pockets before walking back out into the sunshine.

"You were magnificent," Jason told her. "The way you spoke to those people. Everyone listened to you, even if most of them couldn't understand a word you said. That's all you need to do for your presentation."

She grinned. "I remembered what you told me yesterday. You have to want to do it, and I've never wanted anything so much in my life before."

Yesterday! Was it really less than 24 hours since their conversation on the coach? It felt like a lifetime ago.

Chapter Twenty-Two

"Come on, let's get back and check out. We need to find somewhere less salubrious for tonight." The Hotel Manager knew of the previous day's events and personally handled the checkout before stowing their panniers behind reception and insisting they have lunch.

Whilst they did so, he carefully annotated a street map with the location of the Tourist Information Office and a route to get there, avoiding the bus station. "Your things will be safe here while you find somewhere else to stay," he assured them, handing them the street map.

"Shall we try to find the main police station in case the bag has been handed in?" Jason asked as they hurried back into the centre of the bustling city.

Lisa thought it was doubtful they could be that lucky, but she didn't want to be negative; Jason seemed to be feeling a little better, and it was the first thing he'd suggested.

"Yes, if you like."

There was a queue at the Tourist Information Office, and when they eventually left, clutching the details of several lower-priced hotels, Lisa would have preferred to set off in pursuit of alternative accommodation immediately. But Jason had asked the helpful staff to mark the map with the location of the main police station.

"Can we just try there? In case the bag has been handed in," Jason persisted. Lisa glanced at her watch, concerned, but she nodded.

One and a half hours later, seated in a windowless office with a police officer who spoke no English, Jason wondered if it had been a good idea. Despite the police report, it had been a laborious process for them to go through the details of the theft again. The officer had made several lengthy phone calls to obtain advice about applying for temporary passports in Rome and eventually put them on the phone with the American Consulate.

"You're English?" The advisor asked, sounding surprised and at his request, Jason passed the receiver back to the police officer. Following a short exchange, he'd replaced the receiver and then, looking alarmingly close to tears himself, began the process again and eventually put them through to the British Consulate.

With their heads almost touching, Lisa and Jason listened intently to the clipped tones of the government official as he explained in minute detail the procedure to obtain temporary passports. Jason was grateful to the officer for his assistance but overwhelmed at the prospect of making their way to Rome and the process to be endured. He needed fresh air quickly and, like Lisa, was becoming agitated about finding somewhere to stay for the night. Shaking hands with the relieved officer and thanking him, he turned to leave as a head, topped with a thatch of light brown hair rather than the customary jet black, appeared around the door.

"Is that an English voice I hear? I've just come on duty, we've got a tele in the back so we can watch the World Cup. You might be pleased to know England has just scored against Denmark."

After struggling for what seemed like forever to make himself understood, Jason was stunned. "I don't believe it, you speak English!"

"Yes. Mum's from Guildford, I have relatives there."

Quickly, Jason explained what had happened. "I've been trying to ask your colleague if the bag has been handed in, but I can't make him understand, and unfortunately, we don't speak Italian." He grimaced apologetically.

Following a rapid discussion with his colleague, the English-speaking officer walked around to the tall metal filing cabinet at the side of Lisa's chair. "He says only one bag was handed in yesterday." The door screeched on the hinges like fingernails on a blackboard, but there, alone on the middle shelf of the otherwise empty cabinet, was the handlebar bag.

"You're kidding me! No, it can't be. It is. It's ours!" Jason couldn't believe his eyes. The officer passed the bag to his colleague, who removed the contents; two passports and a car key. Checking the names on the passports with the documents he had completed, he confirmed they matched and handed the bag to an ecstatic Jason.

Relief swept through Lisa for the second time in just a few hours as they strolled out into the sunshine. *They had their passports!* There was no need to go to Rome or follow the intricate process at the embassy; they were free to do whatever they wanted, go home or continue with the trip.

"Can you cartwheel?" she asked Jason, grinning broadly.

"No, but I might try anyway." He replied, smiling for the first time in almost 24 hours.

Chapter Twenty-Three

Under cover of darkness, Afrim slipped back into the park and hurried to where Erjon had thrown the bag beneath the hedge a few hours earlier. His heart was beating fast; he was taking an enormous risk but couldn't get the woman with the mass of curly hair out of his mind.

He dropped to his knees and swept his arm beneath the hedge, feeling for the bag; it had to be here somewhere. He was sweating, his breath coming in short gasps. If he were caught, either by the police or, worse still, by Erjon's friends, his life wouldn't be worth living.

Swiftly moving along the hedge, at last, his outstretched fingers felt the canvas bag. He grabbed it and pushed it inside his jacket, trapping it beneath his armpit as he scrambled to his feet. Then he headed across the park to the short stone staircase by the road and the most dangerous part of his plan.

Day and night, drug addicts favoured this place for a quick fix, discarding their syringes into the grimy corners of the staircase rather than into the grass in the park where young children played. It never ceased to amaze Afrim that, even as people's lives were falling apart, somewhere deep inside, there was still a sense of honour, a line they wouldn't cross.

Throughout the day and late into the night, the Carabinieri regularly drove by this spot, attempting to apprehend the addicts. If he left the bag on the steps, there was a chance that the police would find it, but the area was well-lit.

He had left his friend virtually unconscious after his latest fix, but Erjon had connections everywhere. If anyone saw him leave the bag and told Erjon....... he didn't dare to think about what would happen then.

Huddled in the shadows of the trees and bushes, he watched the two young men sprawled on the steps, laughing together and gradually becoming more subdued and supine as the drugs took effect. Renewed panic pulsated through him. *How long had he been here? If he didn't return soon, he would be missed, and how would he explain his absence?*

It would be easy to dispose of the bag and head back, but the memory of the woman persisted.

Afrim had grown up with his parents and two older brothers in Vlore, one of the more developed cities in southern Albania. By 1997, when Afrim was 15 years old, civil unrest was accelerating in response to the failure of a series of pyramid schemes blamed on President Berisha, and there was a threat of civil war.

Chapter Twenty-Three

The rebellion was concentrated in the south, and although the protests were initially peaceful, the rebels eventually took up arms, leaving more than 2,000 dead.

Afrim's older brothers were both injured in the fighting, and fearing for their young son, his parents had persuaded him to board a vastly overloaded ship bound for Italy, only 74 kilometres away across the Strait of Odessa.

On board, he met Erjon, a few years older and determined to make a good life for himself in Italy. But that hadn't happened. Submerged in the crowd that spewed out from the ship, overwhelming the Border Control, they had been grateful to enter the country with neither a visa nor work permit, the requirements for which might well have seen them deported straight back to Albania.

The repercussions had been severe. They had moved around the larger cities for a few years, attempting to find work, but that had been virtually impossible without the necessary visas. Their income had been minimal, their prospects non-existent, and they had resorted to occasional petty crime to eke out an existence.

The situation worsened when Erjon, disillusioned with life at the age of only 20, turned to drugs to drown out the hardships he endured. Afrim had fought hard to avoid becoming an addict himself. He occasionally dabbled when life became too much for him, but he had resisted the heroin that he could see was slowly destroying his friend. Erjon was such a different man now. Gone forever was the laughing, carefree young man who had boarded the ship with so much hope in his eyes.

Driven by the addiction that would send his body into convulsions if he failed to get a fix in time, he had become brutal and ruthless. Work had long since ceased to provide the money required to fund Erjon's habit, and for some time, the two friends had spent their days stealing as much as possible.

Afrim no longer thought about the consequences for their victims; he'd become immune to them. In a world of endless struggle and disappointment, stealing was just something else he had to do out of loyalty to Erjon and to survive.

But then there was the woman. He'd heard her gentle laughter spill across the street as she chased the fluttering bubble wrap, but it was when he was absurdly dancing in front of her, with her full attention, that the sound had suddenly pulled at his heartstrings.

He remembered another young woman looking up at him from where she knelt cleaning the floor, pushing her hair back from her face just as this woman had done, giggling at his antics as a small boy. His mother.

How he wished he could feel her arms around him and see her smiling face. With a sense of horror, he'd watched as Erjon swooped down to pick up the bag, knowing that in that very moment this laughing woman was being swept into misery, and he was partly to blame for that.

In that split second, he had wanted to call out a warning to her, but of course, he couldn't. Erjon would probably have killed him in his ensuing desperation if he had. But it had preyed on his mind for the rest of the evening.

What would his parents think of him if they knew how he was living? They had fought to get him on the ship, to give him a new life, a chance; he was a disgrace to his family, and they would be so ashamed of him now.

Chapter Twenty-Three

Swept into a maelstrom of memories, hopes and dreams, he thought his heart would break. So now, here he was, trying for the first time in a very long time to do something good, something to be proud of for once. But he was scared witless.

Suddenly, the headlights of a slow-moving patrol car lit up the two addicts. Squinting in the bright light, the men hazily realised what was happening and attempted to stand. One was barely upright when he collapsed back onto the steps and was promptly handcuffed and shoved into the back of the car.

The other managed to half-run, haphazardly zigzagging from side to side, before being thrown face down on the grass by the second officer. He, too, was handcuffed and led to the car, which moved off slowly a few minutes later. Now was his best chance. If anyone else were around, they would have moved out of sight. Afrim ran forwards, out of the shadows, down the steps and across the road. As he did so, he unzipped his jacket, raised his arm and dropped the bag onto the steps.

When Erjon eventually arose, groggily, the following day, they walked together to the park and headed straight for the staircase where his cohorts were most likely to be found in varying degrees of consciousness.

Doing his best to look nonchalant, Afrim spotted a scuffed piece of folded white paper lying in the corner of one of the steps.

Edging closer, he could make out the Ryanair emblem beneath a grubby footprint. *A flight ticket. Had it come from the bag, of which there was no sign? Had the police found it?* He could only hope so. Later, following a successful afternoon's work, the two young men returned to the park, as usual, to rapidly check through their haul and dispose of anything of no value.

As they ran up the staircase, Afrim noticed that the piece of white paper had gone and felt an unfamiliar rush of elation. The ticket would surely be useless to anyone but the owner.

Watching Erjon feverishly going through a woman's purse, discarding a passport-sized photograph of a smiling toddler, Afrim knew with utter certainty that the friendship that had sustained him through the long, hard years since his parents had pushed him onto that overcrowded ship was at an end.

With a heavy heart, he waved as a grinning Erjon ran off to meet his supplier, knowing he would never see his friend again. His plan was already forming as he headed back to the squalid apartment to collect his meagre possessions. He would board the first busy commuter train heading for another large city, undetected amongst the masses.

Once there, he would make a new start, report to the appropriate authorities, and attempt to gain asylum and a work permit. If his application failed, he would be deported; but could that be any worse than the life he was living?

Less than two hours before, Jason had turned to shake the hand of the two police officers and casually asked: "You don't happen to know where the bag was found, do you?"

The precise location had been recorded; the side entrance to the park. Urged on by their sudden turn of fortune, Jason and Lisa quickly found the park. "That must be it, where the steps are." Lisa spotted the stone staircase across the road and darted between the traffic before Jason had time to react.

Chapter Twenty-Three

By the time he reached her, she had searched every step, picking her way carefully between the pools of urine and vomit, syringes and makeshift tourniquets. Descending the steps with a small twig in her hand, she called out. "I can't see anything other than this bit of paper. I'm just going to have a look."

"Lisa! Please, wait a minute, let me do that." Jason had never stood in such a hideous place and was bewildered that their possessions had ended up there. Ignoring him, Lisa bent and fought to stop herself from retching due to the evil stench emanating from the corner as she prodded the paper with the twig and carefully dragged it closer.

"Don't touch it!" Jason yelled, but Lisa saw the Ryanair emblem emblazoned on the page. Carefully lifting it from the step and thrilled that, other than a grubby footprint, it appeared to be uncontaminated, she unfolded it and found a second sheet of paper inside.

Disbelief was rapidly eclipsed by euphoria as she turned to Jason, holding the pages aloft and beaming. "Our flight tickets!"

For a split-second, Jason remembered Lisa returning home from work a few weeks before, just as he set off to meet Craig at a time trial. She'd looked immaculate as always; her cream-coloured shift dress set off her blossoming tan, and the red shoes and handbag matched her lipstick perfectly.

He didn't want to think about what people did to themselves and each other in this filthy den of iniquity; she didn't belong here and yet had entered this tragic world without complaint. As she smiled at him triumphantly, she had never looked more beautiful.

Back at the hotel, Rosa couldn't keep up with Lisa's outpouring of excited English, so Jason showed her the handlebar bag and the contents. "My friends!" With tears in her eyes, Rosa ran around from behind the reception desk and warmly hugged and kissed them both.

She waved as they cycled out of the little courtyard half an hour later, the unwieldy bike bags securely stored in the garage until their return. What a lovely couple, she hoped they would now have a wonderful holiday in her country.

"So, what do you want to do?" Lisa had asked as they were getting ready to leave the hotel, knowing Jason had been desperate to return home as soon as possible. "Shall we find a hotel in town tonight and try to get flights back tomorrow?"

"Do you want to go home?" Jason asked. She thought about it, but only for a moment. They had put so much effort into planning the route and had looked forward to this adventure for months.

"No," she replied, "but I will if that's what you need to do."

After considering the recommendations they'd collected from the Tourist Information Office, they settled on a family-run hotel set on a hilltop about 15 kilometres from Bologna. "We can see how it goes and decide what to do tomorrow," Jason suggested.

Pedalling along in the dappled sunlight by the riverside, they both enjoyed the peaceful silence broken only by birdsong and the hum of the distant rush-hour traffic on the snaking main road, soothing the anguish of the previous 24 hours.

Chapter Twenty-Three

As the shadows lengthened, Jason's thoughts began to turn to his stomach. They hadn't eaten anything substantial since their arrival in Italy, and the short bike ride gave him hunger pangs. "It's a bit of a climb up to the hotel." he told Lisa, "And it'll be gone 8 pm when we arrive, they might have stopped serving food. Shall we grab a pizza here?"

A young, budding Italian entrepreneur had thoughtfully positioned a wooden shack close to a small stone bridge over the river where several minor roads converged and offered a limited selection of takeaway pizza. They sat astride the low wall of the bridge with a beer to wait while their pizzas were freshly prepared and watched the fish leaping to catch their supper.

Jason smiled as he wiped the remnants of the Margherita topping from around his mouth using the back of his brand new, expensive, padded cycling mitt. "What a difference a day makes, but I think we need to get going, it'll soon be dark."

The signpost indicated that it was one-and-a-half kilometres to the top of the hill, along a narrow road lined with fir trees on both sides. Before the trip, Lisa had been worried about riding her bike with panniers over the hills of Tuscany. It felt so heavy, and she was afraid she wasn't strong enough, but now, after all they'd been through, riding uphill on her bike held no fears for her.

They set off together in the twilight, but Jason was soon out of sight as the road wound up steeply. Lisa selected the bottom gear and pushed hard on the pedals, determined not to get off; the light was fading rapidly, and there wasn't time to walk up the hill before darkness fell.

She was gulping in air and fighting to control her breathing as Jason suddenly rounded the corner, hurtling back downhill towards her. "Don't stop, I'll catch you up," he called out as he sped past, his voice almost drowned out by the shrill squeal of his brakes.

Just as Jason appeared by her side again, breathing hard with the effort, Lisa heard a rustling in the undergrowth. Then the sound came again, but this time it sounded louder, nearer and a twig or a branch snapped. "What was that?" she whispered, her eyes wide and fearful in the half-light.

"I don't know," Jason replied. "I heard it before, that's why I came back for you. Just keep going, you're doing great." They heard the rustling sound again, but it was fainter now. Whatever it was had moved away further into the trees, and a few minutes later, the lights of the hotel came into view.

It was completely dark when the Night Manager showed them where they could store their bikes for the night. The building resembled an alpine chalet, and they booked a spacious twin-bedded room for the night. "What do you think we heard on the way up? A wild pig, maybe?" Lisa mused.

"Definitely a bear," Jason smiled.

"Gosh! Would you have fought it if it had attacked me?" Lisa teased.

"Hell no! I would have been up that hill like I was jet-propelled."

The air was much cooler on the hilltop than in the city, and they closed the little wooden shutters before showering and heading down for a beer on the terrace.

Listening to the strains of the music floating out from the busy restaurant and lulled by the gentle swaying of the

Chapter Twenty-Three

treetops, silhouetted in the moonlight that bathed the landscape in shimmering silver, it was as though the events of the previous day had never happened.

Jason held out his glass and looked questioningly at Lisa. "Here's to a great holiday?"

She smiled and chinked hers against it. "Cheers to that."

Chapter Twenty-Four

X

Thud. In the semi-conscious state just before waking, Lisa wasn't sure if she'd heard the sound or dreamt it. Thud; there was no mistaking she had heard it that time and then again, thud.

"Are you awake?" she whispered. A grunt came from the tangled pile of quilt and limbs on the other bed. "What is that?"

The sound of chatter mingled with cheering and ripples of applause intrigued her. It was only just after 8 am, but there was a rush of warm air as she opened the wooden shutters. The sun was already high in a cloudless sky, and spread out before her was the lush green expanse of the grassy hilltop, like an oasis amid the surrounding pine woods. A multitude of archers clustered around the numerous targets arranged in lines, spaced for safety, already giving it their all before the temperature soared.

After a delicious continental breakfast taken on the terrace, Lisa and Jason carefully secured their panniers onto their bikes once more and set off toward the Apennine mountains and Florence. "Isn't it peaceful here?" Jason commented. "We've not seen a car since we set off."

The words were barely out of his mouth when they heard the hum of a vehicle approaching from behind. The sound grew steadily louder, and then a scooter overtook them. Then another, and another, and another. Scooters of every type and colour passed by in a steady procession that lasted minutes, some with one rider, others with two, and many cheerily waving.

"You were saying?" Lisa laughed. "I counted over 80 scooters and must have missed at least the first ten." As they began to climb through the foothills of the Apennines, more and more cyclists appeared, mostly male.

"A young man's just tapped me on the bottom," Lisa told Jason when she caught him up at a small roadside water fountain where he was refilling his water bottles. A group of young riders had started to pass her, and she'd felt the gentle tap as a young man with a Colgate smile appeared at her side. "Ciao, baby," he blew her a kiss as his friends laughed good-naturedly. Relaxed and enjoying the ride after the stressful days before, to her amazement, she'd joined in the fun and returned the gesture.

"Really? You would never have let me get away with that." A memory flashed through Jason's mind of Lisa's first attempt to ride a bike at Clumber Park and how she'd swiped at him when he'd tried to hold her up, accusing him of touching her bum. How long ago that seemed to look at her now, dazzling in her coordinating Lycra.

As the wooded valley gave way to open mountain pasture, the heat intensified, and they began to swelter.

Chapter Twenty-Four

Grateful for the shade of the isolated beech trees dotted along the roadside, they paused beneath them just long enough to cool a little before setting off into the blistering heat again.

When the road got too steep, they walked, sweat pouring. "We need to be careful," Jason warned, memories of the sunstroke he'd suffered only a couple of days earlier still fresh in his mind and when, after a couple of hours, they spotted a restaurant seemingly in the middle of nowhere, he suggested they should stop.

Glancing down at the damp patches displayed for all to see on her cycling top and the dust that clung to the rivulets of sweat trickling down her arms and legs, Lisa sighed. "I'm hardly dressed for Sunday lunch."

Undeterred, Jason moved towards the open door, where a petite middle-aged lady with glossy black hair appeared, exquisitely made up and glamorously dressed in a tight-fitting cherry red dress with flounces on the skirt. "Buongiorno! So hot today, you eat something?"

Lisa was grateful that the restaurant was full. "All one family," the lady told them. "But here's okay?" She pointed to the swing seat and a small table on the veranda.

"Perfect!" Jason replied as he slumped down, exhausted. Sipping iced water flavoured with fresh lemon juice whilst waiting for their food, Lisa glanced through an open window into the restaurant. An extended family group was gathered around one long table, ranging from elderly grandparents, or maybe even great-grandparents, down to very young children. They were all dressed in their Sunday best and talking animatedly, taking occasional forkfuls of food.

"They'll be here for hours," Jason told her. "I read about it in the Rough Guide. Sunday is a family day in Italy when everyone gathers to spend time together." He felt a sudden stab of the ever-present sadness he tried so hard to hold at bay; if only he could sit down with his family for a meal and enjoy laughter and conversation with his mum and dad.

Their lunch extended into a leisurely sojourn over a large Caprese salad they shared for a starter, followed by a pasta dish. It was after 3 pm when they left, but if anything, the temperature was hotter than when they'd arrived.

The road climbed steadily, and they rode slowly in the intense heat, frequently stopping to enjoy the views of the forests and grasslands in the shimmering heat haze. With no means of capturing the beauty around them, they tried hard to commit it to memory, but as they arrived at a small hamlet, Lisa heard Jason call out, "Camera!"

"A camera? Where?"

"Over there." Jason pointed to a small sign planted in the grass outside a pretty cottage with red-chequered gingham curtains that matched the colour of the geraniums in the window boxes. "I think 'camera' is Italian for a room or 'B n B'. Shall we try it?"

They propped their bikes against the low wall surrounding a large ornate fountain and left a group of young children carefully inspecting them as they approached the cottage armed with a phrasebook. To their surprise, the owner spoke English. He showed them to a small but comfortable twin room and, with expressive hand gestures in addition to his linguistic abilities, explained where they could find a bar to eat in a village only a short distance away.

Chapter Twenty-Four

"Is there anywhere we can leave the bikes later, please?" Lisa asked.

"Here," the man pointed to the wall of the cottage. "By the door." Lisa looked at Jason and saw that he was as uncomfortable with the idea as she was, even though they had a bike lock. "They'll be safe here," the man said. "No problem."

Still not convinced, Lisa passed him the police report. A deep furrow settled between his brows as he read it before shaking his head. "This is bad, I'm sorry." He showed them to a shed at the rear of the property and gave them the key. When they returned to the bikes, the brand-new cycle mitts Jason had left on his panniers had disappeared. He concluded one of the children must have claimed them as a souvenir; he could live with that.

"It's been a good day, hasn't it?" Lisa asked Jason later, sprawled on her bed in the oversized tee shirt she slept in, partially covered by a thin quilt. In the moonlight that pierced the curtains, she could see that Jason had already assigned his quilt to the floor.

He was silent for a few seconds and then rose and came to sit on the end of her bed. "I shouldn't have left you to sort out all the mess in Bologna on your own, I really am sorry."

"We sorted it out together. You were very ill that first night, there's nothing to apologise for." Against her better judgement, she reached out and covered his hand with her own. She remained rigidly opposed to any display of affection but felt that needs must in the circumstances.

"There is," Jason persisted. "There are things about me you don't know, things that no one knows."

Lisa laughed. "You're not about to tell me you're a closet axe murderer, are you?" she asked, instantly regretting the flippant remark when Jason didn't laugh with her. "Look, you don't need to tell me anything and certainly don't need to apologise."

Jason looked down at her slender hand on his before she quickly withdrew it. It was now or never; he owed it to her to tell her the truth. "There was more to it than the sunstroke. I just wanted to go home, I..... I needed to get home..... to where I feel safe. I'm sorry, this all sounds nuts."

"No, it doesn't," Lisa spoke softly.

"The truth is....... I've never got over losing my parents, really......, not at all, in fact, to be honest. Years ago, I made a ...., I suppose you'd call it a shrine, maybe, for them. I couldn't cope with what happened in Bologna. It was one thing too many, I needed to get home." He bowed his head, ashamed of his weakness, waiting for Lisa to laugh.

"There's nothing wrong with that. I always go to Mum and Dad when I'm upset."

"But, ..., I don't have mine."

Lisa hesitated. "I told you once that I would never ask you anything, but I'd like to make an exception."

He gulped. "Please do."

"The shrine is in your bedroom? You keep the door locked so that no one else can see it and spend so much time there because that's where you feel closest to your mum and dad?"

He slowly nodded, taken aback by the ease and speed with which she understood the situation he'd kept secret for so long. "I should have known you'd be kind, being a Samaritan."

Lisa pulled a curtain back so the silver moonlight suffused his face as she looked deep into his eyes. "I'm not a Samaritan now, Jason, just a friend. After the theft, I would

Chapter Twenty-Four

have given anything to speak to my mum and dad. I was desperate to hear their voices. You needed your parents, and you were desperate to go home to where you feel close to them. It's the same thing, do you see?"

Jason gazed at her in wonder. "I should have told you before. I've kept it secret and told no one, not even my family, because I didn't think anyone would ever understand."

"I'm glad you've told me now. We can go home whenever you need to, let's see how it goes."

Lisa lay thinking about their conversation long after Jason had returned to his bed and began gently snoring. For all his exuberant self-confidence that still made her wary of him, she'd always sensed his sadness but had never imagined for one minute that it imprisoned him. She felt honoured that he'd chosen to tell her what lay behind the locked door and hoped she might be able to help him one day.

They set off early the following morning before the temperature began to climb again and eventually heard a toot from behind when the school bus caught up with them. Jason scanned their hands for his cycling mitts as the children waved enthusiastically through the open windows, but to no avail.

It was just after lunch when Lisa noticed what appeared to be a long, black, shiny line on the road ahead. *It must be scorching, the tarmac's beginning to melt.* Jason was slightly ahead, and suddenly the line began to move towards the opposite side of the road at a rate of knots. A basking snake!

Lisa had endured a phobia of snakes all her life. She felt every hair on her body stand to attention simultaneously, and her pulse quickened, her eyes riveted to the snake as it struck out for the roadside. But then a car appeared, travelling in the opposite direction and at the last minute, the snake turned and started heading back towards her.

Through the sudden adrenalin rush, Lisa saw everything in slow motion. The snake, seeming to be every bit as panicked as she was, was now hurtling her way, and in roughly three pedal strokes, they would collide. She instinctively let out a blood-curdling scream, and at that precise moment, the snake shot up into the air, coiling and looking like it would knot itself. It dropped back to the road and zipped off in the opposite direction for the second time, disappearing into the undergrowth at the roadside.

Alarmed, Jason turned and rode back to her. "Lisa! What's happened? Are you okay?"

Still trying to calm herself, she couldn't even say the word at first. "S....., s......, snake!" she finally forced out.

He burst out laughing and she punched him. "Note to self." He licked an imaginary pencil. "Must find Cornflake the garter snake."

"You've lost a snake?" She was horrified.

He grinned. "No. But a mate at work has."

Later that evening, heads bent close together so that they could study the Rough Guide in the glow from the fairy lights strung through the trees in the garden of their 'B n B', they pondered their next move.

They expected to hit Florence by lunchtime the following day and needed to be careful not to blow their budget. Jason traced his finger beneath the words he was reading from the Rough Guide's list of cheap but acceptable accommodation, according to the author.

"This sounds different, a one-star hotel with shared bathroom occupying part of a 16th-century palazzo located close to the city centre."

Lisa was nervous about riding through the large city; the Italian drivers' reputation for being irate at the best of times preceded them, but she needn't have worried. They might be impatient with each other, but she soon discovered they're remarkably courteous and considerate to cyclists, and they navigated their way to the centre of Florence without any difficulties whatsoever.

After the sun-drenched vistas of the Apennines, the narrow streets seemed dark and oppressive in the shadows cast by the enormous fortress-like houses that lined either side. Despite the shade, the heat was oppressive, and Lisa was relieved when they located the hotel from the tiny street plan provided in the guide.

Entering through a large archway, they found themselves in a sunlit courtyard complete with the obligatory ornamental fountain. The gleaming white ornate wrought iron furniture scattered between pots of vibrant geraniums and shaded by heavily scented lemon trees looked tempting.

"Hi there, come far?" As Lisa and Jason turned to look for the source of the voice, Heather and Ron from Ontario stood and walked over to introduce themselves, explaining they'd arrived only a short time earlier.

Heather pointed to a tandem leaning against the trunk of a miniature cypress tree growing in an enormous terracotta pot. "That's our steed. We're having two months in Italy; we're travel writers."

Over coffee, Lisa and Jason briefly brought Heather and Ron up to speed on their earlier exploits before securing their bikes and heading off to shower and change. Their top-floor room looked immense in the dim light seeping through the closed shutters. The king-sized bed, with its crisp white bed linen, stood like a remote island in the centre of the room, directly beneath the faded remnants of a large and ancient fresco painted on the vaulted ceiling and a gothic-style chandelier suspended from a chain.

In a far distant corner, they could make out the shape of what appeared to be a Tardis but which transpired to be nothing more exciting than a UPVC shower unit that looked as out of place in the antique grandeur of the room as any time machine might have done.

"Wow! This place is something else!" Jason was awestruck as he walked across the scuffed and creaking floorboards, the faint musty smell a gentle reminder of the age of the building, the centuries that had passed since its construction, and the numerous people who had walked across that floor before.

Sunlight flooded in as Lisa opened the shutters, and she gasped. "Look!" Jason joined her by the window. Less than a kilometre away across the rooftops, the magnificent red dome of the Duomo dominated the skyline.

Lisa was almost moved to tears as they strolled across the Piazza del Duomo a short while later. The architecture was breathtaking; the dramatic colours of the intricately patterned marble exterior crowned by the immense dome recognised worldwide. Never before had the beauty of a building filled her with such emotion. Long queues of people patiently waited their turn to enter the iconic space, and Lisa was keen to join them. "Shall we?"

Chapter Twenty-Four

But Jason was on a mission. "It's your birthday tomorrow, and I haven't got anything for you. I need to shop; can I leave you here for a while?"

Ever since the theft, he'd cursed his decision to buy her something in Italy. It had seemed a good idea at the time, but he could hardly splash out now without a credit card or any money of his own.

Despite her protestations, Jason was determined to pursue his quest, so Lisa found a quiet, shady corner of the square to sit with her water and admire the view.

With no idea what to buy and his eyes scanning the brightly coloured window displays like laser beams, Jason quickly established that any gift from the shops littered around the main squares would be well beyond his price range.

Despondent, he decided to try the back streets and hurried along a narrow alleyway. He took several turns and was beginning to think that he was wasting his time when he spotted the small window of what appeared to be a shop.

His heart sank as he scanned the strange assortment of items dumped rather than displayed in the window, and then suddenly, he saw it, almost tucked out of sight behind a garishly painted clown. A plain silver bangle with a clasp formed by the Gemini twins, their profiles back-to-back, identical to the pendant given to his mum by her sister.

A bell rang as he entered the empty, gloomy shop, and a bespectacled elderly man appeared through a door behind the counter. Jason beckoned the man to follow him outside and pointed to the bangle. He was sure he couldn't afford it, but there was no harm in asking. "How much, please?"

The man stroked his chin thoughtfully and tapped a few times on a calculator that had seen better days. "Very old. Long time here, no one came. Twenty euros?"

Jason couldn't believe his luck and laughed. "I get it, it's a pawn shop."

"Porn?" The man looked flustered and insulted. "No! No porn here."

"I didn't mean ..... I'm sorry, I meant......" Realising the scope for rapidly sinking even deeper into hot water, Jason decided to cut and run quickly. "Twenty euros?" He handed the notes over, slipped the bangle into his pocket and hastily left, thrilled with his purchase.

Lisa smiled when he returned, beaming. "I'd almost given up on you. Can we afford a camera, I'd really like to get some photos?" The sun had dropped by the time they returned with the cheapest camera they could find, and the square was in the shade, but the queues had gone, and there were still 45 minutes until the Duomo closed.

"The fifth most capacious church in the world," Jason read from the Rough Guide, "capable of holding a congregation of 10,000." But neither of them were prepared for the vast space that dwarfed them as they entered.

The fresco of The Last Judgement, painted on the ceiling of the dome in the 1570s, impressed them most of all. The colossal artwork was spectacular from ground level, but it was only when they climbed the seemingly endless spiral staircase to the gallery that the enormous scale of the scene became apparent.

In awed silence, broken only by the hushed tones of the handful of other visitors in the church, they slowly circumnavigated the gallery until they reached a guide standing by the side of a small wooden door. "There's just time, five minutes," the man told them.

They ducked to pass through the narrow doorway and climbed a few more steep stairs before they stepped out onto a narrow external walkway around the top of the dome, protected by a high steel mesh fence. Spread out before them in the golden light of the early evening lay all of Florence. They were standing at the very heart of the city.

For a few short minutes, they tried to commit to memory the spectacular views, far too expansive to capture on a simple camera and somehow serene, despite the muffled sound of the car horns far below as the rush hour traffic moved slowly along the arterial roads that fanned out from the city centre like the spokes of a wheel. Then it was time to go back down.

"I don't want to go; this is so wonderful. I want to stay here and watch the sunset." Lisa thrust out her bottom lip like a petulant child as she turned to look at Jason.

The sun had dropped low in the sky, and a golden halo formed around her as she threw her head back, laughing. And that was when it struck him with all the force of a blow from a sledgehammer; he was in love with her.

Chapter Twenty-Five

Lying awake in the early hours, listening to Lisa purring and snuffling in her sleep on the other side of the enormous bed, Jason tried to tell himself again he couldn't possibly be in love with her.

How could he be? He'd decided years ago never to allow himself to fall in love, he loved her as a friend, and that was all. It was just the emotion of the setting that had got to him; it had to be.

The Duomo was indescribably beautiful, and whilst there, he'd thought of his parents and how much they would have loved to see it. *That was it! His emotions were playing tricks on him; he had it all under control, and everything was fine.* But if that was true, why was he still wide awake at 2 am, trying to persuade himself he was okay?

He knew he was really in trouble when he realised it was her birthday. *Dear Lord, what if she gives me that look later today?*

So far, it hadn't cropped up, probably because of the stress at the beginning of the trip and then the exhaustion of their daily cycling exploits in furnace-like conditions. At home, their liaisons were always quick to the point of being almost perfunctory, nothing more than the brief fulfilment of an urgent need, over virtually before they began. Jason always waited for Lisa's signal, that light tap on the door he knew so well.

She always wore a skirt, so she didn't have to remove it, ready to take flight at a moment's notice; he'd never seen her naked. With a sinking feeling of resignation, he realised how much he wanted to hold her, caress the silky smoothness of her skin, kiss her deeply, and make love to her. *This is bad, really bad,* he reprimanded himself, knowing that if he attempted any of that, their friendship would be over in an instant.

That was it then; he must never let Lisa know how he felt about her. Be grateful for what they had together and never hope for anything more; that was the way forward. Relieved that he'd found a solution, he fell into a fitful sleep.

Heather and Ron joined them for breakfast al fresco in the courtyard, where Lisa was opening the cards she had brought from her family. "Happy Birthday! Will you be celebrating later, and if so, can we impose?" Heather asked.

"I'd like that very much," Lisa smiled.

"Thank goodness. I've spoken to the Manager already, and he's recommended a restaurant, The Medici, in the Piazza del Signoria. Shall we book a table for 7.30 pm?"

"Great, I'm looking forward to it already."

Back in their room, Jason handed Lisa an envelope. The card inside bore a picture of a slim, elegant woman wearing red high heels and a wide-brimmed hat, swinging a handbag. She giggled when she read the message written inside: 'Saw this and thought of someone else! Happy Birthday. J.'

"Sorry I haven't wrapped it," he told her as he passed her the bangle.

When she saw the clasp, she gasped. "Thank you so much, it's beautiful. The Gemini twins, it's just like Jayne's necklace!" Jason knew one day he would tell her the necklace had belonged to his mum, but not today.

Half an hour later, Lisa nervously clutched the phone card she'd just purchased as she approached the small canopy that sheltered three cramped public phone booths.

A man dressed from head to toe in white linen, his shoulders hunched as he shouted furiously into the mouthpiece, occupied the centre booth. Positioning herself with her back to him, Lisa pressed the receiver to her ear, dialled the number and then stuck her finger in her other ear to drown out the man's anger.

"Happy Birthday to you, Happy Birthday to you!" Lisa gulped back tears as she listened to her parents singing down the crackling phone line. "I've been worried about you, sweetheart," Kathleen told her. "I thought we might have heard before. Are you having a lovely time?"

Lisa had decided not to tell her parents about the theft until she was safely at home with them, face to face, and they could see she was okay. For now, she would give the impression that everything was good. "Sorry, Mum, it was all a bit hectic when we arrived. I'm having a fantastic time, thanks."

It was only as the words left her lips she realised that, despite the dreadful start to their holiday, they were true.

When they'd finished taking photos of the Duomo in the morning sunlight, Jason wanted to show Lisa the little pawn shop he'd been so fortunate to stumble on the day before, but, despite his best efforts, he couldn't find it again.

Having tried every possible alleyway off the piazza and spending almost an hour trawling the narrow shaded back streets, he eventually gave up, and they made their way to the Piazza Della Signoria to reconnoitre the restaurant.

The scene that greeted them took their breath away. The medieval castle-like structure of the Palazzo Vecchio that, according to the Rough Guide, had served as Florence's Town Hall since 1322 dominated the square.

They could see people walking around the top of the impressive bell tower, but one look at the queue waiting to go inside persuaded them to abandon any thoughts of doing the same. Instead, they strolled through the unique outdoor gallery of numerous ancient statues commemorating significant events in the city's history before sitting for a while by the side of Neptune's Fountain, splashing each other with the cool water like children. "Good birthday?" Jason asked.

Lisa shook her head. "Horrendous!" she snapped, her mouth twitching at the corners.

In the early evening, freshly showered, Lisa slipped on the one dress she had brought, a simple, lightweight red cotton sundress with bootlace straps. She finger-dried her hair into spiral ringlets and applied her only makeup; a flick of mascara and her favourite red lipstick. A pair of black flipflops completed her outfit, and when she could

Chapter Twenty-Five

eventually get into the shared bathroom, she studied her reflection in the cracked mirror.

What she saw looked plain and ordinary, yet she was comfortable with it. *At what point had she lost the need for a disguise, an outfit and a persona behind which to hide to get through the challenges of the day?*

She wasn't sure how it had happened; was it when she'd taken up cycling and got used to looking bedraggled? Was it only when she was with Jason, who had seen her at her most unattractive so many times he probably didn't even notice what she looked like?

No, that couldn't be right because she was content to go out looking like this with her new-found friends. She'd only met them the day before, but already she knew she would keep in touch with Heather and Ron. Their tales over breakfast of adventurous cycling trips across the Rockies had captured her imagination; she'd never met anyone like them before. *Surely it couldn't be that she'd finally become comfortable in her own skin?*

They all enjoyed the meal in the comfort of the popular air-conditioned restaurant, and then, almost imperceptibly, the lights dimmed. The chatter fell silent as a waiter appeared, proudly carrying what looked like a goldfish bowl filled with a lavish ice cream and meringue concoction adorned with fizzing sparklers.

Several waiters moved to join him, singing 'Happy Birthday' at the tops of their voices as they made a beeline for Lisa. *Oh God!* Jason's heart was in his mouth, knowing that she had only agreed to the trip to avoid being the centre of attention at the party her mother longed for. "It wasn't me; I didn't tell them!"

"Sorry, Lisa, it was me; I couldn't help myself," Heather confessed as the waiter set the bowl down in front of Lisa with a flourish while the others gathered behind her to sing again, each in turn stepping forward to present her with a single red rose.

As the other diners clapped and cheered, to Jason's utter astonishment, Lisa stood, took a mock bow and raised her glass to thank everyone before hurriedly sitting back down, flushed but laughing.

"Thanks for a birthday I'll never forget," she told Jason as she climbed into bed that night. She was very tempted to hug and kiss him.

It had been a wonderful day, and she was overwhelmed by the thoughtfulness of the gift he'd given her. *Should she?* She began to turn towards him and then stopped. No, it would be entirely the wrong thing to do; he wouldn't be expecting it, he'd most likely be alarmed, and they'd both be embarrassed.

"Forget it!" the voice inside her head warned, and for once, she listened.

In the early hours, Jason lay awake for the second consecutive night. *This has to stop, right here, right now.* He couldn't forget how she'd looked at him after raising her glass to the other diners. Slowly twirling the bangle around her left wrist as she sat down, she'd smiled, her eyes shining, and his heart had lurched. *Did she feel the same as he did?*

But then the conversation had moved on; the moment had passed. Restless in the darkness, he made a mental list of all the reasons why it was utterly ridiculous to imagine she might have feelings for him. She was wealthy, for a start, out of his league. A memory of the Ferrari came unbidden into his mind and parked there for a second, like a vast red Stop sign.

Her father didn't like him, her brother didn't seem keen either, and most importantly, Lisa herself had told him that she never wanted to be in a relationship again, and he had no chance of getting off with her. *Get a grip if you don't want to end up like this every night!*

Heather and Ron rose early the following day to enjoy a last breakfast together before Jason and Lisa continued their journey across Chianti towards Siena.

"Do you think we'll take them up on their offer of a cycling trip sometime?" Lisa asked as they cycled out towards the Ponte Vecchio.

"Mmmmm. Maybe." Jason was deliberately non-committal but secretly revelled in the possibility that Lisa might consider another trip with him.

There were only a few people around as they rode across the Ponte Vecchio, the oldest bridge in Florence, admiring the glittering displays of jewellery, artwork and less expensive souvenirs in the windows of the centuries-old shops that adorn both sides of the bridge and which would soon be teeming with potential customers. When they reached the other side, they stopped and looked back for a last glimpse of the city, dreamlike and magical in the early morning mist gently rising from the River Arno.

Jason planned to reach the Chianti region by late morning, but they made good progress over the hills dotted with farmhouses, villas and the tall, slender cypress trees so evocative of the region.

By lunchtime, they'd already passed by several vast vineyards stretching out into the distance, decorative billboards displaying the names of the instantly recognisable famous Italian wines.

Although not at all hungry, they stopped at a large wooden table piled high with fruit and olives positioned by the roadside in front of a small cottage. A tiny, stooped lady appeared, dressed from head to toe in black. Her gnarled hands shook slightly as she carefully placed plums, cherries and grapes into paper bags, but her eyes shone as she waved them away, delighted to have made a sale.

When eventually it was too hot to continue, they found shade under a small copse, ate their fruit and fell asleep. It was mid-afternoon when they awoke, rested and ready to continue. On they cycled, transfixed by the colours of the landscape that seemed to intensify as the day wore on. The air was still, and the farmhouses and villas turned golden as the sun began to dip, nestled like jewels in the velvety green folds of the rolling hills on which the vineyards thrived.

When they reached the outskirts of a small village, Jason looked for somewhere to stay, but without success. "How far are we from Siena?" Lisa asked. "Shall we try to get there?"

Siena was still 20 kilometres away, and they would arrive late. Spotting the now familiar canopy of a solitary public phone booth, she decided to try to book somewhere ahead.

Alarm began to set in when the first three places she tried were all full. Fearful the money on the phone card would soon ebb away to nothing; she decided to try just one more. If that failed, she could only pray they would find a 'camera' somewhere but held out little hope as they'd seen no accommodation all day along the quiet route they had chosen away from the main highway.

"Si, si," the man's voice replied. "I have a room, but I will let it go at 8 pm if you're not here. There is a festival."

Lisa didn't know if the last 20 kilometres were hillier than the rest of the route, but it certainly seemed like it, and she was now becoming uncomfortably hungry. Too late, she realised the inadequacy of fruit alone to fuel a day of cycling, even in sweltering weather, and there was nowhere to stock up with supplies. She pressed on, beginning to panic about the deadline and what would happen if they missed it.

Trying to distract herself with the still-stunning scenery, she couldn't help but notice that the sun was dropping rapidly; even the smallest of inclines was a struggle, and the growling in her stomach was getting louder every moment.

"We're almost there." Jason was riding at her side, his hand on her back, doing his best to help her up yet another hill but desperately hungry himself.

Lisa hadn't the strength to reply. She glanced at her watch - 7.30 pm, it was touch and go, and she hadn't a trace of energy left.

Twenty minutes later, light-headed and descending cautiously in the semi-darkness into the city, Lisa felt the sharp sting of tears. They still had to find the hotel, apparently located just off the main square; they were too late.

But Jason knew where he was heading; he'd studied the town plan in the Rough Guide whilst Lisa stopped for water. Like in Florence, all the roads led to the centre; he was confident they couldn't go wrong. A few minutes later, his efforts were rewarded with his first glimpse of the Piazza del Campo and with no time whatsoever to enjoy it, he set about finding their accommodation.

Lisa glanced at her watch; it was 8.10 pm when Jason rushed to the reception of the poky little building he'd been lucky to spot in the darkness, ambitiously described as a 'hotel'. The grin from ear to ear he flashed at Lisa, waiting outside, told her that, incredibly, they still had a room.

But her joy was short-lived; their room was on the top floor. There was nowhere to store the bikes at ground level, and the staircase was too narrow and twisting to take them up. They couldn't stay. Lisa felt her knees buckle and sat down heavily on the stone step. *Now what were they going to do?*

"Wait!" The man at reception called out to Jason. "The fire escape." As he led them along a dark narrow passageway into a rear yard, Lisa was startled by the sudden memory of her hiding place years before on that snowy night in Sheffield.

A dilapidated wrought iron fire escape zig-zagged up to the top floor. The man took pity on them and helped Jason to haul the bikes up to their room whilst Lisa wrestled with the panniers. By the time she'd completed the second ascent, struggling with a pannier in each hand, she felt close to passing out.

After quickly showering in the 'en suite', a grubby, tiled enclosure with no door, lit by a single lightbulb hanging from a cable with exposed wires, they headed out to eat. Across the road was a small open-air restaurant that looked pleasant enough, with multicoloured fairy lights hanging from a pergola and music.

They staggered in and ordered a substantial meal; olives, antipasti, salads, lasagne, garlic bread; the most they'd eaten in one sitting since they'd left home.

Fellow diners, savouring their food, the wine and the ambience of the balmy evening, glanced across in curious wonder as Lisa and Jason devoured their meal at astonishing speed and without speaking to each other or even looking up from their plates.

Sated, they decided to take a short stroll around the Campo, the famous square shaped like the underside of a scalloped seashell where, at the Palio festivals each year, daredevil young men race horses at breakneck speed, bareback, around the perimeter to the roaring cheers of the spectators.

Throngs of people still filled the pavement as they ambled towards the nearby square, and as they turned the corner, the scene before them was breathtaking. The imposing Palazzo Pubblico, another castle-like structure with a high bell tower, stood floodlit at the far end of the square.

The gently sloping medieval red-brick paving was still warm from the heat of the day, and hundreds of bodies littered the ground, some sitting, others lying, enjoying the relative cool of the late evening.

Groups of young people sprawled together, eating ice cream, laughing, softly chatting or singing whilst someone strummed a guitar; parents rocked sleeping toddlers in their arms and encouraged older children to sit and rest, couples nestled close together, watching the world go by.

They completed a circuit of the square around the perimeter, enjoying the contrast of the relaxed, almost surreal atmosphere in the centre and the buzz still emanating from the restaurants dotted all around where waiters, hurrying about their work, still ushered more people to empty tables.

They stopped at one of the numerous gelateria. How to choose from the colourful display of rich, glossy ice cream coaxed into swirling, foaming peaks? The options were endless. Finding a space on the ground to sit and enjoy the delicious dessert, they luxuriated in the friendly atmosphere pervading all around them. As they lay back to gaze at the stars twinkling in the night sky above, all thoughts of their strenuous efforts earlier floated away on the warm air.

It was after midnight when they finally returned to their room, and it was only as she climbed into bed that Lisa realised how exhausted she felt. "Blimey! Have you broken it?" Jason whispered as her bed let out a loud creak.

"That was my knees, not the bed!" she replied, falling asleep instantly when her head hit the pillow. But in the middle of the night, she suddenly let out a shriek and leapt from her bed.

"Lisa! What's wrong?"

"Cramp! Ow, ow ow! It's all the way up my leg." She'd never experienced anything like it, her entire right leg, from ankle to hip, was in agony. She hobbled around in small circles, barely able to walk and gasping in pain.

"Lack of salt, we're losing that much in sweat every day. We'll have to watch that." Jason told her, pummelling her muscles to help relieve the knots whilst she attempted to stretch until, eventually, the cramp subsided.

The following morning, they treat themselves to a leisurely breakfast of fruit juice and freshly baked rolls served with rich, creamy gorgonzola at one of the cafes overlooking the Campo, before making their way to the nearby Piazza del Duomo.

Chapter Twenty-Five

"I was sad to leave Florence," Lisa told Jason. "I didn't think we would see anything so beautiful as the Duomo, but I was wrong."

They were standing outside Siena's cathedral, awestruck by the ornate facade and the bands of black and white marble tiles that give the tower a zebra-like appearance. Enthralled by the splendour of the pillars and arches within the church that echo the same black and white stripes, they soon lost each other amongst the multitude of visitors.

The intricate carving of the pulpit, the magnificent frescoes, the statues, and the marble floor blew Lisa's mind. So exquisite and ancient; according to the Rough Guide, construction was completed in 1382. She wondered what had motivated people to construct such beautiful buildings so long ago. Perhaps even more importantly, when had that motivation ceased and why?

Tired but eager to make the most of their day in Siena, they wandered from square to square, absorbed by the incredible architecture all around them. It was only as the late afternoon sun began to drop that they hurried back to their room to chance another shower. Fortunately, they managed to avoid an electric shock for the second time before returning to the Campo.

"I'm starving!" Jason announced as the sky slowly turned a burnished mix of red and gold. "Can we eat?"

"Hey!" An American voice piped up beside him. "Hope you don't mind me butting in, kids, but there's a great pizza place just around the back of here." A man wearing a red baseball cap, his rotund figure suggesting he should maybe ease up a little on the pizza, gave them a friendly grin and gestured to the Palazzo.

The restaurant comprised a series of long wooden tables with benches on either side, positioned beneath large canvas awnings. The place looked full to capacity, but a waitress approached them as they looked dubiously at each other. "Two?" She asked brightly, leading them to what seemed to be an already fully occupied table, but everyone kindly squeezed up a little more so that they could get on at the end. The waitress handed them the menu. "Wine?"

They had been avoiding wine and settling for cheaper beers, but Jason was tempted here on the edge of the Chianti region. He shot her a disarming smile. "How much?"

"One euro." She handed him the wine list and left them to make their selections. Sure enough, all the wine was only a euro per bottle.

"It's got to be awful, surely, at that price, but........., shall we go for it?" Jason passed the wine list to Lisa, suspecting she knew far more about wine than he ever would.

As they tucked into huge pizzas and an enormous green salad, surrounded by the other diners amiably chatting in several different languages, and sipped the wine that was remarkably good for the price, Lisa thought of the night in Bologna.

At the time, she had been in the depths of despair, struggling to cope with the enormity of their situation. What a difference a week can make; so many beautiful experiences behind her and seven more days of adventures to come. Not wanting to spoil the evening, she kept her thoughts to herself, but unbeknown to her, Jason was thinking precisely the same.

Chapter Twenty-Six

As quietly as possible, they struggled to get their bikes back down the fire escape to ground level early the following morning. It felt oddly cool as they cycled across the Campo; crowd-free for the first time since they'd arrived, revealing the fishbone pattern of the paving that fanned out from the Palazzo in nine separate sections, intended centuries ago to resemble the folds in the cloak of the Virgin Mary. Lisa shivered involuntarily; *was the square really empty or crammed with the spirits of previous inhabitants?*

Having learned the hard way the importance of consuming adequate fuel for the ride each day, after a light breakfast, they bought bread rolls and tomatoes for the journey, then set out in the direction of Montepulciano, the highest of the Tuscan hill towns.

The route took them across an area known as the Crete, described in the Rough Guide as a sparsely populated region of pale clay hillsides dotted with sheep, cypresses and the odd monumental-looking farmhouse. After the previous day's challenges, Lisa didn't relish the prospect of more hills but soon forgot about them as they rounded a bend on a gently climbing country road.

"Oh look, this is what I've been waiting to see!" Before them was the classic image of Tuscany; a narrow, sandy-coloured track meandering from the road between golden fields of crops on either side, with tall cypress trees standing like guards to attention on the approach to the sprawling farmhouse. "It's just like the picture on the ....."

She stopped abruptly, mid-sentence; Jason still didn't know she'd seen the little guidebook. "In the brochures." She finished, hoping he hadn't noticed her hesitation, wondering if he too had recognised the scene from then on repeated many times along their route.

They ate their lunch beneath the shade of a tree overlooking one such vista. "This is like........, utopia," Lisa blushed, embarrassed by her childlike euphoria.

Jason was silent for a moment. "Do you know, I don't think I've heard you complain once?"

"Complain? What is there to complain about?"

"Well, the abysmal start to our holiday, for one thing. Then there's the dive we stayed at for the last two nights, that place should be condemned. And I bet you've never had to drink beer six nights in a row because you don't know if your budget will stretch to wine. Simon, Pietro or any of the others would have had a fit with me before now for suggesting the trip."

Lisa threw her head back and giggled in the way that made him want to wrap his arms around her. "I can't deny there have been some new experiences." For a moment, she

Chapter Twenty-Six

looked serious, contemplating. "But this trip is magical. I'm having the time of my life!"

It was mid-afternoon when they could see the town of Montepulciano, high on a ridge ahead of them. Pouring with sweat, they stopped at a water fountain to refill their bottles before slowly grinding their way up the climb. Halfway up, they stopped to bow their heads and shoulders beneath the soothing cool water gushing from a larger fountain but were soon drenched in sweat again when they resumed the climb.

Trembling with effort and in bottom gear as she passed through the Porta Al Prato, Lisa narrowly avoided being knocked off twice by pedestrians, prone to stepping out with no warning into the narrow road. Dizzy with exhaustion, she walked the rest of the way to the Piazza Grande, the main square that crowns the summit.

The Rough Guide warned that accommodation in Montepulciano is both at a premium and expensive, but Lisa had phoned ahead en route and secured a two-star room located just off the piazza. After their stay in Siena, they feared the worst, but the smiling proprietor led them to a spacious, dimly lit twin-bedded room. A vase of fresh flowers stood on an ancient chest of drawers, and the en suite bathroom smelled of citrus.

Relieved, Lisa could hear a multitude of shrill screeches as she opened the wooden shutters and knew she would never forget the sight that greeted her as long as she lived. It was late afternoon, that special time of the day when everything was still, intense and golden. From high on the ridge, the view across the expanse of the Crete was spectacular, but it was the sight of the birds that mesmerised her.

The sky was teeming with swifts as far as the eye could see, hundreds and hundreds of incredibly agile flyers darting and weaving in every direction, somehow avoiding each other with their high-speed passes.

Enthralled, she forgot about her aching limbs, sweat-drenched body, and parched throat and leaned on her elbows to watch an aerobatic show she knew could not be surpassed anywhere. Intrigued, Jason joined her at the window, and they watched the aerial display together, spellbound.

Showered and changed, they strolled along the narrow streets lined with expensive shops and restaurants, eventually settling on one where the price of spinach and ricotta ravioli wouldn't break the bank.

"Excuse me," Jason called the waiter when their food arrived. "My friend can't eat this." A hush fell across the restaurant. "It's the ham, you see. She doesn't eat ham." The waiter looked bemused. "We didn't know there was ham in it. The menu only says spinach and ricotta......, not ham." Jason tailed off, suddenly aware that everyone was listening.

"But there is always ham in the ravioli," the waiter replied in a tone that implied they were idiots.

The Manager overheard the harassed waiter's remark. No knowledge of Italian was necessary to comprehend that the short barrage of staccato sounds he fired at the hapless man, like a volley of bullets from a machine gun, was a stern rebuke.

A fresh dish of ravioli soon appeared, minus the ham. The Manager insisted they partake of a dessert on the house, rounded off with Limoncello, the piquant taste of which lingered as they wended their way slowly back up the hill for the second time that day.

They left Montepulciano early the following morning to head west across the rolling hills of the Crete before turning north towards San Gimignano. It would be another hard ride in the heat, but they were much stronger than when they started the trip and were looking forward to the challenge.

They had breakfast at a small cafe in Pienza, another picturesque hill town affording magnificent views, before pushing on again to get as far as possible that day. Freewheeling down the winding road behind Jason, basking in the warm sunlight and the glorious scenery around her, Lisa felt a rush of pure joy. She didn't know quite how she'd come to be here, doing a bike tour of all things, but it was as if she was destined for it.

Moments later, a sleek black BMW passed them on a wide bend, and then the driver braked hard, signalling right.

"Lisa!" Jason called out a warning as he pulled on his brakes, swerving hard to his left at the same time to avoid the back of the car as it turned into a gravel driveway leading to a hotel. Jerked out of her daydream, Lisa instinctively braked as hard as she could to avoid running into Jason, but her bike locked up and lurched out of control.

The fiery red brake lights of the car ahead filled her vision. If she released the brakes, she would surely hit the back of it at speed; but if she didn't, she would fall from her bucking bike. Astonished, she saw the smallest of gaps begin to open between the turning car and Jason, released her grip on the brake levers only slightly but enough to resume a straight line, and aimed for it.

They stopped half a mile further on at the bottom, both breathless and trembling at the thought of what might have been. "That was impressive riding, I felt the hairs on your arm as you passed me. I can't believe he turned in front of us like that, we could have been killed if we'd run into the back!" Jason looked shocked and pale, despite his glowing tan. "And they talk about Italian drivers!"

Shaken, Lisa laid her hand on his shoulder. "I know, we took a chance coming here. Let's be grateful that we're safe."

"He wasn't Italian, you know?" Jason shook his head, still stunned by the driver's incompetence. "We've had no problems at all with the Italian drivers. That car had *GB* plates."

With no idea where they might end up by the evening, they decided to make lunch the main meal of the day and stopped at a small, isolated restaurant. "Remember last week?" Lisa asked. "When I wasn't used to eating covered in sweat? Look at me now, I've perfected it."

Jason gave her a wan smile; the close shave hadn't spoiled the day but had taken the edge off it. When they found a pleasant place to stay with breakfast in a small hamlet about 15 kilometres from San Gimignano, he went to rest for an hour, feeling guilty for lying to Lisa that he was tired but needing time alone to grapple with the black thoughts about the precariousness of life that had consumed him all afternoon.

He knew only too well the fine line between joy and sorrow, and this was the very thing he feared the most, that someone else he loved dearly might be snatched away from him in a moment. The near miss had been a stark reminder of why he'd decided never to let himself fall in love. What would he have done if she'd been hurt or worse? No matter how much he tried to reason with himself, persuade himself that he couldn't possibly be in love with Lisa, the way he felt at the thought of losing her left him in no doubt.

"San Gimignano, perhaps the best-known village in all of Italy. A medieval Manhattan, the stunning skyline dominated by the towers built by the feuding nobles of the 12th and 13th centuries," Lisa read from the Rough Guide before they turned out the light.

They set off early the following day and arrived at the majestic hilltop town before the tourist buses began to flood in. "Do you hear that?" Lisa asked Jason as they meandered along the shady streets, gazing up at the numerous towers, some still vertical, others leaning. They followed the sound as it grew steadily louder and turned into a small courtyard where a crowd was rapidly gathering.

Seated in the cool shade within an old barn was a young girl in a tee shirt and shorts, her fingers lightly plucking the strings of a harp. Many watching were visibly moved and dabbed their eyes as the ethereal notes rippled and soared in the still morning air. Lisa glanced at Jason, sitting in the shade of a large oak tree, hunched forwards as he listened intently to the music of angels. She decided to leave him alone with his thoughts.

Jason had never heard anything like it before. His home had always been filled with musicians as he was growing up, and music had always played a significant part in his life, but this was different. It felt like the melody was somehow holding him, soothing him, taking his spirit with it as the notes climbed higher and higher. *Tosh!* He reprimanded himself as they stood to leave when the harpist took a break. *There's no such thing as a spirit. When you're dead, you're dead.*

That thought remained with him as they gazed across the valley to the next hill town they were heading for; Volterra. Standing high on the plateau ahead, the town looked ominously bleak and uninviting despite the bright sunlight.

They made their way carefully down to the valley floor and then, in no time at all, they were climbing yet again in the heat of the day, up and up towards the imposing dark stone buildings of the town. Once through the gateway, the road became cobbled, and they walked the last few hundred metres up the narrow, austere street to a square surrounded by almost entirely medieval buildings.

"This is thought to be the oldest palace of this type anywhere in Italy," Jason read from the Rough Guide, facing the Palazzo dei Priori, a castle-like structure. "Built between 1208 and 1257, can you believe it?"

Lisa brushed her fingertips lightly across the cool stones, wondering who had laid them, who else had stood there and done the same as she had just done, what kind of people they were and what sort of lives they had led; if only buildings could talk.

Despite feeling weary after the ride, they showered and then strolled the length of the town, admiring the floodlit buildings as darkness fell before eating. "Shall we hit the beach tomorrow, piggy?" Jason asked later, sprawled on his bed, waiting for her to turn out the light. Indignant, Lisa jumped up and thrashed him twice around the head with her pillow. "I was referring to the pink around your eyes, not your figure! You look shattered."

Chapter Twenty-Six

After a leisurely breakfast, they had one last walk around the town to take in the spectacular views, the towers of San Gimignano still clearly visible and in the opposite direction, the coast.

"It's all downhill from here!" Jason grinned as he sped off down the hillside towards the ocean, glittering in the distance more than 20 kilometres away. Forty minutes later, standing on the Marina Di Cecina, Jason gave Lisa a high five. "Well done. I thought you might be nervous after the guy tried to take us out the other day."

"Nervous? Me? I was terrified!"

They found a place to stay in Vada, a short distance further along the coast and headed to the beach around 4 pm, just as the local holidaymakers had the same idea. As the Italian families arranged their enormous, brightly coloured beach towels, parasols and chairs before the men began blowing up an array of inflatables, Lisa and Jason unfurled their travel towels.

"What would you go for, head or bum?" Lisa asked Jason. To the amusement of the watching sunbathers, she was squirming around, trying to squeeze both onto something no larger than a hand towel at the same time, tilting her neck at such an acute angle it looked like it might snap, but still failing miserably.

"They're all laughing at my suntan," Jason moaned. He'd developed the classic cyclist's tan; his face, arms and legs were several shades darker than the rest of him, giving him an absurd striped appearance. For half an hour, they swam and read, and then Jason turned to Lisa. "I'm bored, fancy a bike ride?"

The next day they took the train to Lucca. Riding daily in the sweltering heat had been arduous, but as she gazed out of the window at the clear blue sky and the picturesque rolling hills dotted with the farmhouses and cypress trees that were now so familiar, Lisa was surprised to find herself wishing she was on her bike. Jason, sitting opposite her, sensed her longing. "You're thinking the same as me, I can tell."

"I was thinking about a cold beer when we arrive," Lisa lied.

"Told you so. I knew we were thinking the same thing."

Lucca was everything the Rough Guide promised, quieter than Florence or Siena but every bit as elegant. They climbed onto the treelined medieval city walls to stroll and admire the panorama of the city and the surrounding countryside.

Lisa pointed out the Torre Guinigi, a high, battlemented tower built in the 15th century but now famous for the ancient holm oak trees that top it, their roots having grown into the room below and which look like a crown of dark curly hair from a distance.

"I suppose you want to go up?" Jason sighed when she smiled and, a short time later, found himself trudging up yet another seemingly endless spiral stone staircase.

They arrived back in Vada late evening, but the little square was a hive of activity. Young children still played in the fountain whilst their even younger brothers and sisters slept soundly in pushchairs, gently eased back and forth by their parents, oblivious to the clamour of excited voices, chatter and music all around them.

Sitting on the ground with their backs to a tree amidst the hubbub, washing their delicious takeaway pizzas down

Chapter Twenty-Six

with ice-cold beers, Lisa and Jason agreed that life couldn't get much better.

Their last bike ride was along the coast into Pisa. They were both subdued, gazing out over the ocean, sorry that their adventure was coming to an end. Sauntering through the city streets, looking for somewhere to stay, they turned a corner and suddenly, there in front of them were the emerald green lawns, known as the Campo Dei Miracoli, the Field of Miracles, on which stand the Duomo, the Baptistry and the Leaning Tower of Pisa.

"I don't know what I expected, but that is incredible." Lisa was stunned by the sight of the crazily angled tower, supported by a steel girder to prevent it from toppling.

"There's one thing for sure, we won't be going up that one." Jason laughed, but he felt the familiar sharp stab of regret. If only his parents had been able to see this.

They booked into a one-star hotel across the road from the Field of Miracles. It was a shabby little place, but their second-floor room was adorned with ancient frescoes around the walls, the bed linen was pristine and the view from the small wrought iron balcony they gingerly tried out, one at a time, was stunning.

On the way to eat, they passed a sumptuous Ramada Hotel just as a coach party were disembarking in evening dress, stepping through the light that spilled onto the pavement from the dazzling chandeliers as the automatic doors glided open.

Jason sighed. "This is where you belong, not some dingy little moth-eaten place. We could probably afford it, we've budgeted well. Do you want to move?"

Lisa turned to him, surprised. "But this hotel is featureless, it could be anywhere. There won't be any medieval frescoes in there, and they haven't got a view like ours. We're so lucky we found the little place."

In the still warm air of late evening, tired but determined to savour every moment of the view of the floodlit splendour of the Duomo from their balcony, Lisa frowned as she peered at the Rough Guide in the soft glow from her waning torch. "This can't be right, surely. It says construction began in 1063, that's before the Battle of Hastings."

They spent the following day looking around the stunning architecture and magnificent interior of the Baptistry and the Duomo, the numerous statues, carvings and paintings reminiscent of the similar structures they'd visited along the way.

At the little market stalls that had appeared on the lawns, they bought tee shirts for Georgina and Byron, Amber and Jonathon. "I just want to look for something for Mum and Dad." Lisa called out, then spun around, her hand to her mouth. "I'm so sorry, Jason, that was thoughtless." In that instant, he knew that what she'd said to him the night he'd told her his secret wasn't just reassuring words she'd been able to come up with at a moment's notice. Somehow she understood his pain.

He smiled. "Don't be, I'll come with you."

Their meal that night was extravagant, the full works; wafer-thin slices of Parma ham and melon to start, gnocchi in a rich pesto sauce, chicken braciola and tiramisu, accompanied by a bottle of full-bodied Chianti.

Back on their little balcony, Lisa did her best to commit to memory the spectacular view in front of her. *Was it really only two weeks since they'd arrived in Bologna? It seemed like years ago, they'd seen and done so much since then.* "This is such a perfect end to our trip, looking out across the Field of Miracles. It's been a wonderful holiday, one of the best I've ever had."

"It's not over yet, Bologna tomorrow." Jason hoped his smile hid his anxiety; he was dreading going back.

Chapter Twenty-Seven

The train eased into Bologna Central, and Jason reluctantly made his way to the carriage where the bikes were secured. He'd tried hard to relax and enjoy the beautiful scenery but was tense and had spoken little on the journey.

Forcing the events of 14th June to the back of his mind as they began their adventure, he was amazed to find himself enjoying the trip, but the prospect of returning to Bologna had brought back all the bad memories of that fateful day. For the first time since the miserable start of their holiday, he longed to return home as quickly as possible.

As they walked out onto the concourse into the scorching sunshine that had prevailed throughout their trip, Jason noticed several police cars parked outside the low brick building directly opposite. He opened his mouth to ask her if that was where Lisa had been that blisteringly hot afternoon when she seemed to have been gone forever but thought better of it.

They followed the route Jason had planned along the narrow, shaded back streets to the hotel, avoiding the bus station. Only when he saw the sign for the hotel about 50 metres ahead did he let out an involuntary sigh, recalling his excitement two weeks before when he had seen that sign for the first time.

Inside, a handsome young man they hadn't met before stood to greet them with a warm smile. "Ahh, Jason and Lisa. You've made it back to us. How was your holiday?" He quickly explained that he was the Assistant Manager and that all the staff knew of the unfortunate start to their holiday. It was Rosa's weekend off, but she had left a note for them in an envelope on which she had drawn a large heart.

"Please, let me show you to your room," the young man continued. "We've given you an upgrade, no extra charge." He escorted them to a room on the top floor from where they could see the gently leaning towers of Asinelli and Garisenda. "With our compliments, a gift from Italy." He proudly gestured to the bottle of red wine standing on top of a chest of drawers, accompanied by two crystal wine goblets.

After he'd left, Lisa stood for a moment by the window, taking in the remarkable view and recalling other scenes from other windows along the way. "People can be so incredibly kind."

Jason, standing by her side, was overwhelmed. He'd dreaded returning to this place because of its associations with the actions of heartless strangers. But, just as swiftly as that event had catapulted a beautiful summer's day into a living hell, the kind actions of another stranger had instantly replaced dread with pleasure. As he gazed across the tiled roofs glowing in the heat haze, he was surprised by the sudden urge to explore this beautiful city. "Shall we pack up and get out there?"

It was mid-afternoon by the time they'd packed the bikes carefully for the return flight, showered and changed, and strolled into the city centre at almost the same time they had arrived that first afternoon. The day was still hot, but they ambled along the covered walkways with their cool marble floors, scanning the colourful window displays for a suitable gift for Rosa and settling on a heart-shaped box of candies tied with a red ribbon.

After visiting the piazzas, where medieval buildings glowed in the late afternoon sunshine, they made their way to the Torre Degli Asinelli and climbed the 498 steps to the top; rewarded with the spectacular views across the city that the Rough Guide had promised as the sun slowly dipped and disappeared. "This is how it should have started," Jason mused, watching the city shimmer as the sky turned golden.

Lisa smiled. "I'm so happy that it's how it's ended."

As evening seeped across the burnished sky, the city came alive with Friday night revellers, the restaurants and bars scattered all around the piazzas filled with families and young partygoers, merging effortlessly. Eventually, they found a tiny back street restaurant, much like where they could have eaten everything on the menu that first night in Siena. Jason was disappointed. "Not very upmarket for our last night, is it? I should have booked somewhere."

"It's perfect!" Lisa reassured him. "I was fancying pizza and salad. From now on, that meal will always remind me of so many lovely evenings on this trip."

Jason was anxious as they returned to the hotel just before midnight. Would this be the night that she wanted him? The last opportunity, would she give him that look that he knew so well, those beautiful green eyes suddenly so intense, the golden flecks like sparks from the fire within her. He knew his decision to continue as before and not tell her of his feelings was for the best, but putting it into practice wouldn't be easy.

Lying in bed at Jason's side, Lisa felt again the surge of desire she'd resisted throughout the holiday. As she listened to him gently snoring, lying on his side with his back to her, a memory of a dream from years ago came back to her. She could make that dream a reality, move close to him, run her fingers along his thigh, take hold of his shoulder and pull him towards her. *But then what?* The dream had never got as far as what happened afterwards. Would they fall asleep wrapped in each other's arms? *Might that be nice?*

Horrified by her thoughts, Lisa quickly turned away. The trip had been intense and emotional; the traumatic start, the challenging rides, and the incredible beauty of the scenery and the architecture were messing with her head. Better to wait until they were back home and she could knock on his door, stay only a short while and keep her emotions safely in check.

On the final day of the holiday, there was time to take one last stroll around the majestic palazzos before they caught the train back to the airport. Sitting in the shade of a brightly coloured parasol, Jason leaned back against the plump cushions and sighed contentedly. "So, what was the highlight of the trip for you?" Lisa asked.

Chapter Twenty-Seven

He grinned. "That's an easy one, not getting any punctures. There was no way I could have faced blowing the tyres up again with a hand pump in this heat."

Enjoying people-watching from behind the safety of her sunglasses, Lisa realised that Jason had been quiet for several minutes. "Penny for them?" She smiled as she trotted out his well-used phrase, the one he always used when she was quiet.

"I was just thinking about the trip. It has been fantastic, hasn't it? But isn't it strange how that happened after the way it started?" He turned to look at her. "I mean, you were incredible getting the money for us, but weren't we lucky to get the bag back?"

"Well, you were adamant about going to the police station. I had nothing to do with that."

"But why was that? I never really thought we could be that lucky, and wasn't it amazing that just as we were about to leave, that English-speaking guy showed up? Do we have an England goal-scorer to thank for such a great trip? We would never have found the bag otherwise; the other officer hadn't a clue what I was asking. And what about the flight tickets? Who would have thought they'd be able to tell us where the bag had been found? We didn't have time to look for the park, but we did, and there they were!"

"Fate?" Lisa suggested.

But Jason didn't hear her, still lost in his thoughts. "Then there's your bangle." She smiled and twirled it around her wrist so that the clasp with the delicate profile of the Gemini twins lay across the back of her wrist. "I was so disappointed that I had nothing for you on your birthday and no money to spend. I couldn't believe it when I saw it, it's so perfect for you. I know how much you like Mum's necklace."

Lisa frowned, puzzled, and Jason swallowed hard. *Now he'd gone and done it, on the last day as well. Think before opening your mouth, idiot!*

"Your mum's necklace? I thought it was your Auntie Jayne's?"

"I know you did. I'm sorry. I was going to tell you, the time just never seemed right. Auntie Jayne bought it for Mum's 21st, she wears it every day. But how did I stumble on something so similar for you? I couldn't find the place again; don't you think that's odd?"

"Well, there were a lot of narrow little streets," Lisa laughed, teasing him, deliberately avoiding his question in a manner her barrister brother, Neil, would be proud of.

Inside, her mind raced as she glanced back down at her bangle, a connection with a woman she'd never even seen, as Jason hadn't volunteered to show her a photograph. She'd died tragically young in a car crash, and Jason adored her; that was all Lisa knew, but she suddenly felt the urge to learn far more.

"And what about that driver turning across us?" Jason continued, grimacing. "We could have been killed, but somehow, thank God, we're okay." He hesitated. "I know this sounds ridiculous, but do you believe in guardian angels?" Jason wished he could take the words back as soon as he'd spoken them. She would think he was an idiot, and he waited for her to laugh out loud.

The unexpected question caught Lisa by surprise, and she sat back, considering her reply. "I believe I'm watched over and guided by people who love me."

Chapter Twenty-Seven

Jason was so shocked he sat bolt upright. *The phrase was oddly familiar; where had he heard it before?* He rapidly trawled through his memory. *The conversation with Irene when she lost her husband, George, yes, that was it.*

He'd confided in her about the accident to try to comfort her and explain that he knew something of her pain. She'd told him his parents would be watching over him, but he'd dismissed the idea immediately as impossible. He pushed his sunglasses onto his head and gazed intently at Lisa. "You do? No, you're kidding me, right?" He hesitated, not knowing what to think. "Do you really believe that?"

Lisa removed her sunglasses so he could see the truth in her eyes. "I do." She replaced her glasses slowly, deliberating. "People talk about a sixth sense. Have you ever experienced it?"

He nodded. Several times he'd had an odd forewarning of imminent danger. The most recent occasion was on the descent from Montepulciano. The road was clear ahead, he'd heard the car approaching from behind, but there was ample room for it to pass safely. Not knowing there was an entrance to the hotel ahead, for some reason, he'd already started to squeeze the brakes before the car had passed them.

"Well," Lisa continued slowly, "what if sixth sense has nothing to do with us? What if someone else warns us, puts thought into our minds, and protects us? Do you think that's possible?"

"No, I've always thought that when you're dead, you're dead," Jason replied emphatically, but he realised that wasn't strictly true even as he was saying the words. There had been one moment when he'd wondered if there might be some kind of life after death, the day he'd found the dog-eared copy of *The Unexplained* rammed down the back of Simon's sofa.

As he flicked through the pages, he'd suddenly spotted an image depicting something he had experienced firsthand in the hospital just after his grandparents had told him his mum and dad were dead; an out-of-the-body experience. The drawing showed the spirit connected to the body by a silver cord. In the illustration below, entitled *'Death'*, the soul had separated from the body and could move around freely, no longer entrapped.

Jason had been stunned by the concept, but then Simon had spoken to him; he'd shoved the book back where he'd found it and never thought of it again until now.

Lisa wondered whether to continue, teetering on the brink of sharing her deepest thoughts with him, those she kept strictly to herself and discussed with no one.

She twirled her grandmother's wedding band around the fourth finger of her right hand. "Have you ever had a thought that seemed to come from nowhere, completely out of the blue?"

Had he! More than once, and he'd spoken most of them out loud! There was the first time he'd offered to take Georgina and Byron for a bike ride and the consternation that followed. Then there was the invite to Lisa to accompany him to Christophe's birthday party; utterly bewildered, he'd had absolutely no idea why he'd asked her. And he'd startled himself on a dismal day in January when, due to his mouth seemingly working independently of the rest of him yet again, he'd suggested another bike trip. Where the heck had that come from? He nodded again.

"Well, what if someone who loves you placed that thought there? Could someone else have put the thought in

Chapter Twenty-Seven

your head to go to the police station, kept you there until someone arrived who could help, and steered you to the pawn shop?"

Too late, Lisa realised she'd said too much, revealed too much of her inner self. *Why had she done that?* Going far too deep for a sun-drenched morning with her tanned, carefree companion, she knew she was spoiling the end of the holiday and waited for him to ridicule her.

He sat back and thought about love, a maelstrom of memories churning through his mind. There was his love for Rolo, who he still missed every day, the love that bound his family so tightly together wherever they were, the love between friends that had made him and Simon almost like brothers and now his love for Lisa.

He didn't doubt that love was powerful; it had miraculously transformed Pietro from an Italian stallion into a devoted family man, and what about John? To the uninitiated, the most striking thing about him was his outrageous dress sense and over-the-top behaviour. For those who knew him well, however, his most unique quality was his unquestioning love of everything and everybody.

But could love really be so strong that it could overcome anything, even death? He remembered the dark days after the accident when he'd tried to fathom the purpose of living. Was that the answer? To love and to be loved?

Lisa cleared her throat, breaking into his reverie. "I have a confession to make too. When you asked me to look for your toilet bag the first evening, I found a little guidebook in your pannier. I read the inscription, and I thought this trip was special. That's why I asked for enough money to continue, even though you'd told me you wanted to go home."

Jason sighed. "I found the book after I lost my parents. That's Dad's writing in the front. '*Someday*'. Unfortunately, that day never came for them. I hadn't even known they wanted to come here; I couldn't believe it when you suggested Tuscany. I've carried the book around so that at least it made the trip even if they didn't."

Lisa removed her sunglasses again and looked deep into his eyes. "But what if they have made the trip with you? What if we found the passports and the flight tickets because your mum and dad conspired to make their dream come true and share it with you?"

Reeling, Jason lowered his sunglasses and closed his eyes. His mind flew back to the moment in Florence when he had wished his parents could have been there to see the splendour of the Duomo and then to Pisa, standing in the Field of Miracles, gazing at the extraordinary leaning tower. *Had a miracle happened, might they have been there with him? Might they have always been with him?*

His thoughts turned to his bedroom, the photos around the walls and his mum and dad's treasured possessions, the hours he'd spent there, so desperate not to lose his parents from his life that he'd become fearful of being away from home for any length of time. *What if Irene was right; what if they had been beside him all along, and he would never lose them, wherever he was?*

A sudden surge of happiness suffused him, and he realised that for the first time since the accident, he felt a spark of something he thought had left his life forever. Hope.

Chapter Twenty-Seven

"I need to talk to you more about this."

"I thought you might. But not now, we've got a plane to catch, we need to leave soon. Let's talk when we're home over a glass of Limoncello."

"Look forward to it." He sat back again, a smile playing around his lips and closed his eyes. "Five more minutes." There was something special about Lisa, he didn't know what it was, but he knew he was lucky to have met her; good things happened when she was around. Two years before, he'd been worried sick about Christophe's party, frightened that everyone had moved on and his parents' absence would go unnoticed.

"You're good, you should do a gig," Lisa had told him one evening as he entertained the gang at hers with a few songs and that had been the catalyst for his suggestion to Michael that they do a duet. *Or had it? What if it had been his mum and dad's idea, and Lisa had somehow helped it along?* He'd felt so happy that evening when Michael spoke directly to Christophe to the rapturous applause of the entire audience. *Had his parents been by his side then, singing along with him? Could it be possible that they'd been with him for the rest of that trip?*

He'd enjoyed the holiday with Lisa and, to his great surprise, hadn't felt homesick once. The thought of being away for two weeks this time had frightened him rigid; he'd expected to feel terribly homesick, but, other than at the dreadful start to the holiday, remarkably, he hadn't. Lisa somehow freed him, he couldn't explain it, but when he was with her, he could leave the security of the haven he'd created for a while at least.

His mind was made up already; when they got home, he would take her to his bedroom and show her what he'd kept hidden from everyone for so long. He would tell her about his early life, and then, just maybe, he might be able to take a few of the pictures down.

Lisa wondered what was going through his mind as the emotions chased themselves across Jason's handsome face. How much her life had changed since meeting him. Who would ever have thought that she, so timid and shy, would end up here, having adventures with him? She had learned so much about herself from climbing the Tourmalet, but this trip had taken self-discovery to a new level.

Cycling along in the burning heat, not knowing where they would stay that night or even what lay around the next bend, she'd discovered a love of adventure she had never anticipated. What would her brother, Stephen, say when she told him of her exploits this time? And having coped with so much at the beginning, she felt something new stirring within her; she hardly dared to think that it might be confidence.

Jason relaxed and smiled, so different from the man consumed with anxiety who'd sat opposite her at the little table in the breakfast room two weeks before, and Lisa couldn't help herself; she leaned towards him. She saw him tense, sensing her near him and at the last moment, she slid her finger around his coffee cup and plonked a dab of froth on the end of his nose. Laughing, he attempted and failed to lick it off.

"I thought you were going to kiss me. You're allowed to, you know, just once." He pursed his lips comically and waited for the inevitable backlash, but instead, he felt the touch of her lips, as soft and gentle as the gossamer wings of a butterfly against his cheek.

Dawdling back to the hotel along the dappled streets, Lisa recalled their first night in Bologna. She had lain on the bed at the side of Jason, grateful that he was sleeping but fighting mounting panic about their situation.

Her pulse had quickened, and her breath had come in evermore shallow gasps as thoughts of their awful predicament bombarded her. It was when she was close to screaming, alone and helpless in the darkness, that she had silently called out to her grandparents. *Please, help me!*

Minutes later, standing beneath the soothing water in the shower, she'd felt slightly calmer, her breathing slowly steadied, she could think more clearly, and she realised that obtaining money was the place to start. *Had she worked that out for herself, or had her grandparents told her that?*

Her mind went back to the day she unexpectedly met Irene. A right and a left, she had written it so clearly at the end of her directions. She'd read it twice on the approach to the junction, but still, she had taken a left and a right, bringing her to Irene's house. She noticed the tall, fair-haired young man wheeling the shiny red motorbike onto his drive as she left and felt instantly drawn to him. Alarmed, she'd hastily studied her directions to avoid eye contact when she saw him glance towards her.

She'd been even more concerned the first time she'd met him when he'd arrived at her door bearing cupcakes. The last thing she'd wanted was to get involved with anyone else and most definitely not a good-looking charmer like him, but right from the start, she'd sensed a hidden sadness about him. Was that why, totally out of character and on the spur of the moment, she'd invited him and Pietro around to eat? She'd never done anything like that before; she didn't make friends easily. *Had she invited him, or had her grandfather put that thought there?*

Twenty-five years had passed since her grandfather had sat beside her at the little school desk, helping her with her lessons. No one had believed her, not even her parents, until the day when Michelle slipped and fell on the ice in the playground. "Quick, Lisa," he instructed her. "The little girl behind you is falling. Can you help her?"

Mrs Hall, the teacher, had looked surprised when she reached them. "How did you know Michelle was falling, Lisa? Did you hear something?" Lisa hadn't replied, but she'd seen the confusion in the woman's eyes as she fought to comprehend what she'd just witnessed.

She had never seen her grandfather again; over the years, she'd wondered if she'd imagined it all. Had she wanted to believe he was with her so badly that she had made the fantasy a reality?

But then came the evening in the Peace Gardens when Alan, her former Manager, had suggested buying a house. Fleetingly she had glimpsed her grandfather standing beside him, smiling encouragingly at her, and that was when she knew with absolute certainty that she hadn't imagined any of it. In her memories, her grandfather walked with her in the playground and stood by her side. She'd never seen him on his feet when he was alive; she'd only ever seen him in his wheelchair.

For some time, she'd wondered if, like the day he'd found a friend for her at school, her grandfather had somehow played a part in finding Jason for her; a special friend, someone to help her get back on her feet after Mark and Jenni had broken her. Now she wondered if there might be more to it.

She'd been flattered when he chose to share his secret with her and surprised; she had never suspected he, too, was broken. *Perhaps she was meant to help him?*

In a flash of understanding, she knew what she had to do. She would start by telling him about her grandfather and then the secrets she had shared with no one, about the tiny white feathers she had seen floating down together soon after her grandmother passed away, the dream that had helped her to get through her return to work, the events that had led to her becoming his neighbour and how she had kept her head that first night in Bologna.

Only then would she throw caution to the wind, bare her soul and tell him the deepest secret of all, the one she had fought to keep hidden even from herself for so long.

She would tell him that she was in love with him.

x

Acknowledgements

Thank you for your interest in this, my first attempt at writing a novel, a fictional story based on actual events.

Only an exceptional person can trawl through 27 chapters of a novice's work without complaint, painstakingly searching for errors and gaps in the flow. You are that person, Sally. Thank you so much for your constant support and encouragement.

As a child, books were everything to me: treasured gifts, rewards for doing something I didn't want to do, and gateways into an imaginary world filled with wonder and adventure. To be able to hold in my hands a book that I have written is a dream come true. Thank you, Matthew Bird, author of JackFruit Treasure Trap, for guiding me through the process and helping to make my dream a reality.

My grateful thanks also go to Michael Heppell and my fellow 'Write That Book Masterclass' alumni for their invaluable advice, unceasing support and encouragement. I have Gaynor Cherieann, author of *An Adoptee's Journey*, to thank for asking the award-winning author of *Certified*, Roger Wilson-Crane, to write my foreword. I could never have anticipated such wonderful words; *thank you* hardly seems enough, Roger.

Last but certainly not least, thank you to Andrew Buxton, my husband, for the beautiful artwork that forms the cover of this book; the icing on my cake.

Special thanks go to Marilyn, the inspiration for my author name, who sadly left us recently, too soon to see it in print. Remembered with love always.

x

About the Author

Born Deborah Young, Debby grew up in South Yorkshire, the eldest daughter of two. At 16, she left school and started sixth form, but she hated the courses her parents had persuaded her to take. First life lesson: no matter how much people love you and try to help and guide you, go with your gut instinct.

Debby left and fell into a job in the insurance department of British Coal, where she found a niche. Several years of work and study later, Debby became a Claims Manager for a Lloyds Syndicate, specialising in injury and disease claims.

But then she found her way into loss adjusting; the sharp end of the job, out on the road, visiting the accident scene and meeting the witnesses. The job was made for her. Debby covered a large area stretching from the Midlands to the north of England, where she met people from every walk of life and no two days were the same. After 40 years in the insurance claims industry, she had become a good listener and analytical; if it's over-thinking you're looking for, Debby's your woman!

She lost both parents close together and, as a means of distraction, Debby retired in 2018 to go travelling with her husband, Andrew. When COVID put a stop to that, she began her first attempt at creative writing, and this is the result. The greatest challenge was to avoid writing in the style of a legal report.

Debby's hobbies of cycling, walking and travelling have led her to fascinating places and people the world over, and she would love to share their stories with you.

Please contact Debby through the following channels:

www.debbybuxton.co.uk

www.facebook.com/debbybuxtonauthor

www.instagram.com/debbybuxtonauthor

www.X.com@dbuxtonauthor